PRESIDENTIAL AGENT II.

To Mary Craig Sinclair - My Beloved Wife

Into your hands I place the five Lanny
Budd books with whatever honors they
may have won. Without your wisdom and
knowledge of the world they could not
have been what they are. Without your
cherishing love through times of stress and
suffering their author could hardly have
been alive.

TIMELINE

Each book is published in two parts: I and II.

PRESIDENTIAL AGENT II.

Upton Sinclair

Simon Publications

2001

LCCN: 44004916

ISBN: 1-931313-18-0

Distributed by Ingram Book Company

Printed by Lightning Source Inc., LaVergne, TN

Published by Simon Publications, P.O. Box 321 Safety Harbor, FL

Author's Notes

In the course of this novel a number of well-known persons make their appearance, some of them living, some dead; they appear under their own names, and what is said about them is factually correct.

There are other characters which are fictitious, and in these cases the author has gone out of his way to avoid seeming to point at real persons. He has given them unlikely names, and hopes that no person bearing such names exist. But it is impossible to make sure; therefore the writer states that, if any such coincidence occurs, it is accidental. This is not the customary "hedge clause" which the author of a *roman à clef* publishes for legal protection; it means what it says and it is intended to be so taken.

Various European concerns engaged in the manufacture of munitions have been named in the story, and what has been said about them is also according to the records. There is one American firm, and that, with all its affairs, is imaginary. The writer has done his best to avoid seeming to indicate any actual American firm or family.

...Of course there will be slips, as I know from experience; but *World's End* is meant to be a history as well as fiction, and I am sure there are no mistakes of importance. I have my own point of view, but I have tried to play fair in this book. There is a varied cast of characters and they say as they think. ...

The Peace Conference of Paris [*for example*], which is the scene of the last third of *World's End*, is of course one of the greatest events of all time. A friend on mine asked an authority on modern fiction a question: "Has anybody ever used the Peace Conference in a novel?" And the reply was: "Could anybody?" Well, I thought somebody could, and now I think somebody has. The reader will ask, and I state explicitly that so far as concerns historic characters and events my picture is correct in all details. This part of the manuscript, 374 pages, was read and checked by eight or ten gentlemen who were on the American staff at the Conference. Several of these hold important positions in the world of troubled international affairs; others are college presidents and professors, and I promised them all that their letters will be confidential. Suffice it to say that the errors they pointed out were corrected, and where they disagreed, both sides have a word in the book.

An Author's Program

From a 1943 article by Upton Sinclair.

When I say "historian," I have a meaning of my own. I portray world events in story form, because that form is the one I have been trained in. I have supported myself by writing fiction since the age of sixteen, which means for forty-nine years.

… Now I realize that this one was the one job for which I had been born: to put the period of world wars and revolutions into a great long novel. …

I cannot say when it will end, because I don't know exactly what the characters will do. They lead a semi-independent life, being more real to me than any of the people I know, with the single exception of my wife. … Some of my characters are people who lived, and whom I had opportunity to know and watch. Others are imaginary—or rather, they are complexes of many people whom I have known and watched. Lanny Budd and his mother and father and their various relatives and friends have come in the course of the past four years to be my daily and nightly companions. I have come to know them so intimately that I need only to ask them what they would do in a given set of circumstances and they start to enact their roles. … I chose what seems to me the most revealing of them and of their world.

How long will this go on? I cannot tell. It depends in great part upon two public figures, Hitler and Mussolini. What are they going to do to mankind and what is mankind will do to them? It seems to me hardly likely that either will die a peaceful death. I am hoping to outlive them; and whatever happens Lanny Budd will be somewhere in the neighborhood, he will be "in at the death," according to the fox-hunting phrase.

These two foxes are my quarry, and I hope to hang their brushes over my mantel.

Contents:

Book Five: Extravagant and Erring Spirit

Book Six: A Full Hot Horse

Book Seven: The Things That Are Caesars's

BOOK FIVE

Extravagant and Erring Spirit

18

Après Nous le Déluge

LANNY BUDD stepped from the train into the old, large, and poverty-smitten city of Vienna, which he had once described as a head without a body, the result of an anatomical experiment which had been tried under his youthful eyes by the surgeons of Versailles. First they had dissected the Austro-Hungarian body into two halves; then they had dissected away the greater part of the Austrian extremities, and the flesh from its bones, and tossed out what was left to sink or swim, live or die, survive or perish. Eighteen years had passed, and the almost bodiless Vienna had still managed to keep going.

More than a million and three-quarters of townspeople had only four or five million country people to support them; and it might be doubted whether ever in history so highly organized and cultured a group of humans had been suddenly plunged into such extreme and hopeless poverty. A good part of the middle class was condemned to extinction, by a process rapid or slow; rapid if you had no job, for then you had to sell your possessions one by one in order to get the price of a meal; slow if you had a job, for then you could buy enough food to keep you from starvation, and could keep your respectability so long as your clothing held together and you could get enough pieces to patch it with. When your white collar, symbol of social status, became dirty, you washed it yourself and pressed it against your mirror. When it became frayed, you trimmed it with scissors, and confronted with dismay the prospect that it would fall to shreds; for you could not be seen on the street without it, and if you stayed in your room, you would starve.

This socio-surgical experiment had succeeded in producing a fierce class struggle. The workers of Vienna were Socialist, and exercising their democratic franchises they had put their trade-union leaders into political office and proceeded to tax the rich for the benefit of the poor. Lanny had visited here with Irma six years ago, and had never forgotten the horror with which her fashionable friends had told of being taxed for having servants; a graduated tax, increasing with the number you had, and twice as much for men as for women! Owners of great estates and many palaces had known nothing so cheap as servants, and had taken it for granted from childhood that this was the natural condition of the masses; but now came a tax collector, requiring a list of names, and spying, asking questions of your gardeners and footmen, suspecting you of falsifying your reports! Irma had agreed with her friends that Pink Vienna was hardly to be distinguished from Red Moscow.

The situation was complicated by the fact that Socialist Vienna was surrounded by a Catholic and reactionary countryside. The same aristocrats who owned the white marble palaces on the Ringstrasse and in the third and fourth Bezirk also owned great tracts of timber and wheat lands, and they closed their palaces for economy's sake, and moved out to the countryside, out of reach of a confiscatory municipal government. There with the help of the priests they proceeded to organize their peasantry and marshal its votes into a strong conservative party; when this proved not enough, their hotheaded sons proceeded to form the younger peasantry into the Heimwehr, or home guard, which soon became the same thing as Fascism, only it was native Austrian, and supported by Holy Mother Church, as in Spain. As the saying was, they led the village taverns against the Vienna cafés.

Six years ago Lanny had inspected with enthusiasm great blocks of workers' apartments, built by the city of Vienna out of the proceeds of taxes on higher-rent houses and apartments. Two years later he had read with personal grief of the bombardment of these homes by the Heimwehr troops, financed with money put up by Mussolini, and commanded by reactionary officers under the direction of the Catholic Premier Dollfuss. This devout little statesman had suspended the parliament, in which he commanded a majority of one vote; and thus died one more republic and came one more dictatorship to the unhappy old Continent. From that time the history of Austria was a struggle among three kinds of Fascism, each bent upon exclusive rule: Mussolini's, Hitler's, and the native brand run by landowners and capitalists who wanted to keep the almost bodiless head for their private consumption.

II

On his previous visits to Vienna Lanny Budd had been an ardent young Pink. Now he came as an ivory-tower esthete, son of an American millionaire and perhaps one himself, associating only with persons of his own social rank. Such an evolution is generally accepted as normal. All he had to do was to avoid his former bohemian and workingclass acquaintances, and this was easy, because many of them were dead and others in exile or hiding underground; if by chance one sought him out and tried to borrow money, Lanny would give it, but strictly as charity, and with such a manner of reserve as did not encourage a second call. He sought no publicity, but announced his presence by a note to his old friend and client, Graf Oldenburg, who had been living for the past six years on the price which Lanny had got him for a small Jan van Eyck.

Lanny judged that the funds would have run out by now, and this guess was confirmed by the promptness with which the agreeable and self-indulgent old aristocrat replied. He invited the American to lunch, and the food was plain, but prepared with elegance and served by an elderly valet in faded livery and clean white cotton gloves. The wine also was old, and the conversation was about the glories of old Vienna, when Franz Joseph, longest-lived of emperors, had set the tone of society, and the archdukes had entertained the loveliest actresses in the Hotel Sacher. Swarms of two-horse Fiakers had raced through the Prater, a cause of much complaint; everybody danced to the music of Franz Lehár, and a Hungarian nobleman by the odd name of Nicholas de Szemere de genere Huba won more than a million crowns from Count Potocki in a single night of gambling at the Jockey Club.

This invitation to lunch was a small seed from which sprang up almost overnight a garden of the loveliest flowers. Word spread, literally by lightning—since Benjamin Franklin had found out what it was and another American had taught it to carry messages over copper wires. Leisure-class Vienna learned that there was a wealthy American in town, one who was socially presentable, and indeed had a sort of charm which made him almost Viennese. "You remember, he used to be the husband of that frightfully rich heiress—twenty-three million dollars, the papers said—no, not schillings—dollars, I tell you—and he must have kept some of them. His father makes the Budd-Erling airplane, and the son buys paintings—he says they are for clients in

America, but nobody can be sure about that." So everybody who owned a Defregger, or knew anybody who owned one, wanted to meet Lanny Budd. Invitations poured in, and without loss of a day he found himself in the fastest-moving section of the social whirl.

Since the Socialists had been put down, a degree of prosperity had returned to the almost bodiless head. The owners of wheat and timber lands, and of a mountain of iron ore, made money; and those who controlled the marketing of such products, and the speculators who were clever enough to guess the course of prices, all could reopen their palaces. In Vienna luxurious pleasure-seeking had become a sort of delirium, the most hysterical that Lanny had ever encountered. Everybody seemed to know that the present situation couldn't go on much longer; everybody wanted to spend his or her last schilling on one last fling of enjoyment. *Après nous le déluge!*

It appeared that five years of war, followed by eighteen years of economic dislocation, had undermined the sexual defenses of many of the ladies of Vienna. Nowhere had so many in what was called good society pressed their knees against Lanny's when seated beside him at the dinner table. It had always been his habit to wear a pleasant smile when dealing with the other sex, but here he decided that it wouldn't do, and took to looking stern. But that didn't do so well either; that made him appear masterful and military. He remembered the story he had heard about Brand Whitlock, who had been American ambassador to Belgium immediately after the World War. The ladies in the Palace Hotel of Brussels, owned by the King of Spain, had made a practice of knocking upon the doors of unattached gentlemen, and proved embarrassingly hard to get rid of, until the diplomat had the bright idea of purchasing a pair of lady's shoes and putting them outside his door every night along with his own boots to be polished!

III

The founder and chief of the Austrian Fascist army had been Ernst Camillo Maria Rüdiger, Prinz von Starhemberg, who traced his ancestry back to robber barons of the tenth century; the successful robbers had left him a total of thirty-six castles. He was a nephew of Graf Oldenburg, and Lanny met him at a dinner party. He was a man of Lanny's age, tall, vigorous, handsome in a greenish-gray military uniform with a blackcock's tail in his hat. He had served in a dragoon regiment in the war, and ever since had been active in political war against the people's movements of his part of the world. He was one of those whom Lanny had seen marching in the streets of Munich in Adolf Schicklgruber's abortive beer-hall Putsch. Later he had broken with the Nazis and become Mussolini's man in Austria. He was bold, haughty, and opinionated; a reckless gambler and popular with the ladies—in the latter activity it was easier for him to have his own way than in politics.

With him came his latest flame, the young and very lovely actress, Nora Gregor. She sat next to Lanny at the table, and did not try secretly to hold his hand. It was plain that she was completely fascinated by her rather boyish and primitive-minded aristocrat, who was in process of divorcing his wife in order to marry her; this was something unprecedented in the society of Catholic Austria, and meant that Ernst Camillo Maria Rüdiger was through in politics. This he admitted, saying that he was sick of its stupidities and shams, and Austria could go to hell, or Hitler could have it. This, Lanny knew, was sour grapes; Ernst's hated rival with the unprepossessing name of Schuschnigg had ousted him from command of the Heimwehr, and had disbanded this dangerous private army, in the face of Ernst's public statement that it would be done only over his dead body.

Nora Gregor had lovely soft white shoulders, revealed by a filmy pink tulle dress. She had a sweet gentle face, a caressing voice, an innocent manner—in short, the perfect ingénue, in private life as on the stage and screen. She was expecting to become a princess, but said that she was afraid of the world of great affairs, and would much prefer to live in some quiet place in the country. Perhaps it was so— it was the mood of Hollywood, and Nora had been there.

After the fashion of stage people, she talked frankly about her love; she made it seem very lovely—and Lanny wondered, was she saying what she had rehearsed so many times on the stage and before the camera? Manifestly, a woman cannot very well spend her professional hours learning to imitate the tones and gestures of passion, watching her performance before a mirror and trying it out before audiences, without carrying over into real life some of the consciousness of technique. Or was it the other way around—had she given her heart to this arrogant and domineering playboy-politician, and then enacted before her audience the tones and gestures she had practiced upon him? Lanny asked her, and she laughed and said that the web of life was complicated, and she lacked the skill to unravel its many threads.

This much a presidential agent learned for certain: Ernst Camillo Maria Rüdiger, Prinz von Starhemberg, was out of politics to stay, if his future princess had anything to say about it. That, she declared, was a statement never rehearsed before any camera, but straight out of her heart. She told how Ernst had traveled to Rome to interview Mussolini and try to get Il Duce's support against Schuschnigg's intrigues, only to discover that Ernst's own supporters had sold him out, in return for office and promotion. That was the kind of thing that made politics so odious, and caused a star of stage and screen to desire to flee from the *grand monde* and live in a cottage. At any rate, so she told the son of an American millionaire, at the dinner table of a Viennese nobleman, with several men-servants in livery coming and going on velvet carpets, placing reverently before her the choicest wines and most exquisitely prepared foods. Lanny Budd, a devotee of the theater, might well have wondered whether this, too, was a play, and if so, how soon was the curtain to be rung down.

IV

It was a "P.A.'s" business to meet Schuschnigg, the Jesuit-educated doctor of laws who had taken over the destinies of this unhappy country. Lanny wanted it to come about naturally, and without an appointment; he went to one splendid reception after another, and let the word spread that he had recently talked with Hitler. So it wasn't long before members of the government were seeking him out; and when he was introduced to the Chancellor at a musicale, that worried gentleman took him off into the library. Seine Exzellenz was a tall blond intellectual of about forty, with blue-gray eyes, a small light-brown mustache and tortoise-shell spectacles. When he smiled, he revealed even white teeth, and gave the impression of an amiable college professor, a younger Woodrow Wilson.

He started right away asking questions. What did that most dangerous and inexplicable Führer of the Germans really mean? Lanny answered that he really didn't know, and didn't think Adi knew quite yet; Adi was a man of impulses and intuitions. The Chancellor Doktor appeared to shrink at these words. He was extremely apprehensive, and made no attempt to veil or disguise his feelings. He was a man of no great personal force, Lanny gathered; he ruled "with an iron hand," as the saying was, but that seemed rather easy—the police and the military did the dirty work, and the head of the government could smile, or say his prayers if he preferred. It was a form of government familiar to Old Austria—despotism tempered by *Schlamperei*, that is, slackness, inefficiency.

This amiable-mannered Exzellenz talked as if he would like to put his too-heavy burdens off on his visitor. Austria, he insisted, had been created by a *Diktat* of the Allies, who had won the World War and now refused to accept the responsibilities which their victory entailed. "What will France and Britain do, Herr Budd?"—and Herr Budd had to admit the fear that they were in a mood not to do very much.

"Why, a few years ago France threatened war merely because the Germans talked about a customs union with us!"

"I know," said Lanny; "but a lot of water has flowed under the bridge since then. Hitler has built an army, and General Göring a lot of planes."

"*Ach, du lieber Gott!*" exclaimed the pious Catholic. "And what do you in America expect? You came here and broke us down—it was your armies which landed at Salonika and forced the capitulation of Bulgaria—and that was the beginning of the end."

"You may be sure it will be a long time before we do anything of the sort again," declared Lanny, reassuringly. "We thought we were setting the people of Europe free, and hoped they would govern themselves."

"With us," replied the Chancellor, "freedom is taken to mean Marxism, and presently it becomes Bolshevism, and no more freedom for anyone but the commissars. America will have to send us some wise man who can solve that problem for us."

Lanny was sorry, but could not pretend to be that man. Even so, Seine Exzellenz wanted to talk to him, more at length than was possible at a musicale. Would he come to the Ballplatz on the morrow?—and the visitor said he would be very happy. He went and listened to an earnest appeal for American, British, and French protection of Austria; apparently the Chancellor had been told that Lanny possessed wealthy and influential friends in each of these lands. He wanted it understood that while his country was now under a one-party dictatorship, it was a benevolent one, a Christian one, for the good of the country, and having the backing of all the sound elements of the public.

After saying this, the dictator began asking his American visitor how it was that Hitler and Mussolini had managed to get so large a part of the workers behind them. Lanny knew that Schuschnigg had in mind the forty per cent Marxist vote which had been cast in Austria, and which was now sullenly opposed to his regime. Lanny ventured: "If you don't mind my speaking frankly, may it not be because the Führer and the Duce have taken such pains to put forward a social program?"

"*Aber!* I too have a social program, Herr Budd, the best in the world. I am following the program of Pope Pius XI, in his encyclical *Quadragesimo Anno,* which favors neither the rich nor the poor, but seeks equal justice and fraternity between them."

"Unfortunately," replied the visitor, "this appears to be an irreligious age, and a program to be popular has to be rougher and more noisy."

Seine Exzellenz explained that it had long been the desire of the Austrian people to join with the German people in friendship and on equal terms; but to be dragged in by force, and to be governed by such rowdies and gutter rats as the Nazis were hiring here in Vienna—that they would fight *bis zum Tode*—to the death. They would never submit to it, *niemals, niemals*—the Chancellor spoke the word a dozen times in the course of his declaration, and Lanny wondered, whom was he trying to convince, his visitor or himself? Surely he couldn't expect to convince Hitler at this long range!

V

The Führer's ambassador in Vienna was Franz von Papen, known as "the gentleman jockey," a man who had set out to exemplify by his life the formula of Hamlet, that one can smile, and smile, and be a villain. In the first half of the World War this Prussian aristocrat had been an attaché of the German legation in Washington, and had busied himself hiring saboteurs to blow up munitions plants. Shrewd, but never quite enough so, he had kept the stubs of his checkbooks to prove that he had expended the money honestly. On his way back to Germany the British had captured him and his papers, and had turned the latter over to the American government. So now Fränzchen couldn't visit his many friends in Washington and New York—there being a grand jury indictment standing against him.

Lanny had met him first at a reception in the Berlin home of General Graf Stubendorf; afterwards at the Goebbels' and other places. Slender, pale, blond-gray with a blond-gray mustache, urbane and elegant, with a long "horse-face" deeply lined but always smiling, he would tell you whatever he thought you wanted to hear, and he must have the memory of an encyclopedia to remember what he had told each one in the course of years. Once in his life he had tried the experiment of telling the truth and had nearly paid for it with his life. A year or more after the Führer had taken power, the super-diplomat had decided that the regime was through, and had made a speech calling for freedom of the press; as a result, he had been attacked in his office during the Blood Purge and had several of his teeth knocked out.

Hitler would never trust him, but would use him, with a curb-bit and tightly held rein. A year and a half ago he had signed with Schuschnigg a solemn agreement of the two governments to be friends and to let each other's internal affairs alone. A Catholic Chancellor had to assume that the Germans meant to keep their word. But if so, why had the number of their agents in Austria been doubled, and why were they coming and going day and night at the palatial offices of von Papen in the Metternichgasse? Why was the German Travel Agency, with headquarters in the Hotel Bristol, importing salesmen, technicians, students, professors, and plain tourists in constantly increasing numbers? And what was that "Committee of Seven," with headquarters at No. 4, Teinfaltstrasse, composed of the most ardent Nazis, actively buying supporters and never in need of funds?

VI

"Fränzchen," as Papen was called, approached Lanny at one of the smart receptions, chatted amiably, and invited him to lunch. Lanny was pleased to accept, for he was beginning to think that he, too, was a smart fellow, and could get as much out of a gentleman jockey as a gentleman jockey could get out of him. Had Fränzchen by chance learned of Lanny's visit to Hitler? And did he wish to know about it for his own satisfaction, or had Hitler requested him to check on a too-plausible American? Or did Fränzchen suspect that Hitler had sent the American to check on a too-plausible Prussian? Oh, for a practicing telepathist, who could give a glimpse of the system of wheels whirling around in that narrow aristocratic head!

Lanny talked generalities, which must have been irritating to his host, who was paying for an elaborate luncheon in a private room of the Jockey Club. Lanny said that the prosperity which Adolf Hitler had brought to Germany was the wonder of the world. The ending of unemployment was a social contribution; Lanny told what he had heard important men of affairs say on the subject—including his own father. Let Fränzchen quote that to his Führer if he wished!

After a while the guest paused to let his host ask questions, and thus reveal his mind. It soon became evident that Papen was concerned to know what Lanny was doing in Vienna; evidently he didn't believe it was to get prices on Defreggers and photographs of those whose prices were right. Lanny explained that Vienna was a delightful city to live in; the music was of the best, the conversation sophisticated, the ladies beautiful—and the dollar commanded a great advantage over the schilling. To all this Fränzchen smiled assent, and probed more persistently. Whom had Herr Budd met that pleased him especially?

Lanny's fancy had been taken by Nora Gregor; lovely creature, off-stage as on. He mentioned her husband-to-be only incidentally. The Viennese reported him as *borniert*, that is, limited; the Viennese were subtle, and could be counted upon to find exactly the right word. Prinz Ernst was really a man of simple mind; he hated the city, and was much happier among his own sort of people, wearing yodeler's pants and a green cap with feathers in it. In the parliament, before it had been shut down, people had called him "the Loud Mouth," but in private his manner was one of easy familiarity, even gaiety, when he was not worrying about the upkeep of his many castles.

Whom else had Herr Budd met that appealed to him? *Jawohl*, he had had a delightful *Unterhaltung* with the Countess Vera Fugger von Babenhausen, who had just come down from her castle, bringing her four little Fuggers to spend the winter in town. Lanny wouldn't gossip, of course; he would wait until the well-informed ambassador mentioned the love affair which had developed between this wealthy lady and Seine Exzellenz Doktor von Schuschnigg. What an odd thing that both wings of Austrian Fascism should have been loaded down with a divorce scandal at this critical time! The Chancellor himself was a widower, but unfortunately the Countess's husband was still living, which made necessary a tiresome and complicated ecclesiastical procedure.

Lanny knew that Papen himself was a Catholic, so he ventured no comment upon the ingenious devices whereby Holy Mother Church denies divorce to her humble devotees, but can always find a pretext upon which to grant an annulment of a marriage to the heiress of a great fortune—to say nothing of a statesman who was in position to protect the funds which the Church had gained by the sale of such favors to rich ladies. Lanny asked politely how the matter stood now, and learned that the annulment had been approved by the ecclesiastical courts of the city and of the nation, and that a favorable decision was now hoped for from the Rota Court in Rome.

Lanny had carefully studied the technique of giving information which his hearer already possessed, or which could do no harm. He had practiced it upon General Göring, and had managed to establish himself as well-informed and at the same time discreet. Now he employed the method upon one of the world's most cunning intriguers, and must have annoyed that gentleman not a little. Papen wouldn't believe in any man's good faith, of course; but what would he believe? Would he think it over and realize how many clues he had given the American, by the questions he had asked as well as by those he hadn't? It may be true that language was created to conceal thought; but when there are so many thoughts to be concealed—when, indeed, there is nothing of importance which does not have to be concealed —then the most casual word may be loaded with dynamite, and there may be nothing for a super-diplomat to do but eat his lunch alone and in silence.

VII

Lanny rarely ate alone, because there were so many persons in this old city who had fine homes and wanted to hear news from abroad; or perhaps they had fine homes but no money to keep them up, and wanted an American art expert to find purchasers for their paintings. He listened to many people, some of whom spoke in whispers, and casting glances over their shoulders now and then. He collected masses of information and sorted it out in his mind, trying to decide what to believe. He had learned that where freedom of the press has been abolished, rumors thrive like weeds in a garden. One starts, and spreads from mouth to many ears, and next day comes back in a form such that its own creator would not recognize it. Never had the son of Budd-Erling heard so many wild tales as in Vienna under a benevolent Catholic dictatorship. No way to check them, for always the people who knew the truth were people you couldn't ask.

This circumstance caused Lanny to miss what might have been a remarkable "scoop." One morning while he was shaving he received a call from a certain Herr Grüssner, whom he had met six years ago as a dramatic critic for one of the newspapers. Lanny said for the gentleman to come up to the room, and was shocked by the change in his appearance. He had lost his position and was going downhill like so many thousands of others; what hair he had left was white, his face was lined and haggard, and he had a cough. Lanny assumed that this was to be a "touch," and being sorry for the poor devil, was ready to reach for his purse.

But it wasn't that. Herr Grüssner came quickly to the point, as if fearing that this wealthy and elegant American might begrudge him time for a tactful approach. He had certain journalistic connections, concerning which he was not free to give any hint; suffice it to say, he had come upon a piece of information of the utmost urgency—he began to grow agitated as he told about it, and traces of color appeared in his waxen cheeks. He had heard that Lanny had talked with Seine Exzellenz the Chancellor, and this item of news was of such gravity that Seine Exzellenz ought to know it at once.

"You don't know any Viennese who can tell it to him?" inquired the American, surprised.

"You do not understand the situation in our unhappy country, Herr Budd. Anybody who passes such a story on assumes a certain amount of responsibility, and I am a poor wretch who cannot afford to make powerful enemies. I come to you because you are an outsider, and in a position not to be harmed. *Bitte, um Gottes willen,* hear what I have to tell."

"Certainly," said the outsider; "I will hear, but I cannot promise to do anything about it."

Came the ritual of looking outside the door, and then the lowered voice, laden with fear. The story had to do with that Committee of Seven, the Nazi activists who made their headquarters at Nummer vier, Teinfaltstrasse, and were about ready to bring affairs in Austria to a head. Their plan was the old reliable one of provocation; they were going to organize a riot in front of the German embassy, and then blame it upon a prominent anti-Nazi, a member of the Austrian Legion. Ambassador von Papen would be shot, and this of course would excite indignation in Berlin, and divisions of the Reichswehr which were near the border would march in.

"I know, Herr Budd," persisted the one-time critic, "it sounds like melodrama, the sort I have seen many times upon the stage and have considered as deserving my critical contempt. But I assure you it is the truth—I know it as well as if I myself had been present in the office of Dr. Tavs, the secretary and leader of this Secret Seven."

An alarm bell was ringing in Lanny's mind. This might be anything. It might be Fränzchen, trying to find out Lanny's attitude to himself; again, it might be Schuschnigg doing the same; or it might be true—who on earth could guess? Plots within plots, like a set of Chinese puzzle boxes! No doubt the Nazis would be perfectly willing to sacrifice the life of a "gentleman jockey" whom they could never count upon, in exchange for a plausible pretext for seizing the timber and wheat and iron ore of Austria. But, on the other hand, it was just as likely that some enemy of Dr. Leopold Tavs and his committee was seeking to get them into trouble with the police of Vienna. One thing and one only was clear—it was no affair for an American *Kunstsachverständiger!*

Lanny said, very gently and tactfully, that he was here to find a good Defregger for a client, and if Herr Grüssner knew of any, he would be pleased to pay him a small fee; but as for Austrian political affairs—surely Herr Grüssner could see that it would be hopelessly bad taste for a visitor to mix in them.

Tears came into the eyes of this poor sick man. He pleaded that he was thinking about the safety of his country, and what could he do, even by risking his pitiful life? He could not get access to the Ballplatz, watched day and night by the Infantry of the Guard. If he talked to any subordinate, how would he know that the message would get to Seine Exzellenz? The government was honeycombed with spies and traitors; there were Nazi agents everywhere—"literally everywhere, Herr Budd; they may be searching your room, or spying on your callers. For a man like me to act in this matter would mean to be marked, and if they succeed in their plans and some day march into Vienna, I go to a concentration camp."

"I am very sorry, Herr Grüssner, but I cannot take any part in your country's political struggles." Thus Lanny, severely. He weakened to the extent of giving the ex-critic a few schillings, and saw him torn between pride and desperate need, thanking the rich American and begging his pardon for being an unfortunate wretch, *ein jämmerlicher Kerl.*

Lanny might have told this tale in an unsigned letter and sent it off by airmail to Rick. But he doubted its truth, and spent several days wondering what net of intrigue somebody might be trying to spread about his feet. Then all at once the cafés of Vienna were buzzing with the news—only partly told in the controlled press; the police had raided the headquarters of Dr. Tavs and seized a mass of documents proving a conspiracy of the Nazis to stage a raid upon their own embassy in Vienna. Several different revisions of the program had been found. The one to shoot Ambassador von Papen was signed "Heinrich Himmler," and included the idea of blaming it on the Communists. The one to have the Reichswehr divisions stationed near Munich march in was signed "R.H.," which people agreed meant Rudolf Hess.

VIII

The information which Lanny had collected was not so confidential that he was afraid to mail it, of course unsigned. A letter to Gennerich, saying that Austria would be annexed to Germany in the course of the next month or two; that Schuschnigg threatened to resist, but almost certainly wouldn't; that Mussolini knew what was coming, but would pretend not to, because for him to know was too humiliating; that it was the definite policy of the British government to permit this coup to happen, while publicly protesting against it; that Britain wouldn't let France do anything, even if she wanted to, which she didn't. Lanny sent a carbon copy of this report by air mail to Rick, and then took a train for Berlin.

Back at the Adlon, he might have communicated directly with the Führer, but as an act of courtesy he consulted Heinrich, who had been his means of access hitherto. Heinrich thanked him, but said it would be better for Lanny now to make his own approach; it wasn't a good thing for a subordinate to know too much about a great man's affairs, or to seem to thrust himself in where he wasn't needed. The cautious official didn't know anything about mediums and spirits, and maybe the Führer wouldn't want him to. This much advice Heinrich would give: Better to wait a day or two, for again there was trouble in the *Parteileitung* and important persons were in a bad temper.

Whenever this was the case, the person to call upon was Hilde von Donnerstein. "*Ach, grossartig!*" she exclaimed. "Berlin is the most interesting city in the world! Come and have coffee!" So Lanny went, and along with hi. *Kuchen* was offered a delicious *bonbonnière* of scandals. General Werner von Blomberg, Minister of Defense, the man responsible for the rearmament program, had married his secretary. For a high-up Junker this was unthinkable, but Die Nummer Eins and likewise Die Nummer Zwei had stood by him and publicly committed themselves by attending the wedding. Now the haughty warrior was enjoying his honeymoon in warm Capri sunshine, and here in ice-cold Berlin it had been discovered that the bride in her early days had been a lady of easy virtue, to say the least. Number One was furious, and was chewing the costly rugs on the Chancellery floor, according to his practice when his subordinates misbehaved.

Lanny asked about the subject of psychic research, and Hilde said she had talked to several persons who ought to know, but had not been able to learn of Die Nummer Eins having any astrologer or medium in his entourage at present; in fact, one man denied that the great person had ever been interested in this subject, it was all just idle gossip. However, Rudolf Hess, known as the Deputy Führer, lived surrounded by fortune-tellers all the time. Hilde had learned that he was now pinning his faith upon the prophecies of an old woman, a certain "Elsa" in Munich, and that at times he consulted a Berlin "professor" of the occult arts by the name of Bruno Pröfenik.

Hilde didn't know where he came from or what sort of name that was, but he was much talked about by smart ladies. "How could I find him?" inquired Lanny, and she replied: "He ought to be in the telephone book,"—which proved to be the case.

IX

More gossip. The Fürstin told about the latest developments in the Goebbels ménage. "Did you know that Magda fled to Switzerland?" she asked, and Lanny said: "I heard it." If he had been playing fair, he would have said: "I met her there,"—and then what a lovely time they would have had! Instead, he allowed Hilde to report that two husky Nazis in civilian clothes had approached Magda in a Zurich hotel and intimated that unless she returned at once something terrible might happen to her children; so she had come back to Berlin, and she and her "Jockl" were living once more in amity, at least publicly. "*Arme Frau!*" exclaimed Hilde.

A sad world, and the Princess Donnerstein was sorry for all women, herself included. She began telling Lanny about her own situation—concerning which he had learned in the past through Irma. He would have preferred not hearing any more, but to say so would have been rude. Hilde had been married very young, and really a girl didn't know what she was getting in for; titles and worldly glamour produced a great impression on the young, but they didn't make for everyday happiness, not if one had a heart. The Fürst was a stern disciplinarian, and expected his wife to obey him as a sort of higher servant. Hilde had spirit and a will of her own; they had quarreled bitterly and now they rarely spoke except in public—just like Magda and her little Doktor. "Of course Günther"—that was her husband— "goes where he pleases and does what he pleases."

Lanny had no trouble in guessing what all this was leading to. Hilde had considered an American's state of solitary bachelorhood and was sorry for him. She thought that Irma had treated him badly, and could not understand how any wife had been willing to break with such a husband. She wanted Lanny to know how she felt about him; she was paying him compliments, and he had to be appreciative. Just now Günther was away, attending to business matters of his estates which occupied most of his thoughts; no doubt he had some young woman there—the Prussian aristocrat never had any hesitation about asking for what he wanted, it being an ancient custom.

An eligible bachelor, who had been young for many years and still kept that appearance and feeling, had confronted a number of emergencies such as this, and carried with him an arsenal of pretexts, from which at a minute's notice he would choose the most plausible. In each case a friendship would be at stake, and Hilde's friendship was of value to Lanny. He could have told her that his mother had picked out a bride for him; but that might not have made much difference to a lady who was more than slightly neurotic, and whose motto in life was *Carpe diem*, or, as the German song phrases it: *"Pflücket die Rose, eh' sie verblüht."* To have talked about any sort of moral code would have been to claim that he was better than she was, which would have been insulting and might have ended this valuable friendship.

So now, with the most tender consideration and touching frankness, Lanny spoke of a mysterious weakness from which he had begun to suffer, and of certain treatments he was taking. He hoped that Hilde wouldn't say anything about this, and for once he could be reasonably sure that she would comply with his request—for how would she be able to explain that she had gained such an item of information? No, she would be sorry for him, and slightly afraid of him, and the friendship would continue on its agreeable platonic terms.

X

The visitor returned to his high-priced hotel, and on its high-priced stationery wrote a note to Professor Bruno Pröfenik, who resided in a fashionable district of the German capital. Lanny explained that he was an American art expert, an old friend of the Führer and also of General Göring. For many years he had been a student of mediumship and its phenomena, and had heard reports of the Professor's gifts along that line. He was here for a short stay and would like to consult the Professor as a client and, if possible, to have enough of his time to discuss the many ideas which they had in common. Leaving no chance for misunderstanding, he stated that he was expecting to pay for what he was requesting. He sent this letter by special messenger, and was not surprised when the same messenger brought a reply saying that the busy man would postpone other engagements and receive Herr Budd that evening.

Manifestly, this mystic-master was making a good thing out of his talents, whatever they were. He had a fine home and at least one servant in livery. The first thing you saw in his entrance hall was a Japanese dancing demon, a crouched figure three or four feet high, carved of black ebony polished until it shone like glass; it had malevolent yellow eyes made of topazes, and two rows of white teeth carved from ivory. At the end of the hall was a large niche like a shrine, containing not one god but scores; the Professor had been collecting all over the world idols and sacred images of the religions, ancient and modern, and his display would have done credit to a museum.

The master himself was elderly, and had a long gray mustache and two beards, one drooping from each cheek; this made him look like a Chinese scholar, and perhaps he liked the effect, for he wore a black jacket of Chinese silk with small golden swastikas upon it. His eyes were small, dark, and shrewd, and his expression one of cultivated benevolence. With many bows, and greetings in German with an indeterminate accent, he led Lanny into a spacious study which was like an astrologer's junkshop, with globes and zodiacal maps and charts, a cabinet with black curtains, a crystal ball, a ouija board, a Tibetan prayer-wheel, a Congo panther-man's garb and iron claws, a nail-studded cunjur-doll from Haiti, and in one corner a miniature Alaskan totem pole.

On an uncarpeted spot of the polished floor, Lanny observed, marked in black paint, a large double pentagon with a circle outside it. This, so it was explained in course of the evening, was for the enticing and capturing of werewolves—a very ancient practice. Left unexplained was a lovely dark-skinned girl of perhaps fourteen, a Javanese or possibly Balinese, who went about in the comfortably warm study as naked as the day she was born. She brought coffee, and a Turkish bubble-pipe for her master; she evidently understood such orders, but made no sound during the entire evening, so that Lanny wondered if she was a mute. There was an open fireplace with a soft-coal fire in a grate, and a large tiger skin in front of it. When the girl was not doing errands she squatted on this, as motionless as a Buddha, with the reddish light shining on her smooth brown skin.

XI

Seating his guest in an armchair and himself in another, the man of magic expressed his pleasure at receiving a friend of the Führer's, who was a mutual friend and had had sittings with him. He had never heard of Herr Budd, he said, but would not ask any questions because he desired to cast the visitor's horoscope before knowing any more about him. The practice of astrology had been forbidden, but doubtless the law would be relaxed in favor of a foreigner and a friend of the great.

After casting the horoscope, the Professor would go into a trance—a special kind which he reserved for adepts—and see what the spirits would tell him about Herr Budd's future, and about his friends, of whom he no doubt had many in the world where we all have a place reserved.

All this sounded well rehearsed, and Lanny decided quickly that here was a smooth and plausible charlatan. But that didn't mean that he mightn't have real psychic gifts, and be working both methods according to circumstances. Lanny gave the day and year of his birth, and spent half an hour watching and listening while the astrologer prepared a chart analyzing his character and foretelling his very pleasant future. After that the old man entered the cabinet, drew the curtains, and went into a "special" trance—meaning, of course, one which cost more. There came forth some groans and sighs, followed by an astonishingly large booming voice announcing itself to be King Ottokar I of Bohemia.

The communications this personage gave would indeed have been remarkable if they had been genuine. With only slight delay the spirit of Marcel Detaze announced himself, and gave quite plausible messages for his stepson and his widow and his daughter. Marcel was pleased with the use which Lanny was making of his paintings—though on earth he hadn't cared very much about either fame or money. He expressed himself as pleased with Beauty's new marriage. He himself was happy in the spirit world, painting many pictures, better than he had ever done on earth. He had sent Lanny messages whenever he could, and would continue to do so. Also he sent a message to Robbie Budd, to the effect that the military airplane industry had a far greater future than any other branch of armaments production. Robbie was going to be an extremely rich man, and while money wasn't valued in the spirit world, and especially not by spirit painters, Robbie was helping his own country and Marcel's as well as General Göring's. Peace among those three great peoples was to be put upon a basis that would endure for a thousand years.

Most extraordinary; the only thing wrong being that there wasn't a name or a detail which hadn't been published in the Berlin newspapers within the past few years, and all the Professor would have had to do was to call up a friend in a newspaper office and ask for the contents of their *Archiv* on the name of the American Lanny Budd; or, more cautiously, to send his secretary in a taxicab to jot down the data and bring them back. Lanny hadn't the slightest doubt that something of the sort had been done; but it didn't bother him, for he hadn't come here for psychic research, but for an entirely different purpose.

So when the Professor emerged from the cabinet, the sitter told him that his revelations had been amazing and the séance one of the most satisfactory he had ever attended. That made them friends, and they spent the rest of the evening exchanging mystical lore. The Professor soon discovered that this wealthy amateur had really taken the trouble to know what he was talking about; he had a stack of notebooks at home and his memory was stored with significant incidents. His stories were the more impressive because they moved in such exalted circles: Sir Basil Zaharoff at Monte Carlo and Lady Caillard in London, a private yacht cruising in the Mediterranean, palaces all over Europe, a baronet's son being wounded in war and Chancellor Dollfuss being murdered in Vienna. Yes, Lanny told again that tale which he had made up for the benefit of Adi Schicklgruber. He told true tales which revealed the circumstances of his own life and environment—being willing for a Nazi mystagogue to pick up all the data he wanted.

The Professor did his share of talking. He, too, had had remarkable experiences and achieved extraordinary feats. Strange as it might seem, he, too, had been in contact with the monastery of Dodanduwa in Ceylon, and would be able to establish telepathic contact with it at any time. Yes, there were Germans there, and they were spreading the gospel of the *Herrenvolk*. Also, the Professor had known Sir Basil Zaharoff in real life and sometimes had messages from him in the spirit world; if there was any message Lanny desired to send, its safe delivery could be assured. Yes, the Professor had tried hypnotism in many forms, and had the power to hypnotize any medium and cause that medium's astral body to travel to any part of the world, even to Ceylon, and bring back information desired. He could command earthbound spirits as well as those of the celestial regions; in short, Prospero and Cagliostro and Nostradamus were amateurs compared to this National-Socialist wizard, who had all the techniques of modern science at his command —or at any rate all its vocabularies.

XII

Quite casually in the course of this swapping of ideas Lanny introduced the particular item with which he was concerned; putting no special emphasis upon it, and being careful not to dwell upon it too long. "Tell me, Herr Professor, have you ever had the experience of having spirits appear at your séances who seem to be lost, and who come again and again for no discoverable reason?"

"Yes, indeed," said the wizard—he would never admit there was any experience he hadn't had. "In the end I manage to find out who they are and what they want, and I give it to them if possible."

"I have several cases in my notebooks that you might be interested to work over. Shall I give you an example—or am I boring you?"

"Not at all, Herr Budd. It is a pleasure to meet a man who really understands the significance of such phenomena."

"Well there is a spirit who calls himself Ludi; he was a commercial artist here in Berlin, so he says. He died, a painful death, apparently; I cannot get him to talk about it. And either he does not know his last name or else is embarrassed about it. Whenever I press him with questions he fades away and does not return for months."

"Possibly he is a fragment of a dissociated personality."

"That is what I have thought. I ask him why he comes to me, and he answers that he knew me in Berlin. I cannot recall any Ludi or Ludwig who is dead. Of course, I have been about a great deal in Berlin, and have been introduced to swarms of people, sometimes scores at a single *Empfang*. And, of course, as a stepson of Marcel Detaze I have met great numbers of artists of every sort; we had a one-man show in Berlin about four years ago, and all the artists came, the famous and the humble, and in the course of a couple of weeks I must have met hundreds."

"Undoubtedly you met this man, and his thoughts became attached to you. You would have been important to him, because you and your stepfather together represented the things he wanted but couldn't attain to."

"That might be the way. But I haven't told you all."

"Pray go on."

"A month or two ago there came a woman who says she is Ludi's wife. It sounds unlikely—that there should be a couple named Ludi and Trudi—one would take it for a vaudeville team. But that is what the woman says: Ludi and Trudi Schultz; but then again she gives the name Mueller, and doesn't seem to know why she changes. She is looking for Ludi, and he for her, but they never meet."

"Surely your control ought to be able to arrange that!"

"One would think so; but Tecumseh is a peculiar sort of control. Somehow he understands German, but objects to its being used. Anyhow, he says these two spirits fade out when he talks to them, and he has got tired of them. I must admit I have come to have the same feeling."

"Perhaps they had some tragedy in their lives; some crime, or suicide."

"I think that extremely likely. They seem to be harmless creatures, and I try not to hurt their feelings; but they interrupt my researches and make themselves something of a nuisance, especially now that there are two of them."

"We'll see what we can find out about them, Herr Budd. Perhaps if we bring them together they will go their way."

"Spirit hand in spirit hand," said the visitor, smiling; and then, after a moment: "By the way, Herr Professor, I have been told that you have held sittings with Rudolf Hess."

"Many times. He is one of my oldest friends—from the days when the Nazi fortunes were not so easy to foretell as now."

"I can believe that, indeed. I had the pleasure of meeting Herr Hess at the Berghof the last time I was there. I expect to go again before long, and if I see him I will tell him about this meeting."

"I will send my astral body to make note of what you and he are doing, and will tell you about it the next time we meet."

"That will be most interesting, Herr Professor. You may count upon my following up this fascinating subject. I realize that I am only a neophyte, while you are one of the masters."

"A most promising pupil, Herr Budd, and I shall be happy to reveal to you any secrets in my possession."

The time had come for the visitor to take his departure, and he asked this teacher what was the proper fee for the evening's instructions. The Professor said he would make no charge, for he had learned as much as he had taught. But Lanny knew better than to take that seriously. He drew an envelope from his pocket and laid it quietly on the center table, alongside the crystal ball. It contained a check for two hundred marks, about eighty dollars; a reasonably good fee, enough to keep any teacher interested. The check was drawn on a Berlin bank, which gave the elderly wizard a further item of information, and put him in position to get more if he thought it worth while. Again Lanny didn't mind, for he wanted what he wanted, and was prepared to pay.

19

Vaulting Ambition

I

LANNY BUDD had a perpetual problem to wrestle with in his dealings with Adolf Hitler. He hated so to give this most dangerous of living men any information that would be of use to him; but, on the other hand, some information had to be given, otherwise the connection would soon be broken off. Apart from the matter of Trudi, it was surely worth while for a presidential agent to have access to the Führer's home, and a time might come in the future when it would be of crucial importance.

Manifestly, there could be no such thing as restraining this half-genius, half-madman. If Lanny told him things that were calculated to restrain him, he would become irritated; if Lanny persisted, he would fly into a passion and make a speech two hours long. Afterwards, he would realize that he had wasted his time, and would say: "No more of that *Taugenichts!*" No, if you wanted to keep the friendship of a mad king, you had to do like the other courtiers—tell him what he wanted to hear. Watch for the signs of what he meant to do, and then advise him to do it, and he would know you for a wise man. The consequences might be terrifying, but there could be no other way. F.D.R. had hit the nail on the head when he said that it would be necessary to give these dictators rope and let them hang themselves.

So when Lanny received his summons to the New Chancellery, he told Adi Schicklgruber pretty much what he had already written to Gus Gennerich: that the Chancellor of Austria was a weak man who blustered. There hadn't been anything confidential in Lanny's two talks with him; quite the contrary, what Schuschnigg had said was what he wanted the world to know. Lanny told it to the master of the Nazi world, and the Nazi-master beamed, for it was what he wanted to hear. This agreeable American art expert had gone into the heart of Hitler's problem, had talked with the key people, penetrated their thoughts, judged their characters—and come out with exactly the opinions that Hitler held. "Why can't I get my own people to do things like that?" thought Adi—but he wouldn't say it, lest the agreeable American should get a case of swelled head and start raising his price. Two expensive paintings, a Detaze and a Defregger, were enough!

"I doubt very much if he'll resist if it comes to a showdown," said Lanny; and Adi burst out: "What has he to resist with?"

"Not much, I agree; but he could make it awkward—you don't want to kill people of German blood, and you don't want to make too much of an uproar in the foreign press."

"*Die verdammte Judenpresse!*" exclaimed Adi, and began moving restlessly about the room, with those nervous jerks that he gave when something had upset him. He started scolding at foreign journalists, comparing them to a pack of jackals standing around a lion and his kill. Adi, of course, was the lion, and Schuschnigg, presumably, the kill, though Adi didn't say so. What he objected to was the noise the jackals made—for in the neighborhood there was a rival lion, the British, and also a rooster, or whatever symbol you assigned to the French and their army. Hitler dropped his simile, and exclaimed: "My generals are not to be convinced that Britain and France will stay quiet."

"I have heard, Herr Reichskanzler, that your generals took the same position when you wished to move your armies into the Rhineland, and again when you started rebuilding the Reichswehr."

"*Sehr richtig!* The same men, and they made the same speeches— in the Old Chancellery then, and now in this very room."

"Generals are good advisers when it comes to military matters, but for political affairs it takes a different sort of mind, I should imagine."

"That is what I tell them, and I'm going to give them a shaking up that will make their teeth rattle! For five years we have been getting ready, and what is it all for? Am I expected to sit on my tail and let the German Reich go bankrupt because its army leaders haven't the courage to use the forces I have created for them?"

That was almost word for word what Lanny Budd had said to Roosevelt concerning Hitler's problem and his attitude. The "P.A." ventured to repeat: "If a man builds a bicycle, presumably his intention is to ride, and not to go sailing."

"*Ein ausgezeichnete Vergleich, Herr Budd!* You have a happy faculty of finding the word. I am forced to waste my energies arguing with men who have been brought up to obey rules, and who have never had an original impulse in their lives. I tell them: Empires are not made in that way."

II

Lanny wondered: Was the Führer of the Nazis unaware that he was being indiscreet, or was it a calculated indiscretion? Was he thinking of sending this plausible American back to Vienna, to report the iron determination of the Führer and thus frighten a conscientious Catholic scholar? Lanny had another purpose in mind, and he said: "May I make a suggestion, Herr Reichskanzler?"

"I am always ready to hear them from you."

"Why don't you invite Doktor Schuschnigg to visit you at Berchtesgaden? It is a short trip, and if you and he could talk matters over he might discover that your intentions toward the Austrians are not so alarming as he has been led to fear."

"That is what I instructed Papen to arrange, but he has not succeeded. Schuschnigg is afraid, he reports. Does he imagine I would do harm to a guest?"

"I do not know, Herr Hitler. The subject was not brought up in our conversation."

"Do you suppose you could persuade him to come?"

"I am afraid that if I made such an attempt I should destroy any usefulness I might have to you. My advantage lies in the fact that I am an art lover and a citizen of the world. I met the Doktor socially, and we talked as friends; he asked my advice and I gave it. If now I should turn up in Vienna with a message from you, I should forfeit that status and be definitely set down as your agent. When I went to London or Paris, that reputation would follow me, and I should no longer be in a position to hear what my friends in the British Foreign Office are saying, and what they are planning to do with regard to Vienna."

"I suppose so," admitted the Führer, reluctantly—for he hated to give up anything he wanted. Following Lanny's red herring, he demanded: "What *will* the British do?"

"I should say that fundamentally it depends upon one factor, whether or not you succeed in convincing Whitehall that your ultimate goal is Moscow."

"What more can I do to convince them? Have I not promoted and signed an Anti-Comintern Pact with Italy and Japan?"

"That is not quite the same thing as saying that you intend to use your armies against Russia."

"Do they expect me to say that? Where? And how? In a public speech? Do I have to set the date when the advance begins?"

Lanny smiled. "You men of great affairs have your own ways of making things known to one another, Exzellenz. Sometimes a nod suffices."

"*Zum Teufel!* I have nodded my neck out of joint. I have said to every statesman I met that my abhorrence of Jewish Bolshevism is fundamental, and the duty to destroy it is the first of all duties I recognize."

"Do you authorize me to say that for you, Herr Reichskanzler?"

"Indeed I do, and I will be grateful to you for the service, as for so many others."

III

That seemed a good place to leave the subject, and Lanny said abruptly: "By the way, Herr Reichskanzler, shall I report on the matter of the Defregger?"

"By all means," was the reply, and Lanny opened up a portfolio he had brought. He had gone to some trouble to get photographs of half a dozen paintings of which he approved, and now he spent an enjoyable half hour, delivering his suave lecture and hearing his client's responses. Adi really loved art, and never tired of telling his guests that he would have preferred to be an artist, and that if the world would let him he would now retire to paint landscapes and design buildings for the rest of his days.

He liked all these paintings, and said that he would be glad to own them if he could afford it. Lanny, who wasn't thinking about commissions right now, remarked: "The prices of two or three seem to me excessive, and I would advise you, if you are thinking of going into Vienna, to wait until you are established there, and I might be able to do much better for you." He grinned, and the future world conqueror began to laugh and slap his two knees; he looked at Lanny and went on chuckling, rubbing his thighs.

So clever and so disinterested an agent deserved his reward, and the Führer demanded: "What about that Detaze?"

"I have been thinking it over, Exzellenz, and what I want to do is to pick out half a dozen of our best landscapes and either send them or bring them to you and let you make a choice. I will return to the Riviera and attend to that errand now, if you like; and if you are still in the mood to try experiments with my Polish medium, I might bring her back with me. She is an old woman and is not used to traveling alone, especially in a foreign country."

"I am interested in what you have told me about this woman, Herr Budd; but I have to remember that I am the head of a state, and that what I do is an example which millions follow. I must on no account have any publicity to the effect that I am dabbling with spirits."

"There will certainly be no publicity as far as I am concerned, Exzellenz, and I assume that you can control your own entourage."

"You grant me a power which is unattainable by any public man. Whatever goes on in my home is whispered all over Germany in a very few days."

"Permit me to make a suggestion. I recently had a séance with Pröfenik, who tells me that he knows you."

"I haven't seen him for years, but I used to see a good deal of him in the old days. He was a friend of Hanussen, and they sometimes gave stage performances together."

"He mentioned that Herr Hess sees him frequently."

"Yes, Rudi is never satisfied unless some astrologer has approved what he is doing. He can always manage to find one to approve, if he lets them know what he wants."

"It occurs to me that Herr Hess might be the one to invite Madame Zyszynski. Presumably he would do that if you asked it."

"Rudi is my other self; my Deputy."

"Well then, Madame could come to Berchtesgaden as his guest, and you could give it out that you have no interest in her. If she was in the house and you wished to see her, that could surely be arranged without attracting attention."

"*Jawohl,*" said the Führer; "bring her along. You see how it is—I am represented as a self-willed man, doing whatever he pleases, but in reality I am a slave to my German people, and am not master even in my own house."

"You belong to history, Herr Reichskanzler," said the American admirer.

IV

Lanny took the train to Paris, where he had his car and his friends. Zoltan had just come back from New York, full of news about the art shows there; they talked shop quite shamelessly, and had no secrets from each other—except that Lanny was not free to name the important person in Berlin who had just purchased a couple of Defreggers on his advice. Zoltan would assume that it was Göring, and that could do no harm. Inside his shrewd head must have been the guess that this grandson of Budd Gunmakers had not changed his Pink opinions, but was disguising them for some purpose important to himself. The only sign Zoltan ever gave was a slight smile curving the sensitive lips, under a mustache which had once been light brown but was now turning gray.

In the mail awaiting Lanny was a letter from his father, saying that he had made an advantageous deal with Baron Schneider and it would help him over a really desperate time. So Lanny would be doing a filial duty in having lunch with the Baron.

He called at the Paris mansion. When he mentioned that he had had talks with both Hitler and Schuschnigg, the munitions king wanted to hear every word that they had spoken, and there was no reason why he shouldn't hear most. He was especially pleased with what Hitler had said concerning Russia; the pleasure lasted half-way through the meal, but by that time he had begun to wonder, could he believe it, and what did Lanny think on that point? Lanny said: "I would say you may believe it so long as you can make it to Hitler's interest to act upon it." This, of course, was according to the code of a man of great affairs.

In return for Lanny's frankness the Baron brought him up to date on French affairs, which were in a turmoil. The Chautemps cabinet had been forced out, and Blum had been trying to form a "National Ministry." Schneider said he had put his foot down; he wanted unity in France, but not under Socialist auspices, conferring prestige upon that dangerous party. So now there was another Chautemps cabinet, this time with the Socialists excluded; the Baron called that unity—disregarding the fact that the French workers were completely alienated, and ready to do whatever they could to sabotage another government of the *deux cent familles*. The franc had taken another tumble—thirty to the dollar now, and Schneider said it was the doings of the Britisher Montagu Norman. Premier Chautemps was asking for special financial powers and the Socialists were opposing him. Such was *la patrie*, torn in half by a civil war in the very presence of the foreign enemy.

Nothing had been done to punish the Cagoulard conspirators, except that they were still under confinement; the extreme rightist press was hailing them as martyrs, mass meetings were being held in their defense, and Lanny carried off as souvenir a leaflet headed: "*Libérez les de Bruynes!*" He wondered who had paid for the printing—Schneider, or Denis himself, or possibly Graf Herzenberg or Kurt Meissner? Lanny still didn't feel that it was the part of wisdom for him to visit the prisoners, but he drove out to the château to call on Annette.

This lovely young gentlewoman, living in the home which for Lanny had been consecrated by the presence of Marie, didn't know very much about politics, and had only one thought, to free her loved ones. To her the arrest was an outrage committed by the terrible Reds who controlled her beloved France; she went to see each of the martyrs twice a week—they were confined separately—and spent the rest of her time telephoning, writing, and calling upon ministers and persons of influence. She would always be polite to Lanny, but he was sure that in her heart she would never forgive him because he went about his own affairs, instead of dropping everything and trying to help these friends to whom he had stood in such close relationship. All he could say was: "I have assurances that they will never be brought to trial." Also: "I am a foreigner, Annette, and when a foreigner tries to do anything in French politics, it always works backwards."

V

One last duty: at command of the Trudi-ghost, Lanny got a hundred one-thousand-franc notes from his bank. Since they were all new, and the serial numbers consecutive, he spent the better part of two days getting them changed into smaller denominations—mostly by the method of purchasing inexpensive gifts for his family and friends in England and America. He wrote a typewritten and unsigned note to the ex-clarinetist, making an appointment for a dark street, and instructing the man to wear a red carnation and be prepared to give the name of two mutual friends. With the wad of bills wrapped up in a piece of newspaper, as if it were a pound or two of newly bought cheese, Lanny went strolling at the appointed hour, wondering as usual whether this would be the underground or the Gestapo.

The street was dimly lighted and had few persons out on a raw and windy night. There came an elderly gray-bearded German, wearing the proper sign, and Lanny turned and joined him, saying: "*Guten Abend.*" Promptly the man said: "Monck." Lanny said: "*Noch einmal,*" and the man answered: "Weill"—pronouncing it French fashion "Vay," as Trudi had done in Paris. That was enough, and Lanny slipped the package into his hands, turned sharply, and went off into the darkness, looking behind him frequently to make sure he was not being trailed.

VI

Two cords drew his heart to London: Rick, and his little daughter. One morning he climbed into a transport plane at Le Bourget field, and an hour later was set down comfortably at Croydon. What marvels man had achieved—and what use was he going to make of them? Nina

and Rick met him in their small car, Nina driving, as always; the three
of them squeezed into the space meant for two, and they had an hour
in which nobody could intrude on their conversation. An old and tried
friendship, this; a quarter of a century, or two-thirds of Lanny's life,
since he and Rick had become friends. Lanny could tell them everything, save only the name of Roosevelt, and if they guessed that, no
harm would be done.

For the first time he unburdened himself completely about Trudi;
and if the tears came into his eyes he didn't have to feel embarrassed.
"It's rugged, old chap!" said Rick, and that was enough from an Englishman. They listened to every detail of Lanny's adventure in the Château de Belcour, and at the end Rick's verdict was: "It's no go; you
have to count her dead."

Lanny replied: "I suppose so; but I have to make sure. I can't go on
wondering about her the rest of my life." He told of his plan to make
Hitler tell him, and of the progress he had made to that goal.

"It's all right if you can get away with it," was his friend's judgment
—"and especially if you can pick up news as you go along. That was a
ripping story you sent me from Vienna; I had it in type two days
later." Rick put the newspaper clipping into his friend's hand. He had
got twenty pounds for the story, and wanted to go halves. Lanny refused it, for he knew that Rick needed the money, and might have got
twenty pounds every day of his life if he had been willing to write for
the press lords.

"You give me as much news as I give you," the American insisted.
During the time he spent at The Reaches he got a pretty complete
picture of the state of opinion in Britain among those classes which
counted. The "appeasers" had won all along the line. As regards Spain,
the "Non-Intervention" farce was continuing, and while France had
been forced to close her border again, Mussolini and Hitler were sending the Franco crowd all the men and supplies they needed. Hitler
would be allowed to expand his borders, provided only that he didn't
take anything British. Reaction ruled the world, and the masses of the
people weren't even allowed to know what was being done to them.

VII

Nina drove Lanny over to Wickthorpe Castle, and he spent several
days verifying what the pessimistic Rick had said. The renovating of
the castle had been completed, and Irma was safely launched upon that
social career for which her life had been a training. Very interesting to

watch her, so gracious and self-possessed, and to remember her first halting steps, and the guidance she had received from Emily and Margy and the other *grandes dames*, not to mention Beauty Budd and her son. Now she was intending to become the greatest of all the great ladies. Only one rival to dispute her future, another American, Nancy Astor; and Irma had the advantage, because her home was both comfortable and venerable, whereas Cliveden was merely comfortable.

It was in truth a public service to maintain a great establishment with all the comforts of a hotel, where persons of importance could come for stays long or short and discuss the problems of the Empire. Irma had the final say about who should be invited, but she was broadminded about it, consulting not merely Ceddy and his intimates, but anyone of the right sort. If a guest should say: "You ought to know So-and-so," Irma would reply with easy informality: "Bring him along next week-end." She had forty bedrooms, each now provided with its bath. So-and-so might be a high official just returned from Sarawak, or an explorer from the Orinoco; he might be the exponent of a new scientific theory or the author of a best-selling novel; he might even be some notorious leftwinger like Rick, but an English gentleman even so. He might say what he pleased, and be ever so much in earnest, provided he kept his temper and gave the others a chance to answer.

Certainly it was a privilege for Lanny Budd to have the freedom of this establishment. Lanny the man might not be entirely happy here, but Lanny the presidential agent was in his element. He listened to Montagu Norman, governor of the Bank of England, one of the most secretive men in the world, discussing with Gerald Albany the financial techniques by which recalcitrant foreign statesmen were compelled to serve the purposes of the Empire. Baron Schneider accused the British of having caused the collapse of the franc, and "the Governor" wasn't saying anything about it except to the right people. He took it for granted that the son of Budd-Erling, just back from a visit with Hitler, was among these.

Also, a chat with Philip Kerr, Marquess of Lothian, whom Lanny had come to know at the Peace Conference as the secretary of Lloyd George. Kerr, pronounced Carr, had paid a visit of state to Berlin a few months ago, and had come back a complete convert to General Göring's program of letting Germany alone in Central Europe in exchange for a guarantee of security for the British Empire. His lordship was a Christian Scientist, and saw this deal with Germany as the way of reconcilement and readjustment. He was quite sure that when Hitler was satisfied, he would become conservative and gentlemanly like

Lothian himself. The Marquess talked on terms of intimacy with an American who had followed in his footsteps to Berlin and met all the right people. Almost without exception Irma's week-end guests agreed that the ex-painter of picture postcards—they called him a house-painter, sometimes a paperhanger, which they judged humiliating occupations—could not get very far in a career of conquest without tangling with the new Soviet Empire, and that was a spectacle which British Tories were prepared to contemplate with equanimity.

So smooth they were and so elegant; so well informed, and personally agreeable, many of them even charming! They had had an empire for four centuries, and had been trained for their jobs as masters. They were secure and easygoing; they had seen many upstarts upstarting in many parts of the world, but Britannia continued to rule the waves and a lot of the adjacent land. At the same time they were fair; they would listen, and would give way when they had to—no sooner than necessary, and not an inch farther than necessary, but enough to save them and their positions. No French or Russian or Spanish revolutions for them!

Lanny listened to a discussion between Lothian and an M.P. of the old-fashioned Liberal school; that saving minority of Englishmen who believed in morals in international affairs. This Liberal said about the Nazis all the things that Lanny would have liked to say; he said them with vehemence, and made some remarks which Lothian might have taken as personal. But the Marquess took no offense; he was courteous and persuasive, and made those soft answers which turn away wrath. He, too, believed in morals and in fair dealings among states; he wanted everything his opponent wanted, it was merely a question of tactics between them. Listening to this most plausible noble lord, you would have concluded that reactionary statesmen making deals with wholesale murderers were in reality tenderhearted humanitarians and crusaders for righteousness all over the world.

VIII

There was little Frances, several months older, visibly bigger, and still more eager to know about the wonderful world. She had one wing of a palace set apart for herself and her entourage. She was a stepchild, but had apparently not discovered the unhappiness of that status; the fact that her real father appeared only three or four times a year only made him seem the more delightful when he did come. There was a subtle and mysterious bond of blood between them; Ceddy could never take Lanny's place and was too busy to try. His lordship was like the proprietor and manager of a great hotel in which Frances lived, while Lanny was the Prince Charming who traveled all over the world and brought back delightful stories.

The child, too, saved up stories for him, but not much happened to her, she was so well taken care of; she didn't suffer from it, for her routine was normal and satisfying. There were horses and dogs, sheep and deer, rabbits and pheasants on this great estate. There was a French governess, and the child jabbered away to her father, reciting one of La Fontaine's fables. There was a piano teacher for an hour every day, and she played her little pieces for a tolerant judge. Most important of all, there was snow on the ground, and they had a grand time pummeling each other. She couldn't have a pony ride, because the damp snow would ball up under the pony's feet and he might stumble and throw her; but Lanny could pull her about on a sled, and if she fell off, that was a grand adventure to tell her mother about.

Grandmother Fanny, for whom the child was named, had broken her ties with Long Island, and she and her brother had a "lodge" of their own on the estate. The place at Shore Acres was for sale; but who would have the money to buy it? especially now when it appeared that New Deal spending was coming to the unhappy close which everybody had predicted for it, though nobody seemed to have anything to take its place. Just now had come a strange development: a would-be purchaser, the most unforeseeable and incredible of bidders, a large labor union proposing to use the property as a home for its superannuated members! They were actually offering one and a half million dollars, and half a million was cash which they had in their own bank! Word of this horror had got out among the fashionable neighbors, with the result that Irma and her mother had been deluged with cablegrams and letters of protest, and now the neighbors were subscribing to a syndicate to preserve one of the most select of New York's suburban districts. Really, it was a kind of blackmail, and everybody looked at his neighbor, wondering who would be the next to turn up a walking delegate with a yen for high-class real estate.

Frances had heard talk about this, and wanted Lanny to tell her what was so bad about these people. Then she wanted to know: "Papa, will I be an English girl?" He told her: "You will be whatever you want, and you will have plenty of time to decide." He had an idea that the world might change a lot in the next ten years. Stocks might continue to slump and income taxes to rise; the Barnes fortune might cease to be such an impediment to independent thinking. It might even be that

Wickthorpe Castle would come on the market, and some British labor union might have a hundred thousand pounds in its own bank!

IX

A plane returned the traveler to Paris, and his car took him over the well-worn *route nationale* to the Riviera. There Beauty was waiting eagerly to know every detail of the life of her darling. First, Lanny would tell all he could recall, and then she would start complaining because it wasn't enough; she must hear every word that had come from those precious little lips. She would plague Lanny with questions: What did they feed her? How did they dress her? What did she weigh now? Was she really happy? What did she talk about? Men are so uncommunicative; and it was such a shame that Fanny Barnes could have the grandchild all the year round, while Beauty couldn't have her except by disarranging all her affairs and going to camp out in England!

This wasn't exactly accurate, for she and Mr. Dingle could have a cottage on the Wickthorpe estate any time they chose, and a proper quota of servants to wait on them. As for traveling, it had been the major delight of Beauty Budd's life ever since her son could remember. The truth was, it was now the height of the season on the Côte d'Azur, and Emily Chattersworth wouldn't give up entertaining and couldn't keep it up without Beauty and Sophie Timmons to help her. Later, when the hot weather came, Beauty would transport herself and her New Thought husband to England, whither the height of the season would also have moved; there she would divide her time between Wickthorpe Castle and Bluegrass, the home of Margy, Dowager Lady Eversham-Watson, where Sophie also would have installed her husband. These old cronies, all four of them Americans, hung together, unconquered by time and unwilling to give up the delights of spending money and showing themselves to the world—even though they themselves shuddered when they looked at the spectacle in the mirror. Emily was well in her seventies, and Beauty was the only one of the gang who hadn't passed sixty.

Visiting at Bienvenu were Lanny's half sister, Marceline Detaze, and her husband. Marceline had returned because she was going to have a baby; a girl likes to have her mother around at such a time, and Marceline was for the moment less the self-assured and willful playgirl. But her chronic want of money continued, and it was agreeable news to her that Hitler was paying a high price for a Detaze; one-third of this price would be hers, and when would he pay? She started her old refrain: Why couldn't her brother take a little time off and sell a lot of those paintings, as it would be so easy for him to do?

Lanny knew that it was Vittorio who was putting her up to this; it meant that Vittorio was gambling again—if indeed he had ever stopped. He would make glib promises, but what did any promise mean to a Fascist? Evading them was a part of that creed which they called *sacro egoismo*. Il Capitano di San Girolamo was one of those weakminded persons who are always discovering a new "system" for breaking the bank at the casino of whatever city or town they happen to be in. Lanny, who in the course of life on the Riviera had known scores of such persons and seen them all go bankrupt and disappear, strove to convince his brother-in-law that there are laws of mathematical probability which never fail in the long run, and that the odds on a roulette wheel have been calculated on that certainty. But what did it mean to be a Fascist hero, if you had to admit the existence of laws superior to your own desires?

The Capitano had been granted a month's furlough to accompany his wife. He considered that he had earned it, spending a whole year in that God-forsaken hole of Seville where prices had tripled and quadrupled in wartime, and where pleasure was almost unobtainable. Vittorio had begun to open his eyes and discover that it wasn't all a picnic, pulling chestnuts out of the fire for the good-for-nothing Spanish aristocracy and the filthy-rich Juan March; he wondered what Italy was going to get out of it, and especially what a one-armed hero was going to get. He could never fly again, and had to take a desk job which bored him greatly, especially with a small salary and promotion unreasonably delayed. Vittorio was beginning to think of asking for a discharge and settling down on his wife and mother-in-law. If only he could get enough cash to try out the infallible new system which had been explained to him by a lounger in the casino bar!

But none of these personal dissatisfactions ever touched the fundamentals of the Capitano's creed. The ancient Impero Romano was being restored, the Mediterranean was to be "Our Sea," and statues of Il Duce would be set up on the shores all around it. Nice, Savoy, Corsica were the immediate Italian demands, and "Nice" meant this Côte d'Azur as far as Toulon, a necessary naval base. Vittorio's way of strutting, as well as his dogmatic tones, informed the people of Bienvenu, of the Cap, and of Juan and Cannes, that he was to be the future master of this soil. Some day soon the Party would recognize his special qualifications and make him a confidential agent at a high salary. Meantime he sponged on Beauty's rich friends and borrowed money from them, and had his moods of boasting, and other moods of wondering weakly why the French Fascists didn't take him up and admire him, overlooking the fact that the polo-playing and pigeon-shooting *jeunesse dorée* of the Midi had their own program of expansion, which included Italian Sardinia, Italian Tripoli, and even a slice off the Ligurian shore.

Since Lanny had come back from seeing Hitler and was going again, he was well established as a convert and recruit to the Axis, and the Capitano asked questions about the Nazis, their party organization and especially their air force. He revealed that he disliked all Germans intensely, considering them interlopers who had taken over the Duce's ideas and techniques. But there could be no doubt that they had great resources and industrial power, and had a right to expand; only let them do it toward the east, and leave the Balkans and the Mediterranean to the discoverers and creators of Fascism. All this Vittorio expounded at the dinner table of his mother-in-law's home, and Lanny listened courteously. Beauty, no longer sure what her son really believed, was satisfied to see him keeping the peace in the family, and leaving her free to give her thoughts to a soirée at Sept Chênes, where he was to play accompaniments for a singer from the opera company in Cannes.

X

A round of social duties completed, Lanny packed up half a dozen of the best Detaze landscapes and shipped them by express to the Führer at Berchtesgaden. He telephoned to make sure the great man was there, and that a visit would be convenient; then he told Madame to put her belongings into a couple of bags and come for a journey with him. He didn't say where they were going, just to the mountains of Southern Germany; that was enough to set her old heart a-flutter. He wouldn't risk motoring her through the Alps in February. To her it was like a romance, to be with the man whom she adored and who looked so much like the son she had lost. She hoped and prayed that Tecumseh would come on this journey, and not Claribel; so far he always had come, by yacht or train or motorcar. He didn't say how he did it—he was just there, at your service.

These oddly chosen traveling companions got along well, because Lanny liked to read, and Madame liked to play Patience for hours, and then to doze in her seat. They reached Munich safely, and as Lanny had telegraphed the hour of their arrival, there was an elegant limousine awaiting them, with a Nazi chauffeur in uniform and a Death's Head Leutnant riding beside him. "Herr Budd?" inquired the latter, and then: "*Bitte*, may I see your card?" Lanny showed him an engraved visiting card, smaller than it would have been had he been a German. The officer inspected it, and then: "*Bitte, einzusteigen.*" They drove all the way to the town of Berchtesgaden, a matter of a couple of hours on one of those modern superhighways completely cleared of snow. During the trip no word was exchanged; the Führer's guests shared his high status, and were not spoken to unless they spoke first.

From the town the road to the Berghof climbs steadily. Lanny had traveled it two and a half years ago, when he and Irma had taken Trudi out of Germany, and Irma had been so furious about it that she had taken a train to Bremen and a steamer to New York. Such had been the end of Lanny's first marriage—and, as you might say, the beginning of his second, though he had no idea of this at the time. Then it had been night, and the lights of his car had turned here and there with the winding of the road, sweeping over mountainsides covered with tall fir trees. Now it was daytime, and the slopes and trees were covered with deep snow, sparkling in bright sunlight; the air was clear and laden with forest scents.

The private road into the estate was guarded even more carefully than on the previous occasion; there were men of the Death's Head Brigade on patrol every couple of hundred yards or so and they gave their "Heil Hitlers," which the Leutnant returned. At the elaborate main gates they were halted and no chances were taken; not even a Death's Head Leutnant could bring two persons into the Berghof on his own word or guess. Lanny Budd had to present his visiting card again, and to submit to the humiliation of having the fur robe lifted from his knees, lest he might have someone concealed thereunder. The trunk of the car was likewise searched; and all this time the machine guns, one on each side of the steel gates, were kept turned upon the car. The grandson of Budd Gunmakers had had much to do with machine guns in the course of his life, but never before at the wrong end.

When the gates were opened they drove slowly, an SS man walking on each side of them. Lanny had heard that attempts had been made on the Führer's life, and the control had become far more rigid than on his previous visit. He took no chances of making a false move, and at the front door of the residence did not step out, American fashion, but waited for instructions.

There came waddling down the steps of the mansion a rolypoly of a man with a face as round and red as a newly risen harvest moon. Being a Nazi, he said: "*Heil Hitler!*" and then, being a Bavarian, he added: "*Grüss' Gott, Herr Budd!*" It was the one-time Kellner of the

Bratwurst Glöckle in Munich who was now the Führer's majordomo; he knew Herr Lanny Budd, having played the accordion and sung for him on his last visit. Were they afraid that some would-be assassin might have slugged and kidnaped the real Lanny Budd, and with his visiting card be now presenting himself at the Führer's retreat?

"*Grüss' Gott, Herr Kannenberg,*" said Lanny, returning the continuous smile. "Allow me to present my friend Madame Zyszynski." So it was all right; the SS men opened the doors of the car, the guests stepped forth, and their luggage was lifted out for them. Lanny had time for one look about, enough to see that the construction work which had been going on in the autumn of 1935 had been completed, and the simple châlet once called Haus Wachenfels now had a long two-story wing added on each side, so that guests would never again have to sleep in tents. He remarked to his escort the excellent taste of the new work, and the majordomo replied with a tone and expression as if he were singing a psalm in front of an altar: "*Unser Führer ist der grösste Architekt der Welt!*"

XI

Lanny hadn't told Madame to what place she was coming; that was his practice, and she understood that every visit was a test. She couldn't fail to observe all this pomp and circumstance, and perhaps had seen photographs of Der Berghof in the picture papers which she patronized; certainly she would know the most publicized of all faces, commonplace except for a fleshy nose and a Charlie Chaplin mustache. But she wasn't going to see that face for a while; she was coming to visit a different gentleman, whose name was Hess, but it had been arranged that his name also was not to be spoken. The moment she entered the house she was taken in charge by a maid who spoke English, and who escorted her to a room and provided her with every comfort, including lunch and a chance to lie down and rest after her trip.

The rolypoly ex-Kellner took Lanny up in the elevator to another room, and after he had had a bath he made his appearance in the reception rooms on the ground floor. The largest of these was the "great hall," an architect's dream of comfort and elegance. The greater part of its front was of glass, giving a view of the piled-up mountains of the Austrian Alps. The ceiling was paneled, with a dozen heavy beams in one direction and another dozen crossing them, forming squares. They were of some beautifully carved dark brown wood, and from them hung chandeliers, each a ring of thirty slim white candles with electric bulbs in the tops. At the far end was a raised platform, like a terrace, three steps high and perhaps twenty feet deep, extending all the way across the room and along part of one side. Here was a great open fireplace with high-banked lounges in front of it. The walls of the room were wainscoted three or four feet high, and above were paintings, well spaced, and here and there tapestries for which an expert would have undertaken to get several million dollars—but he assumed that they were not for sale.

Awaiting the guest in this sumptuous apartment was a man in a Brownshirt uniform. He was known as the *Führerstellvertreter*, and Lanny had last seen him on a very solemn occasion—standing on the platform before one of the giant Nazi assemblies, calling the roll of the martyrs, those Party comrades who had been killed in the course of more than a decade of struggle for power. He had stood very straight, a tall athletic figure in the simple Brownshirt uniform, and now he wore the same in his Führer's not so simple home. He was a Reichsminister, chief of the Nazi Party, and Number Three man of the *Regierung*, but he did not go in for stage costumes like the Number Two. Following his master, he did not drink or smoke, but set an example to the Party rank and file, and despised and spurned those many who did not follow it.

Walter Richard Rudolf Hess had the face of a fanatic; a mouth which was a straight line, with hardly any lips at all, and another line made by bushy black eyebrows meeting over the top of his nose. His deep-set eyes were a greenish gray, and he was famous for being able to outstare any erring Party chieftain; they were all afraid of the contempt which they saw on his olive-skinned features. There was no trace of the Nordic about him; his hair was black and very thick, and at the top of his head was a long scar where no hair would grow—he had got it in one of those *Saalschlachten* in the early days of the Party, the beer-cellar meetings which had turned into battles with the Reds, and one of the enemy had hurled a beer mug at the head of Adi Schicklgruber's most faithful bodyguard.

IIe had been first an infantry officer and then an aviator in the World War, and afterwards, hearing the ex-corporal make a speech at one of the Munich meetings, had become his adorer and faithful secretary. For his part in the attempt at revolution he had been sentenced to the Landsberg fortress, along with Hitler; and being a man of better education than his master, he had patiently written down every word of the master's outgivings and shaped them into a book. Adi had proposed to entitle this work: "Four and One-Half Years' Struggle Against

Lies, Stupidity and Cowardice"; but Hess, with better judgment, had suggested "Mein Kampf." From then on the pair had been inseparable, and when Gregor Strasser had almost wrecked the Party by resigning and attacking the Führer, it was Hess who had been put in charge and authorized to speak in the Führer's name.

For four years now he had done so, becoming more dour and grim with each day of contact with the frailties of Nazi nature. He seldom appeared at social affairs, having no use for that sort of flummery; so the only time Lanny had met him was here at the Berghof with Irma. On that evening he had had almost nothing to say and had sat looking very glum, watching the two American visitors as if strongly disapproving the Führer's wasting his time on such people.

XII

Lanny had been told that this man could be friendly and even charming when he felt like it, and the visitor wanted very much to see him in that role. "Herr Reichsminister," he began, speaking English, which he knew the other understood and spoke fluently, "you may be interested to know about the first time I ever heard of you. It was at Christmas of 1924, and Heinrich Jung came back from Landsberg and told Kurt Meissner and me of two very wonderful men he had met in the fortress."

"*Wirklich?*" said the dark man; he could hardly say less.

"Kurt and I have been friends from boyhood and I was visiting him at Stubendorf. Heinrich is the son of the Oberförster there, as you perhaps know, and from that time on he never let up on me. I used to get some of your Party literature at least once a month. I stood out against it for years, but in the end I fell under the spell. So you see, Herr Hess, I am a sort of pupil of yours."

This from a guest only four years younger than himself was the extreme of graciousness. The hardest man has something in his soul about which he is sentimental, and that something with Hess was the period he had spent in prison with Adi and the other heroes of the NSDAP. The tight, almost lipless mouth relaxed into a smile, and the man of many suspicions remarked: "Those were great days."

"Greater, I believe, than any of us can realize as yet," replied the visitor. From that time on he was a member of the brotherhood, and no longer felt the eyes of the Deputy Führer following him about with suspicion.

Seated in one of the capacious leather armchairs of which there were a score in the hall, Lanny told about his eight years of dabbling in psychic research. He knew that his host was a believer in spiritualism; when he read that roll of the martyrs to the assembled Nazi throng, he was certain that the spirit of every one of those men was hovering over the scene and thrilling with the same pride as the reader. So now Lanny took that line; Tecumseh was a genuine spirit of a one-time Amerindian chieftain. Lanny had heard also that Hess was a "Moral Rearmament" man, a follower of Buchman, who had come back to America saying: "Thank God for a man like Hitler!" So Lanny spoke of having attended Buchmanite meetings in England, and having recently talked with Lord Lothian.

Lanny knew furthermore that Hess was a believer in faith healing, and had braved the ridicule of the other Party leaders to call a congress on that subject. Lanny knew the language of these many cults, because his stepfather had been teaching him for more than a decade. He told stories about the extraordinary cures which Parsifal Dingle had achieved. The visitor explained his belief that the "faith" which healed had no necessary connection with the Christian religion or the Jewish Bible; it wasn't faith in Jehovah or any other tribal deity, but faith in the creative principle which rules the universe and is in all our hearts. Lanny wasn't sure whether his host believed in Wotan and the old Teutonic panel of gods, but he was careful to leave them out of his condemnations. Also, being socially well trained, he was careful to give his host an opportunity to narrate his own experiences and to set forth the conclusions he had drawn from them; thus they spent a pleasant couple of hours, and at the end of the time were friends.

XIII

The American brought up the subject of Bruno Pröfenik, and told of his visit there. Hess said: "He is a man in whom I would not put too much trust"; and Lanny, not wishing to commit himself, replied: "I know there is fraud in every part of this field; also, I have reason to believe that there are mediums who at times produce genuine phenomena, and at other times, when the phenomena fail to appear, yield to the temptation to help the spirits out."

Hess agreed with this; he had kept his interest in Pröfenik because he was sure the old wizard had produced genuine trance phenomena, and in fact wouldn't dare to produce any other sort for the Deputy Führer. There was a menace in this for the wizard, and Lanny laughed and said: "Don't be too harsh with any of them! Remember that a man or woman in a genuine trance might cheat without being aware of it, or being able to help it."

The Nazi leader said he had never thought of that, and Lanny explained his idea that the subconscious mind has many levels and a variety of forces in it, some good and some evil. "We all have impulses to lie and cheat, and some of us yield to them on the conscious level." He skipped over this quickly, hoping that it wouldn't be taken as an allusion to a literary work of which his companion was joint author. "Why can it not happen that some sly and tricky subconscious personality should take control of a medium in trance, and seek to build up its own prestige and importance by making the medium do and say whatever it finds profitable?"

"That is providing them with a pretty broad alibi," remarked the Deputy Führer, shrewdly.

"Those who are conscious cheats will use everything they can think of. But I am not at all sure that Rudy Schneider ever became a deliberate cheat, or that Eusapia Palladino ever knew that she sometimes helped out her 'ectoplasm' with her foot."

These were cases in the books, and Hess didn't know the books, so Lanny told the stories. Then he said: "Pröfenik volunteered to send his astral body to the Berghof to find out what you and I are doing. It'll be interesting to see if he can make good on that. I wrote him that I would be here today, so no doubt he is trying his arts on us."

"Well, it oughtn't to be hard to guess that we are sitting in two chairs in this hall and talking about him and other mediums."

"I have thought of that," replied the American. "If you are interested in such experiments, let us do something a bit different, and beyond his guessing powers."

"What do you suggest?"

"I have thought of several things. They tell me you are an athlete, and keep yourself in condition. When I was a boy I was taught what was called 'French wrestling,' and what I have since been told all German schoolchildren practice. If the old wizard can say we were doing that, we can be sure he has some supernormal power."

"Either that, or else he has a spy in this household," remarked the dour Deputy.

They took off their coats and took their stand on a vacant part of that well-polished oaken floor; facing each other, but each somewhat to the other's right, with Lanny placing his right foot against the outside of Hess's right foot. They each took a firm stance, with the left foot back, and Lanny took his opponent's right hand in a firm grip with his right hand. So they were ready, and the trick was to keep your own balance while trying to push or pull your opponent off balance; you won a round when you succeeded in forcing him to lift his right foot off the ground. There are many tricks to take him by surprise, but Lanny never used one more than once, for Hess was quick in his reactions and had muscles of steel. Lanny, for his part, was a tennis player, which kept his grip firm; also he played the piano, which is harder work than most auditors realize.

That is what they were at when the master of this household entered the room. They stopped, but he wanted to know what they had been doing, and they went on while he watched them; he wished he had tried this form of diversion in the trenches, he said, when for months at a time there had been nothing to do but wait. However, he didn't offer to try it now; he looked to be flabby, and Lanny had heard that he took no exercise except walking. It wouldn't do for the Führer of all the Nazis to take any chance of being bested at anything. Lanny wasn't sure that his Deputy would have enjoyed such an experience either, and was glad that Hess was able to hold his own so well. When they quit, they were both of them breathing hard, and their Führer said, indulgently: "You are still nothing but boys, both of you." But they were *his* boys!

20

Mohammed's Mountain

I

In THE course of a fortunate life Lanny Budd had been a guest in elegant homes in various parts of the world, and the thing which struck him about them was that the resemblances were so much greater than the differences. There had come to be a standard of leisure-class life, much the same in all great centers. Transportation and communication were responsible for this, and the greatest of these forces was the motion-picture screen, which transported everything and communicated it to everybody all over the world. If the rich man in America had some new luxury, the rich man in Tasmania or Iceland saw it and ordered it. The result was a general level of comfort and culture, with nothing very new or startling to any visitor; the furnishings in the Berghof might have been transported to a mansion on Nob Hill in San Francisco, or on the Avenida Rio Branco in Rio de Janeiro, and would have fitted there.

The same thing had happened to manners and morals. Everywhere were quiet and well-trained servants, and a household seeming to operate automatically; everything was spotlessly clean, and if there was mud outside, everybody wiped his feet before he came in. Everybody spoke in a well-modulated voice and tempers were rarely lost. There might be a great deal of drinking, but people had learned to carry their liquor; they drank until they were beginning to be stupefied, and then went up to their rooms and slept it off. Costumes likewise had been standardized; the gray trousers and blue sport coat which the Führer wore at his lunch-table would have served for an informal meal in the town called Newcastle in Connecticut, or England, or Australia; and the same was true for the white tie and tails of a ceremonious affair.

With few exceptions, the statement applied also in the realm of ideas. The average man of wealth and power took the same attitude toward politics the civilized world around. Details and techniques might differ, but what the rich and great wanted was to keep what they had. That was why Robbie Budd could travel to Paris and Berlin and get along so well with Baron Schneider and General Göring; that was why the movement which had started in Italy had spread so swiftly to Germany and Poland and Rumania and Austria and Spain, to Brazil and the Argentine and Japan; why the Führer's agents could report to him a continuing spread of his propaganda in France and Britain, and in the great democracy which called itself the sweet land of liberty. Those who had property and enjoyed privileges wanted to hold onto them, and when they found labor beginning to organize, call strikes, and use the ballot in its own interest, the masters began to look about for a strong private police. "Fascism is capitalism plus murder,"—so the leftwing Rick had declared after his first interview with Mussolini, eighteen years ago.

II

The household in which Lanny was now a guest appeared to be even more decorous than the average. Its master did not drink, and did not permit anyone to smoke in his social rooms; his guests had to retire to their bedrooms or go outside on the terraces to indulge that evil practice. At the table he served them the customary generous meals, but had put before himself a specially prepared vegetable plate with one poached egg on top, and a one per-cent beer brewed for him. He was so gracious to everybody at the long table, including three women secretaries, that Lanny had to keep saying to himself: "This is the murderer of Trudi, and of Ludi, and of Freddi Robin."

Not that he had killed them with his own hands; but he had established the system and given the orders which included them and thousands of other victims. He was planning at this time the murder of a nation of six or seven millions, and the various generals and officials who came here were giving information and getting instructions bearing on this project. Yes, it was like visiting in the home of Beelzebub, known as the Father of Lies. He, too, no doubt, had a modern and perfectly appointed residence, and his manners were above reproach; but at what moment would the floor crack open and flames and the smell of brimstone burst forth?

After dinner Rudolf Hess asked if it would be convenient for him to make a test with Madame, and Lanny went up to arrange it. He told her that the room was to be dark, and that a gentleman would enter and take a seat; this gentleman was friendly, and would be polite to Tecumseh or whoever might come. Lanny had already explained the procedure to the Deputy Führer, who didn't need much instruction, being familiar with séances. The American would have liked to be present, but was afraid to take the chance; he had got into a jam with Zaharoff through being a witness to his humiliation, and wasn't going to make that mistake with anybody here. What they had in their subconscious minds was their secret. Lanny said, lightly: "Remember, don't blame me if the spirits are impolite." The other smiled and promised readily.

So now Hess disappeared, and the other guests and members of the household were invited into the projection room to see a movie. The Führer was fond of them, and oddly enough preferred American pictures, of course with German titles; he did not understand English, except for "O.K., Chief," and other such standard phrases. This time it was a comedy called *It Happened One Night;* Hitler had had it run several times, and never tired of it. From it he could learn how people traveled on autobuses in America, and how they liked to have their own way—which was something he would surely not wish to introduce into the Fatherland. Lanny wondered, how seriously did he take

American comedies? Had he got the idea that the daughters of American millionaires were accustomed to run away from home and marry some poor but honest young fellow whom they picked up on the road? So far, it hadn't happened in Newcastle, or in the neighborhood of Shore Acres.

When the showing was over, Hess was pacing up and down in the great hall; he took the guest by the arm and led him away, saying: "The Führer also wishes to hear my report." They went quietly to Hitler's study, which was on the second floor, at the front. Seated there before the fireplace, the Deputy said: "Herr Budd, this is really remarkable. Are you certain that nobody has told that old woman my name?"

Lanny replied: "I cannot be certain of that. I can only tell you that I haven't told her, nor told anyone else but you and Herr Hitler. If she got your name, it could only have been from someone in this household."

"That could not have happened, I am sure."

"It is a doubt which troubles everyone to whom I take Madame. Poor Zaharoff tormented himself with it all his life. I can only tell you that I take these experiments seriously, and give you my word of honor that I gave her no hint. Members of my family knew that I was shipping paintings to Herr Hitler, but all I told them about Madame was that I had a friend in Germany who wished to try some experiments. They are used to that, as Madame is."

III

The Nazi *Nummer Drei* proceeded to describe the spirits with whom he had spent the past hour. The first had been a certain Franz Deek, or some such name—Tecumseh was never good at foreign names. Dieckhoff, it was, and Hess had forgotten him, but the spirit brought him to mind; he had been one of those SA men who had aided Hess at the time of the *Putsch*, some fifteen years ago. Hess had not marched in that ill-fated parade through the streets of Munich; it had been his job to kidnap two of the ministers of the Bavarian government, called by the uneuphonious names of Schweyer and Wutzelhofer. The pair had been forced into automobiles and carried off into a near-by forest; they had been blindfolded and stood up to be shot, but had been spared, and carried off to another forest, and stood up again—a form of torture which had been meant to frighten them so that they would obey Nazi orders in future.

"We were naïve in those days," remarked the dark Deputy; "we hoped that we wouldn't have to kill many people."

Lanny thought: "The floor is cracking, and here are the flames and the smell of brimstone!"

Hess told the story of that exciting day. At a crossroads he took the precaution to telephone to Munich and learned that the military attempt had failed. So he turned his captives loose and fled to the mountains, where he remained a fugitive for several weeks. But finally he gave himself up—and that was the most fortunate decision of his life, for they sent him to the fortress where he became a fellow-prisoner with Hitler. They were treated well—allowed liberty within the fortress, and all the books and papers they desired. Hess smiled and said: "No faction could be sure their turn might not come next day, so it was better to be polite to your opponents." Adi smiled at everything his faithful follower said. These two addressed each other with the familiar "du,"—Hess being the only man who took that liberty with his Führer.

Now had come this Franz, or his spirit, reminding the Deputy how frightened he had been when he realized that his opponents were still on top in Munich. At his trial Hess had declared that he never had any intention of killing the two ministers; but Franz knew otherwise, and in the séance joked with him about it. The whole thing had been amazingly convincing. The spirit had spoken with a good Bavarian accent, and Hess wanted to know, did Madame know any German? Lanny replied: "Only a few words that she has heard me use. The spirits use her vocal cords." Ordinarily he would have added: "At least, that is the theory,"—but now he was taking the spirits at their own valuation.

A remarkable sitting, indeed. There had come a World War comrade, one who called himself Hans, and had been with Hess in the trenches at Verdun, and been killed a few minutes after Hess had been shot through the lungs. Hess didn't remember him, but then, there had been so many—fed into that year-long inferno like meat into a sausage grinder. This man had produced evidence, for he had quoted a line of a poem which Hess had written in the trenches. "*He, Franzmann,*" it began, which in English is about the same as: "Hey, Frenchie!" It told this Frenchie in simple language the brute facts about *Lebensraum:* the Frenchies had the land, but the Germans needed it in order that they, instead of the·Frenchies, might survive.

Lanny had never heard that Hess had written poetry, and said so. Hess answered modestly that it wasn't really poetry, just doggerel—but Lanny knew better than to assent. It is in this way that the great are betrayed by their greatness; try as they will, they cannot but absorb some of the flattery which is a part of the atmosphere they have to breathe. Before Lanny got through with this soldier turned party chieftain, the latter had become convinced that his doggerel was a genuine expression of the German *Geist*. Lanny would have said more, only he knew that Hitler would be bored—he, too, having written doggerel, but never having summoned the courage to let it be published.

IV

The Führer agreed that this was a significant psychic demonstration, and he wanted to go at once to Madame's room and make a test himself. But Lanny explained that this elderly woman was exhausted after a séance, and would hardly be able to produce results now; let her have a night's sleep, and any time tomorrow would be all right. Adi preferred the evening; he wanted to sneak into her room and not have any of the servants know it. The presumptuous American grinned and remarked: "For the sake of your reputation, it's a good thing she is so old!"

Hitler always slept badly, therefore he went to bed late, and liked to have company in the evening. These three sat for a long while discussing the nature of the universe and the possible destiny of the human insects which swarmed upon one of its insignificant planets. Hitler did most of the talking—for what else does it mean to be great? The other two listened respectfully, and gave their opinions when asked. Rudi, doglike in his devotion, invariably agreed with every word his divinely ordained Führer spoke. Lanny might venture to disagree, but always in the form of a question, calculated to start *Die Nummer Eins* on another discourse.

Adolf Hitler believed in God; not in the God of any of the established religions, and certainly not in the Hebrew God, or his Son the Christian God; but in the creative force, or spirit—yes, even personality, if you cared to say that—which worked behind the appearances of this mysterious universe. This spirit dwelt in us all, and could be used by us; to say that it answered prayers was merely another way of indicating this use. For a while Lanny might have thought that he was back in Bienvenu, listening to one of the New Thought discourses of Parsifal Dingle. Speak to him, thou, for he hears, and spirit with spirit can meet!

But quickly it became apparent that there was a difference between the transcendentalism of Tennyson and the National-Socialist *Mystik*.

Adi was a practical man, and had a world to conquer and to rule, and his God was approved and worshiped because He was willing to help with this job. No German tribal deity, the Führer hastened to explain, but a pragmatic One, to be judged by His works. That God had a purpose for the Aryan race to fulfill was proved by the fact that He had made them superior to all other races. The Führer said Aryan, for he included the Anglo-Saxons in his classification, and desired nothing so much as a union with the British and American peoples to carry out the great purposes which he envisioned. He didn't say so, but Lanny observed in all his conversation the secret envy which he held for the English with their long-tested traditions of rulership. Men like Lord Halifax and the Marquess of Lothian inspired him with a sort of embittered awe. The last of the Kaisers had had that same feeling, and had aspired to nothing so much as to be an English gentleman; he had got into a war with them, half by accident and half because they had patronized him.

God was a force, said the religious Adi, speaking here in the intimacy of friendship; God was the greatest of personal forces and likewise of social forces. Adi knew the former, because when he retired to his chamber he called upon this force to give him courage and vision, and it responded. Adi knew the latter, because he called upon this force in the hearts of the German people, and got his response in the form of national enthusiasm, will, and power. It was the duty of the seer, the mystic, to make that force real in his private life, and it was the duty of the statesman and the general to bring it into action in the masses. When you had those two personalities in one, then you had a really great leader, the man of destiny, the Führer of the *Volk* and the maker of history—"such as God has chosen me to be," said Adi Schicklgruber, not vaingloriously, but humbly. He never quoted the Hebrew Bible, and perhaps had never read it; but Lanny knew it, and remembered the experience narrated by the prophet Isaiah:

"Also I heard the voice of the Lord, saying, Whom shall I send, and who will go for us? Then said I, Here am I; send me."

V

This God-chosen man went on to discuss the other God-chosen men of history. There had been some who had failed, because they had had only spiritual force, and no way to make it effective; such had been Jesus, whose failure had been most abject—not merely had he been crucified, but his teachings had been perverted and the churches which operated in his name had no interest whatever in what he had believed and taught. The same was true of Buddha, whose doctrines had been even more perverted—his priests had had more time in which to forget him. On the other hand, there were great leaders like Alexander and Napoleon, who had built empires only to have them crumble, because they had relied upon the sword alone, and not upon the spirit, upon God. They had had nothing to teach mankind but materialism, the dog-eat-dog civilization of the moneychangers, the international Jews.

Lanny shivered when he heard these words, fearing that his host would get off on that special private madness of his. But no, Adi was in a constructive mood; he was not fighting his enemies, but building new states, empires, worlds. Said he: "The greatest man who has lived before me is Mohammed." Lanny was startled by this, for in thinking over the Führers of the past he had decided that Mohammed was the one whom this one-time sub-corporal and painter of picture postcards most closely resembled; and of course when Adi called the Arabian prophet the greatest man who had lived so far, it was the same thing as saying that he bore the greatest resemblance to Adolf Hitler. The Nazi Führer explained his prototype: a self-made man who had found God, and had not been content merely to preach Him, but had laid down His law and seen that it was obeyed; in other words, a holy book in one hand and a sword in the other. The result was that the religion Mohammed founded had endured and still endured; his book was still read and his law was obeyed, precisely as he had set it forth. "Do you agree with me, Herr Budd?"

"Indeed I do," replied the guest. "It may interest you to know that I have had this same thought about you, ever since I first read your great book."

"Thirteen centuries have passed since Mohammed died, and the world has changed greatly. It needs a new set of laws, a new revelation. And believe me, I am not relying merely upon the sword, I am not merely forcing people to obey me. I am training their minds and inspiring their souls; I am founding a new religion, one that will last for a thousand years, perhaps ten thousand—until such a time as God may see fit to send a new prophet to supersede me. I am not giving this revelation all at once, but little by little, as God gives it to me, in His good time. I tell you about it, Herr Budd, because you are a man who sees and understands these inner forces and will respect my vision."

"I understand exactly what you mean, Excellency," said the American, reverently.

"The masses of the people cannot live without guidance; they cannot solve the problems of life for themselves, but have to be told what to do. Also they must have a reason for obedience; they must have a faith; they cannot live without God. Rudi has been telling about this fellow-countryman of yours, Buchman—by his name and his ideas I take it that he is of German descent, and it is evident that he understands the religion I am founding, and is preparing America and Britain to accept our National-Socialist crusade. Do you know his Moral Rearmament movement?"

"I have attended some of its house-parties, and I had a talk with Lothian about it a week or two ago. I have had the good fortune to know Lothian—since my youth." Lanny had been about to say: "Since the Peace Conference in Paris," but he realized that this was another of Adi's phobias, and the mention might set him off on a tirade that would last the rest of the night!

VI

Lanny had a hard time getting to sleep that night; he lay contemplating a world pushed back to the seventh century. Adolf Hitler's world would have all modern improvements, such as telegraphs and telephones, radio and cinema and airplanes, but they would all be used for the more rapid subjection of mankind to the will of the new Prophet-Führer. Whereas the Mohammedan crusade on horseback had been stopped in Hungary in the east and in Spain in the west, the Nazi crusade by bombing planes and submarines might not be stopped by either the Atlantic or the Pacific ocean. Lanny composed in his mind a report to Gus Gennerich, to the effect that Adi Schicklgruber was the most dangerous man who had appeared in the modern world.

There was a list of rules posted on the door of Lanny's room, just as in a hotel. One of the rules was that guests were to appear for meals within two minutes of the ringing of the bell. Lanny hoped this didn't mean that he had to appear for the seven o'clock breakfast; he took the liberty of waiting for the second, which the Germans call the "fork breakfast," at nine, and for this he was not corrected. There the Führer took a glass of milk and a couple of rolls spread liberally with marmalade; also an apple. Then he retired to his study, and Lanny was told by others that he spent the morning going through state papers and giving orders to his adjutants. He had private telephone lines to Munich and Berlin, and mail came by plane night and morning.

There was a large staff at his mountain retreat, part of it permanent, and part coming by motorcar or plane whenever the Führer's weariness of office duties and state functions caused him to take flight from the cities. Lanny observed that without exception all these people were young, and he understood this as part of the psychology of a world rebuilder. The old and the middle-aged had been miseducated, they were cranky and set in the desire to have their own way. For almost two decades Adi had been training the young not to want their way, but to want *his* way, and these were the persons he liked to have about him. His military adjutants were a colonel, a commander, and two captains; the former pair under forty and the latter pair under thirty-five. There were three ordnance officers and two personal attendants, one a lieutenant and the other a sergeant; Lanny felt certain that all of these were under thirty and most of them under twenty-five. All were good-looking Aryans, and the same thing applied to the women secretaries and the maids, of whom the visitor must have seen eight or ten.

The Führer's personal physician, also young, took an interest in the guest from overseas. Possibly he had been told to do so; anyhow, he took Lanny in tow and showed him the art treasures of which the châlet was full, told him what he knew about them, and listened with interest to his comments. Later the young architect, who had carried out the new constructions under the Führer's orders, invited the guest to inspect the work which had been done on the estate in the period since his previous visit. Beside the two wings there was the widening of the main terrace and the building of a summer house above it, a garage built into the side of the mountain, barracks for the SS guards, a residence for the staff, and a sumptuous new guest house for important official persons. Everything was of harmonious design, having the background of fir-clad mountains and a view over the tumbled and snow-covered Austrian Alps, including a valley with the lovely little city of Salzburg.

All very splendid, a combination of nature and art; the fairy-story dream of a stepchild who had been neglected and thwarted, of a youth who had wanted to be an artist, but had never been able to get any training, except in the art of killing his fellowmen. He had known abject poverty, unemployment, and the life of a wastrel in a shelter for bums. In the trenches he had been forced to live in rain and mud, in freezing cold and summer's dust and heat, to be bitten by lice, to be blasted and shot at, to suffer wounds and be filled with terrors; all this for year after year—and at the end defeat and humiliation.

Such had been the training of Adi Schicklgruber, and it was hardly to be wondered at that he was a neurotic, and had to take drugs to put himself to sleep, and had moods of exaltation followed by others of suicidal depression; that he fled from his fellowmen in boredom and exasperation, and then fled back because he could not face the thoughts which haunted him alone. Ten thousand murders on his conscience; murders of his best friends, of men who had been his comrades on the battlefield and in the camps, of women who had given him love, or tried to. He believed in spirits, but hesitated to call them because the wrong ones might appear; he believed in God, but had to make Him into a God of war, because Adi himself had never been able to get what he wanted save by threats of war. He could not eat food without elaborate precautions against its being poisoned; he could not go for a drive in the streets of the cities he loved without the thought that at any moment a bomb might be dropped upon his head; he could not take a walk in his beloved forests without looking behind to make sure his sharpshooters were near, and that they were really his own sharpshooters and not his enemies!

VII

In the latter part of the afternoon the Führer had completed his day's labors and went for his daily dose of fresh air and exercise. A "constitutional," Lanny had heard it called by his great-uncle Eli Budd in Connecticut, and now he used this word and explained it, to his host's amusement. There came bounding three beautiful shepherd dogs, also getting their constitutionals; they paid no attention to Lanny, for they were one-man dogs—something the Führer required of all creatures near him. They raced here and there in a pack, and Lanny guessed that it would have gone ill with any stranger venturing into this preserve. A keeper followed to give the dogs orders, and a little farther behind came two of the Death's Head men. The customary automatics in their belts were not enough; each carried a rifle with a telescopic sight, and apparently the Führer had given information as to the route of his walk, for Lanny observed other armed men on the way.

"I am going to show you something that I don't show to many," remarked the master. They started up a mountain path which made him puff not a little, and after a while they came to what was evidently a newly made road, a two-lane highway carved out of the steep mountainside. The snow had been scraped from it, and Lanny could see that it was paved, and also that there had been traffic on it recently. They walked upon it, climbing steadily, admiring view after view. "This is the work of my wonderful Todt, who has constructed all my

Autobahnen. This time he was kind enough to build one for my private use."

Lanny recalled what he had heard from Hilde Donnerstein and others, that the Führer was building himself a secret retreat on a mountaintop called the Kehlstein, and that before this work could even be begun, it had been necessary to construct a road ascending more than half a mile higher than the Berghof itself. This labor had taken some two years; and now Lanny walked around one hairpin turn after another, and looked over the side of precipices a thousand feet deep. The road was beautifully balanced, tilted this way and that so that a fast-moving car would always be safe. Lanny remarked: "General Göring showed me his toy railroad, but you have the real thing." That did not fail to please the host.

He gave out, and stopped at one of the turns, saying: "It is too far to climb this afternoon; but some day next autumn, when it is done, I will take you to it. *Schauen Sie mal!*" He pointed to a spot high up on the mountainside, to what appeared to be a gray cliff. "*Sehen Sie etwas?*"

Lanny could see nothing, and his host explained that he wasn't supposed to; the entrance to the Kehlsteinhaus was expertly camouflaged and invisible from below. The road wound up there and entered into a tunnel cut into the mountain. When it was done, there would be bronze doors that opened automatically at the approach of a car and closed behind it. Inside was a shaft going straight up through the mountain, a distance of some two hundred meters. There was an elevator in the shaft, now used by the workers; when the task was completed, it would be replaced by a guest elevator accommodating eighteen persons. Everything would be run by electricity, of course. At the top would be a real retreat, where nobody could ever interfere with the meditations of a dreamer of new worlds. The house would be small, with just room for the Führer and a couple of attendants. The living room would be glass on three sides, and would overlook these Alps for a hundred miles. "Believe me," said Adi, "the scenery is not to be forgotten."

"It appears that you Germans have the love of mountains in your blood," remarked the visitor.

"That is true. My great teacher, Professor Haushofer, has shown me on a map that our people, emigrating to the east and southeast, have always avoided the lowlands and settled in the higher and more wooded country. And you know what a part mountains and forests have played

in our legends and our art. When the gods ascend to Valhalla on a
rainbow, it starts from a mountaintop."

"I will play you the music when we get back to the house," said the
smiling Lanny. "Will you permit me to suggest a name for your retreat
when it is finished? Perhaps others wouldn't understand, but you and I
and Herr Hess can keep it as our secret. Call it 'Mohammed's Mountain.'"

The Führer of the Nazis looked at his guest for a moment, startled;
then he began to laugh, and was so pleased over the *Witz* that he
chuckled all the way around a half-turn in General Todt's masterpiece
of road construction.

VIII

After dinner the Führer indicated his desire for some music. Brassin's
piano transcription of *Siegfried* was produced, and Lanny played first
the *Waldweben* and then the *Feuerzauber*. This music of forest and
mountain was directed at Adi, a reminder of their recent conversation; it might have been in these Alpine forests that the little bird had
sung to the young hero, and it might have been on the Kehlstein's top
that the magic fire had protected the sleeping maiden. Beautiful beyond
expression was the soul of the German hero, and tragic was his doom,
to have a spear driven through his back by a treacherous foe. Truly
the time had come for a new dispensation, a legend in which that doom
should be averted; someone should warn the hero, and let him be the
first to throw the spear!

The music over, the Führer disappeared, and Hess signed to Lanny,
who went to Madame's room and told her to be prepared for another
visitor. Afterwards Lanny went to Hess's apartment, close to the master's, and they sat and talked while awaiting developments. Lanny was
interested to probe the mind of this silent man and learn about his life.
He had been born in Alexandria, Egypt, and Tecumseh had talked
about seeing a blue sea with many ships, and a dark people; this had
sounded mysterious—but Lanny soon decided that, so far as Hess was
concerned, the mystery was all on the outside, and that the intelligence
behind it was commonplace.

Rudolf Hess was the perfect subordinate; he had only one thought
in the world, which was to please Hitler and help him. Hitler had told
him to run the Party and make it a fit instrument to run Germany; all
right, the Deputy had taken up that burden—which meant filling his

mind with the details of thousands of personalities and as many jobs, making sure that the round pegs got into the round holes and the square into the square. He would follow the pattern of Adi himself, and become furious and terrible, and so get his orders obeyed. He wasn't naturally a cruel person, Lanny judged; he did what his job required. The same thing was doubtless true of Hitler, who had a sentimental streak and was devoted to children, also kept a great many pet birds and was sad when one of them died. Perhaps it could have been said of Mohammed: he would never have killed people if only they had been willing to submit promptly to the will of Allah as revealed to Allah's prophet.

Concerning psychic and occult matters the Deputy Führer was not very well instructed, and Lanny thought it would be easy to take him in, if ever he wanted to—and he might. Hess had accepted the idea of spirits naïvely, and apparently didn't know that there were other theories by which the phenomena might be accounted for. He asked questions about these, and Lanny told what he had read, without committing himself either way. "I don't know" is easy to say, but is unsatisfactory to many minds; and Hess had by now made up his mind that he had talked to the spirits of Franz Dieckhoff and the soldier Hans. Why should a man's own subconscious mind want to play tricks upon himself? It was a silly idea. Lanny could have pointed out many things that seemed equally silly to him, but were in the book which the Führer and his Deputy had composed. They had told the German *Volk* how they were going to deceive the German *Volk*, and had told Germany's enemies how they were going to thwart and defeat those enemies.

"Tell me a little about Pröfenik," suggested the guest, "and why you don't trust him."

"I don't think he has ever played any tricks on me," replied the Deputy Führer. "But he produced physical phenomena for persons I know, and they thought the whole thing was faked."

"I found him interesting," declared the American. "He talked about matters which had puzzled me, and I think he threw light on them. How would it do if you and I were to pay a call on him, sometime when we are in Berlin?"

"By all means let us do it. I'd be interested to see what you make of that old fellow."

IX

Somewhere inside Lanny was a shivering all this time—because Adi was with Madame, and what might be happening? It might be the worst—and so indeed it proved. There came a tap upon the door—one of those good-looking young secretaries, betraying agitation. "The Führer wants you at once; in his study." Hess leaped up without a word and left the room with long strides.

Lanny hurried to Madame, and found her slumped in her chair, writhing as if in pain, and moaning. He knew what that meant; something had gone wrong with the séance, and he had a long job of comforting and consoling to do. She had come out of her trance, and he put his arm about her flabby old shoulders and took one of her trembling soft hands and started talking to her as to a sick or badly frightened child. "Never mind, Madame; it's all right, there's no harm done. I am here and you are safe."

She went on groaning; she suffered pain whenever a séance was broken off abruptly. Lanny half lifted her and half led her to the bed, and there she curled up, weeping; it was a nervous spasm, which she described as something clutching her stomach; he judged it was the solar plexus. He got a bottle of smelling-salts which she kept on her dresser. He went on murmuring words of sympathy and affection, for that was what a poor, lonely, and frightened old woman most needed in the world—somebody to be a son to her and care for her, even if these shocks, which enraged Tecumseh, should cause him to desert her and so ruin her psychic gift.

Presently she murmured: "Who is that man—that terrible man?" Lanny went and shut the door of the room, and then said: "Never mind, Madame; he is a sick man, and perhaps the spirits offended him."

"When I came out of my trance he was rushing up and down the room, cursing and screaming. What is the matter with him?"

"He is a very unhappy man, and something must have pained him deeply; some memory."

"I never heard of such behavior. I am afraid of him. I don't want to stay in the house with him."

"He won't do you any harm, Madame, I assure you. I won't let any harm come to you."

"He heard me groan and he shouted to me to shut up; then he rushed out of the room. I don't want him to come near me again."

"I doubt if he will want to. Don't worry; it will come out all right.

People have unhappy memories, things they cannot bear to be reminded of. Perhaps the spirits insulted him, as they did Sir Basil the
first time."

"I am no longer so young as I was, and I cannot stand such things.
Tecumseh will be furious, I know."

Lanny had to go on soothing this near-child, teasing her a little, also.
He told her that her performance must have been extraordinarily good
—really it was a compliment that was paid her, for a man didn't get
excited about any revelation unless it was true. She was the most wonderful medium that Lanny had ever met, and he had tried dozens of
them. Even if she never produced another spirit she had earned her
place in the books—Lanny was going to have somebody write a book
about her some day, and it would have her picture as a frontispiece.
So on until he got her calmed, and she promised to go to sleep and not
worry about the incident any more. But she would surely lock the
door of her room on the inside!

X

Next morning the Führer appeared at breakfast, affable as usual, but
apt to become preoccupied without notice. He said nothing to Lanny
about what had happened; Hess, meeting the guest in course of the
morning, remarked: "You must excuse that little mishap. Our Führer
has many painful memories in his past."

"I understand, Herr Reichsminister. He has suffered everything the
German people have suffered; if it were not so, he could not represent
them and redeem them as he is doing." A carefully thought-out remark,
which proved to be exactly right. The Deputy was gratified, and
Lanny could be sure he would repeat the words.

"I hope the old woman was not too much upset, Herr Budd."

"I saw her this morning and she is all right. You can be sure she
hasn't the least idea of what goes on at a séance—her trance is complete. So she couldn't talk about what happened even if she wanted to."

"Thank you, Herr Budd. I should like to try her again myself, if
it would be agreeable."

"Certainly—and any of your friends, if you wish. That is what we
came for."

Lanny went to reading the morning papers, which were flown from
Berlin and motored from Munich, along with the mail. He thought the
unfortunate episode was closed, but he failed to allow for the power
of gossip in a small community. Humans are gregarious animals, which

have lived in herds and hordes and households for millions of years; what each of them feels and does and says is of importance to the others—and especially whatever goes on in the mind of the Old Man of the Tribe, upon whose whims the life of all the others depends.

Lanny had received some mail forwarded from Bienvenu, and went to his room to write a letter; there he found one of those attractive young Aryan females, engaged in making the bed. She had already had a chance to look upon him, and had evidently found him good; her smiles told him that if he were to close the door and lock it, and then kiss her, she would not reject his advances. This was in accordance with the Nazi sex-code, but Lanny didn't want any of it. He got what he needed out of his suitcase and was about to leave the room, when the girl said, in a low voice: "*Herr Budd, darf ich etwas sagen?*"—may I say something?

Lanny stopped and said: "*Ja, freilich.*"

She came closer, and whispered: "What happened last night: it was Geli."

"*So?*" replied Lanny. "*Wirklich?*"

"You know that story?"

"It is better not to talk about it," said the proper guest, and went out quickly.

XI

Oh, yes, Lanny knew that story; one which was whispered everywhere by the refugees and other enemies of the *Regierung*. He had never before heard it referred to inside the Fatherland—perhaps because it was too terrible and too dangerous. Greta Raubal had been the child's name, and Hitler had called her Geli, pronounced "gaily." She was the daughter of his half-sister Angela, who had been his housekeeper, first here in the Berghof, after the release from prison, and then in Munich during the days of the Party's hard struggle for power. The child had flowered into womanhood in those desperately unhappy and abnormal times. Had she fallen in love with the dreamer of a new order, or had the dreamer made love to her, in his own strange and terrifying way? The story varied, according to who was telling it.

This much was certain: there had been an affair, permitted by the mother, beginning when Geli was very young and continuing to her death at the age of twenty or so. She was blue-eyed and fair, a tall Nordic blond according to Adi's ideal; she was gentle and submissive, and he, wildly jealous, ruled her with the whip which he liked to carry,

even in public. "When you go to woman, forget not the whip,"
Nietzsche had written, and Adi had read or at any rate heard of this
philosopher, another tormented dreamer on the road to madness.

There had been no happiness between uncle and niece, only fear on
the girl's part and in the end a desire to escape. But if any man came
near her, Hitler drove him away in fury. Otto Strasser told of such an
experience; but people distrusted Otto, knowing that he hated Hitler
as the murderer of Gregor, Otto's older brother. Another Party member, employed as a chauffeur, had learned the story and blackmailed
the Führer to the tune of twenty thousand marks and an important
Party position; this had been an especially unkind cut, since the Führer
had praised the man in *Mein Kampf* as one who had defended him in
the *Saalschlachten.* "My good Maurice!"

Nobody knew exactly what had happened at the end. Geli had tried
to get away and go to Vienna to study music, and the uncle had flown
into one of his hysterical tantrums; he had sent the mother away, and
the girl had been found on the floor of her room with a bullet through
her heart. This had been shortly before Hitler had become Chancellor,
and in Munich he was a powerful man. Göring had flown to the scene
and there had been no police investigation; it was called a suicide and
hushed up. The body had been buried in Vienna, in consecrated ground
—which could hardly have happened if the priest had not believed
that someone had killed her. Subsequently, Gregor Strasser had stated
that the priest on his deathbed had pointed out this fact to him.

So there it was, and you could take your choice: either Adi Schicklgruber had murdered his niece or he had driven her to suicide by
incestuous attentions. For days he had been near to suicide himself.
Too late he had made the discovery that she had been the great love
of his life, and no other woman could take her place, try as they would.
The tortured man had got a permit to visit Vienna incognito, and had
stood by her grave in the Zentralfriedhof late at night and dropped
flowers upon it. Now, half a dozen years later, he was master of all
Germany, and wanted to go to Vienna again. Lanny wondered if that
obscure grave was one of the forces which drew him.

What had happened in the disturbing séance? Had the free-spoken
Tecumseh, a ruler in his own right, dared to say what he thought
about incest and murder? Or had Geli herself appeared, and driven
her whip-wielding uncle into one of his frenzies of grief and fear? "He
that ruleth his spirit is greater than he that taketh a city." But then,
Adi rejected the old Hebrew prophets and did not read them. Suppose
the spirit of Freddi Robin had come and spoken such admonitions? Or

one of Adi's victims, such as Röhm, whom, after a stormy interview, he had had shot in cold blood? Or possibly Gregor Strasser, organizer of the Sturmabteilung. Lanny had once met Gregor in Adi's Berlin apartment, and had heard him get a sound dressing-down from his Führer. Later, after he had been killed in the Blood Purge, his spirit, or what claimed to be that, had been reported by Tecumseh; so evidently he was hovering about this bloodstained scene.

Lanny wondered how this story had got about in the Berghof. Had the beautiful blond secretary been listening at the keyhole? Or did the trusted "Rudi" have some confidant to whom he had whispered the single word Geli? Or had the young Aryan physician been called in to administer restoratives? Anyhow, the rumor was all over the place, and creating such excitement that a beautiful blond maker of beds had risked her job and perhaps her life by whispering to a guest about it. So much for Adi's fond dream that he could sneak into a room at night and consult a spiritualist medium without having the German *Volk* know anything about it!

The son of Budd-Erling realized that in his desire to ascertain the fate of his wife he might have gravely imperiled his privileges as a presidential agent. Hitler would hardly forget this episode; even though he could not blame Lanny for it, he would associate him with it in his mind, and this would surely not increase his desire to see the person. Might it even be that his tormented and suspicious mind would begin to wonder whether some enemy had deliberately prepared this shock for him? And what should Lanny do about the matter? Should he mention it and try to patch it up? Or should he drop some remarks indicating that he had no idea anything had gone wrong?

XII

The guest went down into the great hall and sat in one of the leather armchairs, looking out over Austria. A storm was coming up and dark clouds were scurrying over the tops of the mountains. Political storms, also, were gathering over Austria, and the master of these storms was in the room just over Lanny's head, planning and directing them. He might be standing at his window, said to be the largest in Germany, looking out upon this same scene, watching the swiftly moving clouds. He might be humming the *Walkürenritt*, one of his favorite tunes. Here in these mountains, with dark forests all about him, his mind was full of the myths and images of Richard Wagner, and in his predicament he must wish for Wotan to lend him a thunderbolt, or Loki, god of lies, to come whisper some wily stratagem into his ear.

A limousine came rolling up the drive and halted before the châlet. An officer in SS uniform got out and opened the car door for a woman passenger, tall, elegant, bundled in a heavy fur coat. Recognizing her, Lanny gave a start. Magda Goebbels!

Something new to wonder about! Was this a coincidence, a kindness that chance was doing an overwrought Führer? Or was it a royal command? Had Adi, unable to sleep in spite of his drugs, telephoned to Berlin and ordered consolation brought without delay? Magda would have left Berlin by plane early in the morning, and arrived in Munich an hour or so later.

Lanny rose as she entered the room, this being his duty. When she saw him her sad face revealed dismay for just a fraction of a second. Then, recovering herself quickly, as a woman of the great world learns to do, she greeted him: *"Grüss' Gott, Herr Budd."* He replied: *"Welche Überraschung, Frau Magda!"*

She shook hands with him, which she needn't have done. He saw that she was delaying, to let the SS officer and the man carrying her bags pass on. Then she leaned toward him and whispered, in a voice of tragedy: *"Ich konnt' mir nicht mehr helfen!"*—I couldn't help it— and then swiftly passed on out of the room.

21

Der Führer Hat Immer Recht

I

THE Detazes arrived, and a busy Führer found time for a one-man show. He ordered one wall of the main room cleared and the six French works hung in a row. There they were, land and seascapes, transporting the beholder from the white snowstorms of the Alps to the sun-drenched colors of the Riviera. Everybody was invited to inspect them, even the servants. It took Lanny back to the good old days of German *Gemütlichkeit* which had so impressed him as a boy, when the old Graf Stubendorf had assembled his *Diener* and *Knechte* and made them a speech on Christmas morning. Lanny wondered about this sudden geniality. Was the Führer saying to his household: "You see, this American visitor did not come just bringing an old witchwoman and a bagful of spirits; he is the stepson of a famous painter, and you can observe for yourselves and have something worth while to talk about"?

Lanny had taken the liberty of including one of the paintings which derived from the cruise of the *Bluebird* to the Isles of Greece: an old peasant standing in front of the hut which he had made out of brush, and holding under one arm a baby lamb. The Führer was much taken with this and wanted it. In fact, he wanted them all; a Detaze collection in his Bechsteinhaus, the châlet he had built on the estate for the use of official guests, would tend to show the world how sincere he was in his admiration of French culture, and how desirous of promoting the unity of Europe.

"I want you to understand, Exzellenz," said Lanny, "I didn't bring six paintings here with the idea of selling them all."

"Are they for sale, Herr Budd?"

"Yes, but——"

"Very well; I want to buy them. What is the price of the six?"

They had one of those bargainings in reverse; the Führer making an offer, and Lanny insisting that it was too much. They finally compromised on a price of a hundred thousand marks, a handsome enough figure. Lanny wondered more than ever. Had the great man some errand in mind, or was this just a retaining fee for a high-class agent? Lanny was familiar from childhood with aristocratic methods of hiring; he had listened to innumerable conversations between his mother and his father, and had watched Robbie's devices, such as playing a very poor game of poker, or making a wager on some preposterous thing, such as that the day was Thursday when he knew it was Friday. Adi's method was dignified and honorable in comparison, and perhaps Lanny was oversuspicious; but he could not believe that the Führer of all the Germans would ever do anything that did not contribute in one way or another to his world purpose.

The steward was instructed to obtain a draft on a Paris bank to the honor of Herr Budd, and Lanny was invited to go over to the Bechsteinhaus and see to the proper hanging of the masterpieces. Paintings considered to be inferior were taken up to the bedrooms—a custom prevailing among wealthy art collectors. In his bedroom in the Berghof Lanny had three very commonplace specimens of contemporary

German painting, and he wondered if Hitler had been personally responsible for their choice.

II

Franz von Papen showed up from Vienna and was closeted in his
Führer's study. Other personages kept arriving, generals three or four
at a time, and no effort was made to keep an American visitor from
learning that the screws were being tightened on the Austrian government; Lanny even heard the designations of various Panzer units which
were being moved to the border. He took the precaution to ask Hess
if he was by any chance in the way, and the answer was, not in the
least; the Führer esteemed it a great favor to have the two guests in
his home.

The Deputy himself was having a sitting with the medium every
evening, and was reporting results to his chief. He was telling Lanny
some of the things, but not the most important, Lanny guessed. Hess's
doubts had been completely dissipated; he was having secret conferences with the spirits of old-time *Parteigenossen*, those martyrs whose
names he called at every *Parteitag*. Lanny wouldn't have been surprised
if some day either the Führer or the Deputy had invited him to put a
price on Madame Zyszynski; if he had done so, and agreed to say
nothing about it, no doubt Madame would have stayed right there,
regardless of whether she wanted to or not!

Lanny tried to imagine what was going on in the mind of the new
Mohammed. For seventeen or eighteen years, ever since Adolf Hitler
had taken control of a political party with seven members, he had been
engaged in a guessing game with fate. He had tried violence once and
failed abjectly. Since that time he had acquired a passion for "legality,"
and all the violence he had used had been in putting down those individuals and groups inside his party who rebelled against his determination to preserve the forms of *Gesetzmässigkeit*. Every crime he had
committed had been in the name of law, and any aggression he would
ever commit would be in the cause of peace.

Each decision was a step in the dark, a gamble for life or death. Can
I trust this man, or must I have him killed? (No use to put men in jail,
for when they come out, they are more dangerous than ever; but dead
men tell no tales, nor do they undertake any coups d'état.) Every move
on the chessboard of diplomacy meant a risking of Adi's future; for
after all, his new Reich was a have-not nation, its resources were limited, and its Führer could not afford the luxury of a single blunder.

And if there was any way to lift the veil of the future, or to poke even the tiniest hole in it, how foolish not to make use of that method! If there were people who possessed that gift, why not hire them—especially when their price was absurdly small. Whatever it had been in the past, divination was now the poor man's way.

This ex-painter of picture postcards and possibly of houses believed in astrology, in fortune-telling, in spirits, in the whole kit and caboodle of occult tricks—for he had no means of sorting out the true from the false. His closest friend, his publicly announced Deputy, believed even more implicitly, and right now the pair of them were at a crisis, per-haps the gravest of their common career. Adi was in a struggle with practically his entire military entourage; all the trained intellectual power of the *Wehrmacht*, which he was making into the greatest army in the world. These were the heirs of Germany's greatest tradition; they had spent their lives preparing themselves to carry it on—and now came this upstart, this *Gefreite*, a sort of sub-corporal, or private first class, setting his authority against theirs, and bidding them commit an action which they considered dangerous to the point of madness.

But—it had happened before! They had advised against militarizing the Rhineland; they had advised against the Führer's bold announce-ment that he was going to double the size of the Reichswehr, and again that he was going to introduce conscription. But each time the inspired leader had had his way, and Britain and France had done nothing but enter protests.

And now, here it was again, over the question of the Anschluss. Adi was going ahead; his *daimon* told him to, and was not to be restrained. Just prior to this trip to Berchtesgaden he had shaken up his Cabinet and his army command, in order to get men who would obey him without hesitation. He had taken Ribbentrop, one-time champagne salesman, away from his job as Minister to Britain and made him Foreign Minister—because Ribbentrop was so sure that he had suc-ceeded in bemuddling the British ruling class and that they would take no action to save Austria. He had deposed his oldest and most com-petent generals and given the command to others who were pure Nazis. He had made Göring a Field Marshal, giving him the right to carry a jeweled baton—all because Göring agreed with him and would back him in this contemplated gamble.

But up in that study alone, looking out of the large window over the land of his birth, what agonies of uncertainty must be tormenting the soul of this new Prophet-Führer, this man of destiny without peer in modern times! And in a room under the same roof was an old woman of a nationality whom the Führer despised—but some whim of nature had given her the power to call spirits from the vasty deep. Spirits of friends and of enemies alike—and who could say what they might know, what secret insights they might possess? Even the murdered ones, the former friends, would be Germans before they were enemies; even Röhm, or General Schleicher, or Gregor Strasser who had organized and trained the SA—even such spirits might be appealed to in the name of the holy Fatherland to say what Germany's fate would be, and what was the wise course for her Führer who dared not be wrong.

So what more natural than that Rudi Hess should be stealing off night after night to sit in a dark room and listen to what this stout old Polish woman was saying in her trances! Lanny wondered, could it be possible that Hitler himself was sneaking into that room, keeping the secret even from Madame's patron and paymaster? There was nothing to prevent it; all he would have to do was to make up his mind to endure in silence whatever insults and humiliations the spirits might inflict upon him, for the sake of the secrets they might consent to reveal.

And Hess sitting by, making notes in the dark, or by a dim light behind a screen; writing shorthand, as he had once written down the words of what had become the new German Bible! Would he now get a New Testament, a Book of Revelations of the NSDAP? "Blessed is he that readeth, and they that hear the words of this prophecy, and keep those things which are written therein: for the time is at hand." If anything of the sort should happen, they would surely have to discover that Madame Zyszynski was a changeling, and of pure Aryan blood; or at least that she was illegitimate—the device by which hundreds of Germans with Jewish names had managed to get themselves established as good Nazis!

III

Tension was increasing at the Berghof, increasing hour by hour; you felt it in the air, you saw it in the faces of everybody, high and low. Papen had departed in haste for Vienna, and word spread that he had orders to bring Schuschnigg to the Führer at all costs. Would he be able to do it? Everybody speculated, everybody had an opinion, no matter how presumptuous. It meant so much to them—for here they were, right on the very border; all they had to do was to slide downhill, as it were, and they would be in Austria. The people there were of the same race as themselves, speaking the same language, listening to the same music, eating the same sort of food and wearing the same sort of clothes; they came and went across the border—the German workers going every morning to the Austrian salt mines and coming back every evening. How preposterous that they couldn't be one country!

Lanny had found it pleasant to sit on the high-backed lounge in front of the fireplace and read the newspapers and magazines. Here he would be joined by someone of the household; young officers who had never visited the outside world were curious about it, and discovered that this American visitor knew the key people and possessed a fund of anecdotes. They didn't know why he was there, but they could be sure it was for some purpose important to the Führer, and they treated him as a member of the family. So it was no indiscretion when the young doctor remarked that *Der Paffenknecht*—meaning Schuschnigg—had only three days in which to make up his mind whether he wanted his baroque palace bombed about his ears.

Lanny could have guessed as much from the copy of the *Völkischer Beobachter*, the Führer's newspaper, which lay upon the table at this moment. The newspapers of Hitlerland were like so many searchlights, controlled from a common center and all focused upon the same spot at the same moment. Just now the spot was the Chancellor of Austria. They held this pious lawyer-statesman responsible for all the evils of Europe, and threatened him with dire and dreadful punishments if he did not step out of the pathway of the Nazi chariot of progress—or perhaps in these modern days one might better say the *Hermann Göring Panzer Abteilung*.

It was a technique of provocation which the Japanese had inaugurated in China in the previous autumn: commit an act of violence, blame it on the victims, and then set up a nationwide, a worldwide clamor for the punishment of the aggressors. In the case of Vienna, the criminals were the police who had uncovered the conspiracy of the "Committee of Seven." Dr. Tavs was in jail, with some of his fellow conspirators, and that made them heroes, and their cause was spread over the front pages of all the newspapers of Germany. The demand was that Schuschnigg should reform his Cabinet, putting in an Austrian Nazi as Minister of the Interior, in charge of the police. The conspirators would of course be released, and thereafter the Nazi rowdies would be free to beat up and kill their leading opponents.

IV

Such was the program; and Lanny had to watch it being carried out, without showing any trace of the dismay and disgust which boiled in his soul. He would stand in front of the mirror in his simple but elegant bedroom and whisper the Nazi formulas, watching his features in the meantime to see if he was betraying any trace of improper feeling. Really, he would be equipped for a leading role in any theater when he had got through with this assignment! He came down for the "fork breakfast" on the morning of Friday, the eleventh of February, and found the long table in a clamor with the news: "Schuschnigg is coming tomorrow!" He had no trouble in wearing a look of exultation, for he had guessed what the news would be, and had been rehearsing his comments not five minutes earlier. "The Führer is always right!"—so said the American guest to the magnificent Reichswehr officer who sat beside him at the table—General Wilhelm Keitel, newly appointed Adjutant to the Führer, with cabinet rank. "*Ja, Exzellenz, hier sehen wir wieder einmal: der Führer hat immer recht!*"

Unparalleled excitement throughout the household. Most of the furniture was taken from the great hall, including the fireplace settees on which Lanny had been so comfortable. A large table was moved to the center of the room and on this was spread a great relief map of Germany and all the border lands; "The Distribution of German Population and Culture in the States of Europe" it was labeled, and showed Germany and Austria in bright red, and the border states as pink with so many red spots that you would think they had the measles. The masterpieces of painting were taken down from the walls and in their places were hung greatly enlarged photographs of the damage done by the bombing of Guernica, Valencia, Madrid and Barcelona. The visiting lawyer-statesman was going to get a postgraduate course in the new science known as *Geopolitik*, as well as in the older science known as *Schrecklichkeit*.

Lanny thought it was the part of tact to take Hess aside and say: "I fear that an *Ausländer* will be out of place at this time." But the Deputy hastened to reply: "*Absolut nicht, Herr Budd*. The Führer trusts you, and would be sorry to have you take Madame away at present. May I tell you something in the strictest confidence?"

"Everything you tell me is confidential, Herr Reichsminister."

"I had a most extraordinary séance with Madame last night. The spirit of Hanussen came and foretold the outcome of these negotiations."

"That *is* indeed extraordinary!"—and Lanny didn't have to lie about it. Hitler, launched upon a campaign which had for one of its declared objectives the expulsion or extermination of the Jews of Vienna, was relying for guidance upon the spirit of a Jewish astrologer whom Göring had had murdered as a means of canceling the debts of his dear friend who commanded the Berlin police!

"I hope the prognosis was favorable," Lanny ventured.

"The Führer is greatly encouraged, and I am sure we shall see action before long."

V

Lanny went out for a walk in the forests which had once been the haunts of the witch or evil fairy named Berchta and were now witnessing the birth of a new religion of the sword. He was in the privileged position of those nobles of the *ancien régime* in France, who were admitted to the queen's bedroom to witness her *accouchement* and certify to the genuineness of the event. That would be something to tell to F.D.R., and perhaps to Lanny's grandchildren in the course of time; but just now he was sick of blood and terror, and permitted his mind to wander off to the subject of precognition, popularly known as fortune-telling. A new development in the mediumship of this Polish woman; the spirits she produced had hitherto been content with the present and the past, and never before had ventured upon what George Eliot described as "the most gratuitous form of error."

From the naïve point of view of Hess it was quite simple; the spirit of Hanussen was there, and had been able to foresee the future now as it had while in the flesh. But Lanny was trying to persuade himself that this self-styled "spirit" was in reality some form of subconscious activity, a fabrication or construct of the mind of Madame, combined with that of her sitter and perhaps of others. We speak of "levels" of consciousness because we are unable to think except in terms of space; but in reality the mind occupies no space, and there is no reason for thinking that one subconsciousness must of necessity be partitioned off from all others. It is purely a question of fact: Is it so or is it not? Lanny considered that he had been accumulating evidence disproving the partition hypothesis and proving some sort of commingling.

Why had Madame suddenly taken to foreseeing the future? Lanny guessed it was because a sitter had gone to her firmly convinced of the reality of this power, and consciously as well as unconsciously willing that the "spirits" should tell him what lay beyond the dark veil. Lanny had become convinced, not from any slip of the Deputy's, but from the general tenor of his conversation, that the Führer himself had been stealing into Madame's room, perhaps imitating Hess's voice, and anyhow behaving himself discreetly and taking whatever came. And Hitler was a man of driving will, both conscious and subconscious; perhaps a medium himself, perhaps a hypnotist, and certainly a man with a subconscious personality which drove him and guided him and taught him how to drive and guide others. Lanny had proved that it was possible to hypnotize Madame and direct what spirits or constructs should appear; and now Adi had gone in and commanded that the spirit of his old-time astrologer should be produced, and made to behave as he had when he had been so indiscreet as to announce that Adi had only a few years to live.

What would be the validity of the communications which this fabricated entity would deliver? Would the Hanussen-spirit tell his old-time patron what that patron wanted to hear? Would it have the power to do anything else? The answer depended in part upon whether you accepted the average man's idea of time as something absolute and real in itself, or whether you could manage to accept the teaching of philosophy and of modern physics that time is a form which our minds impose upon reality. Perhaps there is a level of our subconsciousness which is not limited to that form, and therefore a "spirit" might be no more ignorant of the future than of the past. Again it is a question of fact. Do we, or do we not, have dreams which correspond to future events? Lanny had read the books of J. W. Dunne, who had not merely proved by experiment that we do, but had proved by mathematics that we can.

This much any student of history must admit: the *daimon* of Socrates had guided not merely Socrates, but many of the youth of Athens, and later, by the power of the written word, had guided millions of men for a score of centuries. And this *daimon* had known he was doing just that; it had been a living force, foreseeing the future and helping to make it by its own intelligence and will. The same thing was true of the *daimon* of Adi Schicklgruber, when he sat with a medium and mingled his subconscious forces with hers and constructed a future which might be the true and real future because Adi was going to make it that. By will and imagination he renewed his spiritual and mental energy, and became the more able to carry out the purpose he was determined upon. Such has been the role of soothsayers through all time, and Lanny guessed that Adi was going to prove Madame right, and then marvel at her supernormal power.

VI

A stream of visitors kept arriving all that day: General von Reichenau, commander of the Reichswehr divisions stationed near Munich, together with two of his aides and a secretary; then Joachim von Ribbentrop—he had adopted the "von" of an aunt when he married the heiress of a great wine business; then a limousine full of professors, all of whom clicked their heels and bowed from the waist when an American *Kunstsachverständiger* was introduced; one was a geographer, one an agronomist, one a specialist in the history of Central Europe. Evidently they were here for the purpose of arguing with Schuschnigg—but Lanny would have been willing to wager his hundred-thousand-mark bank draft that Hitler would never give one of them a chance to get in a word; and Lanny would have won.

Consultations went on all day and most of the night; Lanny wasn't invited to attend, and thought it the part of good taste to keep entirely out of the way. There had been a thaw and then a freeze, and the snow was hard, so he took a long walk in those dark forests for possession of which Richard Wagner and the Witch Berchta contended in his heart. *Gemsböcke* leaped on the heights far above him, and *Rebhühner* rose with a whir of wings from almost under his feet; he came back tired but exhilarated. Then he looked over the library of the Berghof, and selected from an encyclopedia the volumes "M," "I," and "P," took them to his room, and read all they had to tell him about Mohammed and Mohammedanism, Islam and Pan-Islamism—wishing to know what it was that Hitler so admired, and thus to foresee the future of the world in which he had to live.

The Austrian Chancellor was scheduled to leave Vienna early next morning, and the drive would take five or six hours. He brought with him his Foreign Minister, Dr. Guido Schmidt, at heart a near-Nazi and a poor support; also a military aide and a secretary. Two cars full of private detectives followed, but Hitler ordered these stopped at the border and their place taken by a squad of SS men under the command of an officer who was a renegade Austrian. The party reached the Berghof about noon, by which time the Führer was pacing about biting his fingernails, and members of his staff were slipping outside onto the terrace to smoke a cigarette now and then.

Lanny was invited to take part in the reception. He wondered, did Adi wish to make sure that his guest had been telling the truth about his meetings with Schuschnigg? If so, Lanny would take pains to satisfy

him. He would not speak first to the pale and harassed-looking statesman, but would wait to be recognized. Schuschnigg must have been
surprised to see an American here, for his face lighted up and he exclaimed: "*Grüss' Gott, Herr Budd.*" The art expert replied: "A happy
accident, Exzellenz."

The Führer apparently meant to proceed on the principle that mo-
lasses catches more flies than vinegar. After the fashion of country gentlemen the world over, he took his guests to show them the beauties of
his estate. Lanny tagged along; and when they went into the Bechsteinhaus—named for the rich widow of the piano manufacturer who had
been Adi's main financial support in the early days of the Party—the
Führer called attention to the new paintings on the walls, and remarked: "This is my new Detaze collection. Perhaps you do not know
that Herr Budd is the stepson of this painter. He came here to bring
me these fine works." The Austrian staff would make note of this and
perhaps be fooled by it—who can say who believes what in the game of
Machtpolitik? Presumably they believed Adi when he said that he was
going to build *Wolkenkratzer* (cloudscrapers) in Hamburg, just to
show the Americans that he could do whatever they could. Also he
was going to build a great bridge there; a tunnel would have been much
cheaper, but he wanted to deprive the Americans of the honor of having the longest bridge in the world.

They returned to the Berghof, and the world's greatest *Machtpoliti-
ker* exhibited the relief map, a revelation of his life's dream. Perhaps it
might have been wiser to use some other color than red; however, all
would understand that it was the red of German blood and not of
Jüdisch-Bolshewismus. The thin red lines with arrows at their tips ran
from Berlin to various centers such as Alsace and Schleswig, Prague
and the Sudetens and the Corridor; one of them ran to Vienna, and Adi
didn't have to point it out. He was tactful about it, and didn't say:
"All this is going to be mine." His formula was: "*Unsere gemeinsame
deutsche Erbschaft,*" our common German heritage.

And the same with the greatly enlarged photographs on the walls,
showing the ruin wrought by General Göring's *Luftwaffe* wherever it
had had a chance to try itself out. Adi didn't say: "This is what I am
going to do to Vienna if you refuse to obey my will." No, he said:
"This is what modern war is coming to; a terrible thing to have to
destroy cities like this." He didn't say: "I have had these put up especially for your benefit." He left it to be assumed that this was the
spectacle upon which he fed his soul day and night!

VII

The Führer took the Chancellor and his minister up to his study; Ribbentrop accompanied them, but not the Austrian subordinates or the American art expert. These last sat in the great hall, chatting about the trip from Vienna, the obliging weather, and what other polite nothings men hit upon when they are under extreme nervous tension and are anxious not to show it. Every moment the tension increased and the conversation became harder to keep up; for over and under and in between their polite, well-modulated words came a distant rumble as of thunder, irresistibly commanding their attention and making it impossible for them to think, to say nothing of formulating thoughts into words. They would fall dumb, and then would realize what extremely bad taste they were showing in seeming to listen to what they were not supposed to hear.

Adolf Hitler was making a speech. He had shut the door of his study, and had set armed SS men on guard outside the door, but that made little difference to the laws of acoustics. His voice came down the stairway—or perhaps it came through the floor, or both. It seemed to have echoes, which produced a sort of blurred and booming effect—but then that had always been a characteristic of Adi's oratorical thunder. He had been practicing it for thirty years—yes, fully that, for he had learned to shout down opposition in the shelter for bums, the *Obdachlosenheim* in Vienna before the World War, and had been more than once thrown out because he wouldn't or couldn't keep quiet. After the war he had practiced addressing thousands in the noisy beerhalls which were Munich's meeting places—since no South German could think or even hear without a stein in front of him. In those days there had been no such things as microphones or loud speakers, and survival in politics had been dependent upon the power of the naked voice.

Here today Adi was using that voice upon two persons who were presumably daring to differ with him, to oppose his will. It could happen even without that, as Lanny knew well, having brought it on himself more than once by mere mention of the Jews or the Versailles *Diktat*. He had discovered that, once the Führer got started, an audience of one was the same as one thousand or one million. It wasn't the Führer speaking any more, it was his *daimon*, which perhaps couldn't count; or perhaps it took the mystical view that in the eyes of the Creator one soul is as important as one million. Anyhow, here was that

Supervoice, exactly as all Germany and indeed all civilized mankind had heard it booming and bellowing over the radio. More than ten years ago Adi had told Lanny Budd that he would make the whole world listen to him; recently, when Lanny had reminded him of that, he had replied: *"Mit Gottes Hilfe, ich hab's getan!"*

The Austrian military aide and the secretary had to give up all pretense of not listening; and so did Lanny. Impossible to hear every word, but whole phrases came clearly. The Führer of the Nazis told Dr. Kurt Schuschnigg and Dr. Guido Schmidt that they were a pair of traitors to their German *Blut und Rasse.* He informed them that they had made for years a practice of submitting people of their own blood and race to indignities and outrages, for no offense but that of defending their heritage. The Führer had at his tongue's tip a long list of such outrages, and he brought them up, and with each one his frenzy mounted and his voice became more raucous and more confused by echoes. Now and then would come a pause, in which it might be assumed that the Chancellor or the Foreign Minister was attempting some reply; but it never did any good to reply to Adi—it only made his anger greater and his next speech louder and longer.

VIII

This went on for a couple of hours, until a bell rang, and silence fell. Adi had ordered lunch prepared for his guests, and it was one of the laws of this household that when the bell rang, everybody dropped everything and came trooping downstairs as one company. Adi himself would turn off his rage as if it were water from a spigot; which seemed to suggest that it wasn't something which controlled him, but which he used as a matter of policy. He became once more the gracious host and escorted these blood-and-race traitors to the elevator and thence to the dining hall, where at the long table the Kanzler was seated at the right hand of the Reichskanzler, and the Auslandsminister on his left. Ribbentrop sat at Schuschnigg's right, and then came Hess, and then the Generals and then those of lesser military rank, with Lanny among them, *ars inter arma.* It was the Führer's intention to establish his *neue Ordnung* by whatever force it took, but never to forget that thereafter would come peace and the greatest flowering of culture in all history—so he had assured his art-loving guest.

The Führer had his vegetable soup and vegetable plate and near-beer; the rest of the company had *Hasenpfeffer* followed by *Apfelstrudel,* a very plain meal, almost insulting. Also—and this was the severest part of the ordeal—poor Schuschnigg was a chain-smoker of cigarettes, and here he had no chance for one over a period of nine hours. Immediately after the meal he and his minister were taken back to the Führer's study; the discussion began again—and in a few minutes Hitler was launched upon another tirade. Most of the staff members, the experts and others, retired to their rooms, ostensibly to have a smoke and perhaps a drink; they stayed for another reason—they wanted to hear what was going on without being observed to be listening. When Lanny went to his own room he noted that practically every door in the corridor was open—but just a crack, and heads that were close to the crack disappeared suddenly when his footsteps were heard. All the world knew of this visit to the Berghof, and was waiting to know the outcome; to expect those inside the building not to hear it if they could was to ask more than human nature could achieve.

What had happened in the study Lanny heard later on from Hess. The lawyer-chancellor had brought along a briefcase full of documents which proved to his legal mind that the Committee of Seven had been conspiring to overthrow his government. Hitler shouted at him: "What have I to do with that committee?"—and Schuschnigg, assuming that he really wanted to know, brought forth documents to show that the committee had been financed and directed from Berlin. Of course Adi flew into one of his worst rages—and after that Hess didn't need to tell Lanny any more, for he had been able to stand inside the partly open door of his room and hear the Führer of the Germans telling two Austrian statesmen what he really thought of them and their government and their population.

It was an opinion unprintably low. Adi Schicklgruber called the Viennese a cityful of café loungers and *Bummler*, drunken dawdlers in the *Heurigen* and women-chasers all over the town. As a result of their *verdammte Geilheit* they were a race of mongrels—Czechs, Hungarians, Slavs, Turks and gipsies, niggers, God alone could say what else—all mixed with Jews and dominated by Jew politicians, dancing to Jew music, eating Jew food, sleeping in Jew beds. When Adi got to describing the sexual conduct of the Viennese, he used the language which he had learned as a boy in a village of the Inn valley where they raise cattle, and his similes were such as only a countryman could understand. The louder he shouted, the more raucous his voice became— the effect of a gas injury during the war.

It appeared that Adi's spies had brought word to him that Schuschnigg had been making approaches to the labor leaders and Socialists of the city, with the idea of getting their support. Less than four years ago

Dollfuss had bombed and shot this *Gesindel* into submission and now Schuschnigg was proposing to bring them back into power; that was treason to the German *Volk*, that was *Jüdisch-Bolshewismus*, no less, and brought the loudest screams yet. Hitler said there would be no Red intrigues going on anywhere on his borders, and before he would permit it he would send three hundred planes and bomb Vienna until not one of its elegant buildings was left with a roof over it.

What Adi was demanding was to have Seyss-Inquart, Führer of the Austrian Nazis, become Minister of the Interior, in charge of the police. If the demand was refused, the German army would march. Schuschnigg backed and filled, and finally said he would have to phone to President Miklas in Vienna. This he was permitted to do, and came back reporting that nothing could be decided without a full Cabinet meeting. At this Adi's screams of rage rang through the house; this was *eine Ausrede*, this was *eine Schurkerei*, this was *eine Frechheit!* He shook his fist in the unhappy Chancellor's face and told him that he and his *verdammtes Kabinett* had forty-eight hours in which to make up their *blödsinnigen*—imbecile—minds.

All this Lanny heard, and shivered a little while Hitler told what he would do to the members of the Austrian government if they compelled him to use force. It bore a startling resemblance to what the son of Budd-Erling had just been reading in the encyclopedia under the title "Islamic Institutions." Unbelievers were invited to embrace Islam, and if they did so, their lives, their families, and their property were protected. If they refused, they had to fight, and if they were defeated, their lives were forfeit, their families liable to slavery, and all their goods to seizure. Such was the code, enforced this time, not by lightly mailed horsemen armed with javelins and swords, but by technicians driving mechanical monsters which shot steel and spat flame, and by others flying in the sky and dropping heavy packages of death and destruction. "Under which king, Bezonian? speak, or die!"

IX

It wasn't until night that Adi's near-prisoners were released and allowed to drive home. Then the tension in the Berghof was released, and men emerged from their rooms and admitted that they had heard what they couldn't have helped hearing—or so they could pretend. Dinner was late, a rare event; it was like a birthday celebration—for everybody considered that victory had been won; that miserable pettifogging lawyer would never dare force his country into a war with the

Führer. Or would he? Lanny could sense uneasiness underneath the blustering. How could this story appear to the newspapers of the outside world? Once over the border, the lawyer would be free to tell it as he chose; and what would Britain and France say? What would Mussolini do? Would Czechoslovakia mobilize? And Poland? The military men revealed a tendency to draw off by themselves and talk in low tones.

These were trying days for the Fatherland, and Lanny was not surprised when the Deputy Führer told him that he desired to try another séance with Madame that evening. Was it the Führer himself who was going? It was no part of Lanny's duty to spy, and he didn't; but he heard with interest the report next morning—that the spirit of Paul von Beneckendorff und von Hindenburg had talked with Hess, and had reported himself entirely satisfied with what the Führer was doing. That had surely not been the case during the old gentleman's last days on earth; he had been wont to refer to Adi Schicklgruber as "the Bohemian corporal," a term of contempt and not according to the facts, for Adi was Austrian and had never got as high as corporal. But now the great Feldmarschall was rested and rejuvenated, and with his intellectual powers restored he realized that the German *Volk* were in the best possible hands. All this the Deputy Führer said with a perfectly straight face, and the American visitor heard him in the same fashion—but inwardly wondering if they both hadn't passed through the looking-glass with Alice.

Hess reported that the Führer was obliged to leave for Berlin at once. Would Herr Budd care to come and bring Madame, both to be the Führer's guests? Lanny started making excuses—for he wanted to get off a report to Washington, and couldn't send it from Berlin. He said, quite truly, that Madame was not happy in a foreign environment; the severe climate in the Alps kept her indoors, and she was yearning for the sunshine and flowers of the Riviera. Lanny had some picture business to attend to at home, and would leave Madame there, and proceed to Paris and possibly London. "In a couple of weeks I'll join you in Berlin and we'll try those experiments with Pröfenik, if you're in the mood." Hess replied: "O.K."

That afternoon the two visitors, plus Tecumseh and the spirits, were bundled up and driven to Munich and put on board the night express for Milan. Snow was falling, but it didn't matter to great electric locomotives; snowplows went ahead, and they took their heavy loads of passengers and mail and freight up into the Alpine passes, and through the wonderful tunnels, and down the long winding gap known as *Der*

Brenner, or *Il Brennero,* according to which side you were coming from. The Germans asked if you knew the land where the lemons grew, and sighed to be taken there; the Italians, on the other hand, voiced their fear of invading barbarians who came out of the snow and ice of the north. These barbarians had now taken over the Fascist political creed, but even so, no Latin would ever like them.

X

At Bienvenu all was well. Marceline was in the *hospice de la maternité* in Cannes where Frances Barnes Budd had been born eight years ago; Marceline had a baby boy in her arms, and was proud and happy. As for Vittorio, he was at the bursting point; everything was coming his way—not merely was he a father, but he had won several thousand francs by a new gambling system he had discovered, and the newspapers were reporting a series of victories by his armies, which were pushing down from the north, threatening to reach the sea and cut off Valencia from Barcelona. That dreadful Spanish war had been going on for more than a year and a half, and everything Lanny had hoped for was being crushed and ground into the bloody red dust of the Aragon hills. He found the vauntings of his brother-in-law all but intolerable; but he had to put a grin on his face and keep it there—just as in the Berghof.

His recourse was to pour out his heart through a typewriter onto sheets of paper. Not too many sheets, for he must remember that the Man in the White House had at least one hundred and three confidential agents, and thousands of other people trying to get his ear every day—but surely not many who had been listening behind the door while the Führer of the Nazis browbeat and mauled the Chancellor of the Austrians. Lanny tried to hold himself to the facts; but one of these facts was that relief map, showing the German-inhabited lands which Adi meant to take into his Third Reich. Austria would be the first bite; the second would be the Sudetenland, and the third the Polish Corridor. Meantime Spain was becoming a Fascist state, and a future flying field and submarine harbor for the new Mohammed. "Get ready to meet that," wrote "P.A. 103."

He told his mother what amount of money he had got from Hitler, about forty thousand dollars, but advised her not to let Marceline know, except by slow stages. The child—Lanny still thought of her as that, although she was twenty—didn't really need thirteen thousand all in a lump, and Vittorio would get it away from her and lose every cent of it in one night. Better let them think they were poor, and dole it out to them at intervals. So long as Marceline could live at Bienvenu she wouldn't suffer. Lanny added, with a smile: "I'll keep your share and dole it out to you." Beauty's heart was in a state of deliquescence just now; she was so excited over that marvelous new baby that she couldn't refuse any request of the young madonna.

Lanny took the trouble to cultivate his Fascist brother-in-law for professional reasons. There was quite an Italian colony in Cannes and thereabouts, and Vittorio's friends included several officers recovering from wounds, and several agents promoting Il Duce's cause in the Midi. They talked freely in the presence of Vittorio's rich brother-in-law—why not? Thus Lanny was able to learn the number of Italian troops in Spain—about three times what Mussolini admitted; their armaments, their losses, and the reinforcements expected. They were shipped from the harbor of Gaeta, between Rome and Naples; a small town, rarely visited by foreigners and therefore fairly secret. The cost had been terrific, a couple of billion lire so far, but of course Mussolini would never accept defeat; he had put his hand to the plow and must go to the end of the furrow.

That was what Bernhardt Monck had said nearly half a year ago, sitting under a tree on a hilltop near the doomed town of Belchite. Germany and Italy had to win, and would send whatever men and supplies it took. The Loyalists had men, but no supplies—so now the Italians and Moors had broken through; thousands of those ill-clad and hungry men whom Lanny had seen were dead, and perhaps Monck among them. The presidential agent could have shed tears of grief and rage over these thoughts, but instead he set himself at his typewriter and sent off another report. He permitted himself one sentence of what might have been called propaganda: "Men are dying there in those cold red hills to give us time to wake up and get ready."

XI

On all this Coast of Pleasure, now at the height of a gay and costly season, Lanny Budd knew only one person to whom he could express his feelings. He went in to Cannes, and from there telephoned to Julie Palma, making an appointment to pick her up on the street. He drove her out into the country, and heard all she had to tell about her husband and what he was doing in Valencia. He couldn't write freely, on account of the censorship; anyhow, he was of an optimistic nature, and would go on believing the best in spite of any defeat.

Lanny said: "If the Rebels break through to the sea, the people in Valencia will be trapped. Raoul had better come out now while he can."

"He won't," replied the wife. "He is a Spaniard, and feels that his duty is there."

"Tell him I say he is needed to run the school. He can accomplish many times more that way."

"It would do no good," was the answer. "Right or wrong, he thinks he's needed where he is."

This competent little brunette woman, an Arlésienne, told the news of the school, a center of anti-Fascist agitation in the Midi and greatly hated by the reactionaries of all groups. It had been named to Lanny by Vittorio's friends, and he mentioned this to the woman, warning her again of the importance of keeping his name out of it. Gone were the good old days when Lanny could come to the school and talk to the gang; when the little Red and Pink urchins would greet him on the street. Now he was supposed to have gone the way of the rest of the rotten rich. "The Communists class-angle you," said Julie Palma, with a smile.

He put an envelope into her hands, containing enough bank notes to keep the enterprise going until his next visit. She had invented an imaginary rich relative in Paris who was supposed to be the source of these funds, and she told him about the comments of the school on this lucky find. It made Lanny sad, for he was by nature a sociable person, and now there were so few persons he could talk to. He hadn't told either Raoul or Raoul's wife about Trudi; and now, for what reason he couldn't guess, the Trudi-ghost came no more. One of the first things he had done on reaching Bienvenu was to make a try with Madame, but he got only Zaharoff and Grandfather Samuel and his other familiars. Parsifal got Claribel, and the inmates of the monastery of Dodanduwa. The Trudi-ghost had apparently got lost somewhere on the road between Paris and the Cap.

XII

Vittorio had been driving Lanny's car, which meant that it needed repairs; Lanny waited for these, and then set out for Paris. He had a round of social duties there, and pleasures, if he could take them as such. Selling paintings to the Führer of all the Germans was from the professional point of view no small feat, and Zoltan was delighted to hear about it. Being sent by the Führer as an emissary to Vienna was a feat from another point of view, and Lanny would not fail to tell Kurt and his secretary about that; also Graf Herzenberg and his actress *amie*. It immensely increased his rating with them to know that he had been allowed to stay as a guest in the Berghof while the negotiations with Schuschnigg were going on; from that time on they would talk freely to him and he could pick up many items.

The de Bruynes were out of jail. The agitation of the reactionary papers of Paris had been a source of embarrassment to the members of the Cabinet, some of whom agreed with the prisoners' ideas, and considered them guilty merely of an indiscretion. In other words, the storm had blown over, and so Lanny could visit his old friends without any publicity. All three looked well; they had been allowed every comfort consistent with being in prisons. But all were indignant because they had been compelled to dismantle their lone fortification and agree to purchase no more arms whether at home or abroad, an unprecedented interference with the right of rich men to spend their money as they pleased.

They, too, were interested in hearing about the visit to Berchtesgaden. Lanny was able to reduce their mental distress by pointing out that Adolf Schicklgruber had bought arms and had attempted a *Putsch* and had been imprisoned and compelled to agree to a course of "legality." But that hadn't kept him from getting power. Denis de Bruyne said that meant going into politics, and might be all right for Germany, but in France the politicians were so hopelessly corrupt, they sold out not merely their country but their employers and even one another. The de Bruynes were so depressed concerning the state of *la patrie* that Lanny wondered whether they were ready to invite Hitler in to clean it up. Certainly they were not in the least disturbed by the prospect of having him move into Austria. It was plain to all the world that he couldn't move far to the east or southeast without running into Russia, and that was the development upon which all hearts were set.

There was a long letter from Robbie, telling the news of the family and the business. This man of constantly expanding affairs stressed the importance of his deal with Schneider, so it became Lanny's not unpleasant duty to eat a well-prepared luncheon at the Baron's town house and tell about the various meals he had eaten at the Führer's country house. There was nothing he wasn't free to reveal about this visit, except a few things such as the screaming and bellowing at the Austrian Chancellor; the son of Budd-Erling, well-bred and tactful, would tone that down, so that the Baron might not have the idea that he would go out from the Baron's home and betray secrets.

XIII

So important did the master of Schneider-Creusot consider this account of Hitler's personality and ideas that he asked if Lanny would consent to tell it to a few of the Baron's friends. So, three days later, Lanny was guest of honor at a formal and most elegant stag dinner, served by half a dozen footmen in pink plush livery, and attended by a dozen of the leading industrialists and financiers of Paris. These were the men who really governed the country, putting up the electoral funds, naming the members of cabinets, and being consulted as to all measures of importance. François de Wendel, Sénateur de France and head of the great mining trust; Max David-Weill, representing the bank of Lazard Frères; René Duchemin of the French chemical trust; Ernest Mercier, the electrical magnate—men like these. Not merely the French empire in Africa and Asia, but their satellite states in Central Europe, where their government had loaned many billions of francs and their banks and industries had made even greater investments—all these treasures and dominions were at stake, and the crisis was such that it rocked the political world, and divided even these masters among themselves.

Was this Adolf Hitler a statesman like all the others, whom you could buy at a price low or high? Or was he a madman, one without any price? Here was an American, young compared with those present, the son of a man whom many of them knew, and he had actually lived in the madman's house for a week or more and heard his intimate conversation. They wanted him to tell everything about Adi and what to do about him—provided of course that Lanny would tell them to do what they wanted done. The guest explained that he was embarrassed, for he was no politician but an art expert; his errand to Austria had been to purchase a Defregger for the Führer and his errand to Berchtesgaden had been to take the Führer some examples of the work of Lanny's late stepfather, Marcel Detaze. (Not a bad advertisement for a high-class business, incidentally.)

The story of this dinner would, of course, go back to Berlin very soon; so Lanny had to be careful what he said. He had no objection to describing Adolf Hitler's well-appointed home, his agreeable manners, and what he ate and drank. It was all right to say that Hess believed in spiritualism and mental healing; but better not anything about Mohammed! The facts about the ultimatum to Schuschnigg had been in all the newspapers of the world, so they could be discussed freely. The relief map of German population and culture had been reproduced as a poster and was now being circulated by Dr. Goebbels, so there was no harm in that. The Führer had told Lanny to say that he loved France and hated Russia and that both these feelings were undying; so Lanny carried out these instructions. On his own authority he said that Hitler was determined to control and perhaps annex not merely Austria, but all the adjoining lands whose population was predominantly German; those who did business with him would have to do it on that basis.

After coffee and liqueurs had been consumed, the discussion went on for an hour or two, and even after the guests adjourned to the library they gathered around the guest of honor and wouldn't let him go. There was another Cabinet crisis impending in France, brought on by the Austrian situation. Chautemps was tottering, and Blum was plotting to come in again; these masters had to find somebody to keep him out—but first they had to make up their minds what they wanted done. They were all worried, and Lanny knew of old that men of this sort are the world's best worriers. In reality they were helpless, on account of the firm position of the British Cabinet, which had sold them out in favor of Hitler—at least that is how they saw it. Britain was playing Germany against France according to the ancient practice of *perfide Albion*. Why shouldn't France play Germany against Britain? But then, wouldn't that be playing the game of the Soviets?

They didn't come to any decision that night; but Lanny thought it a good enough story for Roosevelt that in this crisis the secret rulers of France hadn't yet been able to make up their minds whom they wanted for their friends and whom for their enemies.

22

Foul Deeds Will Rise

I

ADOLF HITLER summoned his tame Reichstag into session, a device which he used when he wished to address the world. The Reichstag had two things to do: first, to hear him make a long speech, and second, to vote its endorsement of everything he had said. This vote never failed to be unanimous—since any member who presumed to voice disapproval would be sent off to a concentration camp before that afternoon's sun had set.

This time Adi told the world pretty much the same things that Lanny had told the guests of Baron Schneider. He set forth at length his undoubtedly genuine loathing for the Soviet Union. "We see in Bolshevism more now than before the incarnation of human destructive forces." It was not the poor Russian people who were to blame for this world calamity, he said. "We know it is a small Jewish intellectual group which has led a great nation into this position of madness." And then those Germans on the outside, who had been separated from the Fatherland by the wicked Versailles *Diktat*. "In the long run it is unbearable for a World Power, conscious of itself, to know there are racial comrades across its border who are constantly being afflicted with the severest suffering for their sympathy or unity with the whole nation, its destiny, and its philosophy."

This was a question of philosophy at the moment, for Adi wanted the British Tories to keep quiet while he got Austria into his grip, and then he would take up the next subject with them. But he gave an idea what that was; for when Adi got going, it was hard for him to stop, and when any one of his phobias was mentioned it became impossible for him to control his feelings. He always delivered these tirades extemporaneously and had never yet been known to read a prepared speech. The British press was presuming to criticize his ultimatum to Austria; this was called "freedom of the press" in Britain, and it meant "allowing journalists to insult other countries, their institutions, their public men, and their government." The Führer gave plain warning that he wasn't going to stand this. "The damage wrought by such a press campaign was so great that henceforth we shall no longer be able to tolerate it without stern objections. This crime becomes especially evil when it obviously pursues the goal of driving nations into war."

The British public might have foreseen the result of such misconduct; but the Führer saw fit to tell them in plain words. "Since this press campaign must be considered as an element of danger to the peace of the people, I have decided to carry through that strengthening of the German army which will give us the assurance that these threats of war against Germany will not some day be translated into bloody force." So there it was! Germany was being forced to arm by the British press, and nobody could ever again say that Germany had wanted to do it. Nor was there any use talking any more, so long as the press was free to build up a public opinion, and statesmen in democratic lands had to do what public opinion demanded. Said Adi: "Under these circumstances it cannot be seen what use there is in conferences and meetings as long as governments in general are not in a position to take decisive steps irrespective of public opinion."

II

Lanny listened to this address on his radio while motoring to Calais. It made him rather blue, and his feelings were not improved by a stormy Channel crossing; he was seasick one of the few times in his life, and went to the nearest hotel to spend the night and recuperate. There in the morning papers he read that Anthony Eden, chief object of the Führer's attack, had resigned from the British Cabinet. That would be taken in Germany as an act of submission; in Britain it was taken as a protest against the Prime Minister's course—a very decorous and reserved protest, in the British manner. The Prime Minister received it "with profound regret," and tried to make it appear as a protest against Italy's continued breaches of the Non-Intervention Agreement in Spain.

Lanny motored to Wickthorpe Castle and was welcomed as usual. He played with his little daughter, and in between times read in the newspapers of the hot debate going on in Parliament over the government's course. Secure in his Tory majority of more than two to one, Chamberlain stood firm in his policy of "appeasement"; and over the week-end the politicians and public men gathered at Irma's house-party to discuss what had been said and what was going to be done.

There was a general hush-hush atmosphere, for few Englishmen liked what they were doing. You took things for granted and didn't put them into words, except to a few of the innermost insiders. Germany was hell-bent upon taking back those eastern borderlands which she had lost after the last war; many Britons hadn't approved of taking them from her, and now, to keep them from her would mean a war that Britain wasn't ready for and didn't want. France, which had heavy investments there, would just have to write them off. There had been some sort of understanding with the Nazis—perhaps not in writing, just a gentlemen's agreement with men who rejected that classification. There were hints of it in Hitler's speech; he had said that Germany's colonial claims would be "voiced from year to year with increasing vigor"—which of course was "double talk" for the statement that they weren't being pressed at present. That was the thing which the British ruling class would never stand for—having Hitler become strong overseas, and establish airplane and submarine bases. On land they might have to let him have his way, provided he didn't go too far—but how far would he go? Who could say?

Right at this juncture came Lanny Budd, fresh from a sojourn in the home of this statesman of whims and frenzies, this genius-madman, this uncertain ogre. Incredible, but true; there could be no doubt that he had been there, for he described the pictures on the walls, the decoration of the bedrooms, the size and color and contents of the vegetable plates which the ogre ate. "Upon what meat doth this our Caesar feed, that he is grown so great?" These grave English gentlemen and political ladies thronged about an American art expert and plied him with questions, and some of the most exclusive asked if he would come to their homes and tell another select company what he had seen and heard.

Irma was quite taken aback by her ex-husband's social success. What had come over him? Could it be that he had really changed his mind and dropped his crazy radical notions? Or was this a super-subtlety that he had acquired? From the point of view of a week-end hostess it didn't make much difference, so long as he gave the facts and was so discreet, never intruding his own opinions, but leaving it for his hearers to draw their own conclusions.

Inside this venerable castle was every comfort, and complete protection against the winter's cold; but one heard the fierce gales blowing about the chimneys and rattling the windows. One knew also that political storms were rising, and no amount of English courtesy and

.reserve could keep out awareness of the people's discontent. There were mass meetings in Albert Hall, and huge crowds in Trafalgar Square in spite of unsuitable weather. Mobs shouted against the murder of the Spanish people's government, and British freedom of speech and press was used to print and circulate leaflets, pamphlets, and books denouncing the Fascists and warning of the wars they were preparing. The small ruling group which controlled public policy was being denounced under the name of the "Cliveden set," after the very elegant country home of the Astors. Of course these people vigorously denied that they exercised any such power, and even that there was any such set; Rick in one of his caustic articles had written: "They deny there is a Cliveden set, but will they deny there is a Cliveden sort?"

Irma mentioned this controversy more than once in her ex-husband's presence, and Lanny wondered: Was she a little peeved because Nancy was getting more than her share of public attention? He did not forget that Irma had had several years in café society, both before and after their marriage; and would she have been secretly pleased if the Red and Pink press had taken to denouncing the "Wickthorpe set"? Nancy had the advantage that her husband was a press lord, and she herself a member of Parliament, whereas Irma's husband was a career man in the Foreign Office, and had to preserve an atmosphere of aloofness and impartiality in his home. So that had become Irma's tone, and when she spoke of her rival it was in a gently patronizing vein.

III

Lanny motored to The Reaches, and then what a blowing off of steam there was! All the accumulated pressure of some of the most eventful weeks in the history of both the world and Lanny Budd. He could tell here how Adi had bellowed at Schuschnigg, and even give an imitation of the sounds—which sent Rick and Nina into gales of laughter, for it doesn't take much exaggeration to make German sound funny to English ears. He could tell about the new Mohammed, and what Islam had done to infidels and would still do if it had been able. He could even tell of the dreadful confession of Magda Goebbels, and the degenerate practices of which he had knowledge among the Nazis.

Also he could pour out his heart about Trudi. He hadn't succeeded in getting the information he sought, but he was close to getting it, he believed. "I'll be much surprised if Professor Pröfenik doesn't make use of every tip I gave him," he declared.

"I hope you *do* get it!" exclaimed Nina. "It is such a cruel thing to be kept in a state of uncertainty."

"It is what Trudi herself endured for four years or more. Thousands of others are still enduring it, and will for the rest of their lives."

"I know," said the woman; "but it makes a difference when you know the persons." Womanlike, she was interested in what was going on in the hearts of men, and added: "Tell me how you stand it, Lanny."

"Well, you learn to stand what you have to. It's not so bad in my case, because I'm doing Trudi's work, and I have the feeling that she's always with me. I know exactly what she'd say to everything that comes up, and when I give some money for the cause I feel her satisfaction."

It couldn't be the same, Nina knew; but she forebore to say so, for that would be like probing into a wound that he was managing to heal. Just as the body walls off a foreign substance which has got under the skin, so the mental body walls off suffering. So this gentle woman thought, and Lanny, an old friend, knew the meaning of her silence.

"Our case is hard to understand," he told her. "Few lovers were ever so impersonal. Trudi was so completely absorbed in her cause that really it seemed as if she had no life outside it. I would see her sitting silent, and would never have to offer a penny for her thoughts; I knew that her mind was on the comrades in the concentration camps, or those who were risking their lives circulating our literature. I would try to beguile her, and now and then succeed, but not often—for the pressure was always on her, there was always some new thing coming up that brought the whole tragedy back to life in her heart."

"It's inhuman to be like that, Lanny!"

"Of course it's inhuman; but so are the Nazis, and we who fight them have to be the same."

"What's that going to mean to the future?"

"I leave the problems of the future for the future to solve. The fact is now that we're at war, and have to feel the emotions of war and make the sacrifices of war. The Nazis are not going to be overcome except by men who are as stern as they, and as determined to prevail. There'll have to be a lot of anti-Nazi fanatics, and some of them will be women who think more about saving their comrades than they do about making their husbands happy. Isn't it so, Rick?"

"Right you are!"

"I haven't made up my mind whether I believe in immortality," said Lanny, "but I know that Trudi's spirit lives on in me. I think about her all the time; I suppose it's what the religious people call 'communing.' When I get in a stroke against the Nazis, I hear her saying: 'Good for you!'—and always: 'What next?' The Nazi terror goes on, and our resistance cannot slacken. I suppose I'm becoming one of the fanatics, too."

Nina wanted to exclaim: "Oh, *don't!*" but she was afraid it wouldn't be polite. Instead she asked: "Suppose you learn that they've killed her. Will you go on mourning for her, or will you find another love?"

"A fine chance I'd have to make a woman happy—or to discover one who would live my life!" Lanny smiled—he seldom talked long without finding some occasion to smile. "Did you ever read Sir Walter Scott's 'Outlaw's Song'?" He quoted:

> Maiden! a nameless life I lead,
> A nameless death I'll die!
> The fiend, whose lantern lights the mead,
> Were better mate than I!

IV

Lanny telegraphed Rudolf Hess, asking if a meeting with Pröfenik would now be agreeable, and the reply came promptly that an appointment had been made for two days from that date. So the agent motored to the Channel and had another stormy crossing at the beginning of March. He reached Calais—a town whose name had been written on his heart by the tragedy of the Robin family. An unseasonable snowstorm was making it dangerous to drive, so he put his car in storage and took the train so as not to miss his date.

He was invited to be the guest of the Deputy, but thought it the part of tact to put up at the Adlon and not be in the way. He knew from the newspapers that both Adi and his most loyal supporter were absorbed in what was for all practical purposes a war with Austria, being carried on inside that unhappy country through the agency of Seyss-Inquart and another Nazi who had been forced into the Cabinet. It might have been taken as a comedy war if it hadn't had such grim meaning for the future. The Austrian Minister of the Interior and Public Security granted to the Nazis of Styria the right to wear swastikas and to shout "*Heil Hitler!*"—and then the Cabinet of which he was a member canceled the order. He went to Graz and reviewed fifteen thousand Nazis, many of them in uniform and all giving the Nazi salute in what was an illegal parade. Nobody who knew the Hitler movement could doubt what this meant.

Lanny found the newspapers of Berlin full of clamor concerning the mistreatment of Germans in Austria. Those hateful Nazi newspapers, filled full of lies and abuse! Such a thing as factual reporting was entirely unknown in Hitlerland; it was all the poison propaganda of the crooked dwarf "Juppchen," whom Lanny had come to think of as the vilest human being he had ever shaken by the hand. One glance at any front page in Berlin and you knew what new move the Nazi machine was preparing and who were to be the next victims: Jews, Austrians, Czechs, Poles, Bolsheviks—and now and then a turn at domestic enemies, speculators, black-market operators, refusers of *Winterhilfe,* doubters of the Führer's wisdom—and then pacifists, Catholics, Protestants, Free Masons, and of course Jews and Reds everywhere and all over again.

V

Lanny reported his presence in town and confirmed the appointment; Hess would call for him that evening. Also he called Göring's office, and reported to Hauptmann Furtwaengler that he had orders for two paintings which the Feldmarschall had commissioned him to dispose of. That was always pleasant news; *Der Dicke* had become the richest man in Germany—"But nobody ever has enough money," observed Lanny, and the SS officer chuckled appreciatively. He, no doubt, had had opportunity to observe.

Deputy Führer Hess had not provided himself with a six-wheeled chariot enameled in baby-blue. He rode in a black limousine with a red standard in front and a gold swastika on the doors. A staff sergeant drove, with another SS man beside him for protection. Perhaps the windows were of bulletproof glass—Lanny had no objection to this being the case for the night. As they rode he discussed the Austrian imbroglio, of course blaming Schuschnigg—for what was the sense of appointing a Minister of Public Security and then doing everything to make him insecure? It simply meant that you didn't mean what you said, and the Führer was sick of dealing with people who kept no bargains. The Austrian Cabinet was going to get another shaking up, and this time the double-dealers would be shaken out on their heads.

They talked about Pröfenik, and Hess said the old fellow had had plenty of time to prepare and no doubt would put on a good show for them. It was so hard to find honest and competent mediums—and why did they have to be Poles and low-class people like that? Lanny said he didn't know, but it appeared to be a fact that many of them did come from those Central European lands. The most careful and dependable researchers appeared to be Germans; Lanny named Driesch and Schrenck-Notzing and Tischner. Hess made note of these names, and Lanny wondered if they would receive decorations and be put in charge of a *Forschungs Anstalt für Parapsychologie*.

Before they went into the building Lanny said: "I want you to know, I have not communicated with Pröfenik, or told him anything about you."

The Deputy Führer replied: "He knows plenty about me, and can find out more. But, by God, if he tries any monkey tricks on me, I'll have him skinned alive!"

VI

In that house of mystery nothing had been changed. The black-clad servant took their hats and coats, and the elderly Chinese-appearing gentleman received them with bland courtesy and escorted them into the dimly lighted room. He asked after their health and the Führer's, and said: "We are witnessing great events. I have cast the Führer's horoscope again, and this is the month for him." Hess answered, rather dryly: "He thinks so."

Lanny, watching the wizard closely, noted that his eyes moved warily from one to the other of his guests. "Gentlemen," he said, abruptly, "you have come for advice, and the auguries are favorable. Let us proceed to work, before anything is said that might influence the supermundane forces."

That suited the pair, so without another word the old man entered the cabinet and drew the curtains. They waited, and presently heard a moaning and sort of faint snoring; then all of a sudden the deep bass voice of the "control" who called himself King Ottokar I. Speaking German, he declared: "There is an elderly gentleman here. He has white sidewhiskers but his chin is shaven; he wears a uniform of cream-colored broadcloth with a large gold star on his bosom. He claims to be a great ruler, and gives the name of Franz Josef. Do you know any such person?"

"I have heard of him," replied Hess, not too cordially.

"He is unhappy; he says that terrible things are coming to his beautiful city. The Prussians are marching once more against Austria. He says: 'I don't mind if you kill some of the people—there were always too many of them; but spare my palaces, for they were built to last for a long time.'"

"Tell him that nobody wants to hurt his palaces."

There was a pause, presumably while the old Emperor talked; then the voice said: "He says that if it had been intended that men should fly they would have had wings on their shoulders."

"Tell him," said the Deputy, "that if it had been intended for men to live in palaces, they would have had them growing on their backs, like snails."

Again a pause, and then: "He declares that is no way to talk to *Majestät*, and you will have to be respectful if you desire the honor of his communications."

"I apologize," said the Nazi, for Lanny had impressed upon him that spirits have to be humored. "Ask Seine Majestät if he can tell us what is coming to his country."

"He says many sorrows before any joys; but in the end the name *felix Austria* will be justified."

"That is rather vague. Ask him, please: Will the Viennese resist?"

"He says: 'The Viennese resist everything.' He says, again: 'They have their own peculiar way, which others might not recognize.' "

"What we want to know is, will they resist with guns?"

"He says they will resist with arrows of ridicule; and that it is always better to persuade your opponents."

"Is that all he has to tell me?"

"He says that he really loved the city of his dreams,—'*die Stadt meiner Träume.*' He says: 'I did the best I could, but the world changes too fast for the mind of any man.' "

"Tell him that his place in history is secure," said the Deputy Führer of the NSDAP—and nothing could have been handsomer. "Ask him if he has any suggestions on his mind."

"He wishes you to know that his grandnephew Otto would make an excellent successor to the throne."

"We have heard of the young man, but he has been exiled from his Fatherland—and not by us. Anything else?"

"Seine Majestät thinks that the American gentleman might be interested to know there is a very fine portrait of his Imperial Majesty in the possession of the family of a painter named Husak, in Vienna."

"Ask him for the address," Lanny ventured.

"It is difficult to make out," declared the voice; but finally he gave it, spelling the name of the street. The American gentleman, making notes as best he could in the dim light, did not fail to get this information down. It was the first time the spirits had ever sought to do business with him and he wondered, had somebody offered the Professor a commission on a deal? If so, he was taking a bold chance for a small amount of money, for the communication was certainly not likely to fool the Deputy Führer.

VII

The aged Habsburger faded back into the realm or substance or whatever it was he had come from. They were not sorry to have him go, for his dynasty had never been celebrated for wit or charm. In his stead came a personage who rarely failed Lanny: the Knight Commander of the Bath and Grand Officer of the Legion of Honor. For the first time in his career in this world or the next he addressed Lanny as "Mr. Budd," and for the first time he reported himself as happily reunited with his duquesa. Apparently King Ottokar I was a dispenser of bliss—he had been extremely dictatorial on earth. Lanny was polite, but inwardly skeptical, until the spirit gave him a message for its earthly successor, Baron Schneider, and then a reference to Sir Basil's part in finding the gold of the *Hampshire*.

This was the devilish thing about the business of psychic research; just as you had decided that some medium was a fraud, you would get something that startled you, and then, likely as not, you would think it over and change your mind yet again. Had Robbie Budd's dealing with the owner of Le Creusot been mentioned in any of the Berlin newspapers? Certainly there were important persons in the city who knew about the matter; and that meant also their secretaries and underlings. The same was true regarding the cruiser *Hampshire*. Lanny had told Pröfenik about Sir Basil, though not about this gold; however, it had been only ten years since the treasure-seekers had set out, and the vessel had been equipped in Germany; it had returned to Hamburg, and Horace Hofman had been dined in Berlin, where he had met prominent persons, including Doktor Horace Greeley Hjalmar Schacht. So, if anybody set out to do a research job on Zaharoff in Germany, that was one of the things he might be expected to come upon.

VIII

All these thoughts were driven suddenly out of Lanny's mind, for here came the thing that he was waiting for; his heart began to pound uncomfortably, and he was glad the room was not well lighted. Said the thirteenth-century King of Bohemia: "There is a couple here, Germans and rather young; they speak in low voices and seem embarrassed to trouble Herr Budd. They say they troubled him once before, and now they want him to know that they have found each other."

"What are their names?" inquired Lanny; and really, he could hardly keep from trembling, for suppose this was a genuine medium, and suppose Trudi didn't know that Hess was present, and should blurt out: "I am your former wife." It wouldn't be like the Trudi of the real world, but who could guess what spirits might remember or forget, or how much they might know about the political situation? Truly it was taking a chance to have Hess sitting by—even though the communications might be only constructs of Lanny's subconscious mind!

He was proceeding upon the guess that Pröfenik was no medium, but a shrewd old scamp, making use of the material Lanny had given him. And apparently this was the case. The voice of Ottokar replied: "It is the man speaking and his voice is low. *Bitte, lauter, lieber Herr!* The name appears to be Schultz. Do you know any such person?"

"I cannot recall him."

"He gives the name Ludwig; then he says he is called Ludi. He tries to tell you about the place where he met you. It was in a large drawing-room, many persons present; they served coffee and other refreshments, and his wife was one of those who served as hostesses."

"Does he give the wife's name?"

"She was called Gertrud."

"I cannot recall any Gertrud Schultz."

"He says she was also known as Mueller. I ask, is that her maiden name, and he says no, she changed her name. I ask if they were divorced, and he does not say; apparently there is something very unhappy in their lives. He wants you to know that they are reunited now, and the pain is forgotten."

"Can they tell you anything more about the circumstances of their meeting with me?"

"He says they were artists, both of them, and they told you about their work; you showed an interest, very kindly, but they did not follow it up, because at that time they did not know that you were the stepson of Marcel Detaze, or that you were yourself such a distinguished expert."

"Thank them for me, and say that I wish them well; but I do not understand why they should come to me."

"They had come before and they feared that they had troubled your mind."

"Not at all; I have to confess that I had forgotten them. Have they any art works that I could see and might be interested in?"

"No, they are humble about their work. Ludi says that he was a commercial artist, and such work is only for the day."

"Does he wish to tell me anything about the cause of their unhappiness? Is it a story that I could have heard?"

There was a pause. Then: "The woman is weeping. She says she cannot bear to have it talked about."

"They aren't Jews, by any chance?"

"No, Aryans."

"Jews do not always look like Jews; and they take Aryan names —it is one of their favorite tricks."

"They say they are not Jews."

"Could they have been in any political trouble?"

"They don't want to talk about it; they are turning away; they have their arms about each other, as if they wanted you to know that they love each other deeply."

IX

The rest of the séance didn't amount to much. It was Hess's turn, and the spirit of Horst Wessel announced itself. The Nazi hero-martyr spoke of the song he had written, and was proud of this service to the cause. He told some of the circumstances of his earthly life, but did not mention that he had been a pimp. He made predictions as to the future triumphs of the Party and in general spoke in a way to warm the heart of a Party Führer. His last sentences were a triumphant prophecy that Austria would soon be joined to the Fatherland. He had studied for a year at the University of Vienna, and knew that frivolous people, he declared.

The wizard came out of his trance and emerged from the cabinet. He did not ask anything about what happened, but perhaps he could feel in the atmosphere that he had not scored a hit. He offered to cast the Deputy's horoscope, but Hess said that had been done many times, and he had more important business. Lanny asked if the Professor had tried to send his astral body to the Berghof, and the old man said that he had done so, and had seen Lanny and Hess gazing out over the mountains, and also at something which looked like playing cards—which they hadn't done. No mention of French wrestling!

As they went out, Lanny left an envelope on the table; he noticed that Hess failed to do the same, and wondered if Party chieftains enjoyed the privilege of free séance tickets. When they were in the car, the Deputy said: "That seemed to me pretty thin stuff."

"I agree," replied the other.

"All that about Horst Wessel—he could have got it out of a pamphlet which the Party sells for five pfennigs."

"Zaharoff always called me Lanny; never 'mister' in his life."

"That King Ottokar is a new one to me. Did you ever hear of him?"

"He was a king of Bohemia when it was one of the German states. Grillparzer wrote a play about him."

"No sense in any of it that I can see. We wasted an evening." There was a pause; Lanny waiting to let his companion bring up the crucial subject. He thought it would come, and it did.

"And all that about the Schultz couple. Did you make anything out of that?"

"Not very much. But one thing comes back to my memory—I believe those same people appeared in a séance I had nearly a year ago with a woman medium here in Berlin. There was a spirit who called himself Ludi Schultz, and he was wandering around trying to find his wife who was called Trudi."

"Did you tell Pröfenik about that?"

"That's what I'm trying to get clear in my mind. You see, I had a long talk with him, two or three hours. I mentioned the fact that a number of times I had had reports of spirits who seemed to be just drifting in and then out again. They insisted they had met me somewhere, though I couldn't recall them. It is possible that I may have given the names of the Schultzs; I can't feel sure."

"It makes all the difference," declared Hess. "If you told him, he could easily have made up the rest."

"You know how it is when something seems to be just hanging on the edge of your mind, and you think you've got hold of it but you can't quite. There's that business about women serving coffee and refreshments; there were several places where I was asked to give a talk on art, and of course I met no end of art people, and heard a lot of names."

"Pröfenik could guess that without trouble," insisted the Deputy.

"I know; but I keep reminding myself of this: If a man gets certain facts consciously, those facts are in his subconscious mind also, and they are just as apt to come out in a genuine trance as anything else.

Suppose Pröfenik had read a five-pfennig pamphlet about Horst Wessel, his subconsciousness might weave those facts into a personality without the least dishonesty."

"I never thought of that, Mr. Budd. Few people realize how complicated this subject is."

"You bet! It's a whole universe, whose laws we are only beginning to guess at. Every now and then I have an impulse to follow up some clue. Perhaps you can advise me: would there be any chance of finding a list of commercial artists in Berlin during the last few years? Do they have an association or anything like that?"

"I don't happen to know, but I can find out. There are no associations in Germany that we don't know about."

"It seems to me that would be a good way to check upon Pröfenik. He gave a number of details; and certainly not many Ludis have married Trudis."

Again Lanny waited, and again the trap he had set was sprung. "By the way," said Hess, "didn't the old rascal say the woman was called Mueller also?"

"Yes, I recall that."

"Why should she have two names?"

"That is one of the things we may find out. Often artists take brush names, of course."

"That might be. But a man in my business thinks of another possibility. A lot of artists and people of that sort have been opposing our *Regierung,* and we've had to be rough with them. Maybe we might find that she has some sort of police record."

"By heck! There's an idea! Could you have it looked up, do you suppose?"

"Of course I could. We have a master cardfile."

"I don't want to put you to a lot of bother——"

"No bother at all. I'll tell my secretary to call up the police in the morning, and if there are or were any such persons I'll have the data within an hour."

"I never expected to have the help of the Gestapo in my psychic researches!" chuckled the son of Budd-Erling.

X

Lanny walked into the Hotel Adlon with his feet hardly touching the floor of the lobby. He didn't want to sleep; he wanted to lie on his back in the dark and whisper silently: "Trudi! Trudi!" Once more he felt that she was close to him, and that if he reached out a little farther he would make contact with her. He would say: "Are you there?"—and then argue: "Why should I have to wait on the Gestapo?" He thought of some of the phantasms he had read about, phantasms of the living as well as of the dead. Such stories went back as far as recorded history; also, you would hardly mention the subject in any company without finding some person who had had such an experience, often while refusing to believe it. Lanny had told Trudi a lot about it; she had never known whether to believe it or not, but surely now she would be thinking about it and trying it as he was.

He kept staring ahead of him into the darkness at the foot of his bed, but he saw nothing, he heard nothing, and at last he dropped off to sleep. Then he dreamed about Trudi. Did that mean that she was dreaming about him? Men had been wondering about dreams since the beginning of time, and weaving all sorts of fantasies on the subject. Now came the Freudians, with an explanation which they called scientific; but what would become of their theories if you admitted telepathy into the psyche? A bull in a china shop could do no more damage. Lanny had heard that of late Freud had become convinced of the reality of telepathy, but how could he explain dreams when they might have hopped in from the mind of any other person on earth? Lanny thought about this while he was shaving, and wished that while in Vienna he had called upon the learned Jewish doctor and asked for the answer to that question.

Lanny looked over the morning papers, full of denunciations of the treacherous Austrian government, with demands for immediate action by the insulted Reich. Lanny knew that no Nazi editor ever clamored for action until Dr. Goebbels had tipped him off that action was coming soon. He tried to read on, but could hardly think about Austria's troubles this morning; he thought only of the telephone. What time did Hess reach his office? The Gestapo, of course, would be open all night; its agents came and went, and its favorite time for pouncing upon its victims was at three or four in the morning.

The mail was brought to his room; also a cablegram, which proved to be mysterious and puzzling. It was from New York, and read: "Honored relative will call"; the signature was: "Bessie Budd Host." Lanny didn't have to figure long to realize that this was code for Johannes Robin, who wouldn't risk embarrassing Lanny by signing a name so notorious in Germany. Lanny had taken many agreeable trips on the yacht *Bessie Budd*, and had not forgotten who had invited him and paid the bills. If Johannes had signed the message "Bessie

Budd Owner" or "Bessie Budd Proprietor," that might have sounded phony; but "Host" was an inconspicuous word and might be a name—indeed, Lanny had once met a man who bore it, and if he had married Lanny's half-sister, her name would have been Bessie Budd Host!

Any relative of Johannes was, of course, a Jew; and all Jewish relatives were honored, that their days might be long in the land. Alas, their days promised to be short in Germany, and also in Austria! This would be some person in trouble, of course. Lanny felt a sinking of the heart, for he couldn't help any Jews now, he had another job—and how could he explain matters to his old friend? It might be that all the caller would want was money, and that would be easy enough. But usually what Jews wanted was to get out of Germany, and that might take a lot of money, more than Lanny had in Naziland. Also, they wanted passports to America; and Lanny was one of a hundred and three persons who could make no move along that line.

XI

The telephone rang; the secretary of Herr Reichminister Hess, desiring to know if Herr Budd could call this morning at the Herr Reichminister's office. It was then eleven, and Lanny said he had an engagement to lunch with General Göring, but would come at once and hoped that he could have the interview without delay. He stepped into a taxi, and gave his destination, the headquarters of the NSDAP; then he leaned back in the seat and closed his eyes to the traffic and the signals. Silently, and without movement of the lips, he read himself a lecture and taught himself a role. "*Now!* You're going to get bad news, and how are you going to take it? You might as well make up your mind that she's dead! There's not a chance of anything else; and what are you going to say? You've got to talk telepathy, or spirits, and not show any feelings—not have any feelings, because if you do Hess will know it. Watch every movement, every word, every thought; for this is dynamite."

Silently and without motion of the lips, Lanny practiced what he was going to feel and say if Hess told him that Trudi was dead; then—a still harder task, because less expected—what he would say if Hess told him that she was in a concentration camp. This went on all the way to the large building over which the Deputy and Party Führer presided; all the way up in the elevator; all the way through the closely guarded anterooms and into the great man's presence.

Hess wore the simple brownshirt uniform, probably the same he had worn the night before. He looked stern and impressive at his large flat-topped desk with several telephones and many buttons, the symbols of authority in the modern world. Lanny was treading in one of the centers of the most cruel authority in centuries; this dark, tight-lipped man with the bushy eyebrows meeting over the bridge of his nose might cause serious trouble for a presidential agent unmasked. Or would he do any unmasking? If he had penetrated Lanny's secret, would he not be more apt to keep it to himself and his dread organization, and give Lanny rope with which to hang himself? Treason within treason, and treachery piled on treachery!

The Deputy got down to business, having been told that his visitor had no time to spare. Open before him was a portfolio with many papers and one hand was resting upon them as he spoke. "Mr. Budd, we have uncovered something interesting here. It looks as if the spirits knew more than we gave them credit for."

"Is that so, Herr Reichsminister?"

"I find we have a long record on these people, and of the blackest sort. They were Social-Democratic agitators, Marxists of the reddest dye, over a period of ten years or so."

"Oh, my God!" said the well-rehearsed visitor.

"The man was caught early, and committed suicide in Oranienburg. The woman got away, and caused us trouble for three years or more. She was center of a well-organized seditious group. She took the name of Mueller, and several other aliases—I won't tell them to you, because it might be interesting to see if you can get them through Madame or any other medium."

"By all means! What happened to the woman?"

"She fled to France; but recently she made the mistake of coming back into Germany. She died in Dachau two or three months ago."

So there it was; and Lanny never blinked an eyelash, never changed color by the slightest shade. He spoke the words that he had drilled into his mind: "*Herrgott!* This is really a case of supernormal power!"

"I think we have to admit it. That old bastard has got something after all."

"Well, that's the way it goes, Herr Reichsminister—you meet with disappointments and you are bored night after night; and then, just as you are ready to quit, you run into something like this. I am deeply grateful to you for digging this story out for me."

"Not at all—I am just as much interested as you. We'll go back and try again sometime and see if we can get more details."

"I'll try with Madame, also. Truly, it's a fascinating thing, and when you once get started, you are drawn in deeper and deeper. Imagine those two spirits going off hand in hand—and not wanting to tell their story in your presence! I wonder if they are still afraid of you."

"It's comforting to know they are where they can't do any harm to our cause." Lanny wondered, was this entirely true? Or was there something deep inside Hess that was afraid of what that couple might do to him from the spirit world? Or after he himself had entered that world!

XII

Lanny had time enough to walk to the Ministerial Residence, and he needed it to work off the grief and rage which possessed him. No forecast, no accumulated imagining, could equal the reality of knowing that Trudi was gone forever; that his efforts of the past six months had been futility, and his hope of seeing her again was vain. The scientific monster called Nazidom, the beast with the brains of an engineer, had got her in its clutches, and had treated her as it had treated so many thousands of other victims. Images of what they had done to her swept over him, but he struggled to put them aside—for that way lay madness. He must hate these Nazis, but it must be a cold and quiet hatred, rationalized and organized, scientific like their own.

He told himself that it was war; Trudi had been a prisoner of war, and they had treated her according to their code. They had waged war upon her in their dungeons, first in Paris and then in Dachau, trying to break her spirit, to force her to betray her party and her friends. In this they had failed, Lanny was sure; the fact that he was here, a free man in Berlin, and about to enter the home of the Nazi Number Two, was proof enough of that. With all their ingenuity, their knowledge of physiology and psychology applied to breaking the human will, they had not been able to break Trudi's. She had won that war—or so she would feel, and Lanny must train himself to feel the same.

It was a question about which men would always argue, according to their temperaments and their creeds. The Führer of the Nazis had declared that the greatest spirit could not function when the body in which that spirit was housed was beaten to death with rubber truncheons. Thus the new religion of the sword; and all the soldiers of that religion were taking their prophet's commandment and acting upon it. But Lanny had read Emerson in his youth, and had been assured that the heedless world had never lost one accent of the Holy Ghost. Which was the truth? Which was the word of God and which of Satan? Satan rebelling against God—that was not just a legend, a poet's imagining; that was something that went on every hour in the heart of every man alive. Here, in this Satan's world, with "truth forever on the scaffold, wrong forever on the throne," a man had to fight for his faith in God, and risk his happiness and even his life in the worship of the Holy Ghost.

This much was certain: the spirit of Trudi Schultz lived on in Lanny Budd, and the Nazis could never kill it there unless they killed him—or unless he let it die. It would live on in the hearts and minds of Trudi's comrades both inside and outside of Naziland. It would live in the hearts of other people, if ever the time came that Lanny was free to tell Trudi's story and spread her message. Such was the real and authentic magic of the spirit. Even the Nazis had discovered it, and had their roll of martyrs which they solemnly read, and their song about Horst Wessel, a rowdy whom they had made into a hero because he had been killed in street fighting with the Communists.

The Nazi religion was for one nation, one *Herrenvolk*, which aspired to rule all others. They called themselves a "race," but that was just a piece of nonsense which their fraudulent scientists had invented to make themselves more important; there was no such thing as "Aryan"; there was only German, and even that was open to question. The correct word was Prussian, or more precisely East-Elbian—a little group of proud and bigoted aristocrats whose power was based upon the ownership of huge estates, in a part of Europe where the armies of Napoleon had not penetrated to break up land monopoly. These proud Junkers, nearly all of them high-ranking military men, were using Adi Schicklgruber the gutter-rat as their newest tool, their rabble-rouser and mobdeceiver, and when they were through with him they would send him to join his tens of thousands of victims.

National Socialism versus true Socialism, racism versus humanity—that was the struggle between Satan and God in the modern world. Trudi Schultz had been what her predecessor Heinrich Heine had called "a good soldier of humanity." She had lived and died for her cause, and had passed on her sword to her husband, who must keep it sharp and clean, and use it with that skill and determination without which battles are not won. Lanny would keep the Trudi-ghost alive in his heart, and somehow, someday—perhaps with the help of Franklin D. Roosevelt—he would see that spirit of justice and brotherhood spreading over the world and conquering the forces of bigotry and despotism.

XIII

Right now it was Lanny's job to clench his hands, set his teeth, compose his mind, and go into a granite palace and entertain a big fat lump of vanity, greed, and arrogance dressed up in a pale blue broadcloth uniform with white stripes down the pants. He might have telephoned and said that he had been taken suddenly ill, but that would have been the act of a weakling. Göring was an important man to a presidential agent; from him Lanny got not merely money for the cause, but information and prestige enabling him to get more whenever he wanted it. The Trudi-ghost inside him said "Go!"—so he put his best man-of-the-world smile upon his face, and went up the steps of the splendid building from which the Reichstag-fire criminals had operated. He was welcomed by his old friend Furtwaengler, who, he learned, had just been made into an Oberst—lower rank would not be proper in the exalted regions to which Hermann Wilhelm Göring had recently been raised.

Lanny was escorted to the *Nummer Zwei's* private office, and went to him with hand extended, crying: *"Heil, Herr Feldmarschall!"* and then: *"Darf ich seine Eminenz noch Hermann nennen?"* In reply the great man put his arm over the visitor's shoulder and led him to the flat-topped desk where the jeweled mace of office reposed. He gave an American a chance to see how it felt, and Lanny wielded it with spirit, pointing it in front of him and commanding: *"Vorwärts, Kameraden! In die Zukunft!"*—into the future. He knew where the Nazi future lay, and looking at *Der Dicke* he added, with a grin: *"Nach Wien!"*

They always enjoyed each other's company, because Hermann had a sense of humor, and Lanny the easy-going informality which is supposed to be American. While he ate his broiled salmon and then his breast of chicken with wine sauce, he told his adventures in Austria and at the Berghof. It was easy enough to make fun of Schuschnigg and Stahremberg; and when Lanny came to narrate how the Führer had dressed the former down, and how everybody in the house had stood all day with his ear in a crack of the door, *Der Dicke* roared with laughter so that he came near to choking. Lanny even ventured to imitate the Führer's *forte fortissimo* tones—something which no German would have dared, but which was good clean fun from the land of unlimited possibilities.

Later on they talked seriously, of course. The new Feldmarschall wanted to know all about how England felt and how France felt regarding the Austrian situation. "England," of course, meant the group at Wickthorpe Castle, and "France" meant that at Baron Schneider's stag dinner. Lanny told about both in detail, hereby adding greatly to his social stature. So much so that before they parted *Der Dicke* said, paternally: "*Hör mal, Lanny!* It is absurd for a man like you to be wasting his time selling paintings. Why don't you let me pay you some real money and do some real work for me?"

"*Na, na, Hermann!*" replied the younger man, in filial spirit. "We have had such a pleasant visit, and you want to spoil it! Don't you know that you would feel differently about me if you hired me? Then you would start demanding things, and would think I was lazy and a *flâneur*. But when I come in once in a while like this and enjoy your company, you have a friend and not just one more agent. You learn a lot more from me, because I have been visiting other people in the same spirit—and telling them all about you."

"Nothing bad, I hope," said the fat man, with mock concern.

"What do I know that is bad?" grinned Lanny. "You enjoy my jokes, you have a beautiful wife who is going to present Germany with an heir—and you own the Hermann Göring Stahlwerke!"

BOOK SIX

A Full Hot Horse

23

Les Beaux Yeux de Ma Casette

I

IF LANNY had been a newspaper correspondent or a sight-seeing tourist, he would have headed for Vienna again, for it was obvious that the "big story" was going to break soon. Schuschnigg, casting about in desperation, had hit upon the idea of a plebiscite; the people of his country would be invited to say whether or not they wanted *Anschluss* with Hitler Germany. Nothing could have been calculated to bring matters more quickly to a head, for Adi knew that the people of Austria would vote three to one against him, therefore he took the proposal as a defiance. Schuschnigg must have expected this, for he allowed only four days between his announcement and the proposed vote. The newspapers of Berlin burst forth with stories of Communists in possession of Vienna, mobs attacking Germans on the streets, and Czechoslovakia sending artillery to support the Red uprising.

Lanny knew that this meant immediate action, but it wasn't his job to witness it. Experienced newspapermen would be flying there, and the story of whatever happened would be laid upon F.D.R.'s breakfast tray each morning. It was Lanny's job to find out what was coming next, and he thought he knew. He was seized by a desire to report once more to Washington, and try to persuade his Number One to take some step to stop the new World War before it had spread any further. It was still not too late; if America would show the way, and get England and France together, the smaller states would join, to say nothing of the Soviet Union. The dictators might be halted—and who could guess how many millions of lives might be saved?

Lanny had a picture to get from Furtwaengler, and while he was waiting for this the telephone rang and a man's voice said: "Herr Budd, have you received a cablegram from Herr Host in New York?" When Lanny replied that he had, the voice inquired: "Would you be so kind as to meet me this evening? I will be in the Hotel Eden lobby at eight." Lanny, experienced in conspiracy, replied: "I will be there."

He had not recognized the voice, but assumed that the stranger would know him. He dined alone, looked over the evening papers, and then went for a walk, making certain that no one was trailing him. At five minutes before the hour he strolled into the spacious lobby of the Eden and took a seat. Promptly on the stroke of eight there came a man whom he knew well, though he had not seen him for years—Aaron Schönhaus, elder brother of Rahel Robin, Freddi's widow. Lanny waited until he had passed on, then got up and followed him outside and around the corner. They walked for a block or so, until Lanny was satisfied that no one was following; then he walked faster and caught up.

"Well, Aaron," he said, "glad to see you. How are the old folks?"

"Not too well," was the reply. "Excuse me for meeting you this way. There are reasons which I will explain. I have a car, and it will be safer if we drive."

He stopped in front of a parked car and unlocked it, slipped into the driver's seat, and Lanny took the seat beside him. Lanny was destined to have a lot to do with that car, but he didn't know it and paid no special attention, merely noting that it was a medium-priced sedan of German make and apparently little used. There was a robe and he drew it over his knees while his in-law-once-removed—if there is such a relationship—started the car and drove at a moderate pace on a wide boulevard.

I I

Lanny had met the Schönhaus family soon after Freddi's marriage a decade ago, but he had seen little of them, for they had no special interest in their daughter's Socialist ideas and no aspiration to move in the exalted circles which Lanny frequented. The father of the family was a lawyer on a small scale, and being a Jew, had been forbidden to practice after the coming of the Nazis. He had lived on the bounty of his son, who had some sort of commission business about which Lanny was vague in his mind. Lanny knew that Aaron had a family, and recently had heard that his wife had died; that was all.

The man was several years younger than Lanny, but looked older, for the years had heaped burdens upon him. He was smallish, with a smooth-shaven face and sallow complexion, and wore a black overcoat of no fashionable cut and a hat which showed traces of wear; but that was no proof of his financial condition, for most Jews kept themselves obscure in these dangerous times. He knew English, but not too well, and spoke German to Lanny. He told the status of the family. Mama had developed a cancer, and would not have many years to live; she was not able to be moved to America, and Papa would not leave her, but devoted all his time and thought to taking care of her. They had both been frantically begging Aaron to take his children and emigrate to America; he had money put away, and at any time the Nazis might seize him and torture him to make him give it up. At last he had yielded, and Johannes had managed to get the passport visas. Aaron had paid the necessary bribes here in Berlin and had his exit permits.

He asked Lanny about his sister, who was married again, to a man employed in Johannes's office in New York. She had another baby besides Freddi's son, little Johannes. Lanny reported that they lived with the old folks and got along well; he always saw them when he visited Connecticut. Little Johannes, just eight years old, was the image of his father, and a most lovable child. The Schönhaus family knew what Lanny had done in his efforts to save Freddi from the Nazis—no doubt that was Aaron's reason for coming to him now.

It wasn't a great favor the man wanted; simply to get a little of his money out of Naziland. Said he: "I have always been an independent man; and maybe I think too much about money, but it goes against my nature to land in New York a pauper. I can borrow from Johannes, of course; but he's a dictatorial man—without realizing it, I think—and I prefer to be on my own. You understand, I have made my own way in the world, and earned what I have by hard work. I don't see why I should turn it over to my racial persecutors if I can help it."

"Certainly not," declared Lanny, venturing that far out of his ivory tower.

"Under the Nazi law I'm allowed to take out only fifty marks, and that wouldn't get me and three children very far toward New York. But here is this car, which represents a good chunk of money. I'm guessing that you didn't drive into Germany this time."

"How did you guess it?"

"I read of your arrival in the *Mittag*, so I judged you had arrived in the morning, and I hardly thought you'd have been driving overnight in a storm."

"A good guess. I'm not driving, and I have a couple of paintings to take out."

"That fits right in. This car costs about five thousand marks when it's new, and it ought to bring at least half that in Belgium or Holland. That would be enough to take me and my children to New York and keep us there until I get to work. Nominally the car doesn't belong to me; I have a gentile friend who is so kind as to keep it in his name. He would sell it to you—that is, you wouldn't have to pay any money, but take his receipt for twenty-five hundred marks and the car would be yours. You would drive it to any place you say outside Germany, and I'd meet you there and pick it up."

So there was Lanny being tempted again! Out of the kindness of his heart he would undertake to help some oppressed person—and forget for the nonce that he carried the destinies of his native land and perhaps of the world in his keeping! —Or would he? Doubts assailed him, and he said: "I don't know the law, Aaron. Is a foreigner permitted to buy a car in Germany and take it out?"

"Why not? It's simply export, and the Germans are working like the devil to promote foreign trade. They'd figure they'd be getting good American *Valuta*, with which to buy copper and oil and rubber and cotton and other materials of war."

"But isn't there some sort of permit needed? And mightn't there be a tax?"

"If there's a tax I'll give you the money to pay it with. It wouldn't do for me to be making inquiries, but I'll have my friend, the nominal owner of the car, do it. Or since you have influential friends, you might ask and assure yourself."

III

That was the way they left the matter. In the morning, as chance would have it, Lanny received a cablegram about another of those paintings which Göring had confiscated from Johannes Robin's palace and which didn't happen to conform to the great man's artistic taste. Lanny called up Furtwaengler to make the deal, and at the end of the conversation remarked: "By the way, Herr Oberst, I came in by train this time, and I have several paintings to take home. I have a chance to buy a German-made car at a reasonable price, and I wonder what the regulations are on that subject."

"I don't happen to know," replied the SS officer. "But you don't have to bother about regulations in any case. We'll be glad to fix it up for you."

"I wouldn't want to bother Seine Exzellenz about so small a matter."

"Of course not. I know his wishes without asking, and I'll have the office fix you up with a permit that will enable you to go through without delay."

"That's very kind of you indeed," replied the visitor, and thought, how very convenient is dictatorship—for the dictators and their friends! He felt himself being seduced by the perquisites of office.

He had got the license number and other data on the car, and gave these to the Hauptmann over the phone. The permit, properly signed and stamped, was delivered from the office of the Reichsminister-Feldmarschall that same afternoon, and in the evening Lanny met his Jewish near-relative by appointment and told him O.K. Lanny had been intending to leave at once, but might be delayed a couple of days awaiting a cabled remittance on the new picture deal. Aaron said that was so much the better; he would arrange for the car to have a thorough checking to make sure that it was in order for the journey. They made their arrangements for the sale and the meeting in Amsterdam, where Lanny had word of paintings that he wanted to inspect. Lanny would set out early in the morning, and Aaron would take the night express with his children; they would meet at the Hotel Amstel. Lanny would have offered to crowd them into the car, as he had once done with the Robin family, but they agreed that this would be too conspicuous. A carload of Jews and a permit from Marshal Göring wouldn't fit together very well.

I V

It seemed delightfully simple. Promptly at eight in the morning Lanny paid his bill and had his bags and his carefully wrapped art treasures carried down to the door. There was Aaron, looking like a humble deliveryman, with the car and the bill of sale duly signed. He tipped his hat respectfully and walked off, while Lanny saw his belongings properly loaded. What more natural than that this important American should have bought a car in which to transport himself on a not too raw and windy day in March? He tipped the bellboys and the magnifico of the door, and they all bowed and smiled, and away he went.

"For God's sake, drive carefully," Aaron had said, "for this will be all I have left in the world." Lanny had attached no special importance to this remark, answering lightly that he had motored all over Europe since his boyhood—how many hundreds of thousands of miles he wouldn't attempt to figure.

The *Autobahnen* of the Third Reich had been constructed by General Todt, and their purpose was to take the mechanized armies of Germany to whichever of her borders might be threatened by a foe. Robbie said these roads were a mistake, because in a long war Germany would find herself short of both gasoline and rubber, and be forced to fall back upon her railroads, neglected for a long time. But Adolf Hitler didn't intend to fight any long wars; he intended to overwhelm his foes one by one, and his mind was attracted by everything modern and repelled by everything old. So here were splendid four-lane highways, passing under or over all intersecting roads, straight most of the time, so that you could roll along at whatever speed you chose.

The new car was in perfect order, no rattles or squeaks and no missing of cylinders. The Germans were proud of their cars, and this one sped straight to the west at something like a hundred kilometers an hour. Lanny, used to driving, thought about other matters. Being a sociable person, he thought about the friends he was going to see on this trip; what he was going to tell Rick and Nina about Trudi, what he was going to tell his father about Hitler and Göring; then, the items of news about Austria in the papers which he had glanced at before leaving, and had brought with him for more careful reading. If F.D.R. had read his agent's reports, he would be thinking: "That fellow Lanny had it exactly right!" The fellow Lanny was entitled to what satisfaction he could get out of this reflection.

V

Without incident of any sort he arrived at the Dutch border. It was the second time he had driven up to that black-and-white-painted barrier with a permit from Göring's office in his hand. The first time had been by night and this time was by day, but otherwise there was no difference; the border officials fell into the same state of abjectness, and it was: "*Gewiss, mein Herr*," and "*Selbstverständlich, mein Herr*," and "*Bitte sehr, mein Herr.*" He didn't have to leave the car; he didn't even have to wait while the hood was lifted and the engine number checked. Anything that Göring's office ordered was right. "*Glückliche Reise, mein Herr!*" The barrier was lifted, the car moved on, and there were the Dutch border guards to inspect his passport with its visa.

It was afternoon, and Lanny was hungry; he saw what he judged was a clean and proper eating place on the outskirts of a town, and he stopped, parking his car by the curb and locking it. He took the Berlin papers with him and read them while disposing of an omelette and a salad. Schuschnigg had invited the people of Austria to vote on the question of their independence and had proposed to present them only a ballot marked Yes. If they wanted to vote No they would have to bring their own ballots. But this had caused such a clamor at the last minute that it had been decided to make the ballot secret and to provide spaces for both Yes and No. Lanny thought, how the job-printing concerns of Vienna must be working right now!

VI

His meal eaten and the check paid, he went out to the car. It was still there, but alas, not the same! Some careless driver, or perhaps one swerving to avoid a pedestrian, had struck Aaron Schönhaus's car at the front, on the driver's side, farthest from the curb. At first glance Lanny thought it must have been a terrific crash, for the bumper had been badly bent and the fender crumpled like paper. Whoever had done it had not waited for explanations or apologies; even in well-ordered and law-abiding Holland they had hit-and-run drivers! A few spectators, mostly children, stood looking at the damage.

Lanny's first thought was, had the wheel or the axle been bent? In so serious a crash it was to be expected. But then he saw something that he had never before observed on any automobile in his driving experience: where the fender had been crumpled and the enamel knocked off, there was a bright yellow gleam, such as belonged to no metal used in the manufacture of vehicles. And the bumpers, which are usually of steel with a handsome finish of nickel—where they had been hit the outside finish had been knocked off, and there was the same gleam, which could be only one thing in this world: *Gold!* Gold fenders and gold running boards painted over with black, and gold bumpers painted with some sort of silver—that was the car which Aaron Schönhaus had prepared for his near-relative to drive out of Naziland under permit from the Field Marshal in command of the German Air Force! "By heck!" said Lanny Budd to himself—again and then again.

The wheel was apparently uninjured, and Lanny realized that it hadn't been so serious a crash as he had thought. Gold is soft, and the driver of the other car must have been astonished by the results of a moderate bump. And now, here were people staring—and did they know gold when they saw it, and what were they making of the spectacle? Lanny unlocked the car and slid into the driver's seat; he started the engine, released the brake, and gently tried the car. It moved, and without ceremony he started and left the sightseers behind.

Rolling westward, thinking busy thoughts. So long as he drove, no one would pay attention to a battered car; but as soon as he stopped again, someone would note one of the most exciting of all spectacles.

And of course the same thing would happen in any garage where he might take the car for storage or repairs. Lanny was repeating on a small scale the experience of that humble laborer in the high sierras of California who had been working at repairs to a saw mill, and had noticed the same exciting gleam coming from the bed of a small stream.

Manifestly, the first problem was to cover up that secret. Coming to a town of larger size, Lanny hunted up a paint shop and bought a small can of black enamel and one of silver paint, also two small brushes. Already another crowd had gathered about the car; he left them behind, and outside the town stopped at an unfrequented spot and carefully covered all the exposed surfaces of the gold. He knew that the wind would help to dry the paint, and meantime it would gather dust and look less new and shiny; he would no longer have a treasure car, but just one which had been run into—a sight to be gazed at, but not with revolutionary thoughts, such as of wrenching off a piece and sticking it into your pocket!

VII

The traveler drove, chastened and slow, for he had plenty of time to reach Amsterdam, and must do nothing to risk another crash or to attract attention. Meantime, he did some mental arithmetic. The United States government paid thirty-five dollars an ounce for gold, which fixed the world price; nobody would sell it anywhere for much less. Thirty-five times sixteen is five hundred and sixty dollars a pound. Lanny guessed that the outside appendages of this car, when made of the ordinary material, would weigh at least a hundred pounds. He knew that gold weighs two or three times as much, so it was safe to guess that the clever Aaron had managed to smuggle out of Naziland well over a hundred and fifty thousand dollars!

How had he achieved the making of these parts? It couldn't have been an easy matter, for they are not hammered out by hand but stamped by great machines. It would have to be done where there was an electric furnace, and perhaps in the plant where the car had been made. A group of workmen might do it at night; it would be risky, and involve the payment of a lot of money—to say nothing of the problems of purchasing and turning over to workmen such an amount of gold. Somehow the job had been put through; and Lanny promised himself an interesting story on the morrow. He might have considered that Aaron had played a rather shabby trick upon his near-relative, but he decided to overlook that. He had "got away with it," and no doubt Aaron meant to offer him a fee—which he wouldn't take.

There was nothing to do now but put up at the Hotel Amstel. Lanny took the car to the garage himself. The garagemen were sympathetic about his accident, and asked if he wanted repairs made, but Lanny said No, he had to leave the next day, and would have the work done at home. The damaged parts looked all right, and anyone who noticed the fresh paint would assume that the American traveler had tried to make his car look a bit more respectable. Lanny shivered at the thought of leaving a fortune like that lying unguarded overnight, but it was what the owner had told him to do, and he had no choice. He diverted his thoughts with the afternoon papers and an American movie, and then went to bed and slept the sleep of an honest anti-Nazi.

VIII

Next morning there was *De Telegraaf*, delivered with Lanny's breakfast tray; also *Het Volk*, the Socialist paper, not usually called for by the guests of palace hotels. Both gave news from Vienna; the plebiscite had been called off, and Hitler was demanding Schuschnigg's resignation. Lanny didn't need to read any correspondent's explanations of the whys and wherefores. He could imagine Adi's ravings— perhaps directly to Schuschnigg over the telephone. He could imagine Papen besieging the Chancellery, and the swastika mobs parading, singing about how the world was going to belong to them, and shouting denunciations of that vile form of political sham known as democracy. They would be smashing windows and plundering Jewish shops as proof of their own political and racial superiority.

Lanny bathed and shaved and dressed, and was ready for his guests. The train from Berlin was due, and he could be sure that Aaron wouldn't delay very long to make certain that his treasure was safe. He would probably phone from the station. But no call came, and Lanny decided that the train might be late, or that Aaron was taking a taxi and coming to the hotel. He read a magazine; then he called the office, and learned that the train had arrived on time and other passengers had reached the hotel. Lanny felt a sinking inside him; he didn't need to ask anything more, for he had been through it all nearly five years ago, in Calais where he had waited for the yacht *Bessie Budd* to arrive with the Robin family and it hadn't arrived.

Neither did Aaron Schönhaus arrive, and Lanny never heard from him, directly or indirectly. The art expert spent a miserable day waiting in his room for a telephone call, watching train schedules and imagining calamities. Certainly if anything had delayed Aaron's starting, he would send a telegram, or call Lanny on the phone, or have his trusted gentile friend do that service. Silence like this, a complete blackout, could mean only one thing—that the Nazis had grabbed the unfortunate Jew as they had grabbed his father-in-law at the outset of their *Regierung*. There just wasn't any possibility that with all that treasure at stake, its owner would have failed somehow to get word to its trustee.

What could have happened? Had the Gestapo got word about the gold car? If so, why hadn't they stopped the car at the border? Had Lanny just got through by a few seconds or minutes? And if so, what would be the effect upon Lanny's future? They would surely take it for granted that he had been a fellow-conspirator and was sharing in the loot. And would *Der Dicke* be furious? Or would he roar with laughter, discovering that the son of Budd-Erling wasn't the noble idealist he pretended to be, but was as greedy for gold as *Der Dicke* himself?

Or could there be some other reason for Aaron's arrest, having nothing to do with the car? Had he been so foolish as to try to bring out some money on his person? Or had the Nazis grabbed him on general principles, because he was a Jew, and must have money hidden somewhere. Did they play a cat-and-mouse game with such poor devils, letting them bribe officials and then not get what they had paid for? No, for that would stop the sources of good income. There must have been some other reason, some slip that a too-clever schemer had made at the last moment.

In the case of Johannes and his family Lanny had gone into Germany and worked hard to help them; but he couldn't do that again. His situation had changed and he was no longer a free man. Moreover, he had been heavily in debt to Johannes, and Freddi had been his comrade, whereas Aaron was a comparative stranger—one of thousands of unfortunates whom Lanny was trying to help wholesale but couldn't help individually. He must arrange for the packing and shipping of his paintings, and then go on to his job.

He sent a cablegram to Johannes Robin: "Property here but owner not arrived circumstances compel proceeding England taking property for safety address care Rick." He signed this "Bessie Guest," and did not send it from the hotel but from a telegraph office. If by any chance a Gestapo agent was trying to find the car, there was no reason to make the task easier.

Lanny drove to Calais, where the Channel crossing was short, so that he wouldn't have to leave the car on a ferry-boat all night. He drove to The Reaches, where he told his story to Nina and Rick and discussed what should be done. Obviously, no one in his right mind would desire to drive a gold car, especially when it was damaged; there could be no safe place to store it, and the thing to do was have the gold parts taken off and melted. Rick agreed to attend to this, and if Lanny hadn't heard from Aaron or Johannes in the meantime, Lanny would take a bank draft to Connecticut and turn it over to Rahel Robin, her brother's heir if he was dead. Lanny was never going to put anything into writing about this matter, and would make sure that neither Rahel nor Johannes talked about his part in it.

IX

The English newspapers were full of the details of sensational events in Austria. Schuschnigg had resigned, and the Nazi Seyss-Inquart had assumed authority. "Tourists" who had been visiting Vienna had suddenly turned into *SS Standart Neun und Neunzig*, and occupied the public buildings of the city. All night Nazi mobs had been parading through the streets, screaming *"Sieg heil!"* and the battle-cry of *Anschluss,* which was *"Ein Volk, ein Reich, ein Führer!"* The new government invited German troops into Austria to preserve order—and that, of course, was the "legality" which was Adi's special fetish. At dawn the long motorized columns crossed the border at various places and sped toward the capital. Later that Saturday the Führer himself entered by way of the town of Braunau, where he had been born; the people strewed flowers in his path and hailed him as their deliverer. He visited the graves of his father and mother and told the assembled crowds that he was carrying out "a divine commission." To Rick and Nina Lanny said: "Mohammed!"

It was the end of Austria. The very name was abolished; it was to be the Ostmark, and Seyss-Inquart was to be *Statthalter.* On Monday, March 14, Hitler was driven into Vienna. A plot to shoot him had been discovered, so he showed himself only for a few minutes from the balcony of the Hotel Imperial, and did not make the expected speech. Next day he flew back to Berlin, where he had work to do.

Now was his chance to show the world what a "plebiscite" could be. He would hold one for the whole of Greater Germany, including the Ostmark, asking the people if they approved the *Anschluss;* he would carry on a whole month's campaign of parades, mass meetings, and speeches, in which he would tell the people that this was "a holy vote." And meanwhile the plundering and killing of Jews would go on all over the newly conquered land; women of refinement would be compelled to take off their underwear and get down on their knees and scrub the pavements and gutters with the garments. Thousands were fleeing to the borders, but only a few got across, and many committed suicide.

And not only Jews, but all of Adi's political opponents—for he had no forgiveness in his nature and the idea of chivalry never crossed his mind. Schuschnigg was a prisoner, undergoing torture and destined to be driven insane. A former Vice-Chancellor and Commander of the Heimwehr was murdered, along with his wife and son and even his dog. Other opponents were murdered and called suicides. The men who had killed Dollfuss became national heroes, and the Nazis of the Ostmark were put in command of concentration camps and charged with the duty of tormenting their former jailers. Things like that had been happening in this part of Europe as far back as history goes, but never had there been anything so scientifically organized. It wasn't long before Feldmarschall Göring issued an order to stop the private robbery of Jews, explaining that this was a prerogative of the government and must be carried out "systematically."

X

Interesting indeed to visit Wickthorpe Castle and hear what the ruling class of England had to say about all this! To hear the tall, lean, and long-faced Lord Halifax exclaim: "Horrible, horrible! I never thought they would do it!" Lanny would have liked to say: "Why did you go to Berlin four months ago and give them the green light?" Lanny learned that Ribbentrop had come to London in one of Germany's fast bomber planes, only three days before the march into Austria, and had been wined and dined while carrying on "exploratory negotiations" for a permanent understanding between Germany and Britain. He had talked with Ceddy Wickthorpe and Gerald Albany, and told them about his session with Halifax on the previous day, also with the Archbishop of Canterbury, whose endorsement of the Nazis as the future destroyers of Bolshevism was no secret from anybody at either Wickthorpe or Cliveden.

On Friday, with Hitler's troops poised on the border and ready to roll at dawn, the Nazi champagne salesman had seen the King, and had lunched at Number 10 Downing Street with Prime Minister

Chamberlain. Among the guests had been Lord Londonderry, who was Göring's chum and perhaps the most ardent pro-Nazi in England; Sir Samuel Hoare, the friend of Franco; Sir Alexander Cadogan, pronounced Cadúggan, Undersecretary of State; also Lord Halifax and Sir John Simon and the wives of all these. Several of these noble ladies and gentlemen had revealed to Lanny Budd their belief that the one-time *Gefreite* or sub-corporal named Adi Schicklgruber offered the best hope of safety for the British Empire, provided he could be persuaded to give up his demand for colonies overseas and turn his attention to the east. These ladies and gentlemen were shocked by the rape of Austria, because they had supposed they were at the stage of "exploratory negotiations," and hadn't realized that it was the time for action. For them it was unlikely ever to be the time for action. Why should it be, when they had an Empire on which the sun never set, and all the estates and securities they personally needed; when they all spoke with the right accent, and enjoyed freedom to play the delightful game of political power inside their snug little preserve?

These bitter observations were not Lanny's; they were those of a baronet's son who had the qualifications and might now have been a member of the Cabinet, had he been willing to be tamed and trained like other budding statesmen who had had socialistic inclinations in their youth. Lanny came back to The Reaches and reported what he had seen and heard in his ex-wife's castle; and after he had listened to his friend for a while he said: "When you want to criticize the English, get an Englishman!"

Rick answered, with a smile: "Don't try it otherwise!"

XI

Sir Alfred Pomeroy-Nielson had his man of all work, whose father and grandfather before him had been in the service of the family, take off those unusual car fixtures and cart them away to an electric furnace. Rick had made arrangements and went to see the job honestly done, and then to escort two or three hundred pounds of gold "pigs" to market. While this was going on, Lanny read and played the piano, took long walks and looked at the beautiful country of Hertfordshire which hadn't changed a particle since his first view of it, a quarter of a century ago. Also he thought a bit about his future, and in this had the advice of a wise gentlewoman who had known him since the days when the "Zepps" had been dropping bombs on London.

Nina's hair had been light brown in those days, and now was several shades darker; her complexion, too, had faded, but there was so much kindness in her face that she would always seem a lovely woman. She had managed to keep her interest in ideas, while carrying the burden of a household full of individualists. Sir Alfred had to be amiably checked in his impulse to let his collection of the contemporary British drama crowd out everything else in a rambling old house; in his private study there were so many manuscripts and documents which he intended to read and classify that often he could find no place to sit down. Rick also had a den, where nobody but himself could find anything; and there had been four children, now all at school, and eight servants to manage, and a score of fires to be kept going in the month of March. Yes, Nina had to be a firm and yet tactful character; she knew the facts of life, and looked into your eyes with a frank and steady gaze when she spoke of them.

She came into the library while he was reading. She had her sewing with her, and when that happens, a man knows that he isn't going to read any more. "Rick agrees that I ought to talk to you, Lanny," she said.

"There's no law against it, old dear," he replied. He had told them both the story of how he had got from Hess the definite news of Trudi's death. So now he knew what Nina wanted to talk about. He said: "There's no cure for grief but time."

"Friendship helps," she answered, and he said: "You bet! And when I get too lonesome I head my car in this direction."

"I think you ought to let me advise you, Lanny. You know you won't go on all the rest of your life without love; and neither Rick nor I want to see you make another bad guess like the Irma one."

"I'm not apt to, Nina. I'm older, and also, my circumstances have changed. I have a duty, and I'm doing it. But it makes me a hard matrimonial problem. No woman could get along with a husband who hops from England to New York, and then to Paris, Juan, Berlin, Munich, Vienna, and so on all over again."

"A woman would want to know what her husband was doing on those journeys, of course; but if she was sure it wasn't some other woman, she could stand it. Here on this island of sailors we have thousands of women who don't see their men except at long intervals."

"I know, Nina; but my problem is a special one. I'm playing a role, and getting deeper and deeper into it. I have to be a Nazi; and how is any decent woman going to tolerate that? I can't marry a woman who doesn't know or care anything about politics, because she would bore me to death. I can't marry a woman of the leisure class, because

I'd be lying to her, as I was to Irma, and sooner or later she would find it out and be furious. I can't marry a leftwinger; I can't even meet one without risking the work I've pledged myself to do."

"It isn't a simple problem, I admit, but you exaggerate the difficulty. You are known as an art expert, and that's a respectable role. You don't have to talk politics to a woman the first time you meet her."

"I have to before long. If she shows any serious interest in me, and I don't tell her, I'm giving her a rotten deal."

"Not if she's a leftist. You can keep your pose as a reactionary, tactfully and carefully, and let her try to convert you if she wants to."

"What she'd want to do is to tear my hair out," said Lanny.

"If she does that, you'd know that she was in love with you."

Lanny couldn't keep from laughing. "I suppose it's better to have our rows before we're married than after," he admitted. "You're outlining a unique sort of courtship."

"I'm just showing you that you could meet some woman with brains and character, and find out about her without committing yourself or betraying your secret. If the time ever comes that you're seriously interested, you can give her a hint that she is beginning to persuade you. If she's a woman you want to marry, you would certainly have to trust her with your secret—at least as much of it as you have trusted to Rick and me. If you say to her: 'I have given my word of honor that I will never tell my secret to anyone,' that would be all right. Every Socialist knows there's an underground against the Nazis, and every true Socialist would be eager and proud to help it."

"You would," said Lanny, gallantly; "but I haven't met many like you, Nina." Then he added: "If you or Rick, either or both, know any woman you think I ought to know, I'll be glad to meet her, and be as friendly and polite as I know how. But I can't promise that either of us will fall in love."

"Of course not, Lanny. But it's so much more sensible to talk about love and know what you're doing, instead of just leaving it to chance, and a pretty face or the shape of an ankle."

"One sees a lot of ankles nowadays," said Lanny, with a grin, "but mostly what they support is a poor line of conversation."

XII

Lanny Budd set sail on a Cunard liner, carrying in his pocket a bank draft for forty-two thousand, six hundred and seventeen pounds, seven shillings and fourpence, payable to Rahel Robin. He had deducted the costs of the operation, including a hundred pounds for his friend who had dutifully made sure that none of the gold disappeared at any stage. Lanny had a passage stormy but otherwise uneventful, and was met at the steamer by Johannes Robin and his daughter-in-law. While Rahel wept softly, he told them the sad story. The Jewish man of affairs, already acquainted with sorrow, had guessed the worst and had forewarned the woman. A sum of money for which she had no need would do nothing to compensate for the loss of her brother, and perhaps of her mother and father—for it was a part of the Nazi creed that the sins of any Jew should be visited upon all his relatives.

And the three little ones—what did the master race do with children when they sent the parents to concentration camps? Were they turned out to feed out of garbage cans? Or were they painlessly asphyxiated, or perhaps sterilized and turned into slaves in some proper Aryan household? Lanny couldn't answer those questions, and it was perhaps the worst of Nazi tortures that so many people could never know the fate of their loved ones.

Lanny had invented a very exacting client in Washington, D. C., and said that as soon as he had satisfied this client he would visit his several families in Connecticut. He telephoned Gus Gennerich, and after some delay got an appointment for the following evening. He took the night train, and in the morning made himself comfortable in a hotel and typed out a summary of his recent political experiences—partly to put on the record, and partly to clarify his own memory. Later he took a walk in Rock Creek Park, going over in his mind everything he was planning to put into the mind of the most important man in the world. Mostly it had to be facts, but a certain amount of comment would be proper, and Lanny meant that every sentence should be a high-explosive shell, loaded with accuracy and care.

XIII

In newsreels and newspaper photographs Lanny could see President Roosevelt dressed as the rest of the world saw him; but when he met him face to face, it was always going to be in a pongee pajama coat, blue and white striped, with a knitted blue sweater or a blue cape over it. Apparently he liked to retire early and read in bed—or to hear reports from secret agents. He greeted his caller with a hearty handclasp and a wide smile; his face was rosy and his manner gay—amazing the way the man enjoyed his job and throve under it! Right now, with the stock market at the bottom of another slump, and the men whom he had helped now pouring blame and abuse upon him for the only kind of help that would have done them the least good—right now he was grinning with delight to see a visitor who had been in an ogre's den and counted the piles of human bones in the corners. "Hello, Jack of the Beanstalk!" he exclaimed.

Soon he became serious, and declared: "I want you to know, Lanny, I've read what you sent me. My actions may not show it now, but they will in the end."

"That's what I have to hear, Governor," said the secret agent. "With that, I can keep going for a while longer."

"Tell me what's coming next, Lanny."

"Undoubtedly the Sudetenland."

"Was that taken from Germany?"

"No, it belonged to Austro-Hungary; but Hitler tells the world that it was Germany's, and that he is determined to have it back."

"What has it got?"

"Minerals and forests, and positions vital for military defense. His excuse is a lot of Germans there."

"A majority?"

"It varies from district to district, from village to village; it s all mixed up as if it had been shaken out of a pepper-pot. It's exactly the same as in Stubendorf, where I used to visit my friend Kurt Meissner when I was a boy. That's farther to the east, and was given to Poland. The Poles in the district are mostly peasants and laborers; the Germans are the property owners, the educated people, and so the ones who can make the propaganda."

"You are sure the Czechs will come first?"

"Hitler didn't say it in so many words. You have to listen while he raves and note whom he raves at longest. First came Schuschnigg, and then Beneš. That tells you."

"And will the Czechs fight?"

"I can't tell you that. You know Jan Masaryk—ask him."

"Of course he says they'll fight, but that may be because he wants them to."

"If you're asking for my guess——"

"I'm asking."

"I think the British will make them give way."

"God Almighty, what is Europe coming to?"

"It's coming to Hitler. You can't imagine the present British Cabinet until you listen to them talk. They aren't ready for war, they don't want it and they won't believe it even when it comes. They have made up their minds that Hitler has to be like themselves, because that would be so convenient for them. They are going to 'appease' him, by letting him undo the blunders they made at Versailles—or that the French forced upon them. They are disgusted with the French politicians, because they are greedy and corrupt. They are afraid of the Russians, mainly because of the effect on British labor of letting the Communist experiment succeed. They are sure that sooner or later Hitler is going to come into conflict with the Reds, and then they are going to lie back in armchairs and sip whiskies and soda and enjoy the show."

"How do they think Hitler is going to get by Poland?"

"They don't talk about that very much, because it wouldn't sound good. They expect to appease Poland with part of the Ukraine, which she claims. There's enough land there to satisfy everybody, and it would be saving the world from Bolshevism."

The smile had gone out of the great man's face, and he said in a grave voice: "Lanny, you can surely see why the American people are so determined to keep out of that mess."

"I can see why they want to," replied the secret agent, "but whether they can do what they want is a different question. What will they do when Hitler takes Brazil?"

"Is that on his schedule?"

"Everything is on his schedule until he is stopped. If we let him take Spain, why not Northwest Africa? And when he has the bulge of Africa he's within flying range of the bulge of Brazil."

"We should have to stop him before then."

"Yes, but could we? Remember, it would be air forces, not navies. I can't find anybody in this country except my father who has realized the effect of aviation upon our military situation. From Africa, Hitler would be two or three times as near to Brazil as we are; and he has his agents and his German populations being organized all over South America. Those countries would fall into his lap like so many ripe plums; and we should have the job of landing armies there in the face of land-based aviation. It looks to me, Governor, as if you are going to share the fate of Woodrow Wilson and have to turn your attention from social reform to military strategy."

The frown on the "Governor's" face showed that he didn't relish this prospect; and the visitor went on to add: "It puts me on the spot personally, because my father is making fighter planes and it happens that I own a few shares of stock in the company; so I am one of those 'merchants of death' that I used to be so cross with a few years ago. I would sell the shares, only it would hurt my father's feelings. I'm letting him have the idea that I agree with him these days."

"That's all right, Lanny," said the President, smiling again. "I'll promise never to suspect you."

XIV

A greatly overworked executive was concerned to know how much time he had before these new burdens fell upon his shoulders. Time was urgent, for he could get only limited amounts of military appropriations from Congress. "How long will Hitler wait before his next move?"

"I'll give him six months to digest Austria. He has to put his men into the key positions, and they have to learn their jobs. He has to take over the big industries and fit them into his economy. There's a mountain of iron ore, and Göring will have that; there are steel works, and he'll put them to making cannon. There are huge forests, and Göring was telling my father just recently of the miracles their chemists are doing with wood; all kinds of substitutes, plastics, fibers, and even food, not merely starches but proteins. And food is a weapon, of course; you can say that everything is a weapon, one hundred per cent of the German economy, and it's all working while we sleep."

This line of conversation was calculated to interfere with the sleep of the most powerful man in the world. Lanny was doing it with premeditation—it was why he had crossed a stormy ocean. He went ahead to explain that the "digestion" of Austria would not preclude the softening up of Czechoslovakia. "My guess is that as soon as Hitler has finished with his plebiscite the German press will start up about atrocities in the Sudeten. You understand how it is worked—they send their bullies into the country to provoke disturbances, and when the police put them down, that's an atrocity. By next autumn Hitler will be ready to move; and of course he'll do it legally if he can—but his Panzer divisions will be on the border, and he will be threatening to lay Prague in ashes in an hour. They have rehearsed it on a dozen cities and towns in Spain and they know exactly what they can do."

"Horrible, horrible!" exclaimed F.D.

"Exactly what Lord Halifax said the other day," replied Lanny. "The whole civilized world will say it, but that won't worry Adolf Hitler. He would love to destroy Prague, because it is full of monuments of Czech culture, which he despises. But he won't bomb Pilsen."

"On account of the beer?"

Lanny smiled. "On account of Skoda, which is probably the biggest munitions plant in Europe. Hitler is going to have that, and poor Baron Schneider has guessed it by now, and is sitting in Le Creusot worried sick."

Lanny told about his talks with the munitions king, and the stag dinner in his Paris mansion. He presented his Chief with a new list of code names. "I don't like to use important names in my reports, for one can't trust even the mails entirely, and if a single letter fell into the enemy's hands it would ruin me. But you can count upon the fact that when I tell you I know something, I have got it from some top man."

Lanny had prepared a report on his recent visit to England, and what Lothian and Halifax and Londonderry had said about the raid on Austria. He took his hearer to Vienna, but not for long, for Schuschnigg was now a "dead duck" in the American slang—meaning dead not physically but politically. Better to move on to Berchtesgaden and Berlin, where the live duck was quacking. F.D. had listened to Adi Schicklgruber's recent ravings over the radio, so he could appreciate Lanny's account of scenes in the Berghof while the Führer had been putting the Chancellor of Austria through the softening-up process. The President with a sense of fun guffawed over Lanny's imitation of Adi's bellowings. *Bummler—Geilheit—Gesindel—Schurkerei—Frechheit* —all those were funny words to an American, even though he didn't know what they meant.

Lanny added: "Please be careful and don't tell any of all this to your friends. Remember, the German embassy is very active, and they have a fortune to spend; they know all about you and your jokes, and they have a good idea of what you know about them. If the slightest whisper goes out that you know more than you ought to, they'll start trailing every American who has ever been near the Berghof or Karinhall—and believe me, there aren't very many."

"You are depriving me of some happy hours," replied the President, "but I get your point, and mum's the word."

XV

The President of the United States was never without a sea story or a "whodunit" by his bedside, and perhaps he stole looks into them when he should have been reading grave state papers. Now he listened to a mystery story from real life—the effort to find Trudi Schultz in a Nazi hideout in Seine-et-Oise. That part of a great man which had refused to grow up hung on every word of it, even though he was stealing time from his sleep. When the story came to its bitter climax, tears started down Lanny's cheeks and he did not try to hide them. The grown-up part of his auditor realized that this was a distillation of thousands of tragedies which were going on wherever the Nazi power had penetrated. The unhappy old continent was getting itself ready for another blood-bath, and nowhere within its confines was there sufficient moral or intellectual force to avert the calamity.

"Believe me, Lanny," said the President, "I sympathize with your feelings; but my position as I explained it to you remains unchanged. I have to think about the needs and the demands of a hundred and thirty millions of our own people, and I have only a limited amount of time and thought left for those outside."

"All right, Governor; I have to accept that. But I came to tell you— it means another World War, and we can't possibly keep out of it. What do you want me to do next?"

"I want you to go right on as you have. I cannot go to these different countries, and your travels are an extension of my eyesight. I renew my offer to put you on my secret payroll."

"No, I manage to make picture deals wherever I go."

"Living off the enemy's country," said F.D., again with a smile.

Lanny rose. "I ought not to keep you up any longer, Governor. I expect to be at my father's home for the next couple of weeks, and you could send me an anonymous note, if you wished."

"I doubt if there will be need of that. Just remember that I'm watching you, to see how your prophecies come true!"

"It doesn't need any prophet, Governor; it needs only an understanding of German economy, such as I have obtained from Göring and Thyssen and Schacht and others I meet through my father. I repeated to Hitler what I had said to you, that when a man builds a bicycle he has to ride and he can't sail a boat. Hitler accepted those words as exactly right. He has made the German economy into a war economy, and now he'll be doing the same for the Austrian economy. It's nonsense to say that he will stop when he has got the border territories where the Germans live; for what is he going to do with them? He can't feed the people on machine-gun cartridges and airplane bombs—not even I. G. Farben is equal to that miracle of *Ersatz*. Even if Hitler should die tonight, Göring or Hess would be driven by the force he has created; they have to go after the potato fields of Poland and the wheat fields of the Ukraine, the minerals of the Balkans, and the oil of the Caucasus."

"That's quite a program," said the President, no longer smiling. "Watch him, keep me informed, and trust me to make the best use of the information that I can."

24

God's Footstool

I

LANNY thought that he had earned a holiday, and it occurred to him that he would like to renew his limited acquaintance with his own country. He went up to Newcastle, where they would always find a spare room for him, put a car at his disposal, and let him make noises on the piano at reasonable hours.

The town had grown uncomfortably fast; the staid oldest inhabitants looked upon the changes with displeasure, and found the increase in bank deposits and retail sales a poor compensation for the crowds on the streets and the impossibility of finding parking space. They shut themselves up in their old frame or brick mansions and refused to have anything to do with the new world growing up around them: noise and confusion, bad taste, corrupt politics, unmanageable young people. It was the age of the "jitterbug"; a round-faced Jewish musician stood on a platform and wailed on the clarinet, and the young people swayed their shoulders and swung their hips, or sat in their seats with their eyes closed and their lower jaws dehiscent. They listened by radio all over the land, literally by the millions; Lanny listened also, trying to call it music and to find out what it meant to them. The most popular song of the moment was called "A Tisket, a Tasket." He knew what the first and third word meant, but failed to find the others in the dictionary.

Robbie Budd was partly to blame for conditions in Newcastle, having started a new industry in a town with old and narrow and winding streets; the older Budds—of whom there were many—considered that he should have asked their advice, and they still looked upon him as a headstrong and unsafe man, and were glad they hadn't put any of their money into crazy contraptions to fly in the air. Right now there was a slump, and these seventy- and eighty-year-olds—and two nineties —all said: "We told you so." The men among them still referred to Lanny as "Robbie's bastard," and looked upon him as a young rapscallion; but they were interested to hear him tell about the wickedness of Paris, London, and Berlin.

Robbie played poker with some cronies every Saturday night, and went out with his wife "once in a coon's age," as he phrased it, but otherwise he had no life outside his business. Modern competition called for that, and Robbie glorified it, and was proud of his ability to stand the pace. He had got capable young fellows, including his two younger sons, and drove them hard, and set them an example by knowing every detail of what they were doing. The Budd plant was country and God to them, and the fact that the B-E P12A was now the fastest and most maneuverable fighter on the market was the theme of a song which a girl stenographer had composed and which was sung at banquets, picnics, and other company occasions.

Never would Robbie give up the dream that Lanny would some day be caught by this enthusiasm. Whenever he came, the father would expose him to the contagion and watch for signs that it was taking. He had never been so hopeful as now, for the Pink tinge had faded entirely from his first-born's conversation, and he showed real appreciation of the place of military planes in a competitive world. Of course Robbie wanted to know all about his conversations with Göring and Schneider and other business people; as for Adi Schicklgruber, the idea of visiting that ogre's lair and selling him paintings and buying some for him in Vienna—that was really a tale, and Robbie told it over town, with the result that everybody wanted to hear it, and Lanny became a social lion for the second time—the first having been when he turned up with a twenty-three-million-dollar bride.

People wanted to give him dinner parties in their homes, or at the country club; they didn't ask him to stand up and make a speech, but they would get him talking and then the rest of the table would fall silent, except for questions. The ladies found him fascinating, and were ready to fall in love with him, and not only the single ones. This was a serious matter in these modern days, for it was no longer a question of coy glances and sighs; these were emancipated ladies, who went right after what they wanted. They would press him too closely while dancing, and try to be led off to one of those nooks which architects had thoughtfully provided; if he showed the slightest interest they would think up some pretext to take him somewhere in a car—each of

them had her own—and then anything might happen, and with discon-
certing suddenness.

II

Esther Budd, daughter of the Puritans, now several times a grandmother, knew all about her home town and had been obliged to adjust
her thinking to the changes going on. In Lanny's youth she had distrusted him as a product of the Coast of Pleasure, but now she had
decided that he had turned out much better than her fears, and she
accepted him as "family" in good standing. She knew how strong a
hold he had upon her husband's heart, and she desired to play her difficult role of stepmother with generosity and grace. Lanny had been a
grass-widower now for two years and more, a sufficient time for all
the proprieties and even some of the dangers. Esther decided that it
would be a stroke of statecraft if she could be the means of persuading
him to marry in Newcastle and settle down. Already he came two or
three times every year, and seemed free to prolong his stays at pleasure.

Esther Remsen Budd was a pillar of society in this city which remained a small town in its mind. Her father had been president of the
First National Bank and her brother had recently succeeded to the
post. She was tireless in church work and in every form of what was
called "good works." She had been brought up to believe that woman's
place was the home, but since women had been dragged into politics
and forced to vote they had better vote well than ill; so Esther had
joined a woman's club and inspired it to take a stand for clean
government—which, rather alarmingly, had threatened to bring her
into conflict with her husband's business interests.

They had worked out a compromise, and it had had the rather odd
outcome that this tall and gray-haired, dignified and reserved Puritan
lady became as it were the political boss of her town. When the time
for nominations came around and the local party heads brought Robbie
the proposed slate, he would take it to his wife, who would conscien-
tiously investigate the records of every candidate, and if any of them
were "too raw," would cross them off. Of course a secret like that
cannot be kept, and power like that cannot be held without a lot of
hard work and bother. Deputations would come for this or that, and
candidates to make known their qualifications. And then the barbecues
and political picnics! "You asked for it!" Robbie would say, with a
malicious grin. But the streets were kept clean, and no man who had
ever stolen public funds or neglected his wife and children could rise
to political favor in Newcastle, Connecticut.

III

Esther's way wouldn't be to have a heart-to-heart talk with Lanny, after the manner of Nina Pomeroy-Nielson. In her world these matters had to be arranged with carefully preserved casualness. Esther would try to imagine what sort of young woman would appeal to her difficult stepson, and would invite a specimen to lunch and watch for signs of a spark. If none flew, she would wait two or three days and try another, perhaps at dinner, to make it less obvious. She would make offhand remarks, letting Lanny know who was coming and pointing out her connections and qualifications. There is a saying that in Boston they ask you what you know, in Philadelphia who your ancestors were, and in New York how much money you have. Newcastle lay between Boston and New York, but Esther had the Boston idea and would never speak of money. However, you could be sure that she would never put on the carpet a candidate who didn't have a decent amount.

So Lanny had every opportunity to become acquainted with what beauty, spirit, and talent the land of his forefathers had to offer. Lovely girls and bright girls, some of them sharing his musical and artistic tastes, some of them astonishingly mature and well informed. One of the loveliest, oddly enough, was the daughter of that Adelaide Hitchcock whom Lanny in his callow youth had been the means of turning out of a role in the country-club performance of *A Midsummer Night's Dream*. He had called her a "stick," and had put in Phyllis Gracyn, who had become soon afterwards a stage queen of Broadway and was now acting maternal roles in Hollywood. That social blunder had been forgiven him; and now—my, how time does fly!—here was Adelaide's daughter in early bloom, with her mother's large brown eyes and some of the life her mother had sadly lacked. She was related to Esther and would have scads of money, and when Lanny talked about smart life on the Riviera, she listened entranced. She had been trained for the glory of spending money, principally upon clothes, and wearing them in ballrooms and at dinner tables, and her young heart was a-flutter at the thought of getting started.

What could Lanny have done with such a bride? Leave her here while he went scouting over Europe? Or take her to his mother's home and leave her there? Keep his opinions from her, or else worry and frighten her as he had done with Irma? Certainly he couldn't tell her his new occupation; and when the time came that he got into trouble—as sooner or later he was so likely to do—what sort of time would she have then?

The devil of it was, he couldn't tell either the girl or his kind step-mother, nor could he give them the excuses he had devised for use among the age-old corruptions of Europe. He must be gracious but reserved—which only made him seem the more mysterious and attractive. The eldest son of Budd-Erling became the subject of anxious conferences in many a boudoir in Newcastle and near-by towns. Was he wholly lacking in human feelings? Or did he have some duchess waiting for him in Paris? Or was he perchance looking for another twenty-three million?

IV

Then came to Lanny one of those experiences which befall eligible bachelors, even in the land of the Pilgrim's pride. He had dined with one of the elder Budds, his father's uncle; a duty call, to oblige Esther. It was an early meal, to accommodate an old gentleman and his younger but by no means young wife; frugal fare, a "New England boiled dinner," served on ancient silver plate, in a dining room with a full-rigged clipper ship under a large glass bell, and trophies brought from all the ports of the China seas. Lanny listened to old family stories, necessary to his education; and then, coming home early, looking forward to a quiet read, he passed the central square of what might be called Old Newcastle. In one corner stood the public library, a square brownstone building, long ago the town's pride and now its embarrassment. Esther was one of the trustees and he knew of her efforts to get an appropriation for a new and more commodious building.

Lights were burning within, and Lanny remembered that he wanted some item of information which the meager resources of his father's library did not supply. He parked his car and walked to the building; people were coming out, and just as he entered the central room a bell rang and he saw people getting up—it was obviously the closing bell. The clock on the wall showed nine, and he hesitated, and was about to turn and leave when one of the ladies in charge came toward him. She was of that indefinite age which characterizes librarians and school-teachers; she was slender, and when he thought it over afterwards he guessed that her salary did not permit her to be otherwise. She was obviously very much a gentlewoman. "Can I help you?" she asked, and her voice was in character.

"I am afraid I am late," he replied.

"A few minutes won't matter, Mr. Budd." His picture had been in the local paper, with an account of his delightful occupation and his travels. She would know the vitally important fact that he was a step-son of the great lady upon whom the fate of the new building depended. "I am Miss Hoyle, the librarian," she said. "By all means let me help you."

"I am wondering if you have anything on Italian Renaissance painters —the earlier part of that period."

"We have Vasari," she replied, "and other works with chapters. I will show you."

She led him into an alcove, between closely crowded stacks. She showed him a row of books, and stood by while he glanced over the titles. Meantime, somebody was turning off lights in the building but obligingly left this alcove alone. Lanny was interested in the books and glanced hurriedly into one or two; of course he couldn't fail to be aware of a woman standing close to him, a quiet, self-possessed woman who did not keep up a chatter while he was trying to read, but left him free to make up his mind. When he said: "I think this might serve my purpose," she took out another and said: "You might find something in this, also." Only when he was through with his search did she start to talk, and in a few sentences disclosed the fact that she knew a lot about the Italian Renaissance and its painters. He took the occasion to look at her, and saw that she had delicate features, rather pale, with no make-up; dark hair, and large, dark, admiring eyes.

He knew that when she said: "You wouldn't remember me, but I had the pleasure of being invited to your father's home to see the Goya which you brought from Spain. That was one of the great events of my life. What became of it?"

"It was bought by friends in Pittsburgh."

"Also, I listened to Hansi Robin play at the country club. You have done more for us provincial people than you can have any idea of."

"It is kind of you to tell me," said Lanny. So there were persons in this home town who lived obscure lives and were poor according to his standards, but who eagerly reached out for cultural opportunities! Lanny would be a romantic figure to them. The women would know that manners and morals in France were different, and they might find him a disturbing figure.

Everybody had left, and they were alone, or so it appeared. Miss Priscilla Hoyle made out a card for him, and while she did so he watched her delicate slender hand moving swiftly, and also the fine little dark hairs at the back of her neck. When she gave him the books he said, on an impulse: "Could I have the pleasure of driving you home?"

She was startled, and revealed that there was blood in the marble cheeks. "Oh! But—it is out of your way."

"How do you know my way?" he asked, with a smile. "I have kept you overtime."

"It is kind of you," she said; and then, more precisely: "With pleasure."

V

She turned off the lights and they went together down the steps of the old building. Was Lanny right in his impression that she looked about nervously, to see if anyone was observing this unprecedented behavior? He offered her his arm and she took it; was he right in his impression that her hand trembled? He didn't know her voice well, but he knew it was full of feeling as she explained that Newcastle was culturally a backward town; its body was growing much too fast for its brain, to say nothing of its soul, and those who cared for the higher things of life had a hard struggle here. Lanny understood what this meant; the town librarian was close to the seats of power for a brief period, and if she could cause the stepson of Esther Remsen Budd to take an interest in her library's cause, the scales might be tipped in favor of the appropriation.

Lanny could imagine without being told how she had served for years at this post, coming every weekday for long hours and patiently telling all sorts of persons, old and young, rich and poor, whatever they wanted to know about books. The library was her life, and now she was fighting for it. But was that all? What were her thoughts about this handsome man who must be middle-aged but looked young because he had taken good care of himself; who wore a little brown mustache and was dressed so elegantly, spoke several languages, and had met all the great ones of the earth? She sat alone with him, almost touching him; a prim daughter of the Puritans, strictly brought up, a church member and almost certainly a virgin, or she could never have obtained this post in the town of Esther Remsen Budd.

She had given her address and he was driving, not at break-neck speed. He said: "I know about the library's need, and I'll say a good word for it."

"Oh, thank you!" she answered—and was that more soulful than needed? Was there a voice crying somewhere in this worthy soul: "Youth is passing, and your last chances"?

She had a sweet personality, and he thought it could do no harm if he laid one hand gently on hers, by way of expressing his appreciation.

Immediately then he got his answer to all the questions; she gave the faintest of sighs, and inclined toward him and rested her head on his shoulder. Amazing!

So he asked: "Shall we drive a little?" and she whispered: "Yes." He turned off the road and toward the river. He knew this drive well; there were wooded points, and lanes in which lovers stopped. He knew that there was a moon rising on the other side of the river, toward the east, as is the immemorial custom of moons. It had been a warm day in April, and spring was softening this stern and rockbound coast.

It was a silent petting party. Perhaps both of them knew that the less they said the better. He held her frail hand and it responded to his pressure. When he came to a quiet spot he drew up a little way from the road and turned off the ignition and lights of his car. He put his arms about her and she put hers about him; he kissed her, and she didn't murmur any conventional protest, or feign any reluctance; evidently she had made up her mind that it was now or never; she kissed him in return—delicately, even modestly, but unmistakably.

This was most agreeable; but the question always arises, how far is it to go? Was he meaning to seduce the librarian of his father's, and more especially of his stepmother's town? Seduction it would certainly be called, no matter how willing the lady might be. Once before Lanny had come to almost this same spot and gone through the same procedure, with a girl called Gracyn Phillipson, later Phyllis Gracyn. Then he had been only eighteen, and it had been possible to forgive him; but now he was more than twice that, and it would no longer be possible.

In the course of a fashionable career Lanny had met numbers of men who took their pleasure where they found it, and talked freely about their adventures. Among them more than one had made known that they put only one restraint upon themselves: they would never consent to be the first man. He recalled their phrases: "The first time means so much to a woman; they expect such a lot,"—and so on. These phrases rang a warning bell in the soul of Lanny Budd. If he "went the limit" with Priscilla Hoyle, she would expect him to call at her home, meet her relatives and friends, and escort her on Sunday morning to the First Congregational Church, thus regularizing their courtship. Esther would be astonished, but would accept the strange mishap in the all-powerful name of "democracy."

But again the problem, what would he do with his bride? Set up an establishment in Newcastle, and visit her several times a year? Invent some pretext for never taking her along on his many journeys—not even one honeymoon tour? She might make him a good wife—but how could he know? How could he guess what might be her reaction to his abnormal ideas? He hardly knew her mind; he hadn't even had a chance to ask her what she thought of Newcastle's pet phobia—That Man in the White House!

Thus conscience did make a coward of Lanny Budd, and thus his native hue of resolution was sicklied o'er with the pale cast of thought; thus his enterprise of great pith and moment had its currents turned awry and lost the name of action. The frequency of his kisses diminished, and he began gently stroking the forehead of this estimable lady. Presently he whispered: "This has been very sweet of you."

What had been going on in her own mind? Doubtless the same operations of the conscience; for she said: "Mother will be worried about me." An old-established device for the protecting and preserving of virginity—to mention "Mother"!

Lanny drove her home, asking if he might have the pleasure of calling upon her when he came to town again—he was under the necessity of returning to Europe in a short time, he revealed. Fair warning to Priscilla of the Puritans; the fiend whose lantern lights the mead were better mate than I! He left her with one more kiss, stolen in the darkness in front of the modest cottage in which she and her mother resided. She would cherish this in memory for the rest of her spinsterhood, and would associate the son of Budd-Erling with every line of love poetry she·had read in the course of a life with books. Lanny, for his part, went away half glad and half sorry for his renunciation. Exactly the way he had felt about Janet Sloane, now Mrs. Sidney Armstrong, with whom he had had the same sort of perilous passage-at-arms so long, long ago!

VI

Hansi and Bess lived within comfortable motoring distance, and Lanny spent much time with them. He listened while they practiced for a new concert; then, while Hansi gave lessons to favored pupils, Lanny and his half-sister played four-hand piano arrangements. Bess was going to have another baby, and that was to be all, she declared. Americans had taken an old formula, "Two's company, three's a crowd," and applied it in a new field.

Lanny swore this couple to secrecy and told them the story of Trudi and his efforts to save her; it was a form of release to talk about her and have the sympathy of these dear friends. Lanny had got from his father's safe the sealed envelope containing his will and Trudi's photograph; he had destroyed the will and now carried the photograph with him. He showed it to Hansi and Bess; dwelling on the lovely delicate features, and telling about her ideas, her manners and way of life, untii the young couple had tears in their eyes. Lanny was having the photo enlarged and would leave the copies here; he would not dare to take one with him on his travels.

Of course all this had the effect of setting one more woman to figuring over the problem of finding a proper mate for the incomparable Lanny Budd. Bess saw this dream-woman as a follower of the Party line, who would keep her erratic half-brother in the strait and narrow path. He, of course, treated this line with irreverence, insisting that it had been erratic, while he had held steadily toward the goal of democratic Socialism. But Bess wouldn't give up hoping; there were many ladies of wealth and culture who were classed as "fellow-travelers," and whenever Bess met a new one she wondered how Lanny might hit it off with her. Just how he could go on pretending to fellow-travel with the Nazis while his wife fellow-traveled with the Reds was something Bess hadn't figured out precisely.

Also Lanny visited the home of the Robin family, and kissed his Jewish near-mother, and told once more the sad story of Aaron Schönhaus. Not a word had come from the missing man, and carefully veiled inquiries of friends in Naziland had brought no results. Lanny had to think up an excuse for his own inactivity, and he said: "I am afraid I broke the law, and it would do Robbie great harm if I involved myself any further." Poor Jews, who had to take what crumbs of kindness anybody gave them!

Lanny played with the sweetly serious little eight-year-old boy who looked so much like Freddi Robin, his father. Little Johannes still remembered Bienvenu, and his playmate, Baby Frances, and Lanny told about her way of life in a grand old English castle. It sounded like a fairy tale, and Lanny left it that way; the tale was not apt to come true, for Irma would hardly consent to have her twenty-three-million-dollar baby renew the intimacy with German-Jewish refugees tinged with the hated Pink color.

VII

New York was near, and its call was loud. There was art business to be done, and more to be planned—which meant the acceptance of a certain number of dinner invitations and the pouring out of great gobs of social charm. In the story of Hitler and Schuschnigg Lanny had a passport to the wealthiest circles, and, just as in Newcastle, a full draw-ing-room would hang on his words and ply him with questions. The seizure of Austria had startled the world into attention and forced it to recognize the arrival of a new social force. Men and women who hated the New Deal with such vehemence that they became incoherent when they talked about it, found themselves wondering whether they might not have to follow the National-Socialist lead. If so, they wanted to know how to set about it.

Lanny gave them the benefit of his observations. Adi Schicklgruber had got power because he had spread in the sky of middle- and lower-class Germans a glittering rainbow of hopes. To be sure, he hadn't carried out his promises, save only the plundering of Jews; everything else had been just springes to catch woodcocks. He had caught these birds in the twin snares of nationalism and militarism, and now he had them fast. Lanny didn't say: "Do you propose to do the same to the American people?" He just fell silent and let them talk about when and how it could be done, and where on the political horizon was a leader who had what it took.

Amusing if it hadn't been so terrifying. Their problem was made almost impossible of solution, because they loved their money and their power so that they couldn't contemplate letting any demagogue say anything against it—not even for purposes of camouflage! What they really wanted was another conservative regime, another President Harding, the whole cycle of Harding, Coolidge, Hoover. Lanny was tempted to add: "And another Wall Street smash?" But no, they had forgotten that, and their gratitude to That Man who had enabled the banks to reopen. They just wanted twelve more years of peace and plenty, in which time they could get such a grip upon the nation's affairs as to make it impossible for another demagogue to get started.

They would take the conversation out of Lanny's hands and begin talking about some promising Republican governor in some reactionary state; the visitor would listen, and think that he was back in the days of the Sun King, who had proclaimed: "*L'état, c'est moi.*" But occa-sionally there would be one or two of more intelligence, who realized that this Europeanized American really had something for them; they would draw him aside and ask, where could they get the Nazi Party program to study it? They would fall to canvassing the rabble-rousers of America, in search of one who really had the stuff, and who might be depended upon to stay bought.

A chance for the son of Budd-Erling to learn something about his own country! Huey Long, unfortunately, had been shot; a shrewd devil, he had said: "It will be easy to bring Fascism in America. Just call it Anti-Fascism." That was something to be made note of! There was Father Coughlin—but unfortunately a Catholic couldn't be elected. There were Gold Shirts and Silver Shirts, Gray Shirts and Crusader White Shirts, Ku Klux nighties and many other odd costumes. There was an oratorical fellow named Gerald Smith—somebody ought to make a thorough study of all these friends of the "pee-pul" and choose one who knew where the butter on his bread would come from.

VIII

Departing from one of these Park Avenue parties, Lanny walked to his hotel. A pleasant evening in spring, and he liked to walk, and watch the speeding traffic on this wide avenue, divided into two lanes by a parkway with a four-track electric railroad underneath. He thought about the men he had been talking to; the masters of America—and what were they going to make of their country? They had business dealings with the German cartels, and knew that the German big businessmen as a rule were getting along with the Nazis, working day and night on war goods, earning big profits, and plowing the money back into plant. The gentlemen of Wall Street and Park Avenue were doing the same, and meant to go on doing it; they had the money, and knew that money talks, money makes the mare go, money pays the piper and calls the tunes. Right now they were Nazi tunes, raucous to Lanny Budd's ear.

Crossing a side street, he heard the shout of a crowd, and looking toward Lexington Avenue saw the gleam of torchlights; he stood listening to volleys of sound, and then turned and strolled in that direction. Curiosity, not altogether idle, for it was worth while to know what was going on in this city whose population exceeded that of whole lands such as Sweden and Austria, now the Ostmark. New York was the center of the publishing industry, and impulses which originated here were spread quickly over the three million square miles of America. April was not the time for elections, and this must be some sort of propaganda meeting—Red or Pink, Black or Brown, White, Gray, Silver, Gold, Green, or Purple—there was hardly a shade of shirts or pants which did not have social significance in these frenzied times.

It must be a religious meeting, Lanny thought, because he observed a large white cross standing above the speaker's head in the light of the torches. The orator was standing on a truck, a large man with handsome features and heavy black hair which he tossed now and then. He was evidently at the climax of a great effort, shouting in tones which drowned out the traffic of a busy avenue; the side street, close to the corner, was packed solid with auditors, and every sentence was punctuated by volleys of applause. Lanny was surprised to find an evangelist arousing such fervor in this cynical metropolis; but then he saw a banner: "Christian Front," and realized that this was American Nazism, and the orator a candidate for the attention of the Wall Street and Park Avenue gentlemen.

This one clearly had the qualifications; personality, voice, energy, cunning—and, above all, hate! Hate for everybody and everything that the poor man, downtrodden and ignorant, believed to be his oppressors and his enemies: hatred for the money power, the idle rich, the educated and cultured; hatred for the government, the New Dealers, the bureaucrats, the politicians; hatred for the Reds, the Communists, the Socialists; hatred for the foreigners, the niggers, and above all, the Jews. Roosevelt was a Jew, and his government was a Jew 'government. The New Deal was the Jew Deal: Morgenthau and J. P. Morgan, Felix Frankfurter and Frances Perkins, Baruch and Ickes—the tirade scrambled Jews and non-Jews, and nobody in the crowd knew or cared; they yelled for the blood of each one in turn.

"Is this America?" demanded the orator, and the answer came like the hissing of snakes: "Yes! Yes!" Then: "Are we going to give it to the Jews?"—and the answer like a thunder clap: "No!" "Are we going to restore it to Americans?" "We are! We are!"

It happened that Lanny had been reading *The Island of Dr. Moreau*, a story by H. G. Wells about a scientist on a tropical island who performs surgery upon animals, gives them brains and power of speech, and then teaches them formulas to discipline them and make them behave. So now these half-human creatures stood in the semi-darkness and shouted automatic answers to oft-repeated questions:

"Do we love our little kike mayor?"

"No! No!"

"Do we like to have his cops crack our heads?"

"No! No!"

"Are we going to surrender our rights as American citizens?"

"No! No!"—and sometimes *"Nein! Nein!"*

IX

Lanny, on the outskirts of the throng, observed those about him, screaming, shaking their clenched fists. Next to him a man stopped to catch his breath, and Lanny nudged him and asked: "Who is that?" The reply was: "Joe McWilliams, the greatest man in America." Then, without stopping for a glance at the questioner: "Bully-boy Joe! Give it to 'em, Bully-boy! Down with the sheenies! Kill the kikes!"

It made the son of Budd-Erling feel sick deep inside him. He knew every tone, every gesture, every emotion, every idea. He had heard it first in a huge Munich beerhall more than fifteen years ago; since then he had heard it at a score of meetings in various parts of Germany, and over the radio, and in the Braune Haus and the Berghof. The thought that the land of his fathers had to go through this dreadful cycle filled him with an impulse to flee to some desert isle. But no, there was no longer any refuge in these days of airplanes; this horror had to be faced and dealt with where it was.

So, when a thin-faced fanatical fellow with front teeth missing offered Lanny a copy of the *Christian Mobilizer,* he paid a nickel and put it into his pocket for future study. Then came a red-faced German with a copy of the *Deutscher Weckruf und Beobachter;* then a frail, half-starved girl, selling Father Coughlin's *Social Justice.* Lanny bought everything; even to a button with a white cross on it, which he pinned onto his coat as a preliminary to asking questions.

The speech ended with an appeal to the audience to enroll in the "Christian Front" and give their support to the salvation of America. Many gathered around the truck for this purpose, and it occurred to Lanny Budd that it might some day be useful to a "P.A." to possess a membership card in this organization. He gave his name, together with his hotel address, which wasn't permanent. The card was made out by an elderly woman wearing a black alpaca coat, frayed at the cuffs; she did not fail to note the elegant appearance of this new applicant, and said: "God bless you, brother! Come and see us and give your support to our holy cause."

The paper sellers were busily hawking their wares. There was a table loaded with pamphlets and books, prominent among them the *Protocols of the Learned Elders of Zion.* A strange social phenomenon that! An impecunious lawyer in Tsarist Moscow had adapted this document from a French work of fiction; the original version had had nothing to do with Jews, but the revised version was taken as gospel and had become a hate-weapon of Nazis all over the world. Henry Ford had distributed hundreds of thousands of copies, and wherever his cars traveled people learned on the authority of the world's richest man that the Jews had a secret international organization plotting to destroy Christian society. Later on the Flivver King had taken it back, but few people knew that, or cared. From other literature for sale at these tables you could learn that the Jews had a rite which required the blood of freshly killed gentile babies.

X

Along with other members of the dispersing audience Lanny strolled toward the west, and found himself alongside the hatchet-faced fellow who had sold him the *Christian Mobilizer.* "Hot talk, that!" remarked the visitor, and the reply was: "You said it, brother!"

This sadly depressed specimen of megalopolitan life gazed suspiciously at a spring overcoat of the latest cut and Homburg hat to match; however, he noted the little button with the white cross, and asked: "You one of us?"

"I carry a card," replied Lanny, and showed it in his hand; he didn't mention that he had carried it for only five minutes. "You find a good sale for the paper?"

"We've just started, but it's going big."

"Not with the Jews, I imagine."

Lanny said it playfully, but there was no play in this child of the gutters. "Sometimes we sell to the kikes. They take a good look at us an' guess they'd better."

Among the people walking on this cross street were several other vendors of literature, and others of a sort with whom Lanny would not have cared to be alone on any street. "Where do you go from here?" he inquired.

"We allus go to Times Square after meetings. We get the the-ay-ter crowd, and sometimes we teach the sheenies a lesson. Come along, if you want to see the fun."

Lanny wanted to see everything, and wanted to learn all he could about a "Christian Fronter." An Irish-Catholic boy, raised in the slum known as "Hell's Kitchen" and educated in a parochial school, Mike Raftery had been told by his priest that the bloodthirsty "Rooshians" were trying to destroy Holy Mother Church, and that they were all Jews, or at any rate Jewish-inspired. He had not the least difficulty in believing that Jewish Bolsheviks and bankers were in a common conspiracy to dominate the world; he had but the vaguest idea of what bankers did or what Bolsheviks believed; he had learned from Father Coughlin's papers that the bankers gave money to the Bolsheviks for the undermining of the Catholic religion and the American Constitution. Now he had shifted to the paper of "Bully-boy Joe," which was new and even more violent. "Speeches ain't enough," said Mike. "We gotta have action; we gotta make them kikes pipe down."

What constituted "action" Lanny saw quickly enough. Reaching Times Square, the sellers spread out on the various corners made by Broadway and Forty-third Street. They began screaming: "Buy the *Christian Mobilizer!* Save America! Down with the Jews!" Meantime the group of toughs, the "goon squad," moved from one seller to another; not conspicuously, but one here and one there; Lanny knew them, because he had walked a mile or so with them. When a Jew came along—preferably a poor one—a seller would approach him. "Buy a *Christian Mobilizer*—read all about the dirty sheenies!" If he didn't stop, the seller would try to step on his toes; if he did stop, the seller would poke the paper under his nose. "Save America from the kikes!"

The Jew thus assailed would do well to get out of the way quickly, and to keep his mouth closed. If he said anything angry, or tried to shove his tormenter out of the way, the man or woman would yell and the goon squad would leap in. They carried what appeared to be newspapers, but really were pieces of lead pipe with newspapers wrapped around them. They would bring these down on the victim's head, splitting it open, or cracking his arm if he tried to defend his head; they would leave him bleeding and perhaps unconscious on the pavement, and disappear into the crowd in a flash.

This went on night after night, Lanny was told; and it surprised him, for he had read little or nothing about it in the papers. The New York "cops" were in good part Catholic, and there was no law against their reading Father Coughlin's paper; they came from the same slums as the paper sellers, and in their boyhood had spit upon many a "Christ-killer." The mayor of New York was part Jewish, and was in an awkward position because he was a liberal and had been preaching freedom of speech all his life. The newspapers of New York lived upon department-store advertising, and reports of violence and especially of racial and religious violence were bad for trade; a large part of the buyers who came to the city were Jewish, and what if their wives became frightened and persuaded them to go elsewhere? As for Lanny Budd, playing the good Samaritan in the theater district would surely have been bad for *his* business.

XI

The presidential agent looked up the name of Forrest Quadratt in the phone book and called him. "I have just had the pleasure of spending ten days at the Berghof," he said. "I was there during Schuschnigg's visit."

"Oh, splendid!" exclaimed the poet turned propagandist; he didn't get a call like that very often. "Won't you come up to dinner? I have a friend, a high-ranking personality from overseas who happens to be in town, and I'll invite him. I know you'd like to meet him."

Meeting high-ranking personalities was Lanny's business, so the date was made. He took a taxi to the upper West Side, where the partisan of Nazism had an apartment on Riverside Drive, filled with the trophies of culture. The host had written a shelf of books, including a defense of the Kaiser, whose left-handed relative he was supposed to be. He was a smallish, near-sighted man, suave and gracious, caressing in manner. He had a sweet little wife about whom Lanny wondered, what did she make of the Nazi doctrines concerning her sex? Lanny had the suspicion that both husband and wife had Jewish blood, but this of course would never be put into words.

The other guest was a tall Prussian aristocrat with a round blond head, wearing a monocle and introduced as Kapitän von Schnelling. He had commanded a U-boat during the World War and been one of those who sank their vessels at Scapa Flow. He had most formal manners, and knew Stubendorf, Herzenberg, the Donnersteins, all Lanny's high-up friends in the Fatherland. What he was doing in America was made apparent during the course of the evening, and Lanny realized that he was dealing with a really important man and a shrewd one.

They wanted to hear about his adventures in the Berghof and he told them in detail. He didn't say anything about a spiritualist medium, or about having sold some paintings, which might have turned it into a business affair; he left it to be assumed that his long stay had been owing to the Führer's delight in his company. He talked about walks in the forest and the retreat under construction on the Kehlstein; about a great man's household, his eating habits, his visitors—there could' be no doubt that the teller had actually witnessed these things.

Also he told about Vienna, the interview with Schuschnigg, and the misadventure of the lawyer-doctor in Berchtesgaden. Manifestly, no one would have been permitted to stay in the Führer's home at such a critical time unless he had possessed his host's confidence; nor was this confidence misplaced. The son of Budd-Erling was no *Emporkömmling*, a social climber, but understood the Führer's ideas and his high destiny. He spoke with respect and even awe of a crusader who had set out to chain the wild beast of Bolshevism and put an end to the age-long quarrelings among Europe's petty states.

So the Kapitän could see no reason for secrecy, and talked frankly about his responsibilities in America. He was a sort of inspector-general, making a survey of Nazi educational work all over the country, and at the same time lending his prestige and cultivated intelligence to the task of influencing highly placed Americans. He had completed a tour of nearly two months, in the course of which he had visited a score of cities, all the way from Seattle to Palm Beach, as he put it. He was greatly pleased by what he had found; in most cases the propaganda was in excellent hands and the results most encouraging; America was ripe for a fundamental social change, and with hard work and wise guidance there was every reason to expect that the strong German elements throughout the country would play their full part. The main trouble, as this polished Junker saw it, was the reluctance of the Nazi partisans to Americanize themselves; they wanted to follow the Nazi ways, and to force these ways down American throats, which couldn't be done. The Bund had been ordered to change its make-up, and to print the swastika in red, white, and blue. All this was hard, especially in the hinterlands.

Lanny agreed, but said that he had noted a great many native groups springing up, having the Nazi program, but not acknowledging it as Nazi, and in many cases not even knowing it. They called themselves "Christian" or "Protestant," "Yankee Freemen" or "American Patriots" —it didn't really make any difference, so long as they saw the Red peril and the Jew menace, and fought the New Deal. The Kapitän agreed, and Quadratt put in: "Citizens' Protective Associations and National Workers' Leagues are a dime a dozen in New York right now."

XII

This highly trained aristocrat spoke English without a trace of accent, and had no difficulty in "Americanizing" himself. He was here for America's benefit, he declared, to give the country a chance to profit by the lessons which had been learned in Germany. He had found Americans an extremely receptive people, especially those who were highly placed, and had more to lose from reckless experimentation. He talked interestingly about his meetings with such men. He had spent the better part of a day with Henry Ford, an unusual privilege, and found him in a generous mood. He had spent an evening with Colonel McCormick and found him, as he said, "most congenial." The same for Lammot du Pont in Wilmington; "a really powerful man, with whom we have done a great deal of business, as you know." The same for Mr. Rand, of Remington-Rand, in Connecticut, who had recently had a painful experience with a great strike, and was bitter as a result.

"My father knows him well," said Lanny; and the Kapitän was quick to take that lead. "I have heard a great deal about your father, and would esteem it a privilege to meet him." Lanny couldn't do anything but offer an introduction. Poor Robbie would have to take his chances with this suave and subtle Junker!

The greatest progress had been made in Washington, if you could believe the agent's story. He mentioned hostesses such as Mrs. McLean and Mrs. Patterson who had entertained him, and the senators and congressmen who had heard him gladly and assured him of their sympathy. He was amusing on the subject of Senator Reynolds of North Carolina, who had begun life as a barker in a sideshow, and had got elected by accusing his rival of the crime of eating caviar. "Do you know what caviar is? Fish eggs! Do you want the Tarheel State to be represented in Washington by a man who eats fish eggs?" Now the Senator was congenial to the Nazis, though of course not carrying the label. He was planning a paper to be called the *American Vindicator*, and had shown the Kapitän his idea of the layout. "Pretty poor stuff, I thought it; but I judge the standard of education in the Senator's part of the country is not very high."

Lanny wished that these misguided statesmen might have heard what a Nazi agent really thought of them in private. "Senator Wheeler appears to hate the Administration even more than he loves the Anaconda Copper Company." And then: "Senator Nye, I gather, has been a pacifist for a long time. Now the Führer has got him bewitched, and he is a pacifist for everybody but us." Then a congressman with the odd name of Ham Fish. "I am told that he comes from an old and wealthy family, and was a great football player when he was young. He should have stuck to that."

Forrest Quadratt took up the conversation. He knew Fish very well, and reported him as amiable, but bumptious, and stupid beyond belief. There was a convenient American arrangement known as the "franking privilege," by which congressmen could send out mail free of charge; there was no limit upon it, and some had even shipped their furniture and liquors by that method. Ham Fish had turned over the matter to his secretary, and the secretary had given Quadratt the use of it, a device whereby unlimited Nazi speeches, pamphlets, and books could be distributed to the American people at their own expense. The ex-poet urged his Junker friend to realize the importance of this, and

told about a publishing house which he had set up in a small town of
New Jersey. It was carefully camouflaged to look American, and
Quadratt showed his guests several books which he had written under
pseudonyms and published through this concern.

On another shelf of the same bookcase was a row of the decadent
poets of France, Germany, Austria, Italy, England, and America.
Lanny's eyes ran over them: Baudelaire, Verlaine, Dowson, Symons,
D'Annunzio—and Quadratt's own youthful volume, *Eros Unbound*.
The ex-poet saw Lanny's glance, and remarked, nostalgically: "There
used to be a day when I could recite whole pages from those books;
now, alas, I have had to become a reformer, and my mind is a card catalogue of names and personalities all over my native land." He meant
America, and repeated the wheeze which was his stock-in-trade, that
he was trying to interpret the land of his birth to the land of his forefathers, and vice versa.

XIII

The "inspector-general" of the Nazis had been invited to meet some
of what he called the "key personalities of the American movement."
This was to be on the following evening, and Quadratt offered to get
an invitation for Lanny, who accepted with pleasure. The Kapitän
never made public speeches, he said, but was glad to talk confidentially
with the leaders, and especially those who were in position to put up
the funds, so essential to the building of any new movement. The gathering was to be in the home of a Miss van Zandt, on lower Fifth Avenue, now mostly pre-empted by the dress-making and book-publish-
ing industries. Quadratt explained that this elderly lady was "slightly
cracked, but harmless, and lousy with money." He added that in America it was the women who had the money, and you had to put up with
a certain amount of boredom and inconvenience in order to get it.
Lanny remarked that it was not so different in Germany; he mentioned the Bechsteinhaus at the Berghof, named in honor of the widow
of the piano manufacturer, who had financed the Führer all through
his early struggles. It was a worthy precedent.

At eight on the following evening Lanny descended from a taxicab
in front of an ancient brownstone mansion, and the door was opened
before him by an aged servitor in black. There he met and listened to
the oddest assortment of upper-class intellectuals it had ever been his
fate to encounter. His hostess, tall, thin, white-haired, and wearing
pince-nez, greeted him in the entrance to her drawing-room, clad in a

full-length and long-sleeved black silk dress in which her great-grand-mother might have attended funerals in Grace Church. This lady's ancestry went back to New York's early Dutch beginnings, and she had inherited a small family farm, now covered with skyscrapers paying enormous incomes. When she went for a walk she carried a black silk umbrella faded green, and when she invited guests she gave them rather cheap refreshments, but would not hesitate to write a check for five thousand dollars when a plausible ex-poet persuaded her that he had a new book which would help to oust the Reds from their entrenchments in near-by Union Square.

To this soirée the "slightly cracked" lady had invited persons of wealth whom it might be worth while for a Nazi Junker to meet: among them a White Russian count—White in the political, not the geographical sense—with the difficult name of Anastase Andreivitch Vonsiatskoy-Vonsiatsky. (Lanny never did find out the wherefore of the repetition with variation.) He was a giant of a man with huge hands and thick lips from which came a deep rumbling voice. He had married a wealthy widow more than two decades older than himself, and now he had Nazi Stormtroopers drilling on her immense estate in Connecticut. There also he edited and published a Russian-language magazine called *The Fascist,* and sent arms to the Mexican Gold Shirts —all this quite openly, boasting of it in loud bellows.

And then a round-faced, soft-voiced American with graying hair and the aspect of a scholar, who had inherited a fortune from the paper-manufacturing business and purchased a literary magazine and turned it into an organ of American Fascism. Seward Collins politely explained to Lanny Budd that he had been converted by Hilaire Belloc to "distributionism"; he wanted to go back to the Middle Ages and have everybody cultivate small plots of land. He hated capitalism, and tolerated the Nazis because he thought they were destroying that evil system. He considered anti-Semitism an error, but even so had set up a bookshop for the sale of all sorts of Fascist literature.

Leading brain-truster among this company was a Georgian—the American, not the Russian variety—dark and curly-haired, a Harvard graduate and employee of the State Department in the happy days before the New Deal. Lawrence Dennis had written three books advocating and predicting Fascism for his country, and he now published from a downtown office a bulletin called the *Weekly Foreign Letter.* He was prepared to defend anywhere the thesis that "democracy" was an evil dream, for the masses never had been capable of self-government and never would be. He was ardent in defense of Franco, and in this was supported by two other guests, an elegant old gentleman, Mr. Castle, who had been Undersecretary of State under Hoover, and a shrewd and forceful Mr. Hart, who, Lanny was told, was paid ten thousand dollars a year by certain big corporations to oppose whatever forms of social legislation might come up.

The Army was represented in this gathering by Major-General Moseley, who was treated by everybody with great deference, being looked upon as the future "Nationalist" party's candidate for President; he contributed to the discussion the idea that refugees coming from Europe should be sterilized. The Navy was represented by Lieutenant-Commander Spafford, who, in accordance with Navy traditions, had little to say. The Press was represented by the city's smallest newspaper with the largest circulation.

One of the women guests at this high-class social event delivered Lanny to his hotel, and on the way remarked that if the wealth represented there were totaled up it would amount to a couple of billion dollars. Lanny went to sleep in a state of deep depression, and next morning, to cheer himself up and to pacify the Trudi-ghost he put a thousand-dollar bill in an envelope, together with a typed unsigned note: "To be used for the combatting of anti-Semitism in New York." He mailed this to a liberal clergyman of the city, the same to whom, more than a year ago, he had turned over the profits from the sale of the Goya painting. Before sailing for Europe, the secret agent wrote a report to his Chief, concluding with these words: "America has everything that Germany had during the period that Hitlerism was in the egg."

25

Slings and Arrows

I

LANNY took a steamer to Le Havre, and a very slow train to Calais, where he had stored his car. He drove to Paris, where he met Zoltan, just returned from London with news about the sales at Christie's and other art matters. They went to the spring Salon together, looking for new talent and finding mostly commonplace, for they were two exceedingly fastidious gentlemen. When they got too discouraged about their world they would go to the Louvre or the Petit Palais and commune with the old masters, who had really known how to paint, or so the experts thought. They would have lunch together in an outdoor café at the Rond Point; the spring sunshine was delightful, the crowds gay, and now and then the pollen of chestnut blossoms would be wafted down onto their table, supplying their food with extra quantities of vitamin A. They talked about deals they had made and others in prospect, and life seemed good—so long as you thought only about your personal affairs.

The political situation was truly depressing to any Pink. Franco's armies had cut their way to the Mediterranean, thus dividing the Loyalist forces in two. Everybody agreed that the government's position was hopeless; that is, everybody except the Spanish people, who refused to realize that they had to become slaves. In spite of continual bombing of cities and killing of thousands of civilians, the Valencianos and Madrileños went on fighting desperately in their sector, and the Barcelonese in theirs—something considered irrational and exasperating by all members of the governing classes of Europe. The British and the Italians, having come to an amicable agreement on this and other subjects, put pressure on the French and forced the closing of the border once more. Red Catalonia would be starved until it came to its senses— or rather to British and Italian senses.

A part of the agreement had been over Abyssinia: Mussolini's triumph was to be legalized, and the 101st League of Nations Council proceeded to pass what was in effect an act of suicide, the renunciation of its last hope to prevent war. In harmony with the hypocrisy of the time, it would do this in the name of peace, and the ultra-pious Lord Halifax was chosen as the man for this job. "Great as is the League of Nations," he announced, "the ends it exists to serve are greater than itself and the greatest of those ends is peace." His white Lordship was answered by a frail little black man who looked oddly like a Jew, Haile Selassie, Negus of Abyssinia: "The Ethiopian people, to whom all assistance was refused, are climbing alone their path to Calvary."

Affairs in France stood on the same plane of fraudulence. The Chautemps government had been forced out, because the Socialists had refused to vote it the "special powers" it demanded. On the day that Hitler had invaded Austria, *la grande nation* had been without a government. Then Blum had formed one which had lasted less than a month. Now France had what was called an "anti-Red" Cabinet under Daladier, and for Foreign Minister had a politician named Bonnet, lean and sallow, with a bald head and one of those long beaked noses used for smelling money. Lanny wondered, was any of it Nazi money? The Minister's wife was one of Kurt Meissner's intimates, and Lili Moldau was her constant companion.

The party of these men called itself "Radical Socialist," but had long ago become a party of bribe collectors and distributors. "Envelopes" was the polite word; they were handed to journalists, to publishers, to political manipulators, to ladies who had any sort of influence. They would contain a proper number of bills—never a check that could serve as evidence. Bonnet had a great banking firm behind him, and when public funds were not sufficient for his purposes, the bank would make up the quota.

That was how France was governed now, and when you heard the inside story you despaired of the republic. There were patriotic and honest people left, but they were out of power, and their protests had become stereotyped; the great public, which craved novelties, was bored by them. Blum was a Jew, which damned him, and his party quarreled with the Communists, who repeated Russian formulas and urged Russian techniques—in face of the evident fact that its class enemies had the arms, the planes and bombs and poison gas, and in any attempt at uprising it would be the Fascists and not the Communists who won. The mass of the people read the great press, having no idea that the contents of these papers were for sale to the highest bidders, in many cases the agents of the Fascist and Nazi governments.

II

Lanny had obtained orders from clients in New York and there-abouts, and was planning to set out on another trip into Germany; but something occurred which changed his program in a few minutes. He was strolling, as was his custom, from one fashionable picture dealer's to the next, looking at what they had to offer; this was important, for prices varied from time to time and from place to place, and Lanny's success depended in part upon this knowledge. It wasn't enough to say: "This is a genuine Monet, a worthy example of his art." It would be necessary to add: "I saw one of his works offered in Paris last month for four hundred thousand francs." Right now the franc was down to thirty-four to the dollar, and that made Paris an excellent place to go shopping for art.

The dealers all knew the son of Budd-Erling, and hastened to point out their best. One of them remarked: "I have something that might interest you, M. Budd: a very good seascape by Detaze."

"Indeed?" said Lanny, surprised—for these paintings did not often come upon the market. "I should like to see it."

He was still more surprised when he looked at the painting. He knew all of them by heart, as it were; every brush stroke, of which he had watched so many thousands being put on. He was quite sure that he had had this particular seascape in his hands during his last visit to Bienvenu.

"M. Bruget," he said, "I am embarrassed to have to ask you to set this painting aside and not sell it until I have investigated the matter. I am practically certain that it was in my mother's storeroom less than two months ago; and she never sells a painting without consulting me."

"*Mon dieu, M. Budd!* You mean that it has been stolen?"

"I don't want to say until I have made inquiry. Would you mind telling me where you got the painting?"

"Certainly not. I bought it from the dealer Agricoli in Nice. I thought that was a natural place for a Detaze to be found."

"Did he have more than one?"

"He said he had had three, but had only this one left."

"Would you be willing for me to see the back of it?"

The man hastened to unscrew the back of the frame; and on the canvas, in addition to Marcel's signature, which was always put on both back and front, was a lightly painted number, 94. "That is my catalogue number," Lanny explained. "I have a cardfile at Juan, with the data on every Detaze that I have ever known of. I am sure that I had this one in my hands on my last visit to the storeroom, for I considered it as one of a lot which I was taking to Germany for sale."

"I am greatly disturbed, M. Budd," declared the man. "I hope you understand that I had no means of knowing and no reason to suspect anything wrong."

"Certainly; that idea could not occur to me. I wonder if you would permit me to call my mother's home and pay the charge. I may be able to get some information at once."

Lanny put in a call; and since long-distance service was never very prompt in France, he strolled about and looked at other paintings until he was summoned, and heard his mother's voice. He asked: "Have you sold any of Marcel's works since I was last at home?" When she answered "No," he inquired if she knew of anyone else having sold any. Then he said: "Please do not say anything to anybody about this call until you see me. I will be home late tonight."

"Is something wrong?" Beauty's tone was full of concern.

"I can't be sure until I have talked to you, and to others. Please promise me, nothing until I arrive."

She promised, and the dealer agreed to lock the painting up until he heard again. Lanny took a taxi to his hotel, packed his belongings, and set out on the Boulevard Champs Elysées to the familiar *route nationale*.

III

Lanny drove straight through, and Beauty was waiting up for him when he arrived. While waiting, she had been trying to guess, and he discovered that they had guessed the same thing. He told her what he had learned in Paris, and received once more her assurance that she hadn't given anybody access to the storeroom. He consulted the cardfile which was kept in his room while he was away. Number 94 was marked with an "S," which meant that it was supposed to be in the storeroom. The keys were kept in the top drawer of his chiffonier, and he looked and found them in the proper place.

Getting a torch, he hurried over to his studio. Doors and windows appeared to be intact, and he let himself in, first at the front door, then at the one which led from the main room to the storeroom in the rear. Everything appeared to be as he had left it; rows of deep shelves ran around the walls, and the paintings were ranged on these according to number. It took but a moment to make sure that 94 was gone; what others were gone would require a checking against the cardfile.

Lanny locked up again and went back to his mother. "Somebody has taken one painting, probably three, and possibly more. Either the thief is an expert at picking locks, or he had access to our home and knows where I keep the keys. Either he worked in collaboration with Agricoli, in Nice, or he made that dealer believe he had come by them honestly. I note that he went to an Italian, and that seems to me significant."

"Oh, Lanny, it *can't* be true!"

"I don't want to say that it's true. I'll have a talk with Agricoli in the morning, and see what I can learn. This much I know, and you know it, too—that a man who gambles is always exposed to temptation, and I can't see Vittorio as a very heroic resister. Where is he now?"

"Asleep in their room."

"Well, let them sleep; there's nothing more to be done now."

"Oh, it will be so dreadful if it's true! What shall we do, Lanny?"

"It's always a waste of time trying to cross bridges before you come to them. All I want to know is my own position in the matter. Legally I have no rights in the paintings; they are your property by Marcel's will, and I am merely your agent."

"That is not so, Lanny. I made a definite agreement with you to handle the pictures and divide the proceeds three ways, you, me and Marceline. I should have put it into writing, and I'll do it now."

"Have you paid Marceline all the money that is due her on the Hitler sale?"

"No. I have been giving her a little at a time, as you suggested. She wants more, of course. Oh, Lanny, do you suppose it is possible she could have known about it?"

"My guess is it was Vittorio's own bright idea. But it's futile to speculate. The only sensible thing is to go to sleep, and not worry about troubles that you may never have to face."

"If Marceline doesn't know about it, she will be so horrified!"

"It is important that we don't give either of them any sign that we have noticed anything wrong. The thing for you now is to go to bed. Count your blessings and say your prayers!" The mother had become quite religious under the influence of her husband's example, and when any good thing happened to members of her family, she piously attributed it to her spiritual exercises. Lanny wondered if she had prayed for Vittorio to succeed with his "systems" at the casinos? If so, her faith had been sorely tried!

IV

Lanny didn't sleep much himself. He got up early, dressed, and got a bite to eat, served by the black-clad lame Spaniard who had taken over the management of the home, and who looked upon the young master as one who came down out of the skies in a chariot. After the fashion of servants, José had figured out the relationships existing among the members of this family; unlike most servants, he kept his thoughts to himself, out of loyalty to Lanny. Did he know or suspect anything about the paintings? Lanny didn't hint at the subject; he took a glance at the morning papers, with news of bombings in Barcelona and Valencia, and remarked: "A good time to be in France, José." Then he went out to his car and drove off. He wasn't in the mood for play-acting with the young couple.

In Nice he found the art shop not yet open, and sat in his car reading items of depressing news from all over the world. At about ten there arrived a stoutish, round-faced Italian, with a pointed black beard and the proper morning coat and pin-striped trousers. It was a warm morning, and he had been walking, and wiped the perspiration from his forehead. He did it several times more when the highly respected stepson of Marcel Detaze followed him in and opened up with the tidings that he had been receiving stolen goods. "*Dio mio, Mister Budd!*" exclaimed the dealer, several times without variation.

"Let me relieve your anxiety, Signor Agricoli," said the suave expert. "I don't want to have any publicity, or to make any unnecessary trouble. If you will deal with me frankly, I will consider you an ally and a friend—and I am sure you will find it better that way."

"*Si, si, Mister Budd, sicuramente—naturellement*—with my heart." The frightened man seemed not sure whether he was speaking Italian, French, or English, so he said it in all three.

"I want two things: first, to get the paintings back, and second, to find out who took them, so that I can stop the leak. So far as the money losses are concerned, I am prepared to deal generously with you."

"*Merci, M. Budd—grazie*—I thank you—I will do everything—*tout possible!*"

Hearing the story, Lanny realized that the man had reason to be worried. He had bought three Detazes at an absurdly low price, and had sold them for half what he might have got at the sales rooms of the Hotel Drouot in Paris. Such a procedure seemed to indicate a fear that the paintings had not been honestly come by. According to his story, a young Italian of good appearance had come to him, giving the name of Gigliotto and saying that he had three French paintings which had belonged to his recently deceased father in Genoa. He professed not to know the name of the painter, but had been told that the works were valuable, so he had brought them to France. The pair had bargained back and forth, and the stranger had twice gathered up the canvases and gone out of the shop; finally the dealer had agreed to pay eighty thousand francs. He had the bill of sale, and Lanny inspected it but did not know the handwriting, or recognize the seller from the description. He was interested, however, when the dealer said that he had seen the man two evenings later, coming out of the casino with another young Italian, who wore an officer's uniform with the left sleeve empty.

The dealer named the customers to whom he had sold the paintings. He had carbon copies of his bills of sale, and showed his books, in which purchases and sales were entered. That was all he could do, and all Lanny wanted. Said he: "The paintings are my mother's property, and under the law you will be bound to reimburse the persons to whom you sold them. You will probably not get much back from the thief—since it appears that he frequents the casino. But all this would involve publicity, which my family does not want. I prefer to settle the matter quietly, and I make you the offer that if you will see your customers and buy the paintings back from them, I will reimburse you for the eighty thousand francs you paid to the thief. Does that seem to you reasonable?"

"*Si, si, M. Budd*, most generous—*vraiment*. *Però*—are we not breaking some law?"

"I don't think the law will trouble itself, if no one complains. I am pretty sure I can find out who the thief is, and persuade him to get out of the country and stay out. The French law would be satisfied with that."

"*Mille grazie, Mister Budd*. I will do my best—*sans delai*."

"It will mean a trip to Paris for you—for I think it would be the part of wisdom not to put anything into writing. M. Bruget, I am sure, will be amenable; and if either of your other customers questions your good faith, you may tell him to call my mother's home on the telephone, and either she or I will confirm your statements."

V

So the matter was settled. Lanny drove back to Juan, where he found his brother-in-law on the porch, absorbed in the reading of a yellow-backed novel which he hurriedly shoved into his pocket on Lanny's approach. Il Capitano Vittorio di San Girolamo had a taste for pornographic fiction which he knew his relative did not share. The latter said: "Be so good as to come down to the studio. I have a matter of importance to talk over with you."

Lanny had had time to think over his procedure, and wasted no breath on preliminaries. He motioned Vittorio to a chair and took one himself, then opened up: "Your friend who calls himself Gigliotto has just told me his part of the story, so you might as well tell me yours."

The Capitano had barely touched the chair; now he bounced out of it. "That is a lie!" he cried.

"Don't waste words, Vittorio. I assure you I am in no mood for nonsense. You have one chance to keep out of jail, and that is to tell me the whole story frankly."

"I haven't the remotest idea what you are talking about."

"All I want to know is, did you take any paintings except the ones that fellow sold to Agricoli?"

"It's a God-damned lie. I never——"

"All right, Vittorio. If that's your line, I'll give the police a chance to handle the matter. They are better equipped for such cases than I am." He got up and went to the telephone on his desk, and had got so far as to take down the receiver when the Capitano descended from the aristocratic perch on which he habitually sat. "Oh, all right, I'll talk." So Lanny hung up, and the other resumed his seat and said: "I took three paintings, no more. I was sick of seeing you holding back Marceline's money."

"I'm not going to discuss Marceline. But I point out to you that if you took more, I'll find it out. It's just a matter of checking against my records, which I haven't yet had the time to do."

"You can save yourself the trouble. I only took three. That was all I could carry at once. Marceline was broke and so was I."

"Did she know what you were doing?"

"Of course not. And I hope you're not going to tell her; it'll only make her unhappy for nothing."

"How much of the money have you left?"

"Not a sou."

"What did you do with it?"

"I tried a new system, but I didn't have enough. Just when I got to the point where one more turn would have put me on the road to success, the money was gone."

"It has happened that way ever since the roulette wheel was invented," remarked Lanny. "Now let me inform you, I have arranged to pay Agricoli eighty thousand francs and he will get the paintings back for me. You, for your part, will give me your demand note for the amount."

"What good will that do you?"

"I will put it away in a safe place, on the chance that you may ever have a claim against any member of my family."

"Very clever of you!"

"I hope it is. The other request I have to make is that you will invent a telegram ordering you back to your duties in Spain. In that way you can avoid giving Marceline the information which, as you say, would only make her unhappy for nothing."

"You are going to try to break up our marriage?"

"Just the opposite. If I tell Marceline the truth, it might well break things up; but on the basis I am proposing, she will be free to follow you to Spain if and when she wishes; that will be for you and her to settle. The one thing I have to make certain is that you do not ever come back into France."

"Oh, so you pass a sentence of exile on me!"

"Italy is your native land, and Spain is going to be your colony. There ought to be glory and money enough for you there. I propose that you leave France for my mother and myself."

"Very subtle indeed—but it seems pretty close to blackmail to me."

"I don't know the exact name for the method by which you have been getting your gambling money from my mother and her daughter, and I don't want to bandy words with you. I simply tell you that unless you agree to take the night train to Marseille and a steamer for Cadiz, you will spend tonight in the Cannes jail."

VI

Vittorio de San Girolamo was a young gentleman who thought extremely well of himself; it came naturally to him, and a fond mother had encouraged it. He had pale, well-cut features, and a little sharp-pointed black mustache of which he took great care. He had several medals and decorations which he wore on all occasions, and he had manners which made an impression upon the ladies. Of late he had been feeling himself master of Bienvenu, and had perhaps not been taking the trouble to manifest his best qualities. It occurred to him that now was a time for the quickest possible turning on of his charm.

"Lanny," he began, humbly. "You are taking a very harsh attitude to me, and I beg you to stop and try to understand my position. I may have made a blunder; yes, I know I have, I admit it freely, and truly regret it—but you must realize that it wasn't quite the same thing as a crime. Marceline has a claim on those paintings, much better than your own. She is Marcel's daughter, his own blood; and when she tells me that she is being badly treated, am I not supposed to pay any attention to what she says?"

This was a subject which had been discussed in detail, and Lanny was tired of it. Said he: "Are you ready to give me your answer, or do you want time to think it over?"

"I see that you are hopelessly prejudiced against me, Lanny. How am I to get the money to travel?"

"If you let me know early enough, I will have my friend Jerry Pendleton meet you at the Cannes station and put into your hands a railroad ticket to Marseille, a steamer ticket to Cadiz, and a thousand francs so that you can eat on the way, and travel to Seville. The army, I am sure, will welcome you."

The deflated ex-aviator sat staring in front of him, occasionally biting his lip. He looked like a surly and greatly vexed Fascist, and Lanny thought: "May there be more of them in that state!" Always he saw this brother-in-law in the role of which the brother-in-law was proudest—of dropping bombs upon undefended Abyssinian villages, and mustard gas upon roads where barefooted natives walked.

"You are giving me a rotten deal, Lanny. You must know that Marceline loves me, and wouldn't want this to happen."

"You are at liberty to tell Marceline about it, if you think it will help you; but that won't change my attitude. I am offering you a chance to keep your name clear, and to start life over again, if you have it in you."

"But what in God's name is Marceline to do—and the baby?"

"Marceline is a free agent, and the choice will be hers. If she wants to go with you tonight, I will give her the money. If she wants to stay here and come later, I will give it to her then."

"But sooner or later Marceline will want to come back to visit her mother; and what excuse can I give for not coming with her?"

"I suppose you can plead your military duties. Marceline will be welcome to her mother's home, but you will never come here so long as I live. There is no statute of limitation on felonies, and there will be none on my determination. These paintings have been safe in their storeroom for more than twenty years, and I want to know they will be here the next time I come back."

"You won't accept my word that I am truly sorry, and will never again touch them?"

"Excuse me, Vittorio—you have taught me that your word is worth exactly nothing. My mother has given you money on your pledge to quit gambling, and you have broken it again and again. A home is a place where people believe in and trust each other; and you have excluded yourself from ours."

"Do you want to know what I think about your behavior, Lanny? You're still a Red in your heart. I've believed it ever since you came into Spain to help that God-damned snake Alfy."

"You can believe whatever you please, Vittorio, but don't make the mistake of talking about it. Remember that you took money to do your part in freeing that snake."

"I took the money, but I never did anything. I went to watch you, and make certain that you didn't do any hurt to our cause."

"That's your story; but don't fail to realize what a weak one it is. Your camp is full of spies and traitors, and if you once get that tar on your fingers you'll have a hard time rubbing it off. I'll tell you about myself—I have seen so much of the crookedness of politicians in all the camps that I have decided to attend to my own affairs and let them alone. So far as you and I are concerned, I think it's a fair bargain for me to say nothing of what I know about you, and you to say nothing of what you guess about me. Do you want to give me your decision?"

"Oh, I'll go, of course—what else can I do? I don't want to bring disgrace on my wife, or to handicap my son's future. But I'm telling you, I'll come back to France some day—and on my own terms."

"Perhaps you'll come at the head of an army. If so, I'll hope to get out before the bombs fall."

Lanny seated himself at his desk and wrote: "On demand I promise to pay to Lanny Budd the sum of eighty thousand francs for value received." He dated this, and the Capitano signed it and stalked out.

VII

In the village he took the tram to Cannes, and from there telephoned his wife, saying that he had received at the Italian consulate a telegram ordering him to return to Seville at once; he had made a mistake and overstayed his leave.

Marceline, of course, was greatly upset. What was she to do? Surely she couldn't take a young baby on that long trip, and stay in war-torn Spain, with the midsummer heat coming so soon. "I'll have to wait a while, Vittorio; and perhaps wean the baby and leave him here."

"Oh, Lanny, what have you done!" exclaimed the softhearted mother, in the privacy of her boudoir. "Don't you know how she loves him?"

"It's her hard luck that she made a bad guess," replied the tougher-minded son. "She made her own bed—and she doesn't have to lie in it one night longer than she chooses."

"In Southern Spain, that ghastly climate—and all the mosquitoes! You shouldn't have done it, Lanny! It was too drastic!"

"Hold your horses, old dear," he replied—a phrase he had learned in the rude land of the Yankees. He didn't tell her just how "drastic" he had been, leaving her to guess that the young husband was departing because of his painful embarrassment.

Vittorio explained to Marceline that he had a lot of business to attend to in Cannes, and asked her to pack up his belongings and drive in and meet him. Also, would Lanny be kind enough to have the travel bureau attend to the matter of his accommodations?

Lanny was happy to oblige; he called up his old friend Jerry and promised to mail a check on receipt of bill. He gave Marceline a thousand francs in an envelope, and that was the end of the matter for him. He was glad he didn't have to be a witness of the parting, and persuaded his mother to send her farewells by proxy. Let the young couple have their last hours together and work out their problems in their own way. Lanny himself had no tears to shed; he had always loved his mother's home, but had lost interest in it since a Fascist ex-aviator had been free to spread his ego there. Now Lanny would stay awhile, and go fishing with Jerry, and play tennis, and swim, and let a little of the joy of life seep back into his heart.

VIII

But he couldn't keep out of politics. He had to get in touch with Julie Palma, and take her for a drive, and read the letters that had come from her husband. The government had been moved to Barcelona, and Raoul was there, being bombed almost every day; a strange thing, you got used to it—apparently human beings could get used to anything. You heard the whistle of the bomb, and you closed your eyes for a moment or two—that was automatic; then came the explosion, and the house across the street might be turned to rubble in a fraction of a second. Hundreds of people were being killed in a single day, or worse yet, maimed and pinned under wreckage which might take fire. There wasn't a pane of glass intact for blocks around Raoul. Yet people stayed on and did their jobs, women refusing to leave their men.

Raoul might easily have come out, but he, too, refused. His little wife closed her eyes and the lids quivered as she said: "I won't ask him to come. It's his duty, and I won't be the one to break him down. It's the people's war; it's freedom, it's everything we believe in. We asked for it and we have to stick by it."

Lanny gave her some money and then went back to his home, deeply moved, and troubled in his conscience because he was taking a holiday in a terrible time like this. It was the Trudi-ghost, still working in his soul and giving him no peace. It wanted Lanny to become a fanatic like itself. It filled him with rage at the hypocrisy in high places, at the spectacle of class interest masquerading as patriotism, as piety, as love of peace. He knew how quickly these peace-lovers would start a fight, the moment their own privileges were threatened. You could see that in Spain and hear it talked in smart society on the Côte d'Azur, where the wealthy Spaniards were waiting for their homeland to be made safe again, and where the rest of smart Europe expressed its hearty sympathy.

The farce of "Non-Intervention" went on all that summer, and so, also, did the seeking and finding of pleasure. The French Riviera was now fully established as a summer resort; villas were leased for the year around and hotels and rooming houses were filled to the last garret. The drums thumped and the stopped trumpets blared all night across the Golfe Juan; all day the women lolled in the sunshine with two narrow strips of cloth around them, and the men strolled by and looked them over and took their pick. Day or night it was hard to get near the gaming tables for the crowds, and the dancing floors were so packed that, as the disgusted Sophie put it, you had to learn to dance on a sou.

She was one of those who had bought a luxurious villa on the Cap d'Antibes, planning to spend a life of mild enjoyment, and now resented the invasion of vulgar hordes. The only thing to do was to stay away from public places; entertain your own little group of friends; eat in one another's dining rooms and dance in one another's drawing-rooms, or outside on the loggias. Along the shore were quiet spots with white or pink villas perched upon the rocks, and other villas dotting the slopes of the hills, many of them with extensive and beautiful grounds. The residents divided up into sets according to their wealth and the mysterious thing called "social position," and kept others out in spite of no end of heart-burning. Many who had been considered "fast" when they were young had become pillars of conservatism in their later years, and were now shocked by the doings of the younger set.

Sophie, Baroness de la Tourette, had been a wild one, with henna hair and a loud voice; now she had let the hair turn gray, her laughter was subdued, and her principal diversion was playing bridge for money which she didn't need. Beauty Budd was one of her cronies, and it was a misfortune that Beauty's husband wouldn't learn to play cards. They would try their best to rope Lanny in, and failing in this, would take Marceline. All Lanny wanted was to sit in a corner with a book, or to wander down to his studio and pound on the piano; but this was contrary to the ladies' idea of a social life, and every time they got him here, even for a few days, they would start scheming to interest him in some member of their sex. They wouldn't say "wife," because that had a terrifying sound; but some girl to sit out with on lovely summer nights, and to take sailing on dark blue water whose millions of wavelets sparkled like silver in the moonlight and like gold in the sun.

Just now it was a visiting grand-niece of Sophie's, a lissome young thing just out of finishing school in Mobile. She was a dream made out of the different varieties of roses—cream and pink and red, with the almost black kind for her hair; she had the loveliest soft drawl, if you had time to listen to it, and ran the consonant of one word into the vowel of the next just as if she were French—only the French did it in half the time. Sophie was determined that this was going to be a match, and the bunch of roses was apparently willing to be plucked. Lanny would be invited over to dinner, and then left to stroll in the garden, and he did—but after they had talked about the people they knew and the things they were doing and the places they had been to, what on earth was left?

IX

A funny thing happened. Sophie and her husband, the dignified Mr. Armitage, were in the card room finishing their second rubber with Beauty and Marceline, having won several dollars from their guests. Lanny was sitting outside on the terrace, listening to Lucy Cotton's account of her home on Mobile bay, where the magnolias were now in bloom and the mocking birds singing the whole night long. There came a sound of motorcars and a flashing of lights; two cars stopped under the porte-cochere—it was the fashion to drop in, most any time before dawn, for the nights were delightful, while the afternoons were hot, so you took a long siesta. In the evening, after you had danced, or gambled, or been to a show, you would drop in on friends, and sit for a while sipping iced drinks, and gossiping about the people you knew: She has scads of money— They say her grandfather was a miner— She said this and I said that— And have you heard about Dickie, he's drunk again and Pudzi is threatening to leave him— I have a date with my *couturier* tomorrow, and what are *you* going to do?

One of this company appeared to be different from the rest. For one thing she had no make-up, and for another she wore glasses, which no smart lady will do if she can see to walk down the street without them. This one was of the indeterminate age between twenty-five and thirty-five, a small, birdlike creature, quick in her glances and speech. Lanny had never seen her before, and her name, Miss Creston, told him nothing. He saw that she was watching one after another of the company, and when her eyes met his, she did not avert her glance in the usual ladylike way, but met his frankly, as much as to say: "Well, who are you, and what do you want?" There is a term applied to such a manner; it was "forward."

When she had finished looking at Sophie Timmons, the hardware lady from Cincinnati who had married a French baron and wished she hadn't, and at Sophie's second husband, the retired engineer, and at the one-time professional beauty whose friends had given her that unusual name, and at this too-well-known lady's son and daughter, Miss Creston started inspecting Sophie Timmons' drawing-room, the paneling, the draperies, and the pictures on the walls—which wasn't exactly polite behavior. Then she got up and looked at the books in the bookcase—which was really just like saying that the conversation bored her. Lanny knew how Sophie's books had been chosen; she would get one that people were talking about, and start to read it, but rarely finish, because by that time people were talking about some other.

It happened that somebody mentioned Hitler, and a speech he had just made denouncing the mistreatment of Germans in the Sudetenland. What did the man want, and where was he going to stop? One of the company remarked: "Ask Lanny; he knows him." Another, a stranger, interjected: "You mean, personally?" The reply was: "He was a guest at Berchtesgaden just recently."

That brought Lanny into the spotlight, and the lady with the glasses stepped in and joined him there. Turning from the books, she exclaimed: "My God, do you mean one can actually visit that man?"

Said Lanny, mildly: "One can, if one is properly introduced."

"And how does one get introduced?"

"Well, it happens that the Führer is an admirer of my stepfather's paintings, and I took some there and he bought them for his guest house."

"Oh! It was a business matter!"

"Partly that, but social, also. You would find him a quite charming companion, I assure you."

"I suppose he's fond of little children, and all that!"

"It happens that he is especially fond of children."

"And how does he have them prepared?"

For once Lanny wasn't quick on the uptake. All he could say was: "How do you mean?"

"I mean: How are they cooked? What sauce are they served with?"

The company had stopped all other conversation to listen to this colloquy. Polite persons all, they must have been taken aback, even as Lanny was. However, he managed to smile, and replied: "It happens that he is a vegetarian. The only babies he eats are chicks before they have begun to be; in other words, a poached egg on his boiled vegetables. But he will serve you baby lamb or calf if you desire it."

The woman stood there, as conspicuous as if she were making a speech; and nobody offered to interrupt this duel. "Tell me, Mr. Budd," she said; "do you approve of this charming vegetarian's political procedures?"

"I am an art expert, Miss Creston. I help to find beautiful paintings, mostly for American collections. I have found that it is necessary for me to deal with people who have all sorts of political opinions, and I try not to force mine upon them."

"But you must have a few opinions of your own, don't you?"

Rather awkward for Lanny Budd, who couldn't afford to have the members of this group go out and say that he had evaded such a challenge. This duel was something to be talked about, and would be talked about all over the Cap before the day was over—it was after midnight. He had to make a flat answer, and it had to be one which would satisfy the Fascists and Nazis who swarmed on the Coast of Pleasure.

Said the son of Budd-Erling: "I used to have political opinions when I was young; but when I arrived at years of discretion I found that they disturbed my digestion and my judgment of art works. So now I confine myself to my chosen profession and let more qualified persons run the world's business affairs."

"And if you found that one of these persons was getting world power by means of wholesale murder and lies, that wouldn't disturb you in the least?"

"I am afraid, Miss Creston, I should have to remain in my ivory tower, and leave it for you to deal with that dangerous person."

"Ivory tower, Mr. Budd?" snapped the woman. "It seems to me you might better call it a cave, and yourself a troglodyte."

You could feel the shock run through that well-bred company— for that word had a terrible sound, even though not many knew its meaning.

Lanny still took it amiably. Said he: "My understanding is that the troglodyte was a hairy man, and I could hardly qualify for that."

This gave the company a chance to laugh, and broke the tension. The ladies started to talk very fast about something else; and Miss Creston, realizing that she had said a mouthful, returned to her seat.

X

Lanny's job had brought him close to that state known to psychiatrists as schizophrenia; two minds living in the same body. He was a perfect reactionary, and felt all those emotions—he had to, in order to make them real to an audience. Then he would go apart by himself, and be the perfect rebel. Now he sat quietly, stealing an occasional glance at this stranger, and thinking: "Gosh, what a nerve! Here's a woman who hates every hair on the Nazi beast, and she doesn't mind saying so among people who would like to poison her!"

He remembered the picture which Nina had drawn, of himself being converted by some ardent anti-Nazi girl, and then marrying her! He could be quite sure that Miss Creston would undertake the first part of the job, at least. But how could this operation be carried on, here in one of the world's leading gossip centers? As the story stood at this moment, it was exactly right for a presidential agent: a Red vixen had challenged him, and had called him a troglodyte! "What is that?" the horrified dowagers would ask, and when they were told, "A caveman," they would say, "Oh!" and forever after be sure that Lanny was a good fascist. But if the story were to have a sequel: "Oh, my dear, what do you think? He went to call on her and took her motoring, and they say they are fast friends now,"—no, manifestly that would brand Lanny for the rest of his days.

Or could he call this lady up and ask her to meet him secretly? Not very well. Could he say: "I am completely in sympathy with your ideas, but for reasons of state I have to pretend otherwise?" He would need to know a person very intimately indeed before he could speak such words.

XI

Driving home with his mother and half-sister, he heard what they thought about this episode. "That perfectly odious creature!" exclaimed Marceline; and: "Did you ever hear such insolence in your life?" demanded Beauty.

"Who is she?" Lanny inquired.

"Sophie says she is from New York, and writes stories for the magazines."

"How does she come to be here?"

"She's related to those people who brought her. I'll wager they don't bring her to Sophie's again."

"They won't need to," said Lanny with a chuckle. "She studied the house and everybody in it. We'll all find ourselves in a short story some day."

"I never wanted to scratch a woman's eyes out so much!"—this was Beauty.

"I rather admired her nerve," remarked the wayward son.

"Oh, you would!" countered the mother. "It would be like you to look her up and fall in love. You always did pick out the people who insulted you and patronized you."

"Don't worry, old darling; I don't like that aggressive type. If ever I fall in love again, it will be with some gentle, submissive damsel."

"I'll believe that when I see it," retorted Beauty, so far from gentle or submissive herself. "There's that lovely Lucy Cotton, ready to adore you if you would give her the least encouragement."

It was necessary to deal respectfully with a relative of good old Sophie. Lanny said: "It's not easy for a man to be sure about these amiable young things. They turn out so different after you know them a while. Take Marceline. When she was young, I thought she was the sweetest and gentlest ever; but now you see, she knows exactly what she wants and never gives up until she gets it."

They had been discussing the subject of money on the way over to the party; and in the interim Marceline had lost several dollars because of her mother's card blunders. Now she took up the challenge, in a manner not so different from the Red vixen. "Sell my third of the paintings now and give me the money, so that I can go and live decently in Seville, and you won't ever again be bothered with the problem of my temperament."

"There now, you see!" said Lanny to his mother.

26

Pleasure Never Is at Home

I

Beauty had made all her plans to spend the summer at Wickthorpe Castle, and with Margy at Bluegrass, renewing her acquaintance with little Frances and enjoying the delights of visiting London. But here, unexpectedly, was the problem of Marceline and her infant, doubly dear because it had been named Marcel. The young mother couldn't very well be taken on this tour; she couldn't be left here alone, for she had never been alone, and had no resources within herself. Moreover, she dared not stay too long away from her husband; she said that men were weak and undependable, and Seville was full of idle and predatory women. Marceline agreed with General Sherman on the subject of war.

What she wanted was for her mother to give up the trip and stay in Bienvenu and take care of the baby while Marceline joined Vittorio. It was a lot to ask, but Marceline had never let that stand in her way. She had been brought up to be beautiful, and to live by that beauty; to take care of it, dress it, have it admired and waited upon. She had been taught that only rich people were of consequence, and now she had many rich friends and couldn't keep up with them;

she wouldn't have any other sort, because she looked down upon the others and found them depressing. An unhappy situation for a young woman to be in, and Marceline blamed everybody but herself for it. She complained persistently, and set out with dogged determination to get what she wanted.

Lanny had learned how to meet that attitude to life; he said No and meant it, and let Marceline know that he meant it. But poor Beauty couldn't do that; she said No and meant it, but then gave way, which was the same as not meaning it. She pleaded that it was her duty to see Frances, and not to let that dear child forget her entirely; but Marceline said that was rubbish—what Beauty was thinking about was Ascot and Ranelagh and the balls and parties at Margy's townhouse. It would cost a lot, and Marceline wanted that money to live half-way decently in Seville, where you paid five prices for everything, and maybe ten by now. She argued and nagged: it was just this one season; those hateful Reds couldn't go on with their mad fighting much longer, and then Vittorio could come back with honor, and find something to do that would pay him more than a beggar's wage.

Knowing that she was going to get her way, the young mother proceeded to wean her baby; and Beauty was just on the point of writing letters to call off her trip, when there came an emotional cyclone which turned both mother and daughter on their heads. There had been delivered at Bienvenu a letter addressed to Vittorio; a letter in an unfashionable envelope, addressed in a woman's handwriting of an inelegant sort. Lanny had dutifully readdressed it to Seville and thought no more about it. Then had come a second, and he had repeated the procedure. Now came a third, and this time it was addressed to Marceline, and she received it without Lanny's seeing it. The first notice he got was in the form of a scream, and then a storm of rage and weeping from his mother's room. He went in and found his half-sister lying on her stomach on the bed, kicking her feet in the air, alternately shrieking and biting her handkerchief which she stuffed into her mouth. Beauty was there, pale and bedraggled without her morning make-up; she didn't say a word, but handed Lanny the letter, which Marceline had crumpled up in her rage and then thrown into her mother's lap.

Lanny spread it out. It was in French, and the substance was that the writer had learned Vittorio's real name and had written to him twice that she was pregnant and about to lose her position. She needed help, but Vittorio had left her letters unanswered, and unless the family would make him come to her aid she would be forced to resort to the law. Celestine Lafitte was the name, and the address was a small café in Cannes.

At one moment Marceline proposed to rush off and tear the bitch's eyes out; at the next she wanted to travel to Seville and perform the same operation upon the faithless husband. She used astonishing language, the sort that wasn't printed until the last few years; Lanny was surprised to discover that his half-sister knew such words, not merely in English and French but in Italian. It was like an explosion in a sewer.

"Marceline, dear!" exclaimed the shocked mother. "The servants will hear you!"

"To hell with the servants!" cried the hysterical girl. "To hell with the whole rotten world! That's what I get for marrying a broken-down wreck of a man and sticking to him in spite of every misery and discomfort! The dirty stinking two-timer!"

"You don't even know that he's guilty, my child."

"Of course I know he's guilty; he's a skunk, a wolf! He can't keep his eyes off any good-looking woman—I've watched him, I've given him plenty hell for it. I've heard the talk of those Italian officers when they didn't know I was near."

Lanny would have liked to say: "I told you what the Fascists were,"—but that wouldn't do any good, and he had to leave politics out of it.

"He couldn't wait while I had a baby—that's the sort of dog he is. Jesus, how I hate him! Let him have his Celestine—let her be the one to go to Seville and be his camp-follower! Not me!"

II

It was a long drawn-out scene. A woman who had been petted and spoiled through her almost twenty-one years had had snatched away from her the thing she most wanted, and her way of taking the blow was without dignity or even pathos. She wanted to punish the two persons who had robbed and humiliated her, and the only idea she could think of was that Lanny should go and see this woman, and give her money to travel to Seville, so that she could make Vittorio miserable for the rest of his life. "Give her a gun and tell her to shoot him if he refuses to support her!"

Lanny said: "In the first place, Marceline, I doubt if the woman could get a visa into Franco Spain. All French passports are now stamped: 'Not valid for Spain.' And in the next place, Vittorio couldn't support her in Seville on his pay, even if he wanted to. She and her child would starve to death."

"All right, let them!"

"You overlook the fact that the woman might find some way to get her story into the newspapers. The Red press would find it very much to their taste."

"I don't care what they say—I'm through with Vittorio, his bitch and his bastard."

Lanny, a bastard himself, said no more. He knew that he would have to see this woman, and if she had any evidence that the child was Vittorio's, he would give her enough to tide her over the period while she was incapacitated. He would count that a small price for getting completely rid of a Fascist brother-in-law. When Marceline had got over her hysterics, he thought it the part of wisdom to tell her the reason why her husband had so suddenly departed for the wars. When Marceline heard that, she decided that she had been made a fool of by all the members of her family, and that from this time on she would look out for herself.

She was the child of Marcel Detaze, and somewhere within her was steel. She dried her tears and put war paint on her face, and announced that she was ashamed of her lack of self-control, and from this moment on nobody would see her shed a tear. What she wanted was a divorce from Vittorio as quickly as it could be arranged under the French law. Mlle. Lafitte would presumably serve as a witness, and in that way might earn the money to have a baby. "After all, I'm sorry for the poor brat," remarked the bitter young wife, and then winced, realizing that her own precious infant had the same father.

Lanny thought it over and decided that this was a matter for the family lawyer in Cannes. He consulted this gentleman, who invited the restaurant cashier to his office and found her amenable; she agreed to receive the sum of two thousand francs a month for a period of a year in return for her testimony that she had been seduced by the Capitano. She had some notes in his handwriting, and the lawyer pointed out to her that she would not be compromising her claim against the officer; after the war was over he would presumably return to his homeland, and she might follow him there and bring suit for the support of the child. So everything was "jake," as Robbie Budd would have said if he had been present. The suit was filed, and notice sent to the ex-aviator; then the daughter of Marcel Detaze said to her mother: "Let's give a party right away, a good one, and invite all our friends, so that I can show them I'm not down and out!"

III

The dénouement of this tangle of events was something which nobody could have foreseen. Sophie, Baroness de la Tourette, undertook to give the party, because she had a much larger dancing floor, and admired the "child's" nerve, so she said; she had known Marceline since the hour after her birth, and had helped to keep her a "child" all these years. Sophie made a suggestion that was practically a command: the way for a "child" to display her *insouciance* to the smart world was to do some of that lovely dancing that she and Lanny had displayed off and on for the past ten years.

For Lanny, also, this was a command. Grieving over the already-consummated murder of Austria and the all-but-consummated murder of Spain, he would find it like dancing on a grave; but there was nobody he could say that to, and he really wanted to help his half-sister in this time of trial. He hadn't done any dancing for quite a while, but had kept himself in condition by tennis and swimming, and Marceline had danced even while she was pregnant. Now she fell to practicing in a sort of frenzy. It was a way of defying the world, of answering all the patronizing, the sneers and jibes which she knew were being made behind her back; it was a way of punishing Vittorio, of telling him to go to hell. The daughter of Marcel Detaze was coming back into the *grand monde* again, she was going to have another début and score another triumph.

She and Lanny rehearsed those gay and graceful forms of bodily expression which Lanny had begun while playing with the fisher children on the beach at Juan; which he had disciplined at the Dalcroze school in Hellerau, and had set free again while watching Isadora Duncan through the years. He had begun teaching Marceline when she was just able to toddle, and they had played together on a hundred dancing floors, until they had become as one person, knowing each other's every impulse even before it was born. This ease and grace gave delight to any sort of audience; and Marceline, an extrovert, living to be admired, would catch the crowd excitement, be swept away by it and dance like one possessed.

Of course the gossips had been busy with her story; everybody in this fashionable company knew that her man had "done her dirt," and everybody knew that this was her defiance, her announcement that she wasn't going to whimper or weaken. They admired her for it, and called her out again and again, and warmed the hearts of both the dancing pair. Lanny saw once more what his half-sister was meant to be; and Marceline had known it for a long time.

The consequences were immediate. At lunchtime next day—or rather, that same day, since they had danced until long after midnight —the telephone rang, and a man announced himself as M. Cassin, proprietor of the Coque d'Or, one of the smartest of the Cannes night clubs. He wanted to know if he might come over to talk with M. Budd and Madame Marceline—so he called her—about the possibility of their appearing in his floor show. Lanny said that he might come, and Marceline pretty nearly blew up with delight. She forgot her ice-cold melon and began capering all about the room. The shocked Beauty exclaimed: "My child! Would you be willing to dance in a place like that? And for money?"

"Hell!" said the child. "What do you suppose I would dance for?" Then, seeing the pained look on her mother's face: "Didn't you pose for painters for money?" She didn't have to add "in the altogether," for Beauty knew that several years ago, rummaging in the storeroom, Marceline had come upon that painting of her mother which Lanny had found in an art-dealer's shop and had purchased, but which the respectable widow of Marcel Detaze didn't wish him to hang upon any wall in Bienvenu.

Brother and sister talked it out. Lanny said that he hadn't the time and didn't care for the life. But Marceline begged and clamored; he must do her this one favor, just this one, and she would be off his hands forever; just help her to get a start and she would never trouble him again. This was what she wanted, to be a dancer; she had everything that it took, youth, beauty, grace, verve—she said it herself, knowing that it was true and that Lanny knew it. She wanted money, and this was the way to get it; she wanted independence, a career, a chance to make the headlines and to shine. Never mind if he approved it or not; just grant her the right to be herself, and give her one good push.

Beauty suggested, feebly: "If you would do it for charity——" and the daughter replied: "Charity, the devil!" But Lanny pointed out, it was important to keep her social prestige, to be a Budd as well as a Detaze; she would get more money that way. So then she said: "I'll let it be announced that the engagement is for charity and that will set the tone; then after the first week there can be an engagement for *me*. Oh, Lanny, you *must* do it! Just one week! Then if I make a hit I can get somebody else. You can pick any charity you please, and make all the arrangements. I'll do whatever you say. Oh, please, please!"

So finally Lanny said: "All right; but let me do the talking to that fellow."

IV

M. Robert Cassin introduced himself as an "impresario," and said that he had been told about the triumph which the dancing pair had achieved last night. Previously he had seen them dancing at the casino and other places, and knew about the family and its exalted social position. There was much curiosity concerning the pair in those circles which would like to get into smart society but couldn't. M. Cassin knew that he couldn't tempt them with money, he said, tactfully, but they would give refined pleasure to a great many people, and might help to raise the standard of dancing on the Côte d'Azur, which was far from high at present.

Lanny replied: "This is something quite out of our line; but my sister enjoys dancing, and people enjoy seeing her. If we do it, the money will go to the fund for the widows and orphans of fishermen here on the coast, some of whom were my playmates in boyhood. You might advertise that fact."

"*Magnifique, M. Budd!* That will be *très snob.*" The French had managed to find a worthy significance in this word.

"And how much would you offer us?"

The "impresario" hemmed and hawed. For charity—for widows and orphans of the men who were injured or drowned in these sometimes stormy waters—one would have to be proud to contribute. Would ten thousand francs a week——?

Lanny answered promptly that it wouldn't. That was only about three hundred dollars, less than fifty dollars a night. "My idea is a round fifty thousand francs for the week."

M. Cassin was shocked, or so pretended. They had an argument on the subject of how many smart people would come to the Coque d'Or and how much they would spend for food and drink. At the end they compromised on three thousand francs a night, to be paid each night in cash to the secretary of the fund. The proprietor said he would make a ceremony out of it, he would pay the money after the last of three appearances by the couple, and tell the audience what he was doing. A master of ceremonies likes to have things to talk about, and this would confer great *éclat*.

Lanny added: "If the engagement is a success, my sister might wish to continue. I would not be interested myself, because I have other work which keeps me busy; therefore I suggest that you feature her in the billing. She will use the name Marceline, and you may point out that she is the daughter of one of France's most eminent painters."

"You might add that some of his paintings have been sold for as high as two hundred thousand francs apiece," put in Marceline. Even if she wasn't allowed to sell those paintings, she was surely allowed to advertise them!

V

The hour when this child of fortune first stepped forth as a professional performer was the greatest hour of her life so far. She was shivering with nervousness, but nobody was allowed to see it; she knew what she was doing, and was perfectly right in her statement that she had what it takes. In a night club you perform only for the rich, and Marceline had been one of them all her life, and they knew it. Many in her first audience were the same friends for whom she had danced at Sophie's, and before that at Emily's and in her mother's home. Lanny accompanied her modestly, doing everything he could to put her forward and display her charms. The affair went off like magic; word went out that here was a new sensation—and when the bored victims of *snobisme* discover a new sensation, they pay for it gladly. The night-club gentleman was delighted with his bargain, and told Marceline that he would be happy to have her continue with any partner of her choice.

So, after a few hours' sleep, the new sensation had herself driven to the casino at Nice, where she entered quietly and sat for an hour watching the gigolos, the dancing men who were hired by ladies who because of age or lack of charms had nobody to companion them. Marceline went from one place to another, looking for a boy who was young and agile, and had a reasonable amount of talent; she was going to hire him permanently and train him. She knew what she wanted, and found him without too much delay, brought him to Juan and put him up at a hotel, took him every night to the Coque d'Or to watch her performances, and then, in the afternoons, had Lanny drill him and teach him the steps.

He was an eager if somewhat corrupt youth, and did reasonably well. Within two weeks after the close of the engagement with Lanny, Marceline was ready to show her new partner to the "impresario," and they bargained again; this time Marceline took charge, for she said she might as well learn. She got a two-weeks' engagement at twenty-five thousand francs a week, and there wasn't any nonsense about charity this time; the night club was to have the option to renew for as many weeks as it pleased at the same rate, and that was all right with the dancer, because she could live at home free of charge, and she liked to dance for people she knew and to chat with them between the turns. As for her new partner, she was paying him two thousand francs a week, which was more than he had ever seen in his life before; he had agreed to work for a year on that basis. One other proviso in the agreement: No love-making! "That nonsense is out for me," Marceline told him; and in the privacy of her family she added: "If any man ever makes love to me again, he's going to pay for it, I'll tell the world!"

So that was that, and Lanny could consider that the problem of his half-sister had been solved; no longer would she be complaining, and blaming him for her frustrations. All he could do for her now was to help her think up new ideas—for of course she wouldn't want to go on doing the same old things. She wanted to know about Isadora, and how she had made such a sensation. There would be no "Red" nonsense in the career of Marceline, of course, nor would she waste herself getting drunk, or trying to start a school and teach children; enough if she could teach herself and one indispensable man. When the winter season came, she would want to go to Paris; and what would be the best place for her début, and would Lanny try to pull some strings for her? Emily would give her an engagement at Les Forêts; and what about Baron Schneider, and the Duc de Belleaumont, and Graf Herzenberg, and Olivie Hellstein? Marceline would accumulate a cardfile, like her brother; and Beauty would begin pulling strings—just as she had done for Robbie's munitions, and then for Marcel's paintings, and then for Lanny's old-masterings!

VI

While sharing these events, Lanny was not entirely idle politically. He met influential Fascists on the Riviera, and listened while they discussed their plans for the undermining of the North American states and the taking over of those in South America. As soon as Franco's rule was secure—and it couldn't be long now—his state would become the motherland of a new Spanish-American empire, built upon the Fascist formula. Spain had always been the cultural center for these lands, and Spanish Fascism, standing upon a firm Catholic foundation, would not antagonize the somewhat primitive peoples of South America as Nazism had done. This was explained to the Norte Americano by a Spanish bishop in exile to whom Lanny listened attentively, giving the Most Reverend Father cause to hope that his listener was on the way to becoming a convert. Afterwards Lanny went home and wrote a report—but not for El Papa.

If you stayed on the Riviera long enough, you met "everybody"—meaning, of course, everybody who was rich and important. At Sophie's Lanny ran into Charles Bedaux, Franco-American millionaire who had been one of the guests at Baron Schneider's dinner in Paris. An extraordinary person, he had emigrated to the United States as a penniless laborer and worked as a bottle-washer in a New York waterfront saloon, then as a "sandhog," boring tunnels under rivers. With his eager and alert mind, nothing could keep him down; he had devised a method of timing the motions of every sort of labor; the "Bedaux system" had been installed all over the world, and he had made so much money he had a shooting box in Scotland and palaces all over Europe where he entertained the great and famous.

He knew Lanny's father and mother and Lanny's former wife and everybody in their great world. He had just come back from Salamanca, where he had talked with Franco and Juan March, Franco's money backer. Bedaux admitted that he, too, had invested heavily in Spanish "Nationalist" bonds. He had a châlet on the Obersalzberg where he had spent the previous summer and had visited the Berghof frequently; the home of the Donnersteins was near by, and Hilde was one of his intimates. A big man with a fat face, an eager manner, and a loose tongue, he was a goldmine of information about the big-money world and its denizens. He was all tied up in the Nazi-Fascist schemes, and with money-making on an international scale—always a bit dubious—but he had no reserves with the son of Budd-Erling, merchant of death. All Hitler's intimates, Göring and Goebbels, Ribbentrop and Abetz and Wiedemann, even Max Amman, the Führer's publisher, were investing huge sums outside Germany, and Bedaux was their adviser and silent partner. After talks with him, Lanny had a long report to write.

Also, with his stepfather he continued experiments in psychic research. He tried out the idea of hypnotizing a medium and endeavoring thus to shape the developments of a séance. Perhaps he overworked Madame, or produced confusion in her various subconscious minds; anyhow, the results were one of those dreary stretches which try the patience of psychic investigators. Lanny had been fortunate over a long period of time, but now he got only scraps and irrelevancies, with just enough that was real to tantalize him and keep him trying. Tecumseh resumed laughing at him; and could it be that this malicious old personality was deliberately destroying Madame as a medium, the source of his own being? Was she really the source, or could he wreck her and then go off and enjoy himself elsewhere? Lanny reread Morton Prince's *Dissociation of a Personality*, the case record of a young lady of Boston whose subconscious mind had developed five different personalities. One of them, called "Sally," was a demon, a mischief maker identical with those one read about in ancient fable. Dr. Prince was able to kill her in the mind of Miss Beauchamp, but Lanny's efforts to kill Tecumseh only caused that grim old Amerindian to express scorn.

VII

Also Lanny read the newspapers of London and Paris, which reached him one day late, and watched the slow preparation of that tragedy which he had foretold to F.D.R. Poor compensation to be able to say: "I told you so!" Rick sent him a beautifully written article about the people who had maintained for many centuries the ancient kingdom of Bohemia, and now had built the modern republic of Czechoslovakia, and were trying to protect it in the midst of many angry dictatorships. Lanny had never visited Prague, but he had seen pictures of that romantic old city and had imagined it while listening to Smetana's tone poem of the River Moldau. In Paris he had met Professor Masaryk, son of a coachman and a cook, who had begun as apprentice to a locksmith and a blacksmith, and had ended at the age of eighty-five as founder and president of the most liberal democracy on the Continent. His foreign minister and successor, Beneš, pronounced Béhn-esh, was a peasant's son, one of the few diplomats of Europe who said that he spoke the truth and spoke the truth when he said it.

Now the great boa-constrictor called Nazism was getting ready to swallow this small mountain-girded state. Hitler had had his agitators among the Sudeten Germans from the beginning; their Führer was a bank-clerk named Henlein who had become head of the *Turnvereine*, the gymnastic societies which were camouflage for Stormtroop armies all over the world. Their technique was identical with that used in Austria: agitate, organize, make trouble, and then, when you are suppressed, clamor against "persecution." The Germans in Czechoslovakia were citizens with equal rights and liberties, and that suited most of them; but not the Nazi agitators and terrorists, who had money, arms, and propaganda literature in an unending stream. The Hitler borders had been increased in length by the taking of Austria, and the position of the Czechs was exactly that of a soft woolly lamb in a boa-constrictor's mouth.

Lanny had thought it was all over in the month of May, for Henlein came to London and was received by the leading Tories, and spent a week-end at Wickthorpe Castle. Rick wasn't invited there any more, but living not far away he heard the gossip, and wrote that Chamberlain had definitely decided to deliver the Sudetens as the price of peace in Europe. Hitler declared that this was the last demand he had to make on the Continent, and the British Tories wanted desperately to believe him.

But they had reckoned without the Czechs, who thought something of their liberties and didn't intend to be given away. When the Nazi armies moved toward their borders, the Czechs mobilized and announced their will to fight. The French were pledged to come to their aid, and the Russians were pledged to join the French. Europe hung on the verge of war, and Hitler wasn't ready for it; he backed down, his first big defeat—and Lanny imagined the rug-chewing that must be going on in Berchtesgaden, and wished he had stayed to see the show. But that joy in his heart didn't last very long; he knew that Adi would never give up his purpose, and Rick wrote that the Tories would give up anything that wasn't British. Lanny burned letters like these, taking no chance that they might somehow fall into the hands of his enemies.

VIII

Beauty could be spared now, since Marceline had her career for company, and had got a competent nurse to take care of the baby. Lanny agreed to drive his mother and stepfather to London, with some necessary stop-overs. One was at Le Creusot, gigantic forge of Vulcan; the couple stayed in a smokestained hotel while Lanny spent the night at La Verrerie. He had been asked by his father to cultivate Schneider, and had assented gladly, for the Baron was a pipeline into the center of French financial and political affairs. What this elderly hawk-nosed moneymaster believed and desired affected the destinies of every Frenchman alive, and of millions of other persons who had never even heard his name. It seemed to Lanny Budd a defect in education for democracy, that the people knew so much about the politicians and so little about the men who made the politicians and paid their fares on the bandwagon.

The munitions king had just determined the destinies of Europe, at least for a time. He told Lanny a spy story, a regular movie thriller. He had a "man" in Berlin, evidently a very good one indeed; on Friday, the 21st of May, this man had called the Baron out of bed at two o'clock in the morning, to tell him that Charlotte was ill with appendicitis. Those were not the exact words, the financier remarked with a smile, but it was something like that, and it meant that Germany was mobilizing. Furthermore the man said that Doktor Henry and Doktor Schmidt were in disagreement about the case—again those weren't the right names, but it meant that the British ambassador had had a row with Ribbentrop and accused him of deception, and was now ordering special trains to take British residents out of Berlin—meaning, of course, that he expected war.

"*Mon dieu*, could I let Hitler have Skoda?" exclaimed the Baron. The answer was, "*Jamais*," so he had routed Foreign Minister Bonnet out of bed and told him that France must definitely announce its support of Prague. Said the munitions king: "*Ce malin chauve*"—that bald-headed malicious one—"thinks about nothing but keeping his job and saving the franc; but what will be the value of all the francs if we lose our eastern alliances?"

Now in Lanny's presence the moneymaster was assailed by doubt and depression. He couldn't make up his mind who was his more dangerous enemy, the Brown devil or the Red. "Hitler will never give up, will he?"—and Lanny felt free to say: "Hitler and Pan-Germanism are one and the same."

He suggested that his friend should read Adi's book and see what the Führer had to say about himself. Strange to say, that idea had never occurred to the Baron, and he found it most original. Lanny told about the personality of Rudolf Hess, the real author of the volume; at least, he had seen to it that the greater number of Adi's sentences had a verb in them, and an ending. It did no harm to tell about Hess's interest in astrology and spiritualism, since all the Fatherland knew it; but nothing about the Führer's secret visits to Madame Zyszynski.

All this was of importance to Robbie Budd, since his deal with the Baron involved Pilsen and its great Skoda arms plant. The first thing Lanny did on reaching Paris was to type out an account of the munitions king's distracted state of mind, and mail one copy to his father and the other to Gus Gennerich. He had already warned Robbie that war could not be postponed more than a year or two, and that Robbie's financial arrangements should be based upon that certainty. It was a sign of the changing times that Robbie now took such advice seriously.

IX

There were going to be great doings in Paris; the newly crowned
King and Queen of Britain were coming for a visit of state; they would
be banqueted and presented with French orders and decorations, and
would confer British equivalents upon French statesmen. But Lanny
didn't care for public spectacles, and Beauty was aching to see her
darling Frances, so they drove to the Calais ferry, and direct to Wickthorpe without stopping for any of the delights of London. Beauty and
her husband were installed in a two-hundred-year-old cottage on the
estate—it had been remodeled, of course, and had all modern conven-
iences, but still had a thatched roof and low ceilings, and doorways that
you had to stoop slightly to pass through. Now, in July, it was delightfully rustic, like camping out; there was a vine-covered summerhouse
where Parsifal could say his prayers all day and night if he wanted to.
Frances was having a holiday from her tutors, and could come over and
spend all her time prattling away to her grandmother, who was so
happy that she became a child herself, and neither would bore the
other.

Meantime Lanny put up at the castle, a mass of round towers of
many sizes, and having crenelations on top; the modern parts were at
one side, so as not to spoil the effect. After a brief visit to his daughter,
Lanny became absorbed in his own unusual kind of work. He had happened along at a moment of importance, for the Earl of Wickthorpe
came back from town, bringing a guest to whom Lanny needed no introduction, having met him at the Berghof at the time of the Schuschnigg visit. He was one of the Führer's aides-de-camp, and enjoyed a
specially favored position because he had commanded the company in
which Adi had been a sub-corporal during the World War. Captain
Fritz Wiedemann was a large, powerfully built fellow with heavy dark
eyebrows and lantern jaws; a fanatical Nazi, but also a suave man of
the world. From him Lanny had made certain that he knew exactly
what was going to happen to Austria—in fact, he had been one of the
military men called in to tell the Austrian Chancellor what was going
to happen to *him*.

Gerald Albany had just returned from a highly confidential visit to
Hitler, Ribbentrop, and Göring; undoubtedly he had taken some important proposals of the British government, and now in all probability
Wiedemann had come with the answers. Lanny had read of the Hauptmann's arrival in the London morning papers, together with the offi-

cial denial that he had any diplomatic errand, or had talked with any-one of Cabinet rank. That, of course, meant the opposite of what it said, for British diplomatists proceeded upon the formula that a lie was an untruth told to a person who had a right to know the truth, and the British public was not included in that sacred roster. Before that eve-ning was over Lanny heard from Wiedemann's own lips that he had had an interview with Lord Halifax, the British Foreign Minister, on the previous day. Halifax was accompanying the royal visit to Paris, so Lanny could guess that he was carrying the German proposals to the French.

X

Here was a presidential agent, in the very heart of the intrigue which was to determine the fate of Europe for a long time to come. Never had he had to step more warily, not even on that hair-raising night when he had been helping to burglarize the Château de Belcour. He judged that neither Ceddy nor the discreet Gerald would discuss these ultra-secret affairs in the presence of other guests or of serv-ants; Lanny's problem was to get some one of the group alone, and contrive to have the subject brought up by this person and not by Lanny. Often a man would drop hints without realizing the full signifi-cance of his words.

The first thing was to establish Lanny's sociopolitical position, as it might be called. Exercising his privilege to bring up a new subject of conversation, he said: "By the way, Wiedemann, you remember that you expressed skepticism on the subject of psychic phenomena. Have you had any chance to talk with Hess since he tried his experiments with me at the Berghof?"

"No," said the German. "How did they turn out?"

"One thing that might be of interest to a military man: Rudolf got what purported to be a communication from a soldier who had been in the trenches with him at Verdun, and had been killed a few minutes after Rudolf himself was wounded. Several details were given which Rudi confirmed, and he told the Führer about them in my presence. It made a great impression on both." Then, turning to Irma: "That was Madame, our old Polish medium. I took her to Berchtesgaden for Hess to try his luck."

They talked for a while on a subject which was fascinating and at the same time entirely safe—since the spirits had never been political, at least not so far as Irma or Lanny knew. She told of communications which were supposed to have come from her father; Ceddy told about a ghost which was reputed to appear now and then in the oldest tower of this castle, but which had possibly been disturbed by Irma's recent alterations, since it hadn't shown up of late. This conversation served two purposes of a subtle intriguer. It would enable the Hauptmann to go back to the Berghof and report that the son of Budd-Erling was an intimate of the earl and the countess as he had claimed; and, no less important, it settled in the minds of Ceddy and Gerald any doubts as to the truth of Lanny's claims that he had been in the Berghof at the time of the Schuschnigg visit.

XI

After the coffee and cigars the Foreign Office men excused themselves and took their guest into his lordship's study. That left Lanny alone with Irma, something which might have been awkward for some "ex's," but not for this socially trained pair.

"You have changed your opinions very greatly of late, Lanny," the woman remarked. "It's hard for me to realize it."

"Well, I had to grow up sooner or later," he said.

"If you had made it a little sooner, we might not have had our breakup."

That was kind of her, and Lanny wanted to be no less so. "Then you wouldn't have had this grand old castle," he countered, with a smile.

Irma was *enceinte*, as the polite word had it, and had reached the stage where she moved slowly. "Shall we pay a call on Beauty?" she suggested, and of course Lanny offered to accompany her. They strolled across the grounds through lovely English twilight, which comes late in the month of July. Frances had been taken to bed, for she lived on a strict schedule. It was quite like old times, with Beauty and her husband, and Irma and her "ex." They talked about the child for a while, and then Beauty, most tactful of guests, suggested that Frances' other grandmother might like to share the conversation. Mrs. Fanny Barnes occupied a villa on the estate, where she lived with her brother, the elderly retired stockbroker whom Lanny had learned to call "Uncle Horace." To Lanny he was the world's worst bore, but fortunately he had a touch of the gout and couldn't come.

The large and important widow of the American utilities king summoned her chauffeur and was driven a quarter of a mile or so to "Glavis," as the cottage was called—for some reason that was buried under the debris of time. She proposed a rubber of bridge, and politeness required Lanny to oblige. In former days the two elderly ladies had played against Irma and Lanny, but now Fanny's sense of propriety brought it about that mother and daughter played against mother and son, and won handily. Truth to be told, it was hard for Lanny to keep his mind on his mother's signals, when it wanted to speculate on what the three conspirators over at the castle might be deciding as to the fate of Czechoslovakia. And anyhow, it was always tactful to let Fanny Barnes win.

XII

Luck was kind to Lanny, for when he got back to the castle he found that Gerald Albany was taking Wiedemann back to London that night, and Ceddy was staying on. That meant that after the important guest had departed, the lord of the castle sat in the library with his wife's former husband, and rang for whisky and sodas and a bite before retiring. Did he fear that he might have seemed discourteous in excluding an old friend from a conference? Or was there something that he wanted to get out of Lanny without Lanny's knowing it?

The art expert had thought out his plan of attack while dealing bridge hands, and now he went right to it. "Ceddy," he began, "may I talk to you frankly for a minute or two?"

"Certainly, Lanny—always."

"Why doesn't the British government make up its mind and do something to settle this miserable wrangle that is making every sort of progress impossible in Europe?"

"It doesn't rest entirely with us, Lanny."

"That's where you are making your mistake. You don't realize the position of Britain at the present time, or how much depends upon your decisions. The French simply don't know their own minds; they are staggering around like a lot of drunken men, knocking one another over. I had a talk with Schneider only three or four days ago. Honestly, it is tragic; the man can't keep his mind made up through an hour's conversation."

"Tell me what he says, Lanny."

Was that what the British Foreign Office wanted to know on this critical evening? If so, Lanny would be happy to favor them, in consideration of a fair return. He told what he had heard at La Verrerie, and what he knew about French opinion from other sources. "The French ought to be told what to do and made to do it, and they'll be relieved to get it off their minds."

"It is the most complicated situation we have ever faced, Lanny—perhaps in the whole of England's history."

"I agree with you; but no decision can be so bad as indecision. That means leaving everything at loose ends, and helps nobody but the forces of disorder. I don't feel myself a stranger to Europe, and I suffer from the confusion like all the others, rich and poor. Everybody I know keeps asking: why doesn't England make up her mind? Either say to Hitler: 'Stay where you are or it means war'; or else say: 'We blundered at Versailles, and you can have your border territories back, and let's start over again and be friends.' "

"If it were only that simple, Lanny! But here are all these nations and tribes, like so many wild beasts in a cage, ready to fly at one another's throats. We confronted the possibility of a general war two months ago. And our people don't want war; we aren't ready for it and we don't want to have to get ready."

"All right then, make up your minds to a settlement. Decide what territories you are willing to let Hitler have. Put your cards on the table and say: 'You can have this, and this, and no more.' Put it before the French, not for squabbling over, but as an ultimatum: 'This is the settlement, and you can come in or we make a deal with Hitler instead.' Say to Czechoslovakia and Poland: 'This is our decision, and you have to take it or wage a war by yourselves.' "

"I wish I were free to talk to you about these confidential matters, Lanny——"

"That's all right, old man—it doesn't make any difference, because I'm going back to Paris in a few days, and whatever Halifax is saying to Bonnet, Schneider will tell it all to me in ten minutes. The old gentleman's nerve seems to be broken; he is possessed by the horrid idea that if Hitler gets Pilsen, he will refuse to recognize those pieces of paper which guarantee title to the Skoda plant. So he wants some of my father's fighter planes to protect his property; also he wants somebody to let him cry on his shoulder. Instead of trying to keep secrets from me, Ceddy, it would be more sensible to tell me what you people want and let me help you get it. All I want is to see peace in Europe, so that people can have time to think about paintings again."

"You really do know a lot of the key people, don't you, Lanny."

"It's my blind luck that Budd-Erling is tops right now in the race for speed and maneuverability. Robbie has proudly demonstrated it at several military airfields; so, when I go to Berlin, *Der Dicke* invites me to Karinhall and tells me the most shocking things—I mean, diplomatically speaking. And as for Hitler, when he gets started he tells everybody what he's going to do for the next thousand years. I think it's a calculated indiscretion with him—he's working a gigantic game of bluff." Lanny paused for a moment and added, with a grin: "Would you like me to take a plane to Berlin and send you back a complete report of what Gerald offered to the champagne salesman?"

The Earl of Wickthorpe couldn't keep from smiling in return; it was very disarming. "I don't mind telling you, Lanny, that we've come to be of very much the same mind as yourself. It appears that we have no choice but to let Hitler have a readjustment of his entire eastern boundary."

"And Wiedemann is here to tell you what they demand; and Halifax is taking it to Paris. He is a man of the most upright character, but can he pound the table hard enough to impress those French buccaneers?"

"Many of them require no persuading, Lanny; and Halifax can be stiff-necked when he wants to."

"I hope so. Would you like me to call on Schneider and try to convince him that it's to his best interest to accede to your proposals?"

"I haven't any authority to suggest such a thing, Lanny——"

"Of course not! You don't have to talk protocol to me, Ceddy—that's our Washington slang, as you may know. I'm talking off the record, as one friend of peace to another. I'm not asking for state secrets—there'll be plenty of leaks in the next few days and I don't want to be a possible source. But if I'm to talk to Schneider to any purpose I have to be able to say this and have it straight: Is Britain going to help him preserve his title to Skoda, or is she not?"

The handsome and dignified nobleman looked at his guest with a steady gaze and delayed replying. So presently Lanny added: "I think I ought to make you acquainted with one set of facts, Ceddy. My father has a deal with Schneider, by which Schneider has the right to build Budd-Erling planes in a new plant in or near Skoda. It was a cash deal and my father has no interest in the concern. It would be all the same to him if the Nazis were to grab the plant, for he also has a deal with Göring; thus Göring wouldn't gain anything he hasn't already got, and Robbie wouldn't lose anything he hasn't already sold. I think you ought to know that, so that when we talk about these delicate matters, you won't have the thought that I may be concerned about some family interest."

"I'm glad to have that knowledge, Lanny,—though I had no such thought. You understand, my lips are sealed as to what is going on at the moment, and I would prefer that you didn't mention to anybody that you have talked to me. But, as one friend to another, it can do no harm for me to tell you that Baron Eugène will have to take his chances along with the rest of us. The British government is certainly not prepared to go to war to protect his titles to Skoda, and if France holds out from the settlement we are working out with Hitler, France will have to do her own fighting, and find whatever way she can to help the Czechs. We, unfortunately, lack the means to get there."

"That is plain enough, and I'll tell him," replied the secret agent. "It will have a pacifying effect, I am sure."

Said his lordship: "We can only hope and pray that Hitler means what he tells us, that this will satisfy him, and that he will settle down and reorganize his economy on a peace instead of a war basis."

So Lanny drove up to town next morning and got a room in a hotel, set up his little portable, and hammered out a report to President Roosevelt, setting forth the fact that the republic of Masaryk and Beneš was the next chunk of appeasement that was going to be fed to the Nazi wolves.

BOOK SEVEN

The Things That Are Caesar's

27

Fever of the World

I

LANNY BUDD was living in a world which did not please him; which indeed seemed to be far on the way toward madness. The job he had chosen—or which perhaps had chosen him—obliged him to meet people whose company he could hardly tolerate, and forbade him to meet anybody he really wanted to know. As a result, he stayed alone except when he was collecting information, and found his pleasure in music, or in books, which he was free to read without permission of the Nazis. He was forced more and more in upon himself, and had to fight against moods of depression, and a tendency to brood over his failures and the tragic scenes he had witnessed.

For example, that poor devil he had left behind in the dungeon of the Château de Belcour. It wasn't that Lanny blamed himself for having left him. There wasn't a thing those three intruders could have done; to have carried the man out would have given the whole thing away and ruined the career of a presidential agent. It might have been the part of kindness to smother him to death; but Lanny had never killed anybody, and hadn't even thought of it. Now he kept wondering: was the poor devil still alive, and still being tortured for having tried to give help to Trudi?

The broken figure became a sort of symbol of the cause which Lanny loved and believed in. Not merely the German people—the good Germans, the good Europeans among the Germans—bound, gagged, imprisoned, and condemned to years of torment; but all the other unfortunate peoples whose fate Lanny had been watching: Italians, Chinese, Abyssinians, Spaniards, Austrians—and now the Czechs, the next on the list, standing helpless, watching the assassins gathering about their house. The unhappy Paul Teicher became multiplied in Lanny's imagination by thousands, by millions, by hundreds of millions. It was the destiny of the peoples of Europe and Asia to have their lands invàded, their young men slaughtered and their women raped, their fields ravaged and their homes burned about their heads, their cities bombed to rubble, their leaders and intellectuals shot or hanged or beheaded or shut up in stockades. Such had been the events in incubation during the whole span of Lanny's life—this wonderful new twentieth century which had called itself "modern" and had hoped so much from itself and for itself.

The state of affairs had been getting worse year after year; the crimes had been increasing in arithmetical progression. And now it seemed that what had happened so far was merely a shadow of the holocausts and desolations ahead. The hopes of Spain were going to be completely extinguished. That cold methodical murderer, General Franco, would continue to receive killing materials from Italy and Germany and to blast and rend the bodies of his fellow countrymen, until there was no longer left in Spain a single person of intelligence, of even common decency. Every man and woman in the land who believed what Lanny believed would be slaughtered, or shut up in a dungeon to perish slowly of the diseases of malnutrition. Every child in Spain would be taken and turned into a pious robot, saving his soul by letting some black-robed priest mumble ancient magic over his poor little lice-infested head.

And now it was happening to Austria. *Wien, Wien, du Stadt meiner Träume!*—Lanny heard gorgeous waltz music every time he thought of it; and now it had become a Nazi headquarters, and was being *gleichgeschaltet*—co-ordinated—which meant that in a thousand dark holes were being repeated those hideous iniquities which he had witnessed in Munich and Berlin. And now the beautiful old city of Prague, and the Czechs, one of the most intelligent and democratic-minded peoples of Europe—whose only offense was that their ancestors, nearly a thousand years ago, had permitted many Germans to enter their country and to purchase lands and other property.

These accumulated horrors caused Lanny Budd to ask questions of the universe into which through no intention of his own he had been so suddenly and strangely projected. What ruled this complex of phenomena—a Providence of any sort, or just blind chance? Lanny hadn't seen any works of art or of artisanship brought into existence by blind chance, so he had to believe that there must be some intelligence at work; some mind must have contrived the production of two billions of human creatures on a small planet revolving obscurely in vast and complicated stellar and galactic systems. What that intelligence could be, and how it worked, and above all what it wanted, became harder for Lanny to imagine the older he grew and the more familiar with massed human misery.

Presumably, that Providence or God wanted each human to do his best; and for Lanny that could only mean a great deal of puzzling and worrying. Perhaps this puzzling and worrying was part of the process; perhaps God meant for each of the two billion creatures to go on striving until it learned to think more clearly, and to organize and co-operate with its fellows. Yes, that must be so—but it seemed such a wasteful, a ghastly process. Why couldn't they have learned to co-operate from the beginning? Why couldn't they have been born with enough sense in their heads—instead of with a desire to dominate and oppress, to rob and to kill?

When you asked questions like that, there was only one answer: "God knows." Since God wouldn't tell, that didn't get you very far. The two billion humans were here on this planet, with no wisdom or guidance save what they themselves could devise and provide. If they were ever going to stop dominating and oppressing, robbing and killing, it would be because some among their number had sufficient intelligence to persuade the others to settle down and produce wealth for themselves instead of trying to take it away from their neighbors.

To Lanny's mind this seemed to call for an international government and a world police force. But then he found himself thinking: "Good God, suppose there should be a world police force set up by the new Mohammed!" That was to him just the most horrid thought in the world; and every day seemed to be bringing the possibility nearer to mankind.

II

Politics in England had become so hot right now that Lanny was afraid to go from Wickthorpe Castle to the near-by Reaches. He drove into London and called Rick from there, asking him to come to town; Lanny met him at the station and drove him for a while, as the safest way to discuss the meaning of the Wiedemann visit and the errand of Lord Halifax to Paris. Lanny really didn't have much to tell that was new; the leftwing press had a pretty clear outline of the Nazi-Tory plot to give Hitler what he wanted, in the hope of steering him toward the east. But the leftists couldn't prove it; what they published was shamelessly denied, and the "appeasers" went right ahead with their plotting. Lanny could confirm Rick's ideas, but he couldn't let him publish the evidence, or even hint at it, because Ceddy knew that Lanny and Rick were friends. The playwright would have to do what he had done on previous occasions—pass the information on to others, a little here and a little there, so that in the end readers of the opposition papers would get a fairly clear outline of the picture.

Lanny told about his discontent, and pleaded for the privilege of being with friends for a few days. Why couldn't Nina and Rick take time off and come with him for a motoring trip? Why not drive north and see that Lake District where Wordsworth had managed to live a peaceful life through all the horrors of the Napoleonic wars? "The world is too much with us," Lanny quoted. They would keep off the beaten paths and avoid the fashionable folk who would know them. Rick said "Topping!" and they met by appointment without telling anybody, and felt as gay as three schoolchildren playing hooky.

The Lake District is in the northwest part of the tight little isle, a couple of hundred miles from London. That would have been a week's comfortable journey in the poet's day, and he had taken it rarely during his eighty years. In Lanny Budd's reckoning it was a forenoon's drive if he was in a hurry; but this holiday party took it slowly, stopping to look at ancient landmarks of which every schoolchild hears. The English countryside wore its midsummer dress of dark green, and the natives called the weather hot, but it didn't seem so if you had been reared in the Midi. All England was having a holiday, apparently; a startling thing to come to the land of a contemplative poet's quiet dreams, and discover his roads paved, his lake shore lined with villas and hotels, and the lakes sprinkled with rowboats and canoes. They had to drive some distance away in order to find accommodations.

The poetry of Wordsworth had been given to Lanny at the age of seventeen by his great-uncle Eli Budd in Connecticut, and he had read and marked it dutifully. Rick, whose education had been more of what he called "mod'n," didn't know it so well; however, Lanny had brought along a copy, and they allowed themselves time to read long passages and look for the features described. It was too late in the year for the golden daffodils, and they would hardly have recognized the peaceful vale; but they heard the twofold shout of the cuckoo, and saw the buzzard mounting from the rock, deliberate and slow. They sat upon one of the multitude of little rocky hills and looked down upon the tiny lake of Grasmere, a mile or so long, with its one green island and its rocky shores. They saw the silver wreaths of curling mist, and the earth and common face of nature spake to them, exactly as to the youthful worshiper a century and a half ago.

Ye presences of nature in the sky
And on the earth! Ye visions on the hills!
And souls of lonely places!

III

But there was a limit to the time that men of this age could spend
in the contemplation of natural phenomena. More even than in the
poet's day they were besieged by the fretful stir unprofitable, and the
fever of the world. Just as the mind of the poet had been haunted by
the menace of Napoleon, so the mind of Lanny Budd was haunted
by Nazi-Fascism, and he wanted to exclaim to Rick: "O friend, I know
not which way I must look for comfort!" Surely now, if ever in
recorded time, England was a fen of stagnant waters, and all the poet's
other phrases of grief and despair applied as well to this new age.

The Englishman answered: "Yes, but we survived the Napoleonic
wars, and I fancy we shall pull through again."

Said Lanny: "Every time I go to Germany, and see the preparations the Nazis are making, I grow more doubtful. I don't think you
have ever been in such danger as you are today—certainly not since
the time of the Spanish Armada."

Rick agreed, but added that there were some wide-awake men in
the government, and some real preparing was under way. "Alfy knows
some of the Air Force chaps, and they are working hard, I can assure
you."

Lanny revealed his personal discontent; he couldn't keep himself
persuaded that he was accomplishing anything, that anybody was paying real heed to the information he brought. His friend told him
earnestly: "I don't know what you may be accomplishing in the
States, but I can assure you you're being helpful here. It bucks me
up to get your confirmation, and to know exactly who our enemies
are and what they are planning. I pass on the facts to one key person
after another, and if we all have a clear view of the situation today,
we owe some of it to your efforts. Certainly you are accomplishing
more than if you were to kick over the traces and come out on our
side; you could never again go into Germany, or enter the drawing-
room at Cliveden, or meet people like that in France or the States."

"That's true," Lanny had to admit. "But just now the whole task
seems so immense—so hopeless."

"I'm tempted the same way," admitted the playwright; "but I shan't
give up to it, and neither must you. The house is on fire, and we don't

know whether we can get the people out, but we have to give the alarm, as loud as we can, and as often."

Said the son of Budd-Erling: "In New England they have a heavy iron ring the size of a wagon wheel; they hang it on a chain from a sort of scaffold, and when there's a fire they hit it with a blacksmith's hammer."

"Righto!" replied the other. "You're the chap who comes running with the hammer, and I'm the one who makes the racket. The townspeople are fat and lazy, and hate to have their dreams disturbed, but we keep on banging and little by little we rout some of them out."

IV

Margy, Dowager Countess Eversham-Watson, had been begging Beauty to come and spend a while with her, and Beauty wanted to take Frances, at least for a week-end. Irma and her mother had never got over their memories of the Lindbergh kidnaping, and the precious darling rarely went off the estate; but Lanny agreed to take her and bring her back, and since he possessed the legal right to do so, Irma had to be content with having the child's governess and the child's maid go along. The theory was that everything Frances could need was provided at Wickthorpe, but Lanny observed that nothing could take the place of the outside world; whenever the little one was taking any sort of trip, she was always wild with delight.

When Margy Petries of Kentucky had become the second wife of Lord Eversham-Watson, she had rebuilt and enlarged the mansion and renamed the place Bluegrass. When her husband known as "Bumbles" had died, Margy's stepson, the new heir to the title, had occupied the mansion, and Margy had built herself a villa on another part of the grounds. Beauty was to stay there along with Frances, while Lanny was to be a guest of the stepson, whom he had played with as a boy.

David Douglas Patrick Fitzgerald, seventh Lord Eversham-Watson, was a big, handsome fellow as his father had been; jovial, easy-going, and untroubled by intellect. An ardent sporting man, he had taken over the management of his father's racing stable, whose pure-blooded Kentucky horses had been one of Margy's contributions to the family prestige as well as to its exchequer. The books showed that they had won close to half a million pounds since the World War. Davy, as he was called, was pure-blooded English, but had always had Americans in his home, and delighted himself with American slang.

He was impressed by Lanny's attainments and liked to hear his stories, especially since the •report had got around that this art expert had become a pal of the Nazis One, Two, Three. Everybody wanted to hear about them right now while they were making such bally nuisances of themselves, and Davy had filled up the house with people who wanted to ask questions.

So Lanny spent a week-end in the society of England's "sporting set." Most important among them was a short little gentleman, old, almost doddering, with a fringe of white hair around a bald head and a little white mustache decorating a benevolent smiling mouth. "Old Portland" or "dear Portland" was the way everybody referred to him, for he took them back to what they believed was a kindlier age, when there had been no income and death duties. He had been a duke for more than sixty years and had been Queen Victoria's Master of the Hunt. William John Arthur Charles James Cavendish-Bentinck was his name, and he was K.C., P.C., G.C.V.O., Baron Balsover and Cirencester (pronounced Cizeter), Viscount Woodstock, Earl of Portland and Marquess of Titchfield. He had shot one thousand stags, been in at the kill of as many foxes, and had served ten thousand banquets. All in himself he was an era.

In boyhood Lanny had been taken by Margy and some of her friends to see the enormous Welbeck Abbey, home of this duke; it was in the Midlands, where he owned close to two hundred thousand acres, including coal lands and the sites of several villages. To a boy the most interesting fact was that the Duke's father had been possessed by a passion for building things underground; an underground ballroom a hundred and sixty feet long, an underground carriage road which took him secretly into his village of Worksop, a mile and a half away. He had a garden with ovens built into the walls so as to heat it and ripen fruit quickly; a skating rink for the maid-servants of the Abbey; a riding school with four thousand gas-jets to light it. A boy does not forget oddities like these.

You ran into them frequently in the ruling-class world of Britain. They were individualistic people, especially when they had a great deal of money; they did what they damned well pleased, and there was seldom any law against it. Some of them had come to New England, and their names had been Budd, and Lanny had learned about them and so was used to the idea of eccentricity. He knew there were dukes who set the fashion in clothes, and others who wore any old thing that pleased them. He had heard the great Duke of Norfolk tell a story on himself—how he had been strolling on the grounds of his estate, which he maintained as a park for the public, and had been rebuked by a member of that public for walking on the grass. "Can't you read? Don't you see that sign that says: 'Keep off the grass'? It's people like you that will cause this place to be closed to the rest of us!"

V

There was one of these ill-dressed noblemen among the company at Bluegrass. He appeared in a blue serge suit, worn shiny at the elbows and the seat of the pants, and a hat made of plaid cloth, of a shape known as "ratcatcher." When he dressed for dinner, his black tie was crooked. He had a thin nose, a wide mouth, and a mass of dark hair thrown to one side and having a tendency to fall over his left eye. He looked for all the world like a poet or painter from a Bloomsbury lodging house—of which he would soon own hundreds, perhaps even thousands.

His name was Hastings William Sackville Russell, and when his aged father died he would be twelfth Duke of Bedford, Marquess of Tavistock, Earl of Russell, Baron Russell of Thornhaugh and Baron Howland of Streatham. The father lived quite alone in a Bedfordshire mansion, and Lanny had heard that it was full of old masters, including eighteen Canalettos in a single room. He decided to cultivate the son for this reason, but the son told him it was no use; the old gentleman had sixty rooms ready for guests, and sixty more for himself, but he occupied only three or four, and preferred the company of giraffes and zebras, of which he had a herd. It had been his practice to drive the zebras in harness, and his park was given up to a great number of llamas from the Andes, with a fence around them and guards in green uniforms and cockaded hats to watch over them. Also he had lions and tigers and panthers and what not, and had had an armored train built so that he could drive among them in safety. He could afford to indulge such whims, because he owned large chunks of land on which the city of London had been built, and this land was "entailed"—that is, it couldn't be sold, but only leased, and was handed down to the eldest son.

Thus the Honorable Hastings William Sackville Russell had come honestly by eccentricity. He himself was a lover of birds, and had specialized in the breeding of beautiful parrots. He had been an army officer, but at the outbreak of the World War had decided that he was a pacifist, and had become dishwasher in a Y.M.C.A. canteen. He was still a pacifist, but of that peculiar kind like Senator Nye of

North Dakota, who seemed to except Hitler from his code. The Honorable was greatly interested in the Führer, and Lanny wondered if his haircut was intentionally identical with Adi's. A dozen other noble ladies and gentlemen sat and listened to the questions he asked, and the American was left in no doubt as to the contents of their minds. The familiar problems: Which was the less dangerous, the Brown ogre or the Red, and what were the prospects for getting the pair of them to kill each other off? Lanny thought of that German fairy tale about the little tailor who threw clods at the two sleeping giants and thus provoked them to terrible combat with each other.

VI

The visiting father drove his little daughter back to Wickthorpe, with the governess and maid in the rear seat. All the way the little one chattered about the good time she had had; the beautiful horses, the long-haired shepherd dogs, the kind and friendly people. She asked a string of questions, and again Lanny watched the miracle of a young mind unfolding, a character and a point of view in process of making. He would have liked nothing so much as to take her away and teach her what he believed to be the truth about the world she was to live in. But, alas, he wasn't free to speak a word of that truth, even to hint at it. When she asked about poor people, and why they were that way, what could he answer? If he said anything about the atrocious English land system, the two attendants would hear it and spread the news all over the castle. If he waited until he had the child alone, she would surely blurt it out to her mother: Papa says this, and Papa doesn't think that. He would be breaking faith with Irma, and she would feel it her duty to warn her husband: "Be careful what you say in Lanny's presence; he is still a Red at heart."

No, Frances Barnes Budd must have her mind so shaped that she could live under the English land system without any qualms of conscience. She must believe that by right of birth she was a superior being, entitled to draw off immense sums from the product of other people's labor, and that whenever she returned any of those sums to the people it was an act of benevolence for which they were dutybound to admire and even love her. There were kindhearted countesses and duchesses in England, and some who used their fortunes to carry on Be-Kind-to-Animals crusades. If an elderly white-haired lady leaped from her limousine to stop a carter from beating an old horse with a stick, it might be "Dear Portland's" wife, whom Frances had met at Bluegrass, and who had told her about the pit ponies of the miners which she allowed to fatten themselves on the meadows of her estate at Welbeck. Little Frances might be made into a Lady Bountiful like that; she was being trained by tutors and family to become the proper bride of some one of the great nobles of England, and the best that Lanny could hope was that she wouldn't happen upon one of the eccentrics.

It was a system which had endured since the battle of Hastings, a period of eight hundred and seventy-two years. The dukes and earls and barons were descendants of the Norman conquerors, while the miners and tenants were descendants of the Saxon losers. The two languages had become merged, but in the everyday speech you could recognize the differences between the two groups from a single sentence, sometimes from a word. If the English system had survived and spread all over the world, so that now the sun never set on it, the reason was that the governing classes had possessed the wisdom to yield when they had to, and to treat all conquered peoples with a share of generosity.

Lanny, reading history and watching the events of his time, decided that this was the difference between the British Empire and those which Hitler and Mussolini and Franco and the Son of Heaven were setting out to build. The British always took with them, wherever they went, a saving minority of dissidents, whereas the modern dictators shot theirs, or shut them up in concentration camps and suppressed their ideas. The British practice meant to Lanny that his little daughter had a chance to hear some humanitarian ideas—even without her father's intervention.

VII

The visitor made himself agreeable to the family and guests of this well-run household. English fashion, he was let alone and let everybody else alone. He took long walks, read books from an extensive library, and when the guests wanted music he played for them—nothing too long or too noisy, but properly selected *Salonmusik*. And whenever the occasion presented itself he listened to discussions of the Empire's affairs. He could hardly have chosen a better seat from which to view the procession of events, and to hear them interpreted by those who were directing them, or trying to.

Among other guests at the next week-end came an elderly gentleman who until recently had been plain Mr. Walter Runciman, but now had succeeded to the title of Baron. He was a tremendously rich shipowner and had been a member of the Asquith Cabinet. He had just been yachting at Cowes, where he had acquired a healthful coating of tan; but now the Prime Minister had summoned him and put upon him a duty, which Runciman himself whimsically described as being put adrift in a small boat in mid-Atlantic. He was one of those Englishmen with a wry sense of humor, the sort who read *Alice in Wonderland* and frequently quote it. His forehead was high and wrinkled, his round head visible with little interference from hair. His thin lips smiled frequently, but his eyes betrayed anxiety, for he was going to Prague, supposedly unofficially, but really to persuade the Czech government to assent to the settlement which the British Cabinet had worked out through Gerald Albany and other emissaries.

He had come to Wickthorpe to consult with Gerald and other persons familiar with the fine points of the negotiations. They didn't invite the son of Budd-Erling to their conferences, but they couldn't keep from dropping hints, and then Lord Runciman abandoned pretenses by drawing Lanny off into the library on Sunday afternoon and plying him with questions about the different Nazi leaders whom he might expect to encounter on his mission. Did Lanny by any chance know Henlein? Lanny replied that he didn't, but had heard much about this former bankclerk turned agitator; he told what he knew of such fanatics.

And Ribbentrop? Yes, Lanny had met him several times, but only casually. Doubtless Lord Runciman knew the story of how he had behaved when he had been appointed Ambassador to London; presented to the King, he had given the Nazi salute and exclaimed: *"Heil Hitler!"* The King had gazed at him in amazement, and twice more he had repeated the performance, apparently trying to force His Majesty to return or at least acknowledge the salute. He had been treated to the iciest of English frosts, and ever since then hatred of the country has been his principal diplomatic motive.

"Undoubtedly," said Lanny, "he is the Führer's most evil counselor. Göring is cautious, and pulls back on the reins whenever he can; but Ribbentrop is brash, and tireless in insisting that England will not fight, and cannot if she wishes. Unfortunately the champagne salesman is on top at present, so I am told."

"How can such a man be handled?" asked his lordship; and Lanny had to say: "I am afraid that the program of appeasement which you wish to promote is only likely to encourage his arrogance."

Impossible for anyone to ask questions like these and not betray the secret thoughts of his heart. What was apt to be Hitler's reaction to this proposal and to that? Manifestly, these were the proposals which Baron Runciman of Doxford had been commissioned to make; and before their talk was over he had pretty well abandoned the pretense that the details of the settlement were secret. The British Cabinet didn't want Hitler to get Skoda, for example; but they wanted to give him the mountains in which the Czechs had built fortifications from which alone the Bohemian plain could be defended. "Why," asked Lanny, "should a burglar take the trouble to break into a safe unless he means to carry off the treasure?"

VIII

Rosemary, Countess of Sandhaven, wrote a little note: "Why don't you come to see me, Lanny?" She had a right to ask, being one of his oldest friends, and he having been in the neighborhood for a month. He couldn't think of an excuse, so he went and had tea. How lovely she looked in a light summer dress, with those bold flowered patterns the women were wearing! They sat on a shaded terrace, with two big dogs sleeping at her feet, and drank their tea and chatted about families and friends, and what they had both been doing. Rosemary was interested in people, and events had a tendency to become personal when she talked about them, because she knew the persons who were making the events, and explained everything according to the persons' temperaments and desires.

She was a year older than Lanny, and had three nearly grown children, but showed none of the effects of age; her skin was as fair as when he had first known her, and her two ropes of straw-colored hair had never been cut, but were wound like a coronet about her head. She had taken good care of herself all these years, and had never engaged in any conflict with her fate. She was kind, gentle, serene, and to Lanny a boyhood dream. Her husband had other women, and she had let him go his way, according to the modern custom; she had always been easy-going in sexual matters. Why did Lanny stay away from her?

The political views he now professed were those which Rosemary took for granted, so they could have got along quite harmoniously. If he needed any particular item of information, she would have helped him to get it. They would have had to be what the world called "discreet," meeting in London and traveling together only on the Continent; their friends would have known about it, and no one would have been shocked save a few old-fashioned persons who did not count in their world. The arrangement would have been comfortable, and, from the world's point of view, sensible.

The wrong lay in the fact that Lanny had come to hate that rich and smart world; a parasitic group which didn't even know itself to be that, which hadn't enough brains to realize what it was costing the human race. Some day Lanny was going to break with that group, openly and completely; he couldn't foresee how or when, but meantime he didn't want to compromise with it in his soul, he didn't want to take any chance of weakening his inner resistance. To hold in his arms a woman whose ideas he despised was fair neither to the woman nor himself.

So, talk about the Budd-Erling business, in which Rosemary had a few shares of stock; about paintings which Bertie owned, and for which he wanted too much money; about the Runciman mission—Rosemary knew "Old Walter," as she called him, and said that he was a shrewd trader, for all his whimsical manner, and would probably come away with Ribbentrop's shirt. Rosemary knew the champagne salesman, too, and reported with a smile that he had tried to make a date with her the last time they had met. That had been at Cliveden, and Rosemary talked freely about the visitors there, and what they had said as to the importance of getting France away from the Russian alliance and into some kind of settlement with Germany.

All this was important to Lanny, and he wished the damned business of sex hadn't stood in the way. He had to think up an excuse that wouldn't hurt an old sweetheart's feelings, and on the spur of the moment he told her that he had found a happy love, but was under solemn pledge not to breathe a word about it. Of course that set her on edge with curiosity, but he stuck to his story: Not a word! He could soothe his qualms of conscience by telling himself that it was Trudi he meant. It was really the Trudi-ghost who stood between him and the Countess of Sandhaven.

IX

Lanny studied the newspapers, not only those of London, but those he got from Paris and Berlin. The Runciman mission arrived in Prague and was received at the railway station by the entire Czech Cabinet in top hats. The German papers did their best to make it appear an official effort at "mediation," despite Runciman's own insistence that he was "a purely private person." Also the Berlin papers were full of atrocities in the Sudeten—which meant that the Nazis were determined to have what they wanted, and were beating up the threat of war.

Hitler invited Admiral Horthy, the Hungarian dictator, made a secret pact with him, and showed him a review of the new German battle-fleet, a hundred and ten modern vessels, with the dreadnaught *Gneisenau* at their head. Then he put on a military parade which included huge field guns built so that they could be taken apart and the four parts carried on separate vehicles and reassembled in two hours. Hundreds of thousands of laborers rushed work on the Rhineland fortifications against France. There was a "trial mobilization" of trucks and motorcars, and a million Germans were reported under arms. *Deutschland über Alles!*

Zoltan Kertezsi arrived in London at this juncture. "Everybody" was out of town in late August, but he had some paintings to look at in a country house in East Riding, and Lanny drove him there. Zoltan himself didn't drive, and looked upon motorcars as dangerous toys; but he trusted Lanny, and they liked to be together. They had no end of shop to talk, and the Hungarian revealed that he had a nibble at a couple of Göring's paintings which Lanny had listed with him; he would have to see them, and how about Lanny's motoring him to Berlin?

The political pot seemed likely to boil over any day in Germany and it might be a good thing to be there. No doubt existed in Lanny's mind that Hitler was going to be presented with the western portions of Czechoslovakia, but the question remained, how long was he going to be content with them, and what would he take next, Prague or the Polish Corridor. This would be an important item of information for F.D.R., and Lanny would enjoy being the first to transmit it. It is that way with secret agents; they develop a competitive spirit, and number 103 wants to get ahead of his hundred and two rivals. Lanny said: "It's a date," and got a stenographer and sent off a batch of letters and cablegrams, informing his father and mother and various clients, including Feldmarschall Göring, that his address until further notice would be the Hotel Adlon.

There had been few months in Lanny Budd's life in the course of which he hadn't put his belongings into bags and stowed his bags into a car and driven to some other part of the earth. The procedure had become automatic, so that he could perform it while chatting, or meditating upon the problems of his own life and of the world. Indeed, he had developed two sections of his subconscious mind, one for Britain and the other for the continent of his birth and also for the land of his forefathers; he never forgot which place he was in and gave the wrong signal or got onto the wrong side of the road. It took a few moments' attention to enter a ferry on the left side and come off on the right, but once that was done it was as if a key had been turned, and the British section of Lanny's driving mind was locked away for the duration.

He never tired of rolling along the beautifully paved highways of France, Belgium, Holland, and so into Germany. The world became a panorama unwinding before his eyes; sometimes he noticed it in swift glances, sometimes it was absorbed into his subconscious mind through the skin, as it were. From years of experience he had learned where good food was to be had, and waited till he came to those places; the proprietors remembered and greeted him, and it was pleasant to let his eyes roll over a menu and his appetite indicate a choice. Yes, the world was a pleasant place in the year 1938—if you had looked out for yourself and put money in your purse, and refused to get into a dither over the troubles of the rest of mankind!

X

Arriving at his hotel, Lanny found an invitation from *Der Dicke* to visit him at Karinhall. He called up Furtwaengler and accepted, and at the same time arranged for Zoltan to view the paintings. If he had tried, he could have got an invitation for his colleague to Karinhall; but he didn't, because it was for him a business visit and its secrets could not be shared. The Hungarian was well content; he had affairs of his own, and would learn about *die grosse Welt* of the Nazis from his friend's lively accounts.

Lanny drove himself to the Schorfheide, and there was the fat *Nummer Zwei* and his fair lady, a trinity now, with a tiny baby girl who had been publicized all over Germany as an unprecedented achievement. Lanny, well-trained courtier, knew the proper ritual under such circumstances. He must ask and not wait to be invited to see this royal mite; he must cry out with pleasure the moment the sight burst upon his eyes; he must study every feature and debate whether it was derived from the father or the mother; he must overlook no charm which any of the three possessed, and must end by declaring that in all his experience with bundles fresh from heaven he had seen no one so promising of all the virtues. When he had completed this rite, with every evidence of intense sincerity, Karinhall would be his, and anything in it he chose to ask for.

What he wanted was no earthly treasure, but information, and he began by giving it in generous measure. What could be a better opening than to say that he had spent a week-end with a certain "purely private person," only a day or two before that person had set out on his purely public mission? Göring at once began to ply his visitor with questions. What sort of emissary was this, whose last act before leaving home had been a public prayer in Holy Trinity Church for the success of his mission? Did he really believe in that, or was it just politics in a land of *Dummköpfe*—blockheads? Was he really as rich as reported? He had brought his wife along, presumably to keep other women away from him. Did he drink or gamble, and was he fond of good food, or of money? And how did it happen that he had been prominent in the Liberal Party, but now was working with the Tories? A puzzling thing, this British political system!

XI

Once more it was proved that a man cannot ask questions without revealing what is on his mind. The fat Marshal betrayed to his visitor that behind the Nazi façade of bluff and defiance was a group of greatly confused men, sharply divided among themselves. Before Lanny departed from *Der Dicke's* country place, he managed to bring him to the point of frankness on the subject of Joachim von Ribbentrop; at least to the extent of stating that his country's Foreign Minister was a vain fool, a snob and a charlatan, an upstart, an intriguer, and a sycophant. He had become suddenly wealthy by marriage, and that eminence had gone to his head; he had managed to persuade the Führer by his glib tongue, and had been sent to England, where the aristocracy had twisted him around its finger—making him think that he, not they, controlled the foreign policy of the Empire, and that they were as clay in the potter's hands—a champagne potter!

"You know England, Lanny," said Göring. "Cliveden and Wickthorpe and the other country houses control up to a certain point, but nobody can ever be sure when the mob may rise up and force a reversal of their policy. It's like sailing a small boat on one of those Swiss lakes; everything is so peaceful and still, you think it's a washbasin; but suddenly comes the *bise* and upsets everything."

"I have seen it," replied Lanny.

He had been troubled in his conscience, for fear that he might have been agreeing too freely with the Nazis and thus giving them encouragement. It would be intolerable to think that by so much as a feather's weight he had helped to turn the scales in any of these re-current crises. Now he saw a chance to tip the scales his own way, and he hastened to agree with Göring's opinion of the English "mob"—its instability, its liability to sudden frenzies, and the cowardice of the most powerful political leaders in the face of such a storm. An irresponsible press and an unsubdued labor movement had almost broken the Tory policy over Abyssinia, and again over Spain; now they might easily do it over Czechoslovakia, and Germany would find itself at war with Britain, France, and Russia all at once.

"Give us two years more to get ready," lamented the head of the Air Force, "and we shall be beyond danger. But no, we cannot wait! Ribbentrop is there, like Mephistopheles, whispering into the Führer's ear, insinuating doubts as to the judgment and even the good faith of those of us who try to restrain him, who plead for a little more time. It is a terrible thing!"

Suddenly the great man had a bright idea. "Why don't you talk to him, Lanny?"

"*Me*, Hermann?"

"You know England better than any of us, and he knows that you do. Tell him what you have just told me."

Lanny hadn't really told very much; he had listened to what Göring told, and put in a few words of assent now and then. But it wouldn't do for him to cast doubts upon his own authority. He replied: "You know, it's not easy to talk to the Führer when his mind is made up. *He* does the talking!"

"I know; but his mind isn't made up yet; the thing is hanging in the balance. You might find him in a mood to ask questions. You are one of the few persons he can believe to be disinterested; you have never asked him for anything, and I have told him he can trust you, for I believe you are a good influence upon him."

"Thanks, Hermann. I'm always honored to meet him, because I know he's a great man. You would be interested to see how people everywhere crowd about to ask me questions about him—and about you also. You are looming large upon the world's horizon right now."

"Far too large," replied *Der Dicke*, who had not permitted his high station to destroy entirely his sense of humor. "I am going to have to take a reducing cure. But seriously; let me call the Führer and tell him you are here, and tell him you have talked with Runciman and Wickthorpe and others. He will wish to see you without any suggestion from me. He will probably tell me to have you flown to Berchtesgaden."

"I have my car here," the visitor reminded him.

"*Das macht nichts aus.* We will fly you back here, or send your car to Berlin, or to Berchtesgaden, wherever you prefer. This is a serious matter—the fate of Germany, and indeed of all Europe, may be hanging in the balance."

XII

So it came about that Lanny saw Germany from the extreme north to the extreme south, quite literally a bird's-eye view; a gigantic map unrolling, slowly, silently, except for the roar of a great motor. He sat in the co-pilot's seat, beside a very young Air Force Leutnant, one of the world's best, so *Der Dicke* had declared, patting them both on their backs after he had introduced them. "Take good care of him; he is the Führer's friend,"—so he had told the officer.

So now, through the interphone, the pilot in charge of Lanny's destiny for an hour or so entertained him with the names of cities, towns, and villages, rivers, lakes, canals, forests, mountains, airfields, great factories—every feature of the map below, whether natural or made by man. The greater part of Germany, as seen by a bird, looks like a checkerboard, but with no two squares alike. Different crops have different shades of green or brown or yellow at different seasons of the year; roads are tiny gray ribbons; buildings have only roofs, and these vary according to their materials, and whether they are wet or dry. Such details constitute an airman's life while he is in the sky, and while he is studying photographs, or maps on a briefing-room wall. When he learns that his passenger's father makes the fastest pursuit plane in the world, he gets a thrill and asks many questions, and mentions that the factories of his own land are just on the point of exceeding that record by ten or twenty kilometers per hour.

Lanny was set down expertly on the Führer's private airport, Ainring. A car was awaiting him, and again he was driven into those beautiful mountains. The earth had performed more than half its annual swing about the sun, and early March had become late August. The snow was gone, and the evil witch Berchta had retired to her cave; the landscape was arrayed in dark green, shiny with gleams of the sun; all the good fairies, gnomes, and little men who haunt the German forests were hiding under the fern-fronds, and a million bees were collecting honey for the Führer's table. They had to work overtime, since he, non-smoker and non-drinker, was extremely fond of sweets, especially when they were made into cream tarts or puffs or other delicacies, usually considered more suitable for ladies' palates.

That was one part of the meal he served Lanny at lunch; a much better meal than he had prepared for Schuschnigg on his visit—and surely better than that luckless wight was now getting in the castle where Hitler had him confined. No more proclamations about plebiscites from him; no more insolence over the radio, imitating in a mocking voice the Führer's peculiar modes of speech acquired in the Innviertel! The outside world hadn't heard much about the ex-Chancellor's fate, but Lanny knew that he had been united to his Countess Vera—by proxy, in a ceremony in which his brother took his place, and bride and bridegroom were not permitted to set eyes upon each other!

The master of the Berghof welcomed his guest cordially; but Lanny knew him well enough to perceive at once that he was under great tension. The whole place was on pins and needles, as the saying is; people coming and going, talking in whispers, and watching to be sure that nobody else was listening. Hess was there, and the first thing he said to Lanny was: "You should have brought Madame. She might have been very useful to us now." Lanny answered: "I was planning to consult Pröfenik, but I got whisked away in too great a hurry."

XIII

Right after lunch the Führer invited the guest to his study and seated him in one of those extremely modernistic chairs made out of light stainless metal. "Göring tells me that you have just come from England. Tell me what you found there; it is important for me."

Lanny complied tactfully, beginning with every favorable circumstance he could think of. The British ruling classes were tremendously impressed by the diplomatic skill which a man of the people was so unexpectedly displaying; the military people were awed by the quality of Germany's new armaments; the great industrialists envied him the *Ordnung und Zucht* which he had managed to impose upon German labor. Lanny told of the parade of Mosley followers he had seen in the streets of London; of the admiration for the Führer which had been expressed by highly placed noblemen and their heirs; of the eager questioning by Lord Runciman of Doxford. The Führer beamed, rubbed his thighs, slapped his knees, and gave every evidence that his vegetable plate and temperance beer were setting well upon his stomach.

But then—a *but!* "Of course that isn't all the story, Herr Reichskanzler"—and the great man's face began to fall. "Hermann thinks I should tell you both sides, because you have a grave decision to make, and it is not the part of friendship to withhold any facts."

"By all means, Herr Budd, tell me the worst. What are the difficulties you see?"

Lanny referred to the British press, which boasted itself "free," and understood by freedom the policy of publishing whatever was likely to arouse reader interest and increase sales. A highly competitive press, dominated by commercial motives; under the influence of the late Lord Northcliffe it had thrown dignity to the winds, and gone in for headlines and sensations. There were, of course, still responsible papers. The *Times*, called "the Thunderer," was now owned by Lord Astor, who was the Führer's friend; the same was true of Lord Beaverbrook, who owned the *Daily Express* and the *Evening Standard*, and of Lord Rothermere, Northcliffe's brother, who owned the *Daily Mail* and the *Evening News*, and had gone so far as to give his support to Mosley's Union of British Fascists. All these could be counted upon in any crisis; but there were other papers, able to make a great noise, which catered to labor, to what they called liberalism, democracy——

That was enough to set Adi off, as Lanny knew it would. For a solid half-hour without one pause he poured out his loathing of that licentious capitalistic press and that bastard "liberty" which permitted it to batten on the degradation of the public. It was Jewish-owned and Moscow-subsidized—both these facts the Führer could prove, and it was part of the hideous conspiracy to bolshevize Europe and the entire world. To the thwarting of that conspiracy the Führer had dedicated his life; for that purpose Divine Providence had sent him in this crisis. A complete speech, with all rhetorical stresses and gestures; it might have been delivered with éclat to seven hundred thousand Germans on the *Tempelhofer Feld*, or to seventy millions over the radio, but it was delivered to one American and four dead walls—unless there was a household listening, as in the case of the Schuschnigg tirade.

The orator stopped as suddenly as he had begun—this being his custom, as Lanny had learned. "I am doing all the talking," he said, "and you have information that I need. Please pardon me, and go on."

"The facts I tell you are deplorable, Exzellenz," replied the visitor, deprecatingly; "but you must know that I did not create them. There is no greater service that can be done to a master of men like yourself than to bring him the truth."

"Certainly, Herr Budd; I am not a child and have no wish to be treated as one. Tell me frankly, and be sure that I will consider it an act of friendship."

"What I have to say, Herr Reichskanzler, is that a large section of the British public appears to be in a nervous and excitable state at the present moment; ready to be played upon by any demagogue who tells them that you are not going to be satisfied to get back the territories which are preponderantly German, but that you are aiming at conquests. I don't meet persons of that way of thinking, so I can't say this at first hand, but I know that the governing classes are worried, fearing one of those storms of public emotion that arise, as suddenly as the *bise* on an Alpine lake. It is their prayer that you will make matters as easy for them as possible. Will you give them time, so that the changes can be made with order and by mutual agreement? That is the question I have been asked a score of times in England; and, of course, if you care to give me an answer, I will be happy to pass it on to the key people."

The Führer of all the Nazis couldn't take a thing like that sitting still. First he began to snap his fingers and then to jerk his arms; then he hopped up, and began to pace about. He would stop and start to interrupt, then choke back his words and force himself to listen, as he had promised to do. When he could endure no more, he burst out again, listing the humiliations and insults he had endured from the people and government of England over a period of years, indeed ever since he, the son of Alois Schicklgruber, had become aware of what was happening in the world.

The son of Budd-Erling knew that he wasn't doing himself any good by becoming the target of such a tirade, and at the first break in the deluge of words he exclaimed: "Remember, Exzellenz, I am an American, and you are not to hold it against me when I tell you about people in England."

The great man took this as the occasion to end the interview. "You are correct, Herr Budd. I have to give the historic process time to work itself out. You have done me a service, and be sure that I appreciate it, and hope that you will never hesitate to tell me the truth as you see it. Stay with me a while now, if you can spare the time, and let me ask you for more information."

XIV

That was handsome, and Lanny went to his room with hope that he might actually be helping to bring peace to Europe. This mood lasted for an hour or more; until there came a tap on his door, and there was Rudolf Hess, also seeking information. "The Führer is in one of his black moods. What on earth did you say to him, Herr Budd?"

So Lanny told his story all over again. He wasn't sure what was the personal attitude of Nazi Number Three toward Nazi Number Two, but he thought it proper to state that Marshal Göring had considered his information from England of such importance that the Führer ought to hear it. Hess, who had been raised among Englishmen and knew their ways, assented to this at once; the situation was critical, and it was important that someone should take the onus of pointing it out to the Führer, who didn't know the English people, their language or their literature, and so was in danger of misjudging their attitude. Lanny, groping his way in the mazes of court intrigue, was pleased to discover that Number Three agreed with Number Two, and shared his hatred of the champagne salesman, who had never had a number officially assigned him, but had apparently established himself as Number Four and doubtless had hopes of pushing upward.

The faithful Rudi took it as his duty to explain the greatest man in the world, whose servant and admirer he had been for most of his adult life. Der Führer was a man of action; when the time for action came, he moved with the swiftness of a charging lion, and those were the times when he was really himself. At other times he was restless and uncertain and a prey to many sorts of moods, some of them even suicidal—it was no secret that Hess had had a hard time keeping him from destroying himself after the failure of the *Putsch*, almost fifteen years ago. He was impatient of every sort of detail, and left it to Hess or others upon whom he had conferred authority; he rebuked them when they brought him problems, and told them that all he required of them was that they should succeed—otherwise they were of no use to him and would be replaced.

The prime necessity of his being was solitude. That was the meaning of the long walks in the forest; that was why he had chosen the Berghof, and why, since it had become a great establishment, he had built the eagle's nest on the Kehlstein, where no one could possibly get at him. He had to hearken to his inner voices; he had to give his *Genie* a chance to incubate in secret and give him guidance. For weeks at a time he would be brooding, inaccessible, irritated when anyone forced himself upon him.

"I am sorry if I have made things harder for you," said Lanny, considerately.

The Deputy answered: "Not at all, we are used to it; we have learned to adjust ourselves to the moods of an inspired leader." And then, after a pause: "As a matter of fact, the one who is going to catch it has not yet arrived. I'll not tell him of your part in the matter."

"Who is it?" inquired the visitor. "Ribbentrop?"

"No, Dr. Franck."

Lanny knew the name of Karl Hermann Franck as Henlein's Deputy Führer in the Sudeten. "What has he done?"

"He has taken upon himself to issue a proclamation, canceling the previous instructions to our people there that they should forego the right of self-defense for the present. Franck has told them that they should resist attacks by Marxist terrorists. Of course they should do that, but apparently it is premature, and interferes with something the Führer is planning. He is in a rage, and ordered me to telephone for Franck to be brought here by plane at once. I would not care to be in his boots."

XV

Thus duly forewarned, Lanny stayed in his room. But he took the liberty of leaving his door slightly ajar, according to the custom of the Berghof as he had learned it. When, later on, he heard shouting downstairs, he took his post just behind the door, the best place from which to get an earful—and surely he got it. Apparently the Führer was in such a fury that he didn't wait to have the unhappy Deputy brought up to his study; he rushed downstairs and met him in the entrance hall—which meant that everybody in the place could hear every word.

At the beginning there were a few breaks in the tirade; one could imagine the frightened official trying to interpose explanations or apologies. But after that there were no breaks; the Führer was yelling at him —and never in all his life had Lanny Budd heard such sounds coming from a human throat. The dressing-down of Gregor Strasser, even that of Schuschnigg, had been a summer's zephyr in comparison with this tornado. The unfortunate Herr Doktor was called *Sie Trottel, Sie verdammter Esel, Sie Schweinhund*—and when such ordinary German abuse wasn't adequate, he was called foul names known to the Innviertel yokels. He had exceeded his authority, he had threatened with utter ruin and collapse the Führer's careful policies of legality. Germany might be plunged into war overnight by his insane presumption, and he alone, *der lumpige, abgesetzte, unsägliche* Doktor Karl Hermann Franck would bear the responsibility for it all. A traitor to his Fatherland and his Führer, he deserved to be taken out onto the drive in

front of the Berghof and shot forthwith. Lanny heard the words
erschossen worden at least a dozen times during that lambasting, and
each time he could imagine a terrified wretch cringing and perhaps
falling down upon his knees.

That should have been enough from any master to any servant, so
thought the Anglo-Saxon; but it wasn't enough for a member of the
Herrenrasse. The screams went on increasing in intensity; they became those of a panther rather than of a human being. Lanny had long
ago decided upon "half-genius, half-madman" as a description of Adi
Schicklgruber, but now he shifted the proportions in his mind; he
began to wonder whether the Führer might not be physically attacking his victim, beating him with the horsewhip which for years he
had carried in Munich—though he had abandoned the custom some
time before taking public office. Lanny had heard from Hilde von
Donnerstein and others how Hitler was said to foam at the mouth
during such rages; his lips would turn blue and sweat would stream
down his face. Now it was easy to imagine these things happening.
Lanny was amazed by the ability of a human organism to endure such
protracted effort and strain.

There fell a sudden silence; really quite portentous, and Lanny wondered, had Adi strangled his victim, or had he himself fallen unconscious? Apparently it was the latter, for he heard people running, and
then he thought it proper to open his door and come out. He could
see the stairway, and watched while half a dozen secretaries and staff
members carried a heavy bundle upstairs and into the Führer's apartment. That was all the visitor heard for quite a while; he returned to
his room and shut the door, cherishing the hope that it might be an
apoplectic stroke, freeing Germany and Europe once for all of this
mad Mohammed.

But apparently it wasn't anything out of the usual. When the dinner-
gong sounded, Lanny came down, according to the rules, and here
came the Führer, freshly bathed, shaved, and dressed, smiling like any
well-bred host. The unfortunate Dr. Franck did not appear and was
not mentioned; Lanny was left to wonder whether he had been carried
off to Stadelheim prison, near Munich, where Lanny himself had been
shut up by an unfortunate mistake. But no, he was soon in the news
dispatches again, performing his Deputy's functions in the Sudetenland, but presumably with care not to exceed his authority.

Lanny played, at request, *Elizabeth's Prayer* and the *Pilgrims' Chorus*
from *Tannhäuser*, and then listened to Herr Kannenberg play the accordion and sing Bavarian peasant songs. Later he went to bed, telling

himself that he had helped to prolong the life of the Czechoslovak Republic—possibly for as long as twenty-four hours!

28

The Stars in Their Courses

I

L ANNY telephoned to Berlin, ordering his mail forwarded, and among the letters which came was one from Hilde von Donnerstein. She had a summer châlet on the Obersalzberg and invited him to visit there, adding that her mother was with her, so it would be quite *comme il faut*. The place was a good walk from the Berghof, if you liked hard climbing amid mountain scenery. Lanny paid her a call, and she took him to a summer house on a point of rock, from which you could see all around you, and make sure that nobody was eavesdropping on a shivery conversation. The Fürstin, who lived on gossip, wanted to hear the news about her many friends in England, including Irma, and in return she was ready to pay in kind.

The Führer of the Nazis lived in a glass house, it appeared. His servants told their sweethearts what was going on there, and even some of his secretaries and military aides were not above whispering secrets into one pair of ears. One pair was enough to keep the whole neighborhood informed; and furthermore, if you could believe Hilde, there were high-powered field glasses frequently trained upon that conspicuous house on the mountainside. Anyhow, Hilde knew all about the Dr. Franck episode, and was disappointed to learn that Lanny had been shut up in his room at the time. She knew, or professed to know, all about Geli Raubal, and half a dozen other young women whose happiness had been wrecked by the Führer's peculiar practices. She even knew what Juppchen Goebbels had said to Magda the last time she had come back from the Berghof.

More important to Lanny, some friend had told her what was going on in the Wilhelmstrasse. She knew about the acts of provocation in the Sudetenland, how they had been planned and how they were being handled in the press. She had heard who was going to be put in charge of Skoda when it was taken over—something that would surely be of interest to Baron Schneider! With a nervous glance around the landscape, and after swearing a guest of the Berghof to everlasting secrecy, she told about the recent visit of Count Ciano, Mussolini's son-in-law and Foreign Minister, who had listened to the Führer raving at the Czechs, and coming out, had thrown up his hands and exclaimed: "My God, that man believes his own atrocity stories!"

A curious phenomenon the visitor noted: this sophisticated lady, despising the crude men who had seized power in her country and willing to risk her family's safety for the pleasure of repeating smart gibes about them, was yet in her secret heart proud of what they had achieved. A cynical worldling, she was nevertheless a German. The Fatherland had to expand, she remarked, casually; they were a vigorous people, and had the misfortune to be penned up in a small territory, and shut off from the rest of the world by the British fleet. That fleet, the press reported, was about to flaunt its power in Germany's face by parading forty battleships in the North Sea; something which couldn't, by the widest stretch of words, be called courteous behavior.

Lanny was free to tell about his visits to Professor Pröfenik, omitting the Trudi part. The Fürstin said: "By the way, a friend of mine has just had an extraordinary experience with a young astrologer in Munich. Of course he doesn't call himself that, since it's against the law, but he will practice it for people he trusts. He told my friend the most amazing things about her past and her future—and some of the latter have already come true."

"I don't think much of astrology," answered the visitor. "I have never been able to find a rational basis for it."

"I know; but when things like this happen,"—and Hilde began a string of episodes, the sort of marvels that people tell, doubtless not always getting them quite straight.

The other said: "Hess believes devoutly in astrology. I wonder if he knows this man." He made note of the name, Reminescu—he was a Rumanian—and added: "Perhaps I'll give him a try. I know so many people who would like to have a look into the future right now!"

II

In the course of his dabbling in psychic matters Lanny had naturally met a number of believers in astrology. They studied elaborate charts of the twelve signs of the zodiac, and were firmly convinced that under whichever sign you had been born, your character and destiny were thereby determined. They would cast your horoscope and look enormously wise and speak a recondite and mystifying lingo. You could see on newsstands in London or New York a row of magazines, proving that there were great numbers of persons who believed in this ancient science or art and were willing to pay good money for it. The first time Lanny had heard about the subject had been as a boy, and he had asked the opinion of an old friend at Bienvenu, a retired Swiss diplomat, M. Rochambeau. This student of books and life had answered in words about as follows:

"You see a group of stars in the sky which suggests to you a certain shape, a scorpion or a lion, and you call that a constellation and give it a name. That pattern has not changed very much since the stars were first observed, and it was possible to imagine all sorts of mystical things about it—until modern high-powered telescopes revealed that the stars which make up Scorpio or Leo are millions of millions of miles apart and have no connection with one another, save that they exist in the same universe. It is as if you stood looking out of a window, and saw three flies on the pane of glass, and three leaves on a tree outside, and three birds in the sky and perhaps an airplane, and all these happened at some moment to make a figure, which looked to you like a coffin and suggested death, or like a shoe, perhaps, and suggested that you were going for a walk."

That had sufficed Lanny until long afterwards, when he had become convinced of the reality of telepathy and clairvoyance, and had been led to revise his thinking about all the practices called "occult." We know so little about how psychic phenomena are brought about, and what states of the conscious or the subconscious mind induce them. It might be that studying astrological charts, or the patterns of tea-leaves, or the lines in a person's hand, are forms of autosuggestion, of attaining concentration, of inducing mystical moods or feelings, which might cause some spark to fly, some energy to be released or diverted. Give it whatever name you please, the point is that these modern seers, or the ancients who had observed the flights of birds and the entrails of sacrificial beasts, may have found that they achieved some special mental state by such methods. The mere fact of believing ardently in bread pills has been known to cause some persons to recover from diseases.

So now, returning to the Berghof, Lanny talked with Rudolf Hess, and listened to his ideas about the stars in their courses which had fought against Sisera but now were fighting for Adolf Hitler and his

National Socialist German Workingmen's Party. Lanny remarked: "I have just been told about a remarkable fortune-teller in Munich, a young Rumanian by the name of Reminescu. Have you ever heard of him?" When the Nazi answered in the negative, Lanny said: "There are paintings I want to see in the city, and I might stop in and give him a try—if you don't mind my breaking the law."

"By all means go," replied the other, unsmiling. "We need all the guidance we can get in these critical days."

I I I

The outlawed interpreter of the stars had rented himself a rear parlor in a residential street which was gradually being converted to the uses of art and assignation. A small sign on the door described him as a "phrenologist," and his room was decorated with the customary charts of the head, and with framed letters from satisfied clients. A young woman answered the doorbell, then disappeared, and at once the astrologer came in. He was in his late twenties, Lanny guessed, a rather frail dark chap with sensitive features and a deprecating manner. He wore an ordinary dark business suit, and apparently went in for no hocus-pocus. When Lanny said that he wished to have his horoscope cast, and would promise to consider it strictly confidential, the other looked him over, and said: "You are a foreigner?" When Lanny replied: "Yes," he said: "My charge is ten marks." Lanny produced a bill and paid in advance.

Then began the usual rigmarole. The visitor gave the year, month, day of the month, and hour of his birth, according to what his mother had told him. The man produced his charts from a drawer and began conning them, making notes and calculations. Meantime Lanny watched him in silence, thinking: "He has Jewish blood,"—but one did not ask about that in Naziland. Lanny thought: "He looks worried and unhappy." He had been told that the Gestapo had all the mediums and psychics of the Fatherland on its list and was making life difficult for them.

Suddenly the man got up and moved a chair close to his visitor. "Would you mind if I held your hand for a while?"

Lanny consented and his hand was taken in one that was soft and warm, with delicate slender fingers. He did not look at Lanny's, but closed his eyes and was still. Lanny thought: "He does not trust his stars entirely." He wondered, as many times before, could there be vibrations of some obscure sort which passed from human hands, or from the brain? And if so, what was the sense that received them and interpreted them? Something happened, he was sure.

Suddenly the man remarked: "You are an American?" When Lanny replied, he added: "But I have a feeling that you were born very near here."

That was a bull's-eye, for Lanny had been born in Switzerland, a little more than a hundred miles from Munich. "Yes," he admitted, and the astrologer tried another shot. "The stars tell me that you were born rich, and have become richer."

That might perhaps have been inferred from Lanny's appearance and manner. He replied, discreetly: "Standards of wealth are decidedly relative." To this the other made no comment. Instead he remarked: "It appears that you have been married twice."

Now there were only four persons in the world who were supposed to know that secret: Nina and Rick, Monck, and the President of the United States. Even supposing that Reminescu had recognized Lanny, which was unlikely, how could he know about a secret marriage in England under assumed names?

Lanny took a chance and said: "Only once." The other shrugged his shoulders and replied: "I can only tell you what the stars report."

The client was curious enough to ask: "Will I marry again?" The answer was: "You may wish to, but I doubt if you will." Lanny thought: "Am I going to fall in love with the wrong woman again?" It had been his unfortunate habit.

The next statement came with the suddenness of a shot. "You will die in Hongkong."

As it happened, this remote city was little more than a name to Lanny Budd. He said: "I have no reason for ever going to that place that I can think of."

"You will find a reason," was the reply; "and you will die there. It is in the stars."

"I hope this will not be too soon."

The astrologer went back and studied his charts. Then he announced: "It will be when Saturn is in the constellation Taurus; somewhere between three and four years from now."

"I am not trying to be clever," replied Lanny. "I am sincerely interested in the possibility of precognition, and anxious to understand your methods. Suppose I were to accept your warning and were to refrain from going to Hongkong, would I not thereby cheat this destiny?"

"One does not cheat one's destiny. If you were destined to refrain from going, it would not be in the stars that you would go. There will be some reason for going that will seem to you important, and you will go."

Lanny smiled. "You should not labor too hard to convince me, otherwise you yourself might be thwarting the stars."

"If it were in my power to convince you, it would not be in the stars. You will not accept my warning, but will go away saying to yourself that it is nonsense."

"I'll surely remember it if I ever find myself on the way to Hong-kong!" was Lanny's wisecrack.

IV

That was supposed to be the end of the session; but the visitor wasn't satisfied. He had been intrigued by the statement that he had been married twice—though he couldn't discuss or even mention it. He took another ten-mark note from his pocket and laid it on the table. "I am very curious about this subject, Herr Reminescu. Could I make it worth your while to talk with me a bit longer?"

"Certainly, *mein Herr*. What can I tell you?"

"I am wondering just what part the stars play in your communications, and what part may be telepathy or clairvoyance or some other means. Do you generally hold your client's hand for a while?"

The younger man admitted that when the stars did not give him satisfactory guidance he got it by mysterious "hunches." He told a little about himself and his training, and Lanny in turn gave his name and identified himself as an art expert buying paintings in Munich. They took a liking to each other and chatted for a while—even though another client had arrived and was waiting. Lanny was about to leave, when the astrologer suddenly exclaimed: "Herr Budd, I wonder if I may trespass upon your kindness. I am in trouble, I fear, and greatly need advice."

"With pleasure," Lanny said, and resumed his seat; whereupon the other poured forth a story of difficulties with the German police. It wasn't his illegal profession; that called for only the payment of a little graft. It had been his practice to travel back and forth between Munich and Bucharest, having clients in both cities; and now the police were accusing him of having smuggled jewels out of Germany. Once, he admitted, he had carried a small package for a wealthy client, but he had had no idea what the package contained or that he was violating any regulation. He had been summoned three different times for questioning, and now they wouldn't give him an exit permit, but kept him in a state of anxiety for week after week.

This was a common enough story, and not the sort of thing that Lanny could afford to mix in. There was nothing in the possession of astrological science or of genuine psychic gifts that would keep a man from doing a little smuggling on the side, and of course if he had done it, he would earnestly insist that he hadn't known what he was doing. No doubt the very efficient Gestapo was watching him at this moment, and Lanny didn't want to get on their list as a suspected associate of a smuggling ring. He said:

"I am truly sorry to hear about your trouble, Herr Reminescu. I have no sort of influence with the German authorities, but there is one suggestion I can make. I happen to know a prominent person who is interested in astrology, and if you were to give him a convincing horoscope, or a séance, as you prefer, you might gain his friendship and then tell him your story as you have told it to me."

"Oh, Herr Budd," exclaimed the other, "I have no words to tell you my gratitude! When will this gentleman come, and what is his name?"

"He may prefer not to give his name, but to come anonymously, as I did. I will tell him the circumstances and it will be up to him to approach you in whatever way he sees fit."

"*Vielen, vielen Dank!* I beg you not to delay too long—for you know how the Nazi police are—they move swiftly and one can never know what to expect."

Lanny had an impulse to ask why the interpreter of the stars did not cast his own horoscope and find out whether he was going to die in Stadelheim prison or the Dachau concentration camp. But that wouldn't have been kind, and the son of Budd-Erling would always be kind wherever he had a free choice.

V

Lanny went back to his friend the Deputy Führer and reported: "That is a really extraordinary astrologer. He told me a number of remarkable things—and I'm sure he had no means of knowing my name or anything about me. He told me I'm going to die in Hongkong, and that really gave me quite a start, because I have an old schoolfriend who lives there, and has been begging me to take a trip around the world and pay him a visit. I had been thinking quite seriously of doing so—but now I guess I'll lay off!" Lanny had invented this Hongkong friend as a substitute for his second marriage, which he took as a genuine case of some sort of mind reading, but which he couldn't tell about.

"What you say interests me tremendously," replied the dark Deputy. "I have many questions I would like to ask of my destiny at this moment."

"You'd better not delay," ventured Lanny. "I had a chat with this fellow after he got through with my horoscope, and it seems he's in trouble with the police, and asked me for help."

"Because of his practicing his profession?"

"No; they suspect him of having smuggled some jewels out of the country. He tells a plausible story, but of course I have no means of guessing how true it is. I told him I couldn't have anything to do with a matter such as that, being a foreigner. But I said I had a friend who was prominent in Germany and deeply interested in astrology, and I would tell this friend about the case. Naturally I didn't give him your name or any hint of your identity, so you are free to do what you wish about the matter."

"Thank you, Herr Budd. Give me the man's name and address, and I will make inquiries, and perhaps pay him a visit—or maybe send him the necessary data and let him work over the problem. I am frightfully busy at the present moment."

"The time when you are busiest may be the time when you need help from the stars," remarked the philosopher-friend.

VI

As when two mighty wrestlers struggle upon a mat, locked in an unbreakable grip, heaving and straining, exerting the last ounce of their forces; gasping and panting, they sway this way and that, and their muscles stand out in great lumps, and the cords are as if breaking through the skin, and the veins swell and the eyeballs seem about to spring from their heads; still they increase their efforts, and it appears that one is slowly yielding, but he summons new forces and holds his own; the spectators of this contest catch their breaths, and sway this way and that with the contestants, sharing through the power of the imagination the agony of the effort and manifesting even the physical symptoms of strain: so now it was in the diplomatic arena of Europe, where the once beaten champion Antaeus-like had touched the earth and renewed his forces, and now was coming back for another bout in spite of all the betting odds against him, he being determined, single-hearted and singleminded, while his opponent, grown soft through ease, was confused in his thoughts and hesitant to use the powers which he possessed.

Lanny Budd was watching this international contest from a ringside seat. Telegraph keys clicked, telephone wires hummed, dispatch riders came on motorcycles, important visitors were brought in cars—and the sum total of these communications spread in semi-secret whispers all over the Berghof. Nobody had ever been more skillful at making friends than the son of Budd-Erling, and being an American, he was regarded as a neutral, even a sort of arbiter, a court of appeals, a person not bound by precedents and conventions. "You see what they do to us?" the court physician would say, when some Sudeten German got hurt in a tavern argument and Dr. Goebbels spread it over the front pages of all the newspapers of the Fatherland. "*Sehen Sie, Herr Budd!*" exclaimed the Führer himself. "I take your advice and try to be moderate, and they drive my people to desperation." The man who believed his own atrocity stories!

The Führer took a plane and flew to the town of Kehl, in the Rhineland, to inspect the new fortifications which he was rushing to completion, fronting the Maginot Line. Kehl—the name rang like a bell in Lanny's soul, for it was on that bridge over the Rhine that the Nazis had delivered to him what was left of Freddi Robin after they had got through tormenting him. Only four years ago, and how much water had flowed under that bridge—and how many of the hopes of Europe had flowed away forever! The Führer came back in a towering rage because the French were answering his visit by sending more troops to the border. What else he could have expected was a question that nobody was supposed to ask him.

Diplomats and "purely private persons" were flying back and forth between Prague and Berlin and Berchtesgaden and London and Paris. Henlein and Ribbentrop came to report to their Führer, and Lanny got a glimpse of them. Hess told him they had brought word of new proposals which the Czech government was making. These represented a painstaking effort to satisfy the Germans by giving them every sort of equality, political and educational, and full local self-government in all the cantons—the utmost that was consistent with the preservation of the Czechoslovak Republic's integrity. But that was precisely what the Nazis didn't want, because they didn't trust the Czechs, but regarded them as a lower race of beings.

What interested Lanny especially was the part which Lord Runciman of Doxford was playing in this diplomatic wrestling match. This "private person" with all the prestige of his powerful government behind him was engaged in extracting from Prague a series of concessions which would mean for all practical purposes the end of the republic and its democratic institutions. For one thing, they were to abolish free speech in the country—since it displeased Nazis to have Communists and Socialists and Jews telling the truth about what Nazis were doing. Also, the alliances with Russia and France were to be ended, and there were to be commercial treaties with Germany which would force Prague into economic dependence upon Berlin. These were the things the Nazis were determined upon having, and the noble English gentleman had given up his yachting at Cowes to come and make plain to a long-time ally of Britain that it had to surrender and become a slave of Germany.

VII

As soon as Lanny had made sure of this information, he told his friend Hess that he had some more art business in Munich, and would take the occasion to pay another visit to the Rumanian astrologer. He would stay overnight to attend a concert, he added, and put a bag and his little portable into his car and drove away. But he didn't go into Munich; making sure that he wasn't followed, he turned south, into the high mountains of Austria and thence up the Inn valley to the Swiss border. Across the upper Rhine he stopped at a little inn and got a room and went to work on his big story—two copies, one for Rick and one for Gus. Being afraid that his typing might have attracted attention, he drove to another Swiss town where he dropped the letters at the post office and quickly disappeared. Needless to say, his name was not on them, either inside or out.

Next morning he drove back to Munich, and late in the afternoon called at the office of the stargazer. The young woman answered the door, and the moment she saw him exclaimed: "*Ach, Herr Budd! Die Polizei!*" Her manner was distraught and her face full of fear—which might have been for herself as well as for her employer.

Lanny said nothing until he had come into the room and closed the door. Then: "Tell me what has happened."

"Two Gestapo men came the day before yesterday and took him away, and that is all I know."

"They didn't say what the charge was?"

"They went upstairs to let him pack a bag. I didn't hear what they said up there. They said nothing to me and of course I was afraid to speak."

"You haven't made any inquiry?"

"*Du lieber Gott!* What could I hope for, except to get myself arrested too?"

Lanny told her: "I will make inquiries and see if I can find out anything." With that he excused himself and took his departure.

VIII

But he got only as far as his car. Just as he was in the act of stepping in, a taxicab hove into sight and drew up at the curb. Out of it stepped the astrologer, with a suitcase in his hand. "*Grüss' Gott, Herr Budd!*" he exclaimed. He paid the driver, and then turned to Lanny. "*Um Gottes willen, kommen Sie herein!*"

They went into the house, Reminescu using his key. He greeted the woman casually—his thoughts entirely on Lanny. Shut up in the room he sank onto a couch, exclaiming: "*Jesus Christus!*"—and took out a handkerchief and wiped his forehead. "*Was für ein Erlebnis!*"

"I hope they didn't treat you too badly," said Lanny, by way of being co-operative.

"They treated me as if I were Paracelsus, Pythagoras, and Trismegistus rolled into one," replied the astrologer. "But God preserve me from such hospitality in future!"

"Tell me about it," suggested the visitor, not embarrassed to reveal curiosity.

The still agitated young man lighted a cigarette and took a couple of quick puffs, then began a curious tale. "Two Gestapo men came, the day before yesterday, and ordered me to come with them, no questions asked. 'Bring all your charts and books,' they said, so I packed them up. They took me, of all places on earth, to the Vier Jahreszeiten Hotel, which I am told is now run by the Gestapo. I had a most elegant suite, with Cupids on the ceiling, and a Death's Head SS Major or something saluting me respectfully. 'My apologies, Herr Reminescu; I am carrying out orders from above. It is desired that you should prepare horoscopes for certain important persons. While you are doing this, you will be my guest, and will be supplied with anything within reason that you care to order. No harm will be done you, but unfortunately it will be necessary for you to remain in this suite until the work has been completed. I will put before you the birth data of twelve persons and when your work is done, I will have it delivered, and if it is found satisfactory you will be paid two hundred and fifty marks, and will receive the exit permit which I understand you have applied for.' Did you ever hear anything to equal that, Herr Budd?"

Lanny had to admit that it was a novelty in his experience.

"So, there is a typewritten list, and I spread out my charts and go to work. Such meals as I have never eaten, and such a soft bed with embroidered linen coverlets as I have never seen outside of a museum; and cigarettes, champagne, brandy—truly, I lived like the Shah of Persia, or maybe the Maharajah of Indore. But there I sit, and shivers run all over me, and the sweat stands out on my forehead, and I hardly dare to breathe; for I have run my eyes over the birth dates, and I dare not tell you what I see."

"I can guess, if you will permit me," smiled Lanny.

The other gazed about anxiously; then in a whisper: "*Bitte, sprechen Sie leise!*"

Lanny, replying in a whisper: "April 20, 1889." The other nodded, and fear melted the bones of both, for that was the day when a last and least satisfactory son had been born to the Braunau customs officer Alois Schicklgruber who had changed his name to Hitler.

"It would not be fair to ask me what the stars told me, or what I wrote down," murmured the astrologer, and the visitor replied: "I have not asked you."

After a few moments, Lanny went on: "Do you remember the other dates?"

"They took the list from me, but of course they could not take it from my mind. However, I would not dare give them to you, and it might be very dangerous for you to possess them."

"Quite possibly, Herr Reminescu. And you may be sure I will keep your secret, at least until you are safe in your homeland. I take it, your presence indicates that you managed to please the higher powers."

"I did my best, and the twelve horoscopes were taken away early this morning. A short while ago the officer came and informed me that the work was all right, but that some further questions were to be asked. He had these in writing and I wrote the answers on the same sheet; then he paid me the money and told me that I was free, and that my exit visa would be sent to me. So here I am, and I wait. Do you suppose they will really send it?"

"I do not know, my friend; but if I were in your place I would not mention this experience to anyone else. It happens that I am good at keeping secrets. I have an idea that what has happened was a result of my effort to assist you, and I think I had better not try any further.

I will just say that you were indisposed and unable to do any work for me today. Let me give you my home address in France, so that you can write me and we shall not lose touch with each other. Don't write it down, it is easy to remember."

The stargazer said that his memory was good, and Lanny told him: "Juan-les-Pins, Alpes Maritimes, France." Then they shook hands warmly and parted forever.

IX

Everybody in the Berghof who was entitled to have an opinion of the diplomatic situation wanted to discuss it with Lanny Budd. They had discovered that he knew practically everybody they could mention in England and France; so he found himself once more in the position which he had occupied at the Paris Peace Conference, an interpreter not merely of languages, but of personalities and national characteristics—of manners, climates, councils, governments, himself not least but honored of them all. Word had got about somehow that he considered the British populace to be in a pathological condition, and officers of the household, young Nazis who had been reared upon the idea of the Führer's infallibility, would stop suddenly in the midst of their vaunting and look at Lanny uneasily and ask: "Can it really be so in Britain? How can there be a great nation without any authority, without somebody who knows what it is going to do?"

It seemed to them a most dangerous thing, every bit as bad as Jew-Bolshevism, and indeed the same thing in subtle disguise. The Nazis were going to end it some day, and the only question was when and how? If the possibility occurred to them that they might be moving too fast and running into danger, they would dismiss it from their minds; for of course the Führer would know, the Führer was always right. How could it be possible that the British would be so foolish as to risk defying the German Air Force? And for such a political monstrosity as Czechoslovakia? *Unsinn!*

Adi himself was confronting one of the great decisions of his life; one which might lead him to triumph, or wreck everything he had accomplished thus far. He was in a continuing nervous crisis, and members of his staff kept out of his way when they could. His agency of communication with Lanny was Hess, who would ask this and that about Runciman and Chamberlain and Sir Nevile Henderson, the British Ambassador in Berlin. Once he inquired whether it might be possible for Madame to come to the Berghof again. Unfortunately Madame was laid up with the flu at Bienvenu, and could not travel, even to help determine the fate of Europe.

There came a royal command: Herr Budd was to take a motor ride with the Führer, late in the afternoon, the time when the great man usually went walking with his dogs and his *daimon*. This time he and his guest rode in the back seat, and a staff member in the front beside the chauffeur. They took a road which wound up a mountainside by a series of hairpin turns, and Lanny realized quickly what road this was. "I see you don't forget your promises, Herr Reichskanzler," he ventured, and the reply was: "*Niemals.*"

They were climbing the Kehlstein; but within about five hundred feet of the top the road swung suddenly straight into the mountainside. There was a great bronze door, apparently operated by an electric eye, for it began to swing back, disclosing a grotto, carved out of the solid rock, a chamber paved and walled with concrete, large enough for several cars to enter and turn in. Indirect lighting flooded the place with a warm glow, and when Lanny descended from the car he saw at the far end another bronze door, which also opened automatically. He entered an elevator, large enough to accommodate eighteen persons; but this time only two rode. The Führer pressed a button, and they stood in silence while traveling upward through the heart of a mountain.

When the doors opened, they stepped into a large living room, part of a villa with bedroom, small kitchen, and rooms for two attendants, perched on the very top of a mountain, entirely invisible except from the air. Around it was a terrace from which you looked over what seemed to be all the mountains of Europe: a relief map of deep depressions and swelling protuberances; a study in deep greens, flecked with the bright blue of little lakes and the varied color of villages in the valleys and residences along the slopes. Lanny gazed, and cried several times: "*Herrlich! Herrlich!*"

Adi Schicklgruber, one-time *Gefreite*, had created this and owned it, and the idea that he should not be proud of it was one that had never occurred to him. His heart swelled, and the deepest chords of his soul began to vibrate—his love of the mountains and forests, of music, of the *Herrenvolk* and of his own rulership. He heard those grand open chords by which the Nordic gods ascend over a rainbow to Valhalla; he heard the music of the forging of Siegfried's sword: "*Nothung, Nothung, neidliches Schwert!*" How could a people who had such music calling them to glory ever fail of their destiny?

X

They sat in two striped canvas chairs and watched the sun go down in an explosion of gold and pink, changing to deep red and then to pale violet. Said the Führer of the Nazis: "That is the capitalistic era dying before your eyes. People think that I mean only the National half of my party's name, but believe me, I am not through giving the world surprises. Before I finish, I mean to keep every promise I have ever made."

"I believe it, Exzellenz. I lack the power to read that future in the stars, but I watch day by day to see it happen."

This was a trap Lanny was setting, and his host's foot slipped into it immediately. "Tell me, Herr Budd, do you believe in the influence of the stars upon human destiny?"

"It has always been a problem with me, Herr Reichskanzler. I cannot find any basis in scientific theory, yet it has happened to me to have astonishing predictions made, and to see them come true. The same thing has happened to friends of mine, and I am forced to conclude that there are powers which I do not understand. Just the other day, for example, I went quite casually to a young astrologer in Munich and had him cast my horoscope for me. I am sure he did not know me from Adam, and the things he told me could not possibly be guesswork."

"Tell me about them."

"Well, at the outset he told me that I was an American, but had been born near Munich. It does not happen that many Americans are born in Switzerland, and I am sure I do not carry on my person any signs that I did not enter the world at my mother's home on the Riviera or my father's in Connecticut."

Lanny went on to tell the wonder story which he had partly made up about Hongkong; and it was to be expected that the Führer should display curiosity concerning so capable an astrologer: his name, his age, his personal appearance, his character, so far as Lanny had formed an opinion. "Some of my friends are interested in this subject, and might wish to consult him," explained the great man; and Lanny accepted this tactfully. He wondered: Was Reminescu being considered for a court position? And if that fate fell on him, would he be invited or commanded?

But no, it wasn't that! The Führer of all the Germans had had a horoscope cast, and was trying to make up his mind to what extent he could trust it. In this most dangerous crisis, before which his innermost soul quailed, he needed the help of supernormal powers; but it was so hard to know when you were getting such help, and when you were being victimized by some shrewd self-seeker!

"My own attitude toward these so-called occult matters is very much like your own, Herr Budd. I have seen things which I cannot explain; but I dare not trust the practitioners, because there is so much deliberate trickery, and because even the honest ones might avoid telling me the truth, for fear of displeasing me."

"So!" thought Lanny. "Reminescu has given you a favorable horoscope and you want to believe it!"

Adi was going on: "In matters such as these I have had to learn to trust my own inner voices—intuitions, I suppose is the word to call them. I wait, I listen to all advice, I consider all the factors involved—and then suddenly it is as if an inner light were switched on, and everything becomes clear before my eyes. That is the moment to act, and I never permit myself to hesitate."

"That, Exzellenz, is what the world has agreed to call genius."

It was like touching the button which caused the elevator to rise through the heart of the Kehlstein. Adolf Hitler began to talk about genius. He discussed Richard Wagner, the greatest musician who had ever lived. He discussed Karl Haushofer, the greatest scientist, fortunately still living. He named Napoleon as a military and Bismarck as a political genius. Before long he was explaining the difficulty of combining these various kinds into one. That was something that happened only once in a thousand years or so, and when it did it meant a new epoch in human history. Such an epoch was now in process of being made by himself, the creator of the NSDAP.

The son of Alois Schicklgruber didn't apologize for saying this; he stated it in a matter-of-fact way, because it was the truth, and he always spoke the truth—excepting of course in political matters, where it was necessary to rear elaborate structures of pretense. But here, in the presence of a trusted friend, the former inmate of the home for the shelterless of Vienna told what had been revealed to him by that energizing spirit which dwelt in the deeps of his personality. Outwardly a soft-fleshed, rather flabby man with a bulbous nose and futile small mustache, he saw himself in his soul's mirror as a heroic figure in shining armor, and was carried away by this sublime vision. Standing bareheaded beneath the first pale stars of a twilight sky, he pointed to them and exclaimed: "You, heavenly bodies, once controlled the destinies of men! But now a man has come who will determine his own course, and —who can say?—perhaps, before he has finished, he may determine your courses as well!"

XI

Hess had invited Lanny to be his guest at the Parteitag, the tremendous week-long orgy of racialism and reaction which the Nazi chieftains prepared for their subordinates early in September of each year. It was held in the ancient city of Nuremberg, a hundred or more miles north of Munich. It offered no joys to a secret agent, but many opportunities to meet the Party leaders and hear their purposes revealed; so he accepted gladly.

Since many persons were going from the Berghof, he volunteered to take some members of the household in his car. Thus he enjoyed for several hours the society of three young SS patriots who had never known any other creed or code save that which the Party had taught them. They held rather fantastic ideas about the world outside, and became confidential and revealed to their host the opinion of the Berghof concerning himself—that he must be the person whom the Führer had picked out to become the *Gauleiter* of the North American continent. Manifestly, he had all the qualifications, and what else could be the reason for the favors showered upon an *Ausländer?*

The nine-century-old city has narrow and crooked streets and seems like a Grimm's fairy-story town of houses with high-pitched roofs, peaked gables, and chimney pots; churches with tall spires and every sort of Gothic exuberance; a five-cornered tower with the "iron maiden" and other instruments of torture on exhibition. Now its population of four hundred thousand was multiplied several fold by the swarms of Party leaders of every rank who arrived by train and bus and automobile. Whole tent cities had been erected on the outskirts of the town and army cooking outfits served millions of hot meals each day. Everything had been attended to with German thoroughness; the flags in the streets were like the leaves of a forest, and everywhere were bands of music and uniformed marching men with standards and banners.

Outside the city, on the immense Zeppelin field, had been prepared a breathtaking spectacle. Adolf Hitler, one of the world's greatest showmen, had been working on this for a decade and a half, rehearsing it each year and making improvements. Decorations and scenery like a Wagnerian opera, solemnity and holiness like a Catholic high mass; an appeal to every primitive sentiment, every memory dear to the hearts of the Germans in those dark forests where they had lived through the centuries while preparing for the conquest of the ancient Roman empire. It was Hitler who had devised the ceremony of calling the roll of martyrs, which Rudolf Hess performed early at each Party assembly. It was Hitler who had devised the mystical rite of the dedication of the flags, and he himself performed it, walking down the rows of flags and solemnly touching each with the sacred *Blutfahne*, the flag which had been carried in the Beerhall Putsch of fifteen years ago and was stained with the blood shed in that fight.

Blood was a sacred thing in the German mythology. It was the noblest and best blood in the world, and Germans shed it in battle, not merely for the protection of the Fatherland, but for the extension of its borders, so that there might be more Germans with more of the sacred blood in hearts, arteries, and veins. *Blut und Boden*—blood and soil—was the slogan. The ancient German warrier who died in battle was carried off to Valhalla, and that was a glorious death, whereas to die in bed was ignoble and disgraceful. The Führer was reviving all these ancient barbaric emotions, and his marching legions chanted incessantly about blood and iron and war. "Rise up in arms to battle, for to battle we are born!" The old German God was a God of war, who could never get enough of blood. And now was the time of times, as His favorite new song, *Deutschland, Erwache*, proclaimed. "Storm, storm, storm, storm! From the tower peal bells of alarm!"

XII

Lanny walked about the streets of this romantic old city, home of the Meistersinger, of Dürer and other great artists, now swarming with hordes of red-faced and sweating male creatures with fanaticism in their faces and rage in their hearts, the *furor Teutonicus* which the ancient Romans had dreaded. It made the American rather sick at heart, for he hated war and cruelty, he hated hatred—and these men had been brought up on it, they had been taught it systematically, with all the skill which modern science had put at the service of the teachers. All the arts of the psychologist and the advertising expert had been applied to the inculcation of fanaticism—one of Hitler's favorite words, rarely missing from any speech however brief. ·

Physically Lanny was made as comfortable as a man could expect to be on such an abnormal occasion. He was put up at the Deutscher Hof, the rendezvous of the Party great ones. At the meetings he had a reserved seat among the distinguished guests, which included the diplomats from all countries of the earth. For eight days he was deluged with Nazi oratory, conveyed to his ears by means of bellowing loudspeakers. The keynote was set in the opening proclamation, read for the Führer: "Party comrades! More threatening than ever, Bolshevist danger of the destruction of nations rises above the world. A thousand-fold, we see the activities of the Jewish virus in this world pest!"

Monday, Tuesday, Wednesday, Thursday, Friday—five days of incessant hate oratory, with the crashing of bands, the mass singing of songs, the parading of flags and banners. On Friday night, amid the glare of klieg lights in one of the enormous halls which had been constructed for these meetings, Lanny heard the Führer address a hundred and eighty thousand of his Party leaders of all ranks, and tell them: "At a time when there are clouds on the horizon, I see about me those millions of unflinching, nay fanatical, National Socialists, whose leadership you constitute and for whose leadership you are responsible. Just as I could rely blindly upon you in the days of our struggle, so today Germany and I can depend upon you."

And next day Feldmarschall Göring addressed the leaders of the Arbeitsfront, the Nazi labor battalions. To Lanny Budd, at the hotel where they stayed, he had expressed the same desire for caution and legality as in Karinhall, but under the influence of the crowd and the bright lights he lost his head and raved and bellowed for an hour and a half. He told them how he had saved up food for war and had conscripted labor to complete the *Westwall;* they might have to work ten hours a day for the glory of the Reich. "Our arms industries are going at high pressure in every branch." Referring to his Czechish neighbors he said: "This miserable pigmy race without culture—no one knows where it came from—is oppressing a cultured people and behind it is Moscow and the eternal mask of the Jew Devil." Lanny did not have a chance to ask *Der Dicke* about this sudden change of mood, for when he inquired at the hotel afterwards he learned that the old-style robber baron had been overcome by the violence of his efforts, and had been carried off to the country to recuperate from bronchitis and inflamed legs.

XIII

But the secret agent had plenty of chances to confer with other leaders and listen to their conversation among themselves; he made sure that one and all they were expecting to take over not merely the Sudeten districts but the whole of the Czechoslovak Republic. He heard Foreign Minister von Ribbentrop make statements on this subject which seemed to him so important that he was tempted to bolt to the French border and send off a report to Washington and The Reaches without delay. But such a move might excite suspicion—it would be inconceivable to Hess, to say nothing of the Führer himself, that anybody could leave Nuremberg just before the Führer's closing speech for which all Europe was waiting as for a blast from Gabriel's trumpet.

So Lanny stayed and heard that speech, delivered before what was said to be the largest number of human beings ever assembled in one place—well over a million, and claimed to be more. From the outskirts of the crowd on the Zeppelin field the Führer of the Germans must have seemed a tiny pin-point figure, but by the magic of modern electro-acoustics he had a voice like thunder in the mountains. Over the ether waves it was carried to the whole earth, and few indeed must have been the places where civilized men did not hearken. At the end of every two or three sentences the auditors would hear the wild-beast roar of that mighty assemblage: *"Sieg heil! Sieg heil! Sieg heil!"*

As usual when Adi had a great occasion, he talked at great length. As always, he recited the grievances of the German people; as always, he denounced the Bolsheviks and the Jews; as always, he stormed and threatened at all his foes. It was his purpose to terrify Europe, and especially the statesmen of Czechoslovakia and its allies, Britain and France. Of the Sudeten people he said: "These Germans, too, are creatures of God. The Almighty did not create them that they should be surrendered by a State construction made at Versailles to a foreign power that is hateful to them. . . . They are being oppressed in an inhuman and intolerable manner . . . brutally struck . . . terrorized or maltreated . . . pursued like wild beasts for every expression of their national life." Count Ciano, if he was listening, must have thrown up his hands again.

Adi went on to tell the world what he was doing to protect these Germans; building along the Rhine "the most gigantic fortifications that ever existed." He continued: "On the construction of the defenses there are now 278,000 workmen in Dr. Todt's army. In addition, there are, further, 84,000 workmen and 100,000 men of the labor service as well as numerous engineer and infantry battalions. . . . These most gigantic efforts of all times have been made at my request in the interest of peace. . . . The Germans of Czechoslovakia are neither deserted nor defenseless. . . . We all have a duty never again to bow to a foreign will. May this be our pledge, so help us God!"

XIV

Lanny would have liked to leave right after that meeting and drive all night to the border; but even that might have been dangerous. He had to sit up for hours and discuss the speech with a crowd of excited henchmen; drink beer with them, apologize for his lack of capacity, and endeavor in other ways to justify their idea of him as the future Gauleiter of the North American continent. In the morning he had to thank his host and request him to convey to a busy Führer the guest's compliments upon a magnificent and clear oration. Lanny explained briefly that he was off on a picture deal, and would return to Munich in short order to consult the astrologer and see what further light the stars might throw upon the future of the National-Socialist movement.

At last Lanny was free—as a bird on the wing, or as a motorcar on one of the *Autobahnen* constructed by Dr. Todt's army. Straight to the border at Kehl, where recently the Führer had viewed the most gigantic fortifications that ever existed. The son of Budd-Erling was not invited to view them, but no tourist passing through could fail to see the labors in process on the near-by heights, to hear the rumble of machinery and note the heavy traffic through the town. A hundred and sixty-eight years earlier it had been a tiny village, and in early spring a great cavalcade had arrived there, having traveled all the way from Vienna to bring the fifteen-year-old princess, Marie Antoinette, to marry the future king of France. There had been no bridge then, and several hundred heavy vehicles had had to be ferried across the river Rhine to the old cathedral city of Strasbourg.

Once again the secret agent presented himself at the barrier of the bridge. His papers were in order and he drove onto French soil. He did not go to the Ville de Paris hotel, because he was afraid somebody might remember his stay with Freddi Robin. He put up at the Maison Rouge, locked himself in a room, set up his little typewriter, and went to work to do what one man could to help Britain and America to realize their peril. Adolf Hitler, guided by his own mad *daimon* and egged on by the wounded vanity of Joachim von Ribbentrop, did not mean to rest until he had abolished democratic institutions from the soil of Europe. Said Lanny Budd, in his closing words: "He has the definite purpose not to leave, anywhere in the world, one single person free to criticize his party or his program."

29

The Hurt That Honor Feels

I

LANNY was sick of the Nazis; of the sight of them marching in uniform, the sound of them yelling and singing, the smell of them in closely packed mobs. He wanted nothing so much as to get into his car and drive to Bienvenu, to a studio in a quiet garden facing the sunsets. There was a piano, there were paintings on the walls and a couple of thousand well-selected books on shelves. The water would still be warm for swimming; he could go fishing with Jerry Pendleton, play tennis, and perhaps persuade Nina and Rick to come for a visit, take them sailing, and talk over old times.

But the Trudi-ghost said No. He had promised to help in keeping the underground alive, and in keeping the people of France and Britain from falling under the spell of the bad witch Berchta and her flock of sheep in human form. Regardless of his own happiness, he had to go on earning money and distributing it where it would count, and supplying Rick with information instead of tempting him to holidays. Also, that job he had undertaken at Hyde Park, a little more than a year ago. What excuse could he give F.D.R. for not watching the events that were shaking the world?

He got the London and Paris and Berlin newspapers. Two hundred thousand troops of the Wehrmacht had been moved to the Austrian frontier, facing Czechoslovakia; that country was shaped like a badly stuffed sausage, and the heavily motorized army, facing the middle of it, could cut it in half in a single day. They had done it to Austria, and all Adi had to do was to say the word and they would do it again.

All over the Sudetenland Nazis were attacking Czech public buildings and stoning Czech policemen; and this could only be under orders, its purpose being to work up feeling in Germany and justify the Führer in his next move. The French were mobilizing—could that be the rumble of camions and tanks which Lanny heard in the night under the windows of the Hotel Maison Rouge? If the war started,

Strasbourg would be one of the first points at which the Germans would strike, repeating the air smash they had rehearsed so thoroughly at Guernica and Barcelona and Valencia and Madrid. They might do it without any warning, a new technique called *Blitzkrieg* which Göring and his staff talked about freely. Make up your mind, Lanny! East or west doesn't matter—any place but No Man's Land between the two marshaling hosts!

<h1 style="text-align:center">II</h1>

He had left Zoltan in Berlin, promising to get in touch with him as soon as the visit to Berchtesgaden was ended. They had talked about paintings in Munich for which they might find purchasers; they would help each other and divide the commissions. Now Lanny telephoned, saying: "I can be in Munich this evening." The other replied: "I will take the night train."

The secret agent packed his belongings, paid his bill, and set out. Not wishing to attract attention to himself, he drove down the Rhine on the French side and crossed into Germany by the first ferry. To Munich was a couple of hundred miles, a pleasant day's drive, with time off for a leisurely lunch, and stops to look at the Black Forest and admire the snow-clad Alps from their foothills. In between these pleasures the traveler meditated upon the state of the world, and now and then turned on the radio to hear "spot news" of Europe's impending crisis.

The ex-bankclerk Henlein had decided to settle the problem by direct action. His followers had been plundering Jewish shops, and the Czech government had declared martial law. That Wednesday morning Henlein issued an ultimatum, demanding the withdrawal of Czech troops and police from the Sudetenland; when the government paid no attention to this challenge, his Stormtroopers attempted to seize barracks and public buildings, using hand grenades, machine guns, and even tanks which they had brought in from the Fatherland. Fighting went on all that day, and one or two hundred men were killed on each side; but the Czech government stood firm. By suppertime, when Lanny reached Munich, even the Nazi radios had to admit that the *Putsch* had failed. The Henleinists were everywhere in flight into Germany, where the Nazis hailed them as heroes and martyrs, and denounced the Czechs as terrorists and murderers.

Lanny didn't have any uncertainty as to the meaning of such a series of events. He could be sure that Henlein, and his Deputy, the well-chastened Dr. Franck, had not attempted a private revolution, nor was Juppchen Goebbels celebrating martyrs for any purpose of his own. Adi was getting ready to move; or at any rate he was telling the world that he was doing so—and it came to the same thing, since he couldn't afford to let his bluff be called a second time as he had done in May. He had discussed that episode in his Nuremberg speech, saying in substance that he had let it happen because he hadn't been ready; but now he had got ready, and the world was on notice. How long would he wait? Lanny guessed that he wouldn't wait more than a day or two, perhaps not more than an hour or two.

The traveler put up at the Regina Palast and got a light supper, with an evening paper to keep him company. When he went to his room he turned on a new gadget which had come on the market, a portable radio set which didn't have to be plugged in to a light socket or the generator of a car. With this he listened to an official statement from the British Foreign Office, given by the Munich radio both in English and German. Prime Minister Chamberlain had sent through his Ambassador in Berlin a message stating that he proposed to fly at once to Germany to consult with the Führer in an effort to find a peaceful solution to the existing crisis. He had asked the Führer to name a place for a meeting, and the Führer had replied accepting the proposal. "The Prime Minister is, accordingly, leaving for Germany by air tomorrow."

III

It was to be doubted if there was any person in the city of Munich to whom that news meant more, or who was in better position to interpret it. The presidential agent could transport himself in mind to Wickthorpe Castle and listen to Ceddy and Gerald planning the move—in all probability one of them had suggested it. They were in a state of bewilderment, almost of despair. It was hard for them to conceive of a man like Adolf Hitler holding power in a European country; they didn't know how to deal with him, and had even been reduced to the hope that an American art expert might be able to smooth him down and temper his rages. Sir Nevile Henderson, their ambassador, had been powerless to do it; Lord Runciman of Doxford was failing abjectly; the Marquess of Londonderry, the Marquess of Lothian, the Earl of Perth, Sir Alexander Cadogan, Viscount Halifax— a string of the noblest and most plausible of English gentlemen had been running to Berlin and Berchtesgaden over a period of years, with no results worth mentioning. And now plain Mr. Neville Chamberlain, a commoner who manufactured small arms in Birmingham, was going to make one last try.

Lanny had met this statesman only casually, but had watched him closely at public and social affairs. He was tall and lean, with thin sallow face, prominent nose, and long neck with conspicuous Adam's apple. He dressed in black, wore an old-fashioned wing collar, and might have been taken for an undertaker. Since he lived in a land where rain comes frequently, he never went out without a proper black umbrella, tightly rolled; the cartoonists, on the lookout for oddities, took this up eagerly, and before long the world had accepted a black umbrella as the symbol òf a political point of view.

This attitude Neville himself called "practical," but more properly it might have been called "commercial"—of course on a·large scale. He was a businessman, which meant that he bought things and sold them for more than they had cost; he believed in this procedure—of course on a large scale—and thought that if it was continued long enough and over the whole world, everything would work itself out and all problems would solve themselves. He came from an old family of trade aristocrats; he had been Lord Mayor of Birmingham, and so had his father and five uncles and a cousin. Personally, Neville was a dry and unimaginative old man, interested in birds and fishes more than in human beings. He was a pacifist who made instruments of killing; he thought he could go on making them on a large scale without having them used, and it had apparently never occurred to him that if his customers did not intend to use them, they would stop buying them.

I V

Lanny learned from the newspapers that the Führer was at the Berghof, and it was a safe guess that the conference would take place there. He might have called up Hess and got himself invited; but what good would it have done? He surely wouldn't be asked to act as interpreter at this supremely important affair, and he could be sure there wouldn't be any yelling in the house. Adi had great respect for the British ruling classes and desired most earnestly to have them consent to what he was determined to do. He had always been polite in dealing with them, and on this occasion would try his best to behave like a Birmingham undertaker.

Lanny could foresee what was going to happen almost as well as if he had been on the scene. This meeting, over which the whole world was agog, was in fact a sort of stageplay, of which Lanny had attended the rehearsals. The details of the settlement had been worked out by Gerald Albany in Berlin and by Wiedemann at Wickthorpe and Cliveden. Adi had made his demands and they had been granted. The present dramatic journey of the head of the British government had to do, not with the what, but rather with the how and the when. Could not Seine Exzellenz be persuaded to display better table manners and not grab suddenly with both hands and thus risk upsetting the soup tureen? Could he not persuade the Sudeten Germans to endure a few days longer, while Mr. Chamberlain and his friends made clear to the French that they must repudiate their engagements with Czechoslovakia, and to the Czechs that they had not a friend in Europe and had no choice but to surrender?

That was what this dramatic flight would be for, and when the Führer conceded a few more days it would be a triumph for British diplomacy, heralded to the world with radio trumpets. The facts about it, hammered out on Lanny's typewriter in a London hotel, had been on President Roosevelt's desk for several weeks, and all that Lanny could get now was the melancholy satisfaction of saying: "I told you so." This being true, he would refuse to get excited over anybody's oratory, but would have his sleep, and in the morning would not suggest taking Zoltan to the airport to join the throngs who would cheer the Prime Minister's arrival. Rather the pair would go to view paintings, and would talk about prices and customers, just as if Europe were not supposed to be hanging on the verge of a second World War.

Zoltan's own mind was in a confused state. He was a man of peace, a man of international mind, a good European who had no quarrel with anybody on the ground of race, creed, or political ideology. He met people on the pleasant sunlit fields of art. His occupation, which was at once a business and a delight, took him all over the Western world, and he had learned to listen politely to what other people said, and, if they tried to draw him into controversy, to tell them that an art lover had to live above all battles. Now it seemed to him that the world was going mad, that civilization was committing suicide. He accepted at its face value the stageplay which came to be known as "Munich." Chamberlain was really trying to save the peace of Europe, and Zoltan awaited the outcome in painful suspense. Such was the mood of the average uninformed man all over the world, and Lanny had to join with millions of others in saying: "God help him!"

V

The man with the black umbrella landed at the Munich airport and was taken at once to the Führer's armored train, which carried him on to Berchtesgaden. Cheered everywhere by crowds, he was motored to the Berghof, and the Nazi radios told how the Führer had come out barebeaded in the rain to welcome him. For three hours the two statesmen sat in Hitler's study, with only an interpreter present, and afterwards the official communiqué announced that they had had "a comprehensive and frank exchange of opinions." Later on, telling the House of Commons about it, the Prime Minister said that he had there got the impression that "the Chancellor was contemplating an immediate invasion of Czechoslovakia."

Chamberlain went on to record: "In courteous but perfectly definite terms, Herr Hitler made it plain that he had made up his mind the Sudeten Germans must have the right of self-determination and of returning, if they wished, to the Reich." In these last words the Prime Minister was repeating one of Herr Hitler's favorite lies, and it was hard to believe that he was doing it naïvely; for certainly Gerald or Ceddy or some other of his permanent Foreign Office men must have informed him that the Sudeten Germans had never belonged to the Reich, not since they had left Germany nine hundred years previously. And as for "self-determination," those Germans had never been consulted; the Nazi agents and agitators had done the "determining," and among their determinations was that a fair plebiscite should never be held in that region.

Here was the author of *Mein Kampf*, demonstrating his thesis that the bigger the lie the easier to get it believed, and that all you have to do is to keep on saying a thing often enough and you can make it the truth. Adi had made it the truth that he was master of Germany, and he was going to make it the truth that he was master of all the lands where any number of Germans lived. Such was the *Blut und Boden* doctrine. Adi had moved two-thirds of his army to the borders of Czechoslovakia; and would he have dared to take that risk unless British statesmen had "made it plain" that they were not going to defend the threatened country? Chamberlain expected the Commons to believe that he would, and presumably they did so, for they let him continue in his role of the statesman who was saving Europe from a devastating war.

The Prime Minister had obtained a promise that the German armies would not move until he had time to return to London and consult with his Cabinet, and also with the French. These consultations began, and continued day and night. Premier Daladier and his Foreign Minister, Bonnet, came to London, and there was endless speculation over the radio about what they were deciding. In Germany there were heavy penalties for listening to foreign broadcasts, but Lanny could lock the door of his hotel room and turn on a whisper and listen in safety; the gravity of the offense began when you told other persons what you had heard, and this he had no wish to do.

As a matter of fact there wasn't much to choose between Nazi and British radios in this crisis, so far as moral character was concerned; it was all "propaganda," serving the purposes of governments which didn't want their publics to realize what they were up to. Lanny knew the pale, flabby, and tricky politician who had become Premier of France, and likewise his Foreign Minister who was in his heart a Fascist and whose wife chose German agents for her intimates. Chamberlain wouldn't be having to spend a day and a night persuading such men to indorse a treacherous bargain. No, they would be talking as "practical" men. Just what promises could they get from Hitler that would make their surrender appear less abject? Just how should they present it to make the dose less bitter to the world? Such would be the subjects debated at No. 10 Downing Street, and it wouldn't be worth Lanny's while to fly to London for the details of such a conference.

VI

Tired of listening to lies, the "P.A." put on his rainproof coat and went for a walk. He had promised to look up the Rumanian astrologer, and this was an hour for consulting the stars, if ever. He found the rooms empty and the *Pförtnerin* not especially communicative; Herr Reminescu had moved out, and the young lady also, and had left no address; no, the police had not come, the tenants had just moved and said nothing. So that was that, and Lanny thought: "I will get a letter some day at Juan." But he never did get a letter, and never heard a word from or about the young mystagogue. That was one of the unpleasant aspects of dictatorship as Lanny had observed it in operation for a decade and a half. People disappeared, and that was the end of them so far as relatives, friends, clients, customers, and everybody else was concerned; it might be dangerous to ask about them, and unless it was someone especially dear to you, you decided that discretion was the better part of curiosity.

So, look at old masters and get prices on them, call in a stenographer and write letters and cablegrams to your clients and await their replies. There is no law against taking art works out of Germany, for the Nazis need foreign money to buy oil and tin and rubber and the other raw materials of war which the Fatherland lacks because other nations got there first and grabbed the desirable colonies. All that is going to be changed soon, and meanwhile we let the art-loving *Ausländer* come in, and we serve them politely and pretend that we like them; but *Der Tag* will come—it is not so far off now—and then we will take back what we have lost, with interest at rates which we shall fix ourselves.

There was good music to be heard in Munich, there were dramas to be seen, and paintings to be looked at; also charming people to be met —people who did not greet you with the Hitler salute and did not talk nonsense about blood and soil, blood and race, blood and iron, blood and guts. There was Baron von Zinszollern, from whom Lanny had bought a painting years ago while trying to get Freddi out of Dachau. The Baron's fine home was mortgaged, so he was glad to see an art expert again, and still gladder to see two. Since they were socially acceptable persons, he not merely showed them his collection and talked prices, but invited them to stay to lunch and spent most of the afternoon in conversation.

He was a typical Bavarian, with round head, dark hair and eyes, and plump features; genial but skeptical and worldly. He got pleasure out of life as he went along, and after he had made certain that he was dealing with two good Europeans, he told amusing stories about the kaleidoscope of history in which he and his fellow *Münchner* had been living for the past half century. A monarchy with mad rulers, a World War, a Socialist republic and a Communist revolution, a democratic republic and a Nationalist revolution—the Baron smilingly declared that he couldn't keep track of them all, and didn't remember the name of the particular kind which they had at this moment.

He was out of politics, but never out of humor, apparently. When he learned that Lanny was an investigator of occult matters he asked if he had met Fräulein Elvira Lust, a little old lady who lived on Nymphenburgerstrasse here in Munich; you would find her in the telephone book as a "graphologist," since astrology was forbidden. She was all tied up in knots with arthritis, but the Führer sent a car for her every now and again and had her brought to the Berghof. It was said that she was used by high-up Nazis to give him advice which he would take from the stars but not from mere humans.

Lanny didn't say that he had been a guest at the Berghof, for that might have stopped the flow of urbane gossip. He inquired concerning a young Rumanian astrologer whom Hess was reported to have patronized, but the Baron had never heard of that one. He declared that the best known of the *Regierung's* occult advisers went by the one name of "Elsa," and lived just across the street from the Führer's Munich apartment; she was toothless, and used a pack of black rubber cards without markings so far as anyone could observe. A friend of the Baron's had consulted her a few days ago, and had paid her ten marks to shuffle the cards and tell him that he had come to consult her about the chances of war—a safe guess about anybody at the moment. Her answer had contained only five words: *"Kein Krieg in diesem Jahr."* The skeptical nobleman was not impressed, for he said that Hess and other members of the Führer's staff consulted Elsa frequently, and she quite certainly had information about his purposes.

So talked Baron von Zinszollern, and others of the well-to-do folk whom Lanny met during his stay in this capital of good beer and *Gemütlichkeit.* The Nazis had been able to abolish many of the liberties of the *Münchner,* but not their liberty to be amused. And yet, strange as it might seem, this pleasure-loving gentleman referred quite casually to Germany's need of colonies and her right to expand. Indeed it had been years since Lanny had met in Germany a single man or woman who didn't think that Germany had to expand. He had decided that the last of such persons must have got caught and been either beheaded or shut up in a concentration camp.

VII

On the morning of Monday, the 19th of September, the radios of Europe blared forth in a babel of languages the result of the deliberations of the British and French heads of government in London. It was an ultimatum which had been presented in Prague. With hypocrisy not often matched even in the diplomatic world, the two great governments informed a small and helpless government that it was to be torn into fragments in the cause of "the maintenance of peace and the safety of Czechoslovakia's vital interests." The small nation was required to turn over to the Reich "the districts mainly inhabited by the Sudeten Deutsch." A reply was called for "at the earliest possible moment," on the ground that "the Prime Minister must resume conversations with Herr Hitler not later than Wednesday, and earlier if possible." The ultimatum didn't say what would be done to the Prague government in the event of refusal to comply; presumably Herr Hitler would attend to that part of the procedure.

For Lanny Budd it was like finding out that Trudi was dead; he had been sure the news was coming, and still he was sick at heart over it. He shut off the radio and walked up and down his room for a while, swearing vigorously; then he reminded himself that he was a presidential agent, and called up Hess at the Berghof. He had already written a "bread and butter" letter to thank the Deputy for his hospitality. Now he said: "The Führer has achieved a great feat of diplomacy." The reply was: "He is far from certain about it. Come and tell him."

So Lanny drove, on a warm sunshiny afternoon, with a soft haze over the mountains and no breath of air stirring the millions of fir-tree needles. By the time he arrived, he had thought out his program carefully, and was once more the suave courtier and admiring friend.

The Führer was taking a bath, one of his aides explained; this was his practice whenever he was under nervous strain. Lanny agreed that warm water was relaxing, and didn't ask whether it was true, as reported in Munich, that the Führer took three baths every day. A certain "nature-cure" Dr. Bummke of that city had prescribed the regimen, and the Führer followed it although he had quarreled with the elderly adviser. It was as hard to know what to believe in Munich as it had been in Vienna—two cities where a sense of humor seemed to prevail over strict concern for facts.

In the great hall Lanny encountered a young woman wearing an English walking costume; a tall, straight blond with lovely regular features, the perfect embodiment of a Führer's Aryan dream. Lanny had met her once at a race meet in England, but she didn't recall him and he had to remind her of the occasion. She was one of the two daughters of Lord Redesdale, an ardent supporter of Nazism; her name was Unity Valkyrie Freeman-Mitford, and her sister was twice married to Sir Oswald Mosley, leader of the British Union of Fascists, the second time in Germany, with the Führer serving as best man. Unity made Nazi speeches in Hyde Park, and had got herself celebrated in the newspapers as one of Adi's infatuated admirers; she followed him everywhere he went, and gossip had it that she planned to marry him and thus bring about the union of the two countries. How far Adi went along with this program was uncertain, but it was well known that he liked to look at beautiful girls, and Unity was adapted to that purpose. She had golden curls hanging to her shoulders—at the age of twenty-four.

Lanny politely assumed that she had come for the same purpose as himself, to congratulate a great man upon his diplomatic triumph. He tried to make himself agreeable, talking about the wonders they had witnessed at the Parteitag; but he noticed that the lady seemed restless, and kept looking in the direction of the stairs. Abruptly she excused herself and went up, and at the same time Lanny observed Rudolf Hess entering the room. Without especially lowering his voice, the Deputy remarked: "I wish somebody would kick that bitch all the way down."

So once more Lanny observed that these little Nazi children did not always obey the injunction to love one another.

VIII

The hydropathic regimen had apparently not been entirely effective in this crisis, for when Lanny was escorted to the Führer's study he found him almost wild with nerves, pacing the floor, snapping his fingers, and manifesting a peculiar jerking movement of one leg. His face made Lanny think of those he had watched in the gambling casinos of the Riviera; faces of men and women who were staking everything they owned upon the turn of a card or the spinning of a wheel. Hitler was doing much the same, and a moralist might have observed that one does not achieve world power without paying for it.

"*Diese verdammten englischen Staatsmänner!*" he burst out. "Can anybody believe a word they say?"

"I think you can believe what they say in this case, Exzellenz," replied the visitor, mildly. "They have committed themselves before the world."

"Yes, but have you read the text of that statement?"

"I have heard it over the radio, in both English and German." This involved an admission, but Lanny didn't mind making it, for he was accepted as a member of the *Herrenrasse*, and the Führer would hardly object to his listening to news from whatever source.

"Do you see the tricks they have put into it? They mention a plebiscite, and the fact that the Czechs have objected to one; but they leave it as a possibility that the Czechs may change their minds."

"I thought the English were unusually shrewd, Herr Reichskanzler; they tell Prague that they are taking it at its word, and state clearly that they anticipate the method of direct transfer."

"But then they go on to talk about negotiations, provisions for adjustment of frontiers, and so on. I have never read so many weasel words in my life. They are making the greatest mistake if they think they can tie me up in red tape, and make me listen to the quibbling of what they call 'some international body, including a Czech representative.' I don't want any Czech representative anywhere near me—ever again while I live!"

"If you want my opinion, Exzellenz——"

"Of course; I am asking it."

"Well, you followed a course of legality for many years inside Germany, and I heard some of your followers complain that you had a 'legality complex.' But you know that it paid you well in the long run, and I think it will pay you to deal on a basis of legality with the British also."

"Is that what they tell you to tell me?"

Lanny didn't have to pretend to be shocked. "Nobody in England is in a position to tell me anything, Herr Reichskanzler. I am an American, and my only interest is in having peace prevail in Europe. You cannot expect to have friends unless you can bring yourself to trust them."

"*Ja, ja, Herr Budd, Sie haben recht.* You must understand. I am under heavy strain. They have kept me dawdling about this matter for months; and I am by nature a man of action."

"Of course; but could any man wish to provoke war when by steady pressure and patience he can gain the same ends without war?"

"You are right; I have to admit it. Tell me about this incredible Chamberlain. Can it be possible for any human being to deceive himself to such an extent as he appears to?"

So Lanny delivered a discourse which might have come out of Emerson's *English Traits;* he explained that peculiar combination of religiosity and sanctioned avarice which enabled a man to become Lord Mayor of Birmingham in the stage of capitalism's approaching collapse. Elderly English Tories dreaded the future, dreaded every sort of change, and in this crisis couldn't make up their minds whether to trust to their dreadnaughts or their prayers. Runciman had prayed publicly before setting out for Prague, Halifax prayed several times every day, and Chamberlain's wife had been praying for him in Westminster Abbey while he was in flight to Munich. At the same time the forty British battleships had been parading in the North Sea.

In answer to a direct question, Lanny said he had no doubt whatever that Chamberlain intended to see that the Czechs turned over to Germany those parts of the Sudetenland whose population was more than fifty per cent German. Any danger to the Führer's plans came, not from the insincerity of British statesmen, but from the volatility of British public opinion; it was possible, but not probable, that such a storm might arise that the government would be overthrown and the deal canceled. "If that happens, it means war!" exclaimed Adi; and his visitor replied: "They know it, and that is why it is unlikely to happen."

IX

It had been agreed that the next meeting of the two heads of government should be at a place nearer to England; Hitler had made the suggestion, so Chamberlain stated it, "to spare an old man another such long journey." The spot selected was a summer resort on the Rhine near Cologne, where the river is inside Germany. The place was Godesberg, which is old German for Hill of the Gods; the old gods, of course, those deities of *Blut und Eisen* whom the Führer and his chief mystagogue, Rosenberg, were bringing back to life. Godesberg was a favorite resort of the health-seeking Adi, and the newspapers reported that he had visited the Hotel Dreesen no less than sixty-seven times. It was in this place, a little more than four years ago, that he had received urgent and terrifying phone calls from Göring, as a result of which he had taken Goebbels and flown to Munich to order the murder of one· of his best friends, Ernst Röhm, and a thousand or more others; those dreadful days and nights of the Blood Purge which had come so close to ending the career of a presidential agent before it got started.

Lanny might have hinted tactfully at the idea of being on hand for this new conference. He had thought of it but decided that it would not do. There would be a swarm of newspapermen on hand, and their presence was reason for him to be elsewhere. Many of the old-timers knew him from the days when he had been a "Pink," and he didn't want the job of explaining to them when and how he had changed his color. When any reporter sought to interview him he replied that his visits to the Berghof had to do with the sale of art works, on which the Führer was considered to be an authority.

The Godesberg conference began on the 22nd. Hitler stayed at the Dreesen, and the Prime Minister at the Peterhof on the opposite side of the river. Chamberlain crossed by the ferry, and they held council all afternoon, after which Chamberlain issued an appeal for patience and order in the Sudetenland. That was enough to start reports that all was not going well. Next day the pair met again, and later the Prime Minister went back to his side of the river, and they took to sending notes back and forth, a procedure which justified still more alarming reports. Chamberlain came back, and they argued all evening, and at half past one next morning, when they parted, Chamberlain stated: "I cannot say it is hopeless,"—which was about as ominous as could be. Terror spread over all Europe. The French and British governments notified the Czechs that they could not "continue to take responsibility of advising them not to mobilize"—which was the same as telling them to prepare for war. The horrified Czechs proceeded in haste to obey, and the Goebbels newspapers went wild, reporting more outrages in every new edition. The Hungarians and the Poles put in demands for parts of Czech territory, and now the Russians warned the Poles that if they moved against Czechoslovakia the Russians would denounce their non-aggression pact with Poland. That was the way it was in unhappy old Europe; the nations were like a row of tin soldiers standing close together—you pushed the first one and down went the whole row. The French called up half a million troops, and in London gasmask stations were opened and swarms of people gathered to be fitted. Armies of men began piling sandbags around public buildings, and digging trenches in the parks so that people might hide from flying bomb fragments. The government organization known as Air Raid Precautions began issuing elaborate instructions over the radio and with loudspeakers in the streets.

In short, it was war; and what did it all mean? Lanny could make a guess that Adi had voiced his strenuous objections to being "tied up in red tape" and forced to listen to "the quibbling of an international body, including a Czech representative." He was demanding the right of military occupation of the Sudetenland at once, and a praying English gentleman was trying to restrain him, claiming that the Führer was increasing his demands over what had been agreed upon in Berchtesgaden. Chamberlain was a man of his word, while Hitler was a man of what he wanted, and that was the difference which had caused them to take to sending notes back and forth across a river.

Of course they were trying to bluff each other; they both had shrewd bargainers with them, and were playing close to their chests, with the future of Europe as stakes. Both were afraid, Lanny could be sure, but he guessed that Adi had the advantage, because he was half mad and his rage would overcome his fear. Thinking the matter over, day and night, Lanny wondered whether this diplomatic duel was altogether sincere. Might not both parties have decided, perhaps without voicing it, that it was necessary to give the public another scare, to increase the demand for peace and reduce the protest of those elements in Britain and France which were denouncing the program of "appeasement"? Knowing what the diplomats had been discussing among themselves for the past several months, Lanny found it hard indeed to believe that anybody was seriously thinking of war over the issue of Czechoslovakia.

X

Munich had its share of the terror. The Czechs had an air force, less than a half-hour's flight away. Suppose those treacherous sub-human creatures should decide to strike first, instead of waiting for the *Herrenvolk* to do it! Marshal Göring's flyers at the Oberwiesenfeld warmed up their motors, and the young men of the city were put into uniforms, loaded into freight cars, and hauled away toward the frontier. The performances of the Führer's favorite comic opera, *The Merry Widow*, which were given every night at the Theater am Gärtnerplatz, with a very young and lovely dancer, entirely nude, rising on a platform through the center of the stage—these performances lost nearly all of their dancing men, and the promotion of what the Nazis called "a healthy eroticism" received a sudden check.

There was an annual event in Munich, the October Fair, beginning in the middle of September and running for a month. In the Theresienwiese, an enormous meadow below the Exhibition Park, was held a combination of all the various forms of public entertainment known to the Western world: Coney Island and Luna Park, Crystal Palace and Vauxhall Gardens, Mardi Gras, Barnum and Bailey, and the state fairs of the forty-eight United States of America. Anybody who wanted to be considered a good *Münchner* had to go and ride on roller coasters and merry-go-rounds, listen to the bands, throw coconuts at the heads of clowns, and learn to eat Bavarian horseradish along with pretzels and beer.

Lanny and Zoltan went on Monday evening, two days after the Godesberg conference broke up. A quarter of a million South Germans had come to enjoy themselves in the open air, and two foreign visitors wanted to watch them at play. The visitors forgot that this was the night which the Führer of all Germany had chosen to make his report to his people, and what that would mean to the festival. All day, and until the middle of the evening, joy was unconfined; huge crowds milled here and there amid bright lights and lavish decorations; they burst into singing on the slightest occasion and danced with their *Mädels* wherever there was a smooth floor or turf underfoot. Music echoed everywhere, the barkers of sideshows orated, bells rang, roller coasters roared, and people yelled with laughter or with simulated fright.

Then suddenly came the bellowing of loudspeakers; the Führer was about to address the world from the Sportpalast in Berlin. All other sounds died away as if by enchantment. Dancing stopped, talk stopped, and a quarter of a million men and women halted in their tracks. And it was the same with all other activity, everywhere in Germany; all work in factories, all showing of motion pictures, sales in shops, serving in restaurants, walking on the streets—everything halted, and seventy million people, excluding only the babies, listened to one monstrous Voice. To fail to listen or to walk away was a crime, and had landed many a person in a concentration camp. Said Adolf Hitler:

"If I am now the spokesman of this German people, then I know: At this second the whole people in its millions agrees word for word with my words, confirms them, and makes them its own oath! Let other statesmen ask themselves whether that is also true in their case!"

XI

This Voice, roaring over the hundred acres of the Theresienwiese and over the air waves of the whole earth, told not merely what the German people were doing at this second, but what they had been doing for the past twenty years and what their great Führer had been doing for them. In the course of an address of some six thousand words, the Voice used the words I, me, my, and mine a total of one hundred and thirty-four times. Said this Voice: "I have offered disarmament as long as it was possible. But when that was rejected, I then formed, I admit, no halfhearted decision. I am a National Socialist and an old front-line German soldier. I have in fact armed in these five years. I have spent milliards on these armaments: that the German people must now know!"

It was the policy of this supremely cunning statesman to deal with one enemy at a time. Therefore in this speech, an ultimatum to the Czech Republic, he set to work to eliminate methodically all other opposition. With Poland, he said, "permanent pacification" had been achieved. As to the English people, he hoped that "the peace-loving parts would gain the upper hand." As to France, there were now "absolutely no differences outstanding between us. . . . We want nothing from France—positively nothing!" With Italy, under the "rare genius" of its Duce, there had been established "a true union of hearts."

All these matters having been disposed of, the Voice came to what it described as "the last territorial claim which I have to make in Europe." This problem, it said, existed because of "a single lie, and the father of this lie was named Beneš." The lie was "that there was a Czechoslovak nation." This lie had been told to the Versailles statesmen and they had believed it. The rest of the long speech was a recital of the duel of wills between this liar and his lie on the one hand and the Führer of the Germans and his truth on the other. This struggle had now come to its climax. Said the Führer: "I have demanded that now after twenty years Mr. Beneš should at last be compelled to come to terms with the truth."

On October 1, five days later, the hated Czech was required to turn over the Sudetenland to Adolf Hitler. It was an ultimatum, and none of the rascal's wrigglings and evasions would do him any good. "Mr. Beneš now places his hopes on the world! And he and his diplomats make no secret of the fact. They state: it is our hope that Chamberlain will be overthrown, that Daladier will be removed, that on every hand revolutions are on the way. They place their hope on Soviet Russia. He still thinks then that he will be able to evade the fulfillment of his obligations.

"And then I can say only one thing: now two men stand arrayed one against the other: there is Mr. Beneš, and here stand I. We are two men of a different make-up. In the great struggle of the people, while Mr. Beneš was sneaking about through the world, I as a decent German soldier did my duty. And now today I stand over against this man as the soldier of my people."

The Voice went on to thank Mr. Chamberlain, and to repeat the final assurances which had been given him before, "that the German people desires nothing else than peace. . . . I have further assured him, and I repeat it here, that when this problem is solved there is for Germany no further territorial problem in Europe. . . . We want no Czechs!"

Then, at the end, this all-powerful Voice addressed his faithful flock throughout the Reich:

"And so I ask you, my German people, take your stand behind me, man by man, and woman by woman. In this hour we all wish to form a common will and that will must be stronger than every hardship and every danger. And if this will is stronger than hardship and danger, then one day it will break down hardship and danger. We are determined! Now let Mr. Beneš make his choice!"

As a piece of oratory it was vigorous beyond dispute, and as an example of diplomatic strategy—which precedes war or continues war

—it was a masterpiece. How did it seem to the German people? To Lanny it was as if he were witnessing a plebiscite being taken on the Theresienwiese. A quarter of a million Germans were asked if they wished to "be stronger than every hardship and every danger," and they cast their vote, not in words but in actions which speak louder than words. There was not one handclap, not one cheer, not even one smile. The quarter of a million Germans, assembled to enjoy the simple pleasures of the poor, had been invited to become heroic. The men, ordered to take their stand behind their Führer, man by man, behaved like dogs which had been kicked with a heavy boot; the women, ordered to take their stand, woman by woman, bore the aspect of hens which had been doused in a tub of soapy water.

Every particle of life went out of the October Fair. The merry-go-rounds started to whirl, but nobody wanted to ride; the barkers started shouting, but nobody listened; the sausages started sizzling, but nobody wanted to eat. The people strolled away and went home, or gathered in little groups, talking in low tones. There would be no chance for a pair of strangers to hear what they said, but their woebegone expressions were eloquent enough. Man by man and woman by woman, they took this speech to mean war; and full as it was of subtle falsehoods, it had contained one incontrovertible truth—that the German people desired nothing else than peace.

30

Hell's Foundations Tremble

I

THE next two days were a nightmare to the people of Munich. Everybody believed that war was certain; everybody who knew Lanny Budd wanted to ask what he thought, and he could only say that he didn't know any more than they. In his secret heart he was sure there wouldn't be war—not yet. Britain and France would give way, as they had done in case after case. But this was an opinion not to be voiced, even to Lanny's friend and colleague in art experting. His conclusions had long since been placed in the hands of Rick and F.D.R., so now he had nothing to do but listen to the radio, read the newspapers, and await the event.

The papers published a cablegram which President Roosevelt had sent to Hitler and to Beneš, pleading with them not to break off negotiations. Officially, the President could hardly avoid taking that position, and Hitler's reply was likewise according to formula—another long tirade, rehearsing his grievances against Czechoslovakia. Lanny pictured his Chief lying in bed in the White House, reading that sheaf of telegraph sheets—and what would he be making of them? Would he believe what he read, or would he have in mind the facts his "P.A." had provided?

The night after the Hitler speech the British fleet mobilized; that cost a lot of money, and certainly looked serious. Then Poland broke off with Czechoslovakia—which meant that Poland's dictator had swallowed the bait, sugared with flattery, which Adi had held out to him; Poland was going to take a chunk of the plundered country, and block off Russia from giving its promised aid to the victim. No doubt the British Tories were back of that action—since of all things in the world they wanted least to have the Soviet Union take part in a successful war on Germany and make it into a Communist state. Lanny recalled a conversation between Gerald and Ceddy during the crisis over Abyssinia; they had agreed that they couldn't afford to let Mussolini be unhorsed, because of the certainty that some sort of leftist government would take his place in Italy.

Lanny would have liked to be in London now, to hear what these friends were saying; but he knew it could do no good, for the crisis would be over long before he could get any word to Roosevelt. No, an agent's business was here, in the Führer's playground; the Führer would come back from this crisis with his heart high, and would boast about what he meant to do next. If there was anything one could be certain about in this mess, it was that Adi's statement concerning his "last territorial claim in Europe" was a piece of nonsense, a bait for suckers.

II

Two days after the Sportpalast speech, the British Prime Minister arose in the House of Commons to make his report. Solemnly, as if presiding at a funeral, he told the long story of his negotiations. His hands were full of papers, and trembled as he read them; the notes which had been exchanged, the proposals which had been made, the memoranda of his two visits and what had been said at them. He declared that he had cast aside all thoughts of self, and of the dignity of his office; he had sought to preserve the peace of Europe. He revealed that he had just sent one last letter to Hitler, offering to make a third visit to Germany, and pledging the power of the British and French governments to see that agreements arrived at would be "carried out fairly and fully and forthwith." Also he had written to Mussolini, begging him to join the conference, and to use his influence with Hitler "to agree to my proposal which will keep all our peoples out of war."

A dramatic incident. Just as Chamberlain had reached this part of his speech a messenger from the Foreign Office rushed upstairs to Lord Halifax in the balcony and delivered an envelope. Halifax read the contents and passed it on to Gerald Albany, who hurried downstairs and passed it to the Prime Minister. The latter read it, and a smile of relief dawned upon his haggard features. "That is not all," he announced. "I have something to say to the House yet. I have now been informed by Herr Hitler that he invites me to meet him at Munich tomorrow morning."

That was as far as the speaker got; the House forgot all its rules, and burst into a frenzy of cheering, clapping of hands and stamping of feet. The dry and frigid Prime Minister wept, and others of his sort made no attempt to restrain their feelings. There wasn't going to be a war after all! The head of the British government was going to forget his dignity once more, and give Adi Schicklgruber a chance to wring still further concessions from him. "It's all right this time!" cried Neville to the crowds who cheered him in the streets. The Queen Mother went out weeping; the whole nation wept—and nobody stopped to think how the Führer of the *Herrenvolk* might use this revelation of the great dread of war which possessed the "degenerate democracies."

III

For Lanny this arrangement was most convenient; he had decided against going to London, and now London was coming to him! Just as he finished reading in the morning papers the news of the dramatic scene in the House of Commons, two planes from the Heston airport near London arrived at the Oberwiesenfeld airport, and from them stepped the Prime Minister and his staff—including Lord Wickthorpe and Gerald Albany. They were to be put up at the Regina Palast, where Lanny and Zoltan had a suite; many persons had to be suddenly thrown out, but needless to say a friend of the Führer would not share such a fate. The two visitors received special cards which enabled them to pass the SS guards who surrounded the hotel, and outside in the streets they could know when the distinguished guests arrived, because of the thunderous cheers from crowds surrounding the building. Munich had come to life again, and the man with the black umbrella had taken a place even higher than the Führer in the hearts of all Bavarians.

Hitler had gone in his private train to the frontier to meet Mussolini, so that they could have a conference in advance. On their ride back the Duce labored to persuade his Axis partner to be reasonable, and at the railroad station there were more cheers for Il Duce than he was getting now at home. The Prinz Karl Palace had been hurriedly dusted off for the Italian staff, while the French were taken to the Vier Jahreszeiten, under the charge of the Gestapo. It happened to be a beautiful day, and flags flew everywhere, and the radio told the people where to go and whom they were to welcome. The heads of three great states had come at the Führer's bidding, and everybody knew what a triumph that was; everybody trusted the magic of their divinely inspired leader, who had brought them safely thus far and would guide them to a happy ending.

Lanny sent in his card to Ceddy, and was called to his lordship's room for an exchange of hurried greetings. The perfect blond Aryan was engaged in "washing up," and the visitor came close and handed him a tiny slip of paper with a typewritten message: "Don't forget that your room is pretty certainly wired." Ceddy read it, and lifted his eyebrows. "Really?" he said, in the English fashion which makes it sound like "rarely" without the second "r." Lanny answered: "Take my word for it," and then handed a second slip, reading: "Tell the Old Man to stand firm. The other side will back down if they have to." To that Wickthorpe replied by putting his ear close to his friend's and whispering: "I won't have a chance to. It's all settled." Lanny held out his hand for the two notes and tore them into small pieces; he dropped them into the toilet bowl and pulled the lever—a technique he had learned from his father long ago.

They had time for a few words about family matters. Lanny had read in a London paper the news that Irma had presented her husband with a son and heir to his great title and estates. Ceddy was extremely proud, and of course Lanny congratulated him cordially. Lanny said that he would be returning to England as soon as he had got through with some picture deals. While they were chatting, there came a summons for Ceddy; the visiting delegations were going to have luncheon at the Führerhaus, and after that the discussions would begin. "The people seem glad to see us," remarked his lordship out loud—that being a statement to which the Gestapo would take no exception.

IV

The rest of the day, and until after midnight, all the world waited upon that conference. It had been known in advance that the Führer was insisting upon military occupation of the Sudetenland on Saturday, four days later, but beyond that all was uncertainty. Lanny stayed in his room, to keep out of the way of the newspapermen who swarmed in the hotel, and who, in the absence of real news, would have been glad to get hold of·a man who had been a recent guest at the Berghof. The radio would give the results as soon as there were any; and meanwhile, take the most interesting book you could get hold of and do your best to lose yourself and forget the agony of the world! Lanny had an American book, dealing with ranch life in the wide open spaces of the great southwest; some tourist had left it behind, and it had caught Lanny's eye on the open stall of a secondhand-book store. It was a part of the world which he had never visited, but it was his homeland nonetheless. In spite of mountain lions and rattlesnakes and tarantulas and bandits, he would have chosen it as a place of residence over any city of old Europe on the verge of war.

At one o'clock in the morning, such Germans as had stayed awake learned over the radio that their Führer had put his signature to a Four-Power Pact, providing the methods by which the Sudeten territory was to be turned over to Germany. The evacuation by the Czechs was to begin on the next day and to be completed within ten days. The German troops were to enter zone by zone to each of four zones marked on an accompanying map. Both sides were to release political prisoners, and the inhabitants of the ceded territory were to have six months in which to decide which citizenship they wished to enjoy. All these matters were to be in charge of an international commission, and the four heads of government agreed to guarantee the new boundaries of the Czechoslovak State against unprovoked aggression.

So there it was; peace in Europe had been saved. The three visiting delegations went home in rain, and when the British arrived there was a rainbow in the sky over Buckingham Palace, and crowds singing and shouting a tumultuous welcome. They told Chamberlain that he was a jolly good fellow, which must certainly have surprised his friends. In return he told the crowd that it was "peace with honor" and "peace in our time." Premier Daladier said afterwards that he had expected to be mobbed when he reached home; but he too was cheered and sung to, all along a twelve-mile drive into Paris. Arriving, he was carried on the shoulders of a multitude to the Tomb of the Unknown Soldier. Only a few grumblers and Czechs had any fault to find with the settlement, and Lanny Budd knew few of either. When, later in the day, he read that the Assistant Secretary of State of his own country had praised the achievement, he felt himself the forgotten man.

A tragic time indeed for clearsighted men and lovers of justice; the greedy ones were rubbing their hands and the butchers were sharpening their knives all over the world. Every gain that had been made in the World War had been thrown away, and every principle for which Woodrow Wilson had fought had been mocked. Each day became a series of fresh humiliations, and it took all the fortitude that a presidential agent possessed to keep him from throwing up his job and going back to lie on the beach at Juan and let the world go to hell in its own way.

The Führer went to Berlin, and of course had a triumphal progress. Promptly at the hour set, his troops crossed the border from Upper Austria, and soon afterwards he followed, the first day into Eger and the second into Karlsbad. At the same time Poland served an ultimatum, demanding Teschen—a district which, during the days of the Peace Treaty, Lloyd George had admitted never having heard of. The Poles had remembered it, and now they took it; also the Hungarians proceeded to take their bites out of the stricken carcass. The Nazis took everything they wanted, and the "international commission" in Berlin decided all disputes their way. The hated President Beneš resigned, since it was obvious that he could no longer do his country any good, and what was left of the carcass became a dependency of the Nazis. Pilsen was taken over in the very first days, and the great Skoda plant started making war materials for Hitler's next campaign. Lanny Budd got one feeble smile, wondering how Baron Schneider was enjoying that.

V

Life came back to Munich as to a drought-stricken garden after a thunder shower. The bands played and the merry-go-rounds whirled and the shoot-the-chutes roared on the Theresienwiese, and all good *Münchner* laughed and sang as of yore. Those who had permitted doubts of their Führer to creep into their hearts were shamed and tried to forget it; he was the world's greatest wonder-worker, and from now on they would follow him without question, certain that he could do whatever he wanted with the rest of Europe.

Zoltan had to return to Paris, but Lanny stayed on, because he wanted to catch the Führer in an unbuttoned mood, and the Berghof was the place. Sooner or later he always returned, generally on impulse and without notice. Meanwhile Lanny attended to his picture business, making money among the rich and friends among all classes.

Among those he had met at the Berghof was Adolf Wagner, Gauleiter of Bavaria, and one of Adi's oldest pals, having marched with him in the Beerhall Putsch and helped him in the Blood Purge. He was a big man and had an even bigger voice than Adi; he had taken pains to imitate every tone of his master, so he was officially known as "the Führer Voice," and read speeches for Adi on many occasions—among them always the opening of the Parteitag. He had a wooden leg from the war, but managed to get his great bulk around on it. "Big Adolf" was a political boss of the sort that cities in America are used to, but he had no law to interfere with him. When it rained in Munich, as it did frequently, and his stump ached, he would send some Catholic priest to Dachau; when, on the other hand, the sun shone and he had loaded up with *Münchner* at the great Artists' House which Big and Little had designed and built, his friends could get anything they wanted from him.

The artistic tastes of the Bavarian Gauleiter were not the same as Lanny Budd's, but Lanny had kept that fact to himself. The blusterous gang leader was proud of his love of culture and had appointed himself State Minister of Education, Culture, and the Interior; he patronized all the arts and all artists, especially those who were young and pretty. Anyone whom the Führer entertained must be all right, so Lanny had the keys to the city. He didn't care for Bierabends, and pleaded lack of capacity; but right now, when all Germany was celebrating, he had to accept some invitation, so he went for a raft ride on the Isar River, a unique sort of excursion.

The waters come down, clear and cold and green from the glaciers of the high Alps, and on them float logs from the carefully supervised state forests. When the stream is big enough they are tied together with chains, and presently there is a raft. When a political boss wishes to entertain his friends he has planks nailed on top of such a raft, and has a special car hitched onto a train and takes the party overnight to Bad Tölz, where he has a brass band to welcome them at the station and Aryan peasant girls to dance with them. After a breakfast of sausages washed down with the native beer they march to the raft, which has comfortable steamer chairs on it, also baskets of *leberwurst* and *schweitzerkäse* sandwiches and of course a keg of beer.

The raft is poled out into the stream and away it goes, under bridges lined with cheering crowds—no trouble getting people to cheer in Germany in October of 1938! You see a lot of fine scenery, and you have exciting times sliding down sluices past the various dams in the river. You stop at a monastery for a fry of river fish, and finally you arrive at Munich's favorite bathing place. There you go ashore, while the raft continues on its way to the beautiful blue Danube, perhaps to become part of a house in Vienna or Budapest.

VI

Feldmarschall Göring had built himself a châlet on the Obersalzberg, having had the bad taste to build it high and looking down upon his Führer's. To this place he had retired with his bronchitis and swollen legs, and now he had recovered and was sticking pigs in his forest. He invited Lanny for a visit, and Lanny was pleased to go, but preferred to watch the pig-sticking from a distance. He didn't lose caste by that, for the operation was admitted to be dangerous, and *Der Dicke* was satisfied to display his prowess and be admired by weaker men. The job was done on horseback, and two keepers with rifles rode close behind, to be ready in case of accident; but none happened, and three great shaggy boars were pierced through the heart by the fat man's well-aimed lance.

After supper they sat before a blazing fire, with a backlog so huge that it had to be brought on a little rubber-tired "dolly." They talked about the state of the world, and the marshal was as proud of his Führer's stroke of statecraft as he was of his own stabs at the pigs. "Was there ever such a man since the world began?" he inquired, and Lanny didn't try to think of another. He lent *éclat* to the occasion by telling what he knew of its risks; it had been touch and go, for the British statesmen had been almost broken by the pressure of public opposition.

It was all right for Lanny to say: "I had a few minutes with Ceddy Wickthorpe in the Regina Palast, just before he went in to the conference. He was a badly worried Englishman, *glauben Sie mir*." That was slang in American, but oddly enough wasn't in German.

"I don't mind telling you that I had very little sleep for several nights," admitted *Der Dicke*. "The Führer is hard to deal with at such times; he has a way of calling you on the telephone when he can't sleep."

"What is he going to do next?" inquired the visitor.

"*Weiss Gott!* I doubt if he knows himself."

After such a question and such a reply, a skillful spy would pass on quickly, so as to seem casual. Said he: "The newspapermen pestered me so that I shut myself up in my hotel room all the time of the conference. I read a book about hunting in the American southwest, and one story seemed to have some bearing on what was happening at the moment. It was in the Rio Nueces country of Texas; a man had located a place where wild turkeys roosted at night, and he went just at sundown to get them. He tied his horse to a tree some distance away and crept to the spot and waited, and when the moon came up he shot six turkeys with his shotgun. He tied the turkeys together and hoisted them onto his back and started to carry them through the brush; but before he got very far he discovered that he was being followed by a mountain lion."

"They have lions in Texas?" inquired Göring.

"It is the panther, or cougar; it has a number of names—in South America the puma."

"I see."

"This mountain lion has a most terrifying scream, and the man realized that he was in grave danger; his shotgun would be of no use against a sudden charge in the dark. The creature had smelled the blood of those turkeys, and didn't mean to let them get away from him. So the man stopped and cut off one turkey and left it lying in the trail. That sufficed for a while; but then the man discovered that the lion was stalking him again, so he dropped another turkey. That went on, and every time the man dropped a turkey, he was safe for the time, but then to save his life he had to drop one more. Finally he used up his last turkey; then, by good fortune, he reached his horse, and leaped on, and, as they say in that country, 'tore a hole through the brush.' The story goes on that when he got home he told his wife of the adventure and she saw that he suddenly began to tremble; she asked: 'Why do you tremble now that you are safe?' He replied: 'It just occurred to me, suppose I had shot only five turkeys, what would have happened?' "

Der Dicke had got the point of this story before it was half told; at the end he burst into laughter, the loudest the visitor had ever heard from that capacious throat. "*Wunderbar!*" he exclaimed. "*Herrlich!*" Then he added: "The woman should have made an answer."

Of course it was up to Lanny to ask: "What would the answer be?"

"She should have told him: 'If you had not shot any turkeys at all, the lion would never have troubled you.' " So then it was Lanny's turn to chuckle, and the pair of them had a gay time over the plight of a British Prime Minister whose shotgun was a black umbrella and whose turkeys were called Abyssinia and Spain and Austria and Czechoslovakia and Poland and—who could say about Number Six?

"Perhaps it will be called Turkey," suggested the son of Budd-Erling.

VII

Lanny thought that he knew the Nazis by now, and didn't expect any more surprises; but Göring provided one. Lifting his considerable bulk from an overstuffed chair, he went to a near-by cabinet and took out a phonograph record. "Here is something that will answer questions in your mind," he said, and put it on the machine and pressed the lever. Then he resumed his seat, and Lanny listened to a voice discussing the attitude of the British government toward the Reds and "their so-called Socialist Soviet Republic." It was an English voice, cultivated, deliberate, with a touch of Oxford. It would say two or three sentences and then stop, and another voice would translate the sentences into German. The English voice would resume, declaring that the British government would raise no objections to moves which the German government might make toward the east, provided that they would make a satisfactory arrangement with the Poles; that the British government were firmly convinced that Communism was a great menace, and would be disposed to look upon the spread of its power as highly deleterious to European civilization.

There was nothing new in this point of view; Lanny had heard it expressed many scores of times by Ceddy and Gerald and their guests, and by other highly placed ladies and gentlemen at Bluegrass and at Cliveden. The voice to which he was now listening was speaking with slow precision, evidently on some formal occasion; it was a vaguely familiar voice, suggestive of Parliament, and Lanny thought: "It couldn't be Londonderry. It couldn't be Runciman. Could it be Nevile Henderson?" Not until a third voice broke in, asking a question in German, did it suddenly dawn upon a "P.A.'s" mind what he was listening to. The English voice was that of the Prime Minister, and the occasion was the first of his conferences with Hitler, in which he had settled, or thought he had settled, the destinies of Europe for the next generation.

The twelve-inch record was completed, and Lanny, younger and more movable, got up and stopped the machine. He stood by it, staring at the fat Marshal. "By God, you've got him over a barrel!" he exclaimed.

Der Dicke chuckled until he shook all over. "Can you imagine such a fool?"

"Does he know you have this recording?"

"*Herrgott, nein!* We have a new and marvelous invention, that catches the faintest whisper."

Lanny shivered inwardly, recalling the scene in Karinhall when his father had written little notes to caution him about being too cordial to Hermann's wife; also the occasions when he had gossiped with Hilde, and when he had been tempted to gossip with Ceddy in the Munich hotel. Had there been any place where he had yielded to the temptation?

"This is just a few extracts which we have put together on one record," added the Marshal, still grinning. "I would play you the whole thing, only it would take several hours, and would be very boring."

Lanny said: "I tried to keep myself busy looking at paintings while that conference was going on, but I found it difficult to keep my mind on them." Then, after a pause: "Tell me, Hermann, am I at liberty to tell my father about this?"

"I haven't asked you to keep it confidential, have I?"

"No, but there are some things that are understood among gentlemen."

"Put your mind on this situation. The British have been doing everything in their power to block our moves in eastern Europe. Everywhere we turn we hit our shins against obstacles they have set in our path. Some day in an emergency I may invite some of our Russian friends who understand English to listen to this recording; and it is barely possible that if Mr. Neville Chamberlain knew that we had it, he might be tempted to reduce the ardor of his diplomatic agents. You know, we don't want any unpleasantness that we can avoid."

"You have provided me with a delightful item of conversation at my next visit to Wickthorpe Castle," replied the son of Budd-Erling.

"You don't have to say where you heard the recording; just say what you heard, and the man with the umbrella will remember what he said."

Lanny went to his room convinced that he had indeed got a delightful item, but by the time he was ready for bed he had begun to wonder whether he had got anything at all. That was the way with the Nazi code of lying—they made it impossible to believe anything they said. What would be easier than for Göring to have had such a record faked? Some blackguard Englishman with a cultivated accent could be hired for a few pounds and be set to studying real records of Chamberlain's mannerisms. As for Hitler—well, if he didn't want to take the trouble to "frame" a record, Adolf Wagner could do it for him, and no Russian could tell the difference. Lanny decided that he would do some investigating before he helped to spread that delightful item.

VIII

Back in Munich, Lanny paid a visit to that crippled lady in the Nymphenburgerstrasse who enjoyed such a high reputation among the Nazi élite. Evidently the profession of "graphologist" was well rewarded, for the lady had a fashionable apartment and a maid in cap and uniform; Lanny was seated in a luxurious drawing-room, dimly lighted so that the waiting customers might avoid being stared at. When his turn came, the maid asked for his ten marks in advance, he being a stranger.

He was escorted to a table in a little cubicle, with some light on him and none on the lady; he could see that she was stooped, and wore a dark blue robe, hiding a crippled figure. "Be so good as to write a few words on the pad," she murmured, and he took a fountain pen which lay before him and wrote the German equivalent of: "Now is the time for all good men to come to the aid of the party." That had its meaning in Germany as in America.

The little old woman took the pad in her gnarled fingers and for a long time sat studying the script. Part of the time Lanny guessed that she was studying him. Finally she exclaimed, in a cracked voice: "What a strange man! What is the matter with you?"

The visitor guessed that was a rhetorical question, and did not answer. "You are an unhappy man," she went on; and then: "I do not like you!"

"I am sorry," he replied, humbly.

"You are two men, and they are at war. Presently you will not know which you really are. Make up your mind, or it will go badly with you. I see a tragic fate in store for you."

There was a pause; then Lanny asked: "Can you tell me where that fate is to be?"

He wondered if she was going to say "Hongkong." Even if she had, he wouldn't have been satisfied, of course; he would have called it "telepathy"—"that old telepathy!" in Tecumseh's phrase.

The woman said: "I am disturbed by your presence. I cannot do any more for you. I am sorry."

The rejected client did not ask for his ten marks back. He went out thinking hard about this strange world of the subconscious, so greatly neglected by orthodox science. Somehow he had taken it for granted that any power of mind-reading which a medium possessed would deal with aspects of his life such as a munitions-making grandfather or a Transcendentalist great-uncle. But suppose—just supposing!—that some old witch-woman should call up Gestapo headquarters in the Wittelsbacher Palace and report: "I have just been reading the mind of an American *Kunstsachverständiger*, and he is here for the purpose of spying on Number One, Number Two, and Number Three."

Lanny decided that for the present he would discontinue psychical researching inside the Third Reich!

IX

Rudolf Hess was back in Munich. He had his home here, with a family which he did not publicize as did others of the Nazi leaders. He was personally the most decent of those whom Lanny had met, the most agreeable because of his international upbringing and outlook. He was fanatically loyal to his leader, but where Party matters were not concerned he had a sense of humor, and with persons whom he trusted he put off his grim exterior.

Lanny paid him a call at the Braune Haus, the Party building whi h the Führer had purchased and made over according to his taste. It was on the Briennerstrasse, a fashionable neighborhood, with the papal nuncio right across the street. It was a four-story building, set well back and protected by high fences. Outside were SS guards, and inside was a riot of swastikas of all sizes, on grillwork, lamp brackets, windows, doorknobs, ceilings. Hess's office was simple and unostentatious; its windows looked out upon the Führerhaus, one of the magnificent structures which Adi had built since taking power, and in which the recent world-shaking conference had been held.

Naturally they talked about that event and its consequences. The Deputy Führer explained that for him it meant a great increase in duties and responsibilities; he had a new Party province to govern, and since the Party administration was everywhere more important than the political government, Hess had his hands full right now. He explained that the type of men suited to agitation and guerrilla warfare was not the same as that needed for administration after a victory, so he had a lot of demoting and promoting to do, and many heads to knock together. Lanny listened sympathetically, and was glad in his heart that he didn't have either to administrate or be administrated.

This was the period during which Hitler was increasing his demands on the Czech carcass day by day. The "international commission" which was supposed to decide disputes consisted of one Nazi official, one Czech, and the British, French, and Italian ambassadors to Berlin. These last were busy gentlemen, and didn't want to be bothered by complaints or talk about fair play. When the Nazis set up a claim that a certain section of the Bohemian plain had more than fifty per cent of German population, the ambassadors didn't go to make a count, nor did they pay heed to the fact that the territory contained some mineral resource or industrial enterprise which the Führer needed for his war preparations. They just voted the Czech delegate down and the German troops in.

Of course it meant friction, and lamentations from the Czechs, some of which got into the foreign press and annoyed the Nazis. Herr Goebbels had dropped his press campaign against this fragment of a state, but now he was taking it up again. Lanny said: "You can't get along with those people; they are too different from Germans."

"I am afraid you may be right, Herr Budd," conceded the Deputy.

"The Führer said: 'We want no Czechs'; but my guess is, he'll be able to find work for them if he has to take them over." The secret agent said this with a grin, and the dour Deputy grinned in return. No more words were needed between friends.

Lanny added: "I am wondering why the Führer had to go so far as to give a guarantee to Czechoslovakia. The British wanted it, of course; but did he have to give way?"

"He always knows what he is doing," replied Hess. *(Hitler hat immer Recht!)* "What he gave is a guarantee against unprovoked aggression, and you may be sure that if there is any, the Czechs will do the provoking." The smile had gone from the Deputy's face, and he meant this statement without any trace of irony. Anyone who heard him would have been glad not to be a Czech.

X

Adolf Hitler did not like the cold and formal city of Berlin, and stayed there only when ceremonies and diplomatic etiquette required it. Munich was his playground and the birthplace of his party; his own kind of people were here, and he would dump responsibilities into the laps of his subordinates and fly to his mountain castle. From there Munich was only a couple of hours away, and he would step into his black bullet-proof Mercédès, followed by three cars full of SS men, and speed away to his peculiar pleasures.

He liked to visit the Schwabing district, which was Munich's Quartier Latin, and dine in the Osteria Bavaria restaurant, where his vegetable plate was prepared by a chef who knew his tastes. He liked to put on black chamois shorts and a green *Loden Frey* hunting jacket and visit the October Festival, mingling with the people and being photographed with children around him—his plain-clothes guards keeping carefully out of the camera's eye. He liked to dress in black trousers and immaculate white jacket and visit the Theater am Gärtnerplatz —now giving Strauss's *Fledermaus*—and see his personally selected "Beauty Dancer" giving her performance in the second act. Adi would arrive during the intermission, and his Führer Standard would be hung from the railing of his box; before the performance was resumed, the plain-clothes men scattered through the audience would give the Hitler salute, and the entire audience would rise and make their thrilling response. Then, in the interest of a healthy eroticism, the Führer would sit with a pair of high-powered glasses fixed upon the young, supple, and entirely nude Dorothy van Bruck displaying her many charms.

Or perhaps he would visit the Künstlerhaus on the Lenbachplatz, which he had just rebuilt. This had been in the old days a clubhouse for world-famous artists, and Adi, who was pleased to be hailed by his adorers as the "Greatest Artist in the World," had made it over on a scale of magnificence suited to his New Order. A suite had been set apart for him, and when he discovered that a large Jewish synagogue interfered with his view, he ordered the building torn down and the site used for the parking of Nazi cars. All self-respecting artists stayed away from the place and it had become in effect a night club for the Party bosses. Beautiful girls with theatrical ambitions were always on call, and companies gave private performances at command. Such shows as the American Acrobats and the Can Can Ballet, with French dancers giving the Hitler salute with one leg instead of one arm—these helped to divert the mind of a world conqueror from his cares. The Number One would go home at three or four in the morning, and then the real fun would begin for his champagne-soaked subordinates.

XI

Such was the "Artists' House"; and still more grandiose was another structure just completed in the Englischer Garten, called "The House of German Art." It was, in a way, a monument to one of the most significant events in the life of Adi Schicklgruber, his rejection as an art student by a committee of judges in Vienna. All his youthful hopes had been centered upon such a career, and when he submitted his work and was coldly told that he had no talent, it had meant for him a sentence to sleep in the shelter for bums and to earn his bread by painting and selling postcards. When by his political genius he had made himself master of Germany, one of his burning desires had been to prove himself the Fatherland's greatest critic and patron of the arts. So had come that colossal marble structure, built on swampy ground at tremendous cost—but nothing mattered in the cause of proving how great had been the error of the Vienna committee!

After four years the work was done, and the wits of Munich had dubbed it the "Greek Railroad Station." It was an unusual art museum, in that it was also a restaurant, a beerhall, and a night club. Had not the Nazi Party been born in a beerhall, and had not all the Führer's early speeches been delivered in such places? The new order was pledged to the extermination of Christian-Jewish asceticism; eating, drinking, and making merry were the order of the new day, and all young Germans were told to build strong bodies and to bring new strong-bodied Aryans into the world as early and often as possible. Most Nazi temples provided an abundance of private rooms in which a beginning might be made at any hour of the day or night.

Lanny Budd visited this temple of art, and found it not easy to keep his shudders from becoming visible. Not that there were no good paintings to be seen, for Munich had been a home of art for centuries, and not all the good painters were in concentration camps. When they painted landscapes the places were recognizable, and when they painted Bavarian peasants they frequently revealed sympathy. But when they painted a naked Aryan Leda in the embrace of the swan, it made one think of the "feelthy postcards" which were peddled all over the Mediterranean lands. When they painted Stormtroopers in uniform and Nazi implements of war, it seemed that the work belonged in the Department of Propaganda and Public Enlightenment, presided over by a crippled little dwarf.

The visitor stood before a large and extremely bad painting called

The Spirit of the Stormtroopers, depicting a column of Nazi youths marching in the brave old days when they were engaged in making the streets free to the brown battalions. Concerning this work the gossip-monger of the old regime, Baron von Zinszollern, had told a most awful story, having to do with the festival called the "Day of German Art" in the previous July, when this and thousands of other new works had been revealed to the world. One of the curses of the Nazi regime had been homosexuality, and at the time of the Blood Purge Hitler had used this as his pretext for ordering the murder of Ernst Röhm and others of his oldest associates. It had been necessary to outlaw the prac-tice, and the crime had been described in Paragraph 175 of the Crimi-nal Code. Since it has always been the practice of civilized man to find some subtle way of alluding to things that are not nice, it had come about in Germany that *"hundertfünfundsiebzig"* had become the Ger-man way of whispering a reference to this form of abnormality.

And now, here came this magnificent art show, trumpeted to the world as evidence of Nazi love of the higher things of life. Several hun-dred thousand catalogues had been printed, intended to be sold for one mark, twenty-five pfennigs each; and was it the operation of blind chance or of some malicious trickster on the hanging committee that the number assigned to a painting entitled *The Spirit of the Storm-troopers* should be that much-whispered number? The discovery was made by an American correspondent, who reported it to the Gestapo, with the result that all the catalogues were destroyed, and if rumor could be believed, somebody high up in Munich art affairs lost his life. When the "Greek Railroad Station" opened, the marching Nazi heroes were found with a harmless number, while *hundertfünfundsiebzig* was assigned to a *Vase of Flowers.*

XII

Lanny Budd went to call on the Führer in his elegant Munich apart-ment in the Prinzregentenstrasse. He found the great man as happy as the cat that has swallowed the canary and has not been spanked for it. He did not refer to the fact that a wise and understanding American had advised him how to proceed, and Lanny was, of course, too tact-ful to hint at it; he judged that the occasion called for a good stiff dose of flattery, and he told the greatest statesman of modern times that the world marveled at the diplomatic finesse he had displayed; above all the sense of timing, which had been the essence of this most difficult job. Such a humiliation for a British Prime Minister—and such pitiful efforts in Parliament to dignify himself! There had been nothing like it since King Henry had come to Canossa.

The Führer behaved as cats do when they lie in front of a warm fire and have their fur stroked the right way. He appreciated the discernment of this sympathetic visitor, and presently when the visitor hinted that there might be a weakness in the Führer's position, he asked at once what it was; when told that it was the guarantee against unprovoked aggression given to Czechoslovakia, he smiled slyly and said that this was a guarantee against the aggression of other states. See how he had reduced the demands of Poland and Hungary for Czech territory! But that was far from meaning that the Czech politicians were free to carry on their intrigues against Germany abroad, and if they kept it up they would soon find they had no guarantee against German discipline.

"We Nazis have learned that diplomacy and war are two sides of the same shield," declared the Führer. "Very surely we shall not allow anyone to make war on us unpunished." He spoke of the fact that the Foreign Minister of Poland had just been to Rumania in an effort to make an agreement for mutual defense. Of course such an agreement could be aimed at no one but himself, declared Hitler, and proceeded to denounce the Poles as another subhuman tribe, victims of priestcraft and clerical intrigue. "The cross and the swastika cannot exist side by side," declared Adi. "The Versailles *Diktat* has put the Poles in position to blockade Germany from East Prussia, and who but our enemies could imagine that I will permit such a thorn to go on festering in the body of the Reich?"

"Aha!" thought the "P.A."—another territorial claim in Europe! Said he: "That remark interests me for a personal reason, Exzellenz. May I talk about my own plans for a moment?"

"I am always interested in my friends' plans, Herr Budd."

"A few months ago I was passing through the Corridor, and chanced to see a little place that I thought I would love to own. You know how it is—you proved it here at the Berghof, if you start with a place already built you save a lot of time; you have the roads, and the beautiful trees that would take a lifetime to get, and a place to live while you plan improvements. I inquired about this little property and found that it is within my means. Only one thing deterred me—I could not bear to live under a reactionary Polish dictatorship. I thought: 'I will wait and see what happens.'"

"You won't have to wait indefinitely, Herr Budd; that much I can tell you."

"I don't want to commit an impropriety and put myself in the position of a real estate speculator. If I should make the purchase, it would be to have a home for the rest of my days; and one of my reasons would be that it is in convenient driving distance of Kurt Meissner, and of yourself, if I may make so bold as to count upon your friendship. I should probably wish to become a citizen of your Third Reich."

"You will be most welcome, I assure you. And certainly you can count upon the fact that all the impositions of Versailles are going to be wiped off the books of history. If the place you speak of is in a district in which the Germans are a majority, or in which they were a majority before they were driven out by Polish misgovernment, you can be sure that it will come under my protection very soon."

"*Herzlichen Dank, Herr Reichskanzler!* There is no reason why I should pay more than necessary, so I think I'll wait until your intentions have become manifest, and the Poles will be more disposed to sell."

Lanny said this with a smile, and the Führer broke into a grin. He had a sort of ghoulish humor when it was a question of his ability to outwit his opponents. "Wait about six months, Herr Budd, and I will promise to soften the price of your future home!"

XIII

The Führer had just ordered the new puppet government at Prague to break off its Russian alliance, and the order had been obeyed. He said now that he hoped soon to see the French people come to their senses and realize that dalliance with the monster of Bolshevism could do them nothing but harm. This dalliance represented the nadir of depravity to which venal politicians could descend; French newspapers and Cabinet members had been bought outright by Russian gold, and so long as such men held power there could be no friendship between France and Germany. That was what the Führer meant by the statement that diplomacy and war were two sides of the same shield; the Russian alliance was a perpetual act of aggression against his *Regierung*.

Lanny remarked: "You are aware, of course, that many statesmen in both France and Britain are hoping that you will put down Bolshevism for them."

"While they sit and watch me bleed to death! Believe me, Herr Budd, I am nobody's monkey and pull nobody's chestnuts out of the fire. When the war on Bolshevism begins, they will help, and I'll be certain they are all the way in before I put in one foot."

"Tell me," said the visitor; "have you thought of the possibility that you might make a non-aggression pact with the Soviets? That would give Britain and France quite a jolt."

"Indeed it would; and be sure that I don't overlook any cards in my hand. I am well aware that Britain and France have been doing their best to set the Bolsheviks against me, and it is no part of my program to let my enemies move first."

"When I go to London," remarked the art expert, "Lord Wickthorpe is going to ask me as to your views. Shall I tell him that?"

"Tell him anything that I have said to you. That is the advantage of my position; I tell them the whole truth, and it is as if I had said nothing, for they do not believe me."

"You are something unique in the history of Europe, Exzellenz, and they do not know what to make of you. I have never before called you '*Mein Führer*,' but I think from now on I shall have to do so."

And after that, of course, a presidential agent was free to share in all the secrets of Nazi diplomacy!

31

Courage Mounteth with Occasion

I

LANNY had got the information he wanted, and was through in Munich. He had found a purchaser for another of Göring's superfluous art works, and would drive to Berlin, pay for the painting, and take it out with him; he made it a rule never to ship anything from inside Naziland, dishonesty having become so rampant in the country that he was unwilling to trust even the German employees of the American Express Company. He would pay duty calls on several persons in Berlin such as Herr Thyssen and Dr. Schacht, who were free talkers; he would listen to General Emil Meissner tell about the newest technical achievements of the Reichswehr; also, he wouldn't fail to collect a few tidbits of gossip from the Fürstin von Donnerstein.

The day before he left the Bavarian capital a dreadful piece of news came over the radio. A Jewish youth in Paris, a refugee crazed by his personal sufferings and those of his people, had shot Eduard vom Rath, official of the Germany embassy whom Lanny had met in the Château de Belcour. The Nazi radio burst into a frenzy, blaming the crime upon the incitements of the British press, which had persisted in publishing stories about the persecution of the Jews in Germany. It happened that the day of the Paris shooting was the anniversary of the Beerhall Putsch, so all the Nazi leaders were in Munich. That night Adolf Wagner gave the order, and a wild pillaging of Jewish shops began; Lanny in his hotel room heard the crashing of glass and the yells of the Stormtroopers, and went out to watch the disciplined marauders smashing plate-glass windows and showcases with sticks and stones, filling their pockets with watches and jewelry, tying up bundles of furs, lingerie, silk stockings—whatever they thought might please their lady friends.

That wholesale looting went on the whole night, and many of the Nazis in their greed got badly cut with flying splinters of glass or with the sharp edges in showcases. Lanny witnessed one of the strangest of sights, a battle royal between the Stormtroopers and the SS guards of Marshal Göring in front of the Bernheimer establishment which dealt in oriental rugs, antiques, and objets d'art. He supposed it was a brawl over the possession of these treasures, but later on he learned that Herr Bernheimer was an "honorary Aryan," the only one in Munich; he had supplied the fat commander with all the furnishings of Karinhall, and thus was entitled to protection.

Next morning when Lanny set out upon his drive, the street-cleaning department of the city was engaged in sweeping up the broken glass and loading it into trucks, and the looting was no longer an enterprise for the rank-and-file Nazis, but was being systematized in proper German fashion. Members of the city's Kulturkammer had been commissioned to ransack Jewish homes and carry off to the museums all works of art of whatever character which might interest the Aryan public. All the male Jews of Munich were being rounded up by the Gestapo and carted off to Dachau; some who had learned what went on in that place of horror were shooting themselves or jumping out of windows.

It was the same all over Germany; more than sixty thousand Jews were put into concentration camps in this dreadful "November Pogrom," and the number who were murdered could never be guessed. Lanny, who had started late, stopped for lunch in Regensburg, home of one of Göring's great airplane factories. He there observed an elderly bearded Jew sneaking along the street like a frightened animal, doubtless trying to get to his home or some other place of hiding. A gang of half a dozen of the Hitlerjugend, boys of no more than fourteen or fifteen, set upon him with clubs and with their "Daggers of Honor." The poor man screamed for mercy, putting his head down and hunching his shoulders to protect himself from the blows. They beat him to the ground and then pounded and kicked him and slashed his clothing and his flesh with the daggers. They quit only when he was such a mess of blood that they could not touch him without ruining their brown uniforms. They went off singing the *Horst Wessel* song, leaving the motionless form lying in the gutter.

There was nothing Lanny could do about it. He was safe because he was an Aryan and looked it, but he would have ruined his career forever if he had made any move to interfere with the German effort to protect their "racial purity." Grief took away his appetite, and he got back into his car, depriving the busy city of Regensburg of the two or three marks he would have spent in one of its cafés.

II

The same scenes were taking place in all the towns along the Munich-Berlin *Autobahn;* looted shops gaped with broken windows and empty shelves, and trucks were loaded with wretched Jews, many of them having faces and clothing red with blood. Nowhere was the situation worse than in Berlin; organized brutality prevailed for a week, and turned the cold and proud capital into a charnelhouse for Lanny Budd. Impossible to have any sort of pleasure there; impossible to read a newspaper, to take part in social life, to enjoy rational conversation. Painting, poetry, drama, music, all had been poisoned by this systematized lunacy. You might say that you would go to a concert hall and hear great music out of the past; but Bach, Beethoven, and Brahms were mocked by modern Germany—their scherzos were like dancing on a grave, their adagios became the unbearable agony of a great and noble culture being dragged down and defiled.

Two cultures, in fact, the German and the Jewish, equally worthy, and reciprocally dependent. Lanny had met many Jews in the Fatherland; all sorts, both good and bad, as was the case with Germans. He had observed that there were characteristic Jewish faults, as there were characteristic German faults, and he saw little to choose between them; he liked the domineering German just as little as he liked the devious Jew. On the other hand he liked the ardent idealistic Jew as much as he liked the genial and warmhearted German, and he knew that these types supplemented each other; he knew that they got along well together, for he had seen it happening.

The tragic events of the time were really a family quarrel, for the Jews had been in Germany for many centuries, and thought of themselves as Germans before they were Jews. They had prospered, and had their share in the country's history and the building of its culture. They had been proud of themselves, and looked down upon the Jews of Poland and Russia as an inferior breed. Now the Nazis were beating them down to a level below the dogs of Germany—for that same Hitlerjugend who had murdered the old Jew in Regensburg would love and cherish their dogs.

In Lanny Budd the souls of Heine and Toller, of Mendelssohn and Mahler, Marx and Lassalle, Ehrlich and Einstein and a hundred other great German Jews cried out against this horror. It was really not the German people who were perpetrating it, but a band of fanatics who had seized a nation and were perverting its youth and turning them into murderers and psychopaths. Germans would awaken some day as from a nightmare, and contemplate with loathing and dismay the crimes that had been committed in their name. They would do penance for centuries, having to read the pages of history on which these deeds were recorded; they would bow their heads and shed tears upon the pages, knowing that to the rest of mankind the name of German had become a byword and a hissing.

Lanny thought of cultivated and gracious Jews he had known in this nightmare land. Those in Munich who were not dead or in Dachau would be seeking refuge in the woods which bordered the river Isar, or in the Alpine foothills, depending upon the charity of the peasants for food. Those in Berlin, if they had not cut their own throats or jumped into the city's canals, would be hiding in cellars, coming out at night and trying to escape in a freight car or canal boat. Suppose one of them were to telephone to Lanny at the Hotel Adlon, saying: "I am in peril of my life. Help me!"—what would he answer? In the old days he had done what he could for the Robin family, but what could he do now for the Hellsteins or the humble Schönhaus family? He couldn't say: "I am a secret agent, and my duty is elsewhere." He could only mumble some excuse which would mean to the hearer: "I am a coward and a man without human feelings."

III

Lanny attended to his affairs in Berlin, and then on a day of heavy and cold rain he drove to the Belgian border, and straight on, without stopping except for a meal, to Paris. There, in his hotel, he wrote his latest report on Germany, and put it into the mail.

For a few days *la ville lumière* seemed like home; Zoltan was here, and Emily, old friends whose hearts were warm and whose minds were not perverted. His mother had gone back to Bienvenu, and he called her on the telephone and got the family news: Marceline was soon to get her divorce; she was dancing her head off; the baby was well; Madame had got over the flu. Lanny reported that he was going to' London and then to New York, where he had a lot of business, some of it urgent.

There was the autumn Salon, worth a day of any art expert's time. There was a lot of nude flesh, but no marching Nazis, and the number 175 was represented by a harmless landscape with sheep. Also there was a visit to the de Bruyne family, eager to hear the latest news from *la patrie's* new ally; they deplored but excused the pogrom, and looked upon the Four-Power Pact as the most fortunate event in French history for many a year. The hated Franco-Russian alliance was for all practical purposes dead, and now Daladier had got emergency powers and was able to govern "by decree"; a plague of labor revolts would be put down without the customary weak compromises.

In short, French politics looked more hopeful to a family of French aristocrats than it had for a generation. They were proud of their personal martyrdom, and considered what had happened at Munich as their vindication. They talked freely, as usual, and Lanny listened to the latest details of wire-pulling by the "two hundred families," who collectively had decided upon a compromise with Hitler as the cheapest form of insurance. "It means the surrender of our power in Central Europe," admitted Denis père, sadly; "but we still have North Africa and the colonies, and we are safe behind our Maginot Line. Above all, we don't have to make any more concessions to revolution at home."

It wasn't Lanny's business to educate this self-made capitalist, but only to make remarks that would draw him out. The same was the case with Schneider, who was at his town house and invited the son of Budd-Erling to lunch. The elderly munitions king was carrying his burdens not too easily; he seemed worried and far from well. His interests were spread all over Europe, so he was not so optimistic as

Denis. He reported on the arrangements he had made about Skoda; he would remain the owner and get generous profits, but would not be able to take them out of Germany; he would have to turn them into extension of plant, or building of new plant, as a government bureau in Berlin would direct. "In plain words, I am giving my time and skill to making armaments for Germany; and if I don't like it I can sell out for what they offer me, which is practically nothing." The Baron shrugged his shoulders in the French fashion. "What can a man do, in these strange times?"

Lanny couldn't tell him what to do. He could only report what Nazis Number One, Number Two, and Number Three had said about what was coming to the rest of Czechoslovakia, and to Poland, and then to Hungary and Rumania and the other turkeys. The most staggering thing of all was the suggestion that if France and Britain didn't hurry up and make their peace with the Führer, he might turn to Russia for a friend; that truly was like seeing the world turned upside down and shaken. "Has the man no principles whatever?" demanded the master of Le Creusot. By his own principles he had managed to preserve his munitions plants from bombing during the World War, but he couldn't see how he was going to achieve that feat a second time. "Your father is the wise one," he remarked. "He got cash, and took it out of Europe!"

IV

One more report to Washington, this time on the situation in France. Then Lanny stored his car in Paris and took flight to London. At Wickthorpe he was welcomed, and inspected the lovely new baby and paid all the proper compliments. This tiny mite of life with the pink cheeks, golden down on the head and lips forever sucking, was the Honorable James Ponsonby Cavendish Cedric Barnes Masterson—named for various relatives, including his American grandfather. Already he had put Frances completely into the shade, and would keep her there the rest of her days.

Lanny could now talk safely in an Englishman's home, his castle in which there were no dictaphones. Interesting indeed to hear what had gone on inside the conference room of the Führerhaus in Munich; the little details of personality and manners of the four men who had settled the destiny of Europe. His lordship had been called in at one stage of the drafting, because he had made a special study of the courses of rivers and the boundaries of towns involved in the transfer. The discussion had been carried on in the German language, and every word had to be translated to the Prime Minister. Il Duce thought that he knew German, but his efforts were terrible, and did him no good with Hitler, who made faces. The Führer's own German was far from perfect, but that didn't trouble him.

Lanny had much to tell, and told it freely, on the principle that fair exchange was no robbery. To hear a permanent official of the Foreign Office react to Hitler's latest outbursts was to know pretty surely what the Tory government of Britain were going to do in the course of the next few months. (The government of Britain were plural—that was one way you could tell an Englishman from the rest of the English-speaking world.) The government were going to do everything possible to avoid offending a touchy Reichskanzler, even to the extent of censoring British opinion on the subject of "Munich." American news-reels which ventured criticism were barred, and a strict rule against censure of Chamberlain was being enforced by the British radio.

But the ghost would not stay laid; for there was no way to keep individuals from voicing their sense of outrage in print and at public meetings. Just now a hot controversy was going on over the part played in the settlement by Colonel Lindbergh and Lady Astor. "Lindy" had been in Germany in August, being shown all the secrets of the Air Force, and then he had gone to the Soviet Union and been treated as an honored guest. He had come back to England, right at the critical moment while the crisis was at its height, and, so the story ran, had told Nancy's guests at Cliveden that Soviet aviation was "utterly demoralized," and that Göring's Air Force could defeat the combined forces of Britain, France, Czechoslovakia, and the Soviet Union. That, insisted the critics, had turned the tide and brought about the decision to surrender; so now the "Cliveden set" carried on its already burdened shoulders the blame for the greatest diplomatic defeat in Britain's history.

A story ready-made for the Reds and their fellow-travelers! In all the pubs of Britain, and likewise in the drawing-rooms, the issue was debated with heat. Lady Nancy, *née* Langhorne of Virginia, Conservative gadfly of the House of Commons, declared that the whole story was "Communist propaganda." First she said that Lindbergh had not been at any Cliveden dinner recently and had not discussed the Soviet Union there. Then her memory was refreshed and she said that he had been at a luncheon, and had "talked about Russia in general," but she couldn't recall what he had said or who had been present. The makers of Communist propaganda found this unlikely, and it only added fuel to the flames.

Lanny knew that Roosevelt had met the mistress of Cliveden, and that he was interested in personalities; so a conscientious agent collected the names of those who had been present at the famous luncheon. Members of the "Cliveden set" found it amusing to be called that, and said that of course they had tried to learn all they could about German versus Soviet aviation, being concerned to protect their country from getting into a fight which it might not be able to win. War would be no bally joke these days, because it wouldn't be confined to the troops in the field but would involve everybody at home, and what was to keep a bomb from being dropped on Buckingham Palace or the House of Commons? What statesman would want to run such risks to oblige the Reds or their fellow-travelers—or to save for a mongrel nation like Czechoslovakia a strip of land which ought never to have been taken away from Austria, and which should go to Germany now because she had already got Austria?

V

In short, the British government were committed to the policy of satisfying the Führer, and must continue in that course, even though it meant stubbing their official toes many times. It meant being told that the Führer was highly incensed at a speech by Mr. Lloyd George, and then at British criticisms of a nationwide pogrom. It meant taking up a discussion of the limiting of air forces, and having the Germans express willingness, on the basis that they were to have three times the strength of the British. The government rejected this, but did decide to modify their building program to meet Hitler's wishes; they would have fewer bombers, meant for attack, and more fighters, meant for defense. When Gerald Albany told Lanny about that, Lanny's reply was that it would bring his father over to England in a hurry!

As part of the appeasement policy there must be a settlement with the Duce—all according to that world conqueror's wishes. They would recognize his title to Abyssinia and his right to intervene in the Spanish war. The Loyalists there were still holding out, in spite of Franco's frequent announcements that they were beaten. Now the British would recognize Franco's belligerency, and would force the French to do the same. Il Duce's reply to this courtesy was most elegant; when the French ambassador came before the Italian deputies to present the gift, the deputies shouted: "Tunisia!"—which meant that they wanted to take this French colony, presumably by the method of Hitler in Austria and Czechoslovakia. Outside in the streets the Fascisti were shouting: "Nice! Savoy! Corsica!" Those cries had special interest for Lanny Budd, who had not forgotten the idea of his ex-brother-in-law coming back to France with his army. In Nice, the city where Vittorio had disposed of the stolen paintings, he would be only ten miles from Bienvenu; and just where would his Duce draw the boundary line?

VI

For Prime Minister Chamberlain and his Cabinet, life had become "just one damn thing after another." The Führer had solemnly promised that if he got the Sudetenland with British help, he would forget the subject of colonies for a few years; but now he was talking colonies —and in that rude and harsh manner which he had brought into the diplomatic drawing-room. "We wish to negotiate, but if others decline to grant us our rights we shall secure them in a different way." And what were the British government going to do about that? It was the business of a presidential agent to meet the key people and tell them what he had heard the Führer say on the subject, thus luring them into stating their reactions. Needless to say, no British government ever gave up anything that belonged to Britain; but there were Togoland and the Cameroons, belonging to France, and perhaps the Führer might be contented with that brace of turkeys.

The inquisitive agent heard various suggestions, all having to do with sacrifices to be made by other nations. It was the British fleet which protected the little fellows in their colonial possessions; if Britannia ever ceased to rule the waves, what chance would there be for the French Empire, the Belgian, the Portuguese, or the Dutch? Was it not reasonable to expect these dependent nations to contribute at least one turkey to Adi Schicklgruber's Christmas feast? Lanny heard in British tea parties references to sections of the earth which hitherto had been mere names to him, and obliged him to consult the large globe in the library of Wickthorpe Castle. French Equatorial Africa, a huge territory, from which slices of dark meat could surely be cut. The Belgian Congo was likewise enormous, and very fat. Portuguese Angola was small, but then, so was Portugal; she had had a treaty with Britain for some six centuries, the oldest still valid treaty in the world, so Gerald declared. It had been several centuries since Portugal had been in position to protect herself, and surely now she might be asked to pay a long-standing debt. Security cost money in these times, said a pious high churchman.

Lanny went to London and met Rick, according to their new arrangement. They had lunch in a hotel room for greater privacy, and exchanged secrets which would surely have caused each individual Aryan blond hair of Ceddy or Gerald to stand on end. According to his custom, Lanny put a couple of hundred pounds into his friend's hands, to be used in promoting the anti-Nazi cause in England. Having friends among the Reds, Rick could reveal that Hitler had just recently made approaches to Moscow on the subject of a *rapprochement*. "Will they consider it?" Lanny asked, and the answer was: "Good God, no!"

Lanny wanted very much to believe that; but he was living in a mixed-up world where one could not count too much upon anything. He made this remark to his friend, who replied: "That is one thing I would stake my life upon. It is a question of ideological differences, utterly irreconcilable."

VII

For the first time in his life Lanny Budd found himself coming to think of America as home. America hadn't as yet got as far in corruption as old Europe; people were kinder there; less sophisticated, less highly cultured, perhaps, but also less dangerous. The social conflicts which were rending the old world were developing in the new, but they hadn't progressed so far; there would be at least a few years of respite. Lanny decided that he was tired of wandering, and might find a wife, or let his wise and kind stepmother find one for him; he would settle down, read some books, refresh his piano technique, and enjoy the luxury of saying what he thought.

He boarded one of the big ocean liners at Southampton and had a stormy passage near the end of November. The flight of time was accelerated by a charming widow from California, a state which Lanny had never visited; she looked and acted as if she had money, and made it plain that she liked the son of Budd-Erling and might be willing to console his mysterious melancholy. He danced with her, and avoided any chance of displeasing her by the expression of unorthodox opinions. But when she invited him to visit the Golden State, he told her that he had to be about his father's business—and did not intimate that it was the Great White Father in the Great White House.

Ashore in New York, he was driven to the airport, and called Gus Gennerich in Washington. He was shocked to learn that the man had died while accompanying the President on his trip to South America in the previous August. There had been no way to let a secret agent know about this. He was wondering what to do, when the voice, a woman's, inquired: "Are you calling on official business?" When he answered that he was, she said: "Call Mr. Baker," and gave a number. So Lanny put in another call, and when a man's voice said "Baker," he replied: "Zaharoff, 103, phoning from New York." The voice instructed him to come to a certain street number in Washington.

He had time before the plane left to call Robbie and report his arrival. He was off on a picture deal, he said, without saying where. He didn't want his father to get Washington fixed in his mind, and start guessing about Lanny's errands. Instead, he told what "Baron Tailor" had said about Robbie being so lucky; also the news that Britain had changed the proportion of fighters over bombers—which drove all other thoughts out of the father's head.

There being still time, Lanny called Johannes at his office, and promised him a load of news before long. All the family were well, its head reported; Hansi was playing in Carnegie Hall next week, and no news had come from Aaron Schönhaus. "Oh, Lanny, that awful pogrom!" exclaimed the exiled financier, with a catch in his voice. Lanny said: "I saw a little of it, and will tell you."

VIII

Up the movable steps into the luxuriously fitted plane, and then that miracle of flight to which Lanny could never grow indifferent. Younger men might take it for granted, but not one who had seen it born into the world. Lanny had been a grown boy when his father had taken him and Rick to see with their own eyes the dream of Icarus and Leonardo made reality. That had been on the Salisbury Plain in England, just before the outbreak of the World War; and now the mature man sat at ease and looked down upon the land of his fathers from a viewpoint which they had never been able to attain: cities and villages that were all roofs, roads with tiny dots moving on them, rivers with boats that seemed fixed in glass, farmhouses with painted roofs and fields dark with wetness. Then, in one hour, the white marble structures of the capital, ever multiplying as the interest of America shifted from business to politics, from Wall Street to Washington. More softly than a duck sliding down into the water the plane settled onto the runway, and Lanny stepped forth with his two light suitcases. He checked them in the station and stepped into a taxi.

At a small brick dwelling he rang the bell, and the door was opened by a vigorous youngish man with a businesslike manner. "Baker," he said, and Lanny replied: "Zaharoff." Invited in, the visitor said: "I only just learned of Gus's death."

"What is it you wish?"

"To see the Chief."

"You understand that you have to identify yourself to me."

"I am under orders not to give my name."

"I know that. You can tell me about Gus, and the procedure you followed with him."

Lanny recited all the details that came to his mind. "Gus Gennerich was a big blond fellow, quiet and decided in manner; he used to be a New York policeman, so the Governor told me. Gus never talked about himself, in fact he didn't talk to me at all. I met him on the street at night, by appointment; he picked me up in his car and took me into the White House by the 'social door.' We went up by the stairway to the second floor; always at night, and the Chief was in bed, propped up reading. He wears pongee pajamas, blue-striped or plain blue, and a blue coat sweater, but the last time he had a blue cape. He always has a stack of papers, and a mystery or a sea story. There is a typewriter in the corner at the right, beyond the foot of the bed. A colored valet sits outside the door. Is that enough?"

"You must understand, I wouldn't take any stranger into that room without searching him. After the Chief has O.K.'d you, it will be different."

"Certainly," answered Lanny. "Do you mean now?"

"I mean before we go in. I have made an appointment for you at ten tonight."

"That's all right. Shall I come here?"

"I'll pick you up as Gus did." The man named a corner, and Lanny jotted it down for safety. His mind was greatly relieved, for he had feared that he might not be able to get to the President without betraying his identity.

IX

The traveler got his bags and put up at the Mayflower. Then he went for a walk, to see the new sights of his country's capital, which had been nearly a century and a half a-building, and had grown more in half a dozen years than in its first century. White marble appeared to be *de rigueur*, and Adi's House of German Art in Munich was being put in the shade by a National Gallery of Art which was to cost fifteen million dollars and to house many great collections, beginning with the banker Mellon's. In the bad old Coolidge days this two-hundred-times millionaire had been called "the greatest Secretary of the Treasury since Hamilton," and it had been his sad fate to lead his country's finances into collapse, and then be forced to admit that he had no idea how to put Humpty-Dumpty together again.

Lanny dined alone, read the evening paper, and took another walk, to get clear in his mind what he wanted to report to his boss. He had made up his mind to ask for a release from further duties; he wasn't going to criticize what the boss was doing or failing to do, but merely to say that he didn't feel that he, the secret agent, was accomplishing very much. He wanted to throw off his camouflage, tell the world what he really thought about Nazi-Fascism, and do what one American could to arouse the democratic peoples to the peril into which they were drifting. If it wrecked the art-experting business, all right; the son of Budd-Erling had enough to live on. He might even go into the business of making fighter planes—upon which the future of the world appeared to depend.

Promptly on the minute he stepped into Baker's car. There was another man driving, and while the car rolled on, the new arrival was subjected to a going-over by swift and well-trained hands; not merely all his pockets, but under his armpits and in his trouser legs, where a small weapon might be concealed. Even the inside of his hat was not overlooked. "O.K.," said the searcher, at last, and apologized: "We don't take any chances these days."

"I hope not," replied Lanny, with feeling.

X

Once more he retraced the familiar journey and found himself in the presence of that big man with the powerful shoulders and the exuberant smile. His greeting left no doubt in the guard's mind that this was the real and right "Zaharoff." The man took his departure, closing the door behind him, and the visitor seated himself by the bedside and underwent the scrutiny of F.D.R.'s bright and lively blue eyes. "Well, Lanny!" said the warm voice with deep overtones. "You have waited a long time between calls."

"A lot of things were happening, and I kept on the trail of them. Have you received my reports?"

"Every single one, in order as numbered. I have them in a special file. Incidentally, I have them in my head. Tell me what is coming next."

"Hitler is going to take Prague and what is left of Czechoslovakia. You can place your bets on that."

"And how soon?"

"By the end of the winter, I should guess. That will be six months after his Sudeten move. It appears to take him about that long to consolidate an acquisition, and to carry on his softening process for the next one. According to that he should be ready for Danzig and the Polish Corridor by next autumn."

Lanny went on to give his reasons for these beliefs: what Hitler had said, what Göring had said, what Hess had said. In the middle of it the President broke in: "Hell's bells! Will you be telling me they have put you in charge of their military operations?"

Lanny laughed. "It is due in great part to my father's prestige; he has what they need and understand. That got me next to Göring, and when Hitler saw me solid with Göring, he thought I must be all right—and so it has gone. I lay myself out to entertain them, and I tell them things about France and England which they need to know. Also, I put in a touch of sauciness, of a sort they consider American; they have a peculiar attitude toward us—they envy us and imitate us, even though they wouldn't acknowledge it, even to themselves. Hitler, Göring, Hess, any one of them would smack down a German who dared say to them what I say. My turkey story, for example."

Lanny told the story, and his auditor threw back his head and laughed, almost as heartily as Göring had done. "That tells a lot," he commented. "Göring doesn't resent seeing his Führer as a beast of prey!"

"Göring always has a lion cub as a pet, and Hitler until recently carried a riding whip everywhere he went. They have a Death's Head brigade of the SS, and many such symbols of cruelty and terror. They have committed themselves to that course, and cannot turn back if they would."

Lanny went on with his recital. He told how he had watched the Munich crisis develop, and what the British and the French had said and done in the face of it. He described Chamberlain, Runciman, Halifax, Londonderry, Wickthorpe—appeasers all, and the part they played in the ignominy. As Lanny had foreseen, F.D. wanted to know all about Lindbergh and Lady Nancy, and just what had really happened; he was pleased by Rick's epigram that there might not be a "Cliveden set" but surely was a "Cliveden sort." He wanted to hear about Adi Schickl-gruber's secret interest in the occult arts; the idea of locking an out-lawed astrologer up in a Gestapo hotel and compelling him to cast a dozen horoscopes he called a story out of the Arabian Nights—but Lanny assured him it had really happened, and it really had.

This busy great man, with the cares of a hundred and thirty million people on his shoulders, took hours off from sleep to ply Lanny Budd with questions concerning events and personalities of Western Europe: what Schacht had said about German finances; what Thyssen had said about how industry was controlled; what Schneider had revealed concerning his Skoda arrangements; what the de Bruynes had told about Laval and Bonnet and their intrigues with Kurt Meissner and Otto Abetz; about Daladier's noble *amie*, the Marquise de Crussol, and her intrigues; about Ceddy and Gerald and their hope that the Nazis would keep agreements as to arms limitation; about "Old Portland" and "Young Bedford," and Mosley and his Blackshirts, and even about Unity Mitford and what she was doing at the Berghof. In the course of this unrelenting quiz Lanny could make sure once for all that not merely had his reports been read and digested, but that his ideas had become a part of the mental make-up of his country's Chief Executive.

XI

So the secret agent never got a chance to offer his resignation; or, at any rate, he never took the chance. The idea just quietly melted away in the warmth of this great man's sympathy and gratitude. The nearest Lanny came to a complaint was to say that he found it damned discouraging, wandering about Nazi-Fascist Europe and never meeting a person to whom he could speak an honest word. The President's answer was: "Consider yourself a soldier under orders. The scout who goes into the enemy's camp at night feels the same way, but he goes."

"If you put it that way," Lanny replied, "of course I have to stick it out. But sometimes I wonder if I am really doing any good."

Said the President, looking suddenly grave: "Do you imagine I never wonder about my job, Lanny?"

"At least you can do something now and then."

"Not as often as I want to, believe me! If you think otherwise, it is because you haven't given much study to the American Constitution, and to our political system. I am not only well checked and balanced,

I am under orders, as much so as any private in the army. The American people are my boss, and I have the job of finding out what they want, and doing it. I might bull something through, but what good would it do if the people repudiated it at the next election?"

"I suppose that is true," admitted the visitor.

"I know just how you feel in Europe, Lanny. You see the horrors piling up, and you send in your reports—and nothing happens! But you must understand, I am no Hitler or Mussolini whose will is law. I have my private opinions, of course, but I have to remember that I speak as the voice of the nation. Incidentally, I am the leader of a party. I have only two years more as President, and I cannot take an action without thinking what will be its effect upon the party's future; otherwise I might throw away my six years' work, and have the humiliation of seeing a successor undo the entire New Deal. If you saw the election returns early this month, you know that the Republicans made gains; so I have to stop and ask myself, what have I done to cause it, and what can I do to check the trend and keep it from becoming a landslide?"

"I must admit all that makes a difference," said the agent, greatly chastened.

"It is my duty to lead the people, but I can only lead them as fast as they will follow. As I think I explained to you before, if I go faster, I lose contact, and somebody else becomes the leader. Never forget that it takes time to change the thinking of a hundred million people, or even of the educated part of them. You go to Europe and see the events with your own eyes; but the people do not go, and the tragedy seems far-off and unreal to them. If I had denounced the rape of Czechoslovakia, and given any hint of aid to England and France, do you imagine for one moment that the American people would have got behind me?"

"Only a few, it may be."

"I should simply have been handing the government over to the appeasers and the reactionaries. When there comes some ghastly thing like this pogrom, I can voice my abhorrence; I have recalled our ambassador from Berlin, and shall probably not send him back—a gesture which your high-up Nazi friends will not fail to understand. Also, I can tell the Congress that these are perilous times, and that it is necessary for us to increase our means of national defense. That we are doing, I assure you. But for the rest, I have to await events, and the education which they will give to the people. Facts are the only teachers who will be heeded."

"What keeps me unhappy, Governor, is the fear that the lesson will be learned too slowly."

"Don't think that you are the only one who has that fear. It has kept me awake many a night, and tempted me to what are considered indiscretions. You saw what happened when I let you persuade me to make that 'quarantine speech.' I haven't been forgiven for it yet."

"I hope you have forgiven me," said the visitor, troubled in conscience.

XII

Lanny had been over this interview many times in his mind, and had stowed there a number of items that he wanted to "get across." Most important of all was this question of the time limit within which his Chief had to work; a schedule not of Roosevelt's making, but of Hitler's. Now, speaking earnestly, Lanny said: "Governor, I want to put a question which you may not care to answer. You don't have to, but you ought to have it in your mind."

"All right—shoot!" said this informal great man.

"The question is this: What, exactly, would you do if you should be waked up in the middle of the night and told that London has just been bombed to dust and rubble?"

There was a silence; then: "I don't think I could answer that question, Lanny—not without a lot of reflection."

"It would be wise to think it over. And this, also: Suppose the British Prime Minister should call you on the telephone and tell you that you have twenty-four hours in which to decide whether to send Britain aid, or else the fleet will have to be surrendered."

"Good God, Lanny! You mean that seriously?"

"I am quite sure it is one of the possibilities."

"And how soon?"

"I don't think war can be more than a year or two away. I can tell you for certain that that is what the Nazi leaders believe. Göring is the most conservative, and two years is what he is asking for. Of course I can't tell whether his Air Force can do what he thinks it can; but undoubtedly he means to try. The British leaders all know it, and that is why their bones have turned to putty. If he were able to wipe London out, I don't see how the British government could continue, except by taking the fleet to Canada. But what good would that do, unless we promised them support?"

There was a pause, while a Chief Executive who had learned caution weighed his off-the-record words. "I don't think the American people would ever let the Germans come to Canada," he remarked, at last. "Also, I admit the fact that our country has lived in safety for more than a century behind the shelter of the British fleet. We haven't realized it, but in such a crisis it might be possible to make the American people realize it. You understand, all this is for you alone."

"Rest assured, Governor, I have never quoted a word that you have said to me, or even mentioned that I have met you—not even to my mother or father."

The face which was usually so genial and smiling had become somber, and the man who was stealing time from his sleep sat staring before him, frowning. "Do you know the Bible?" he asked, suddenly. "There are some words—I think St. Paul's: 'God is not mocked.' "

" 'Be not deceived; God is not mocked: for whatsoever a man soweth, that shall he also reap.' "

"I think that applies to nations as to individuals, Lanny. I don't attempt to guess how it is coming, but I refuse to believe that men can commit such crimes as the Nazis have committed, and not raise up some agency of justice against them. If it should appear that the American people have to shoulder that burden, I trust they will not shrink from it."

Again a pause. Then the President, watching his agent's face, inquired: "Do you know much about Lincoln?"

"I am ashamed not to know my own country as well as I do Europe."

"Take my advice then, and read a good life of Lincoln. He was a man of peace who was compelled to fight a long war. Observe his wise patience, his shrewdness in reading the public mind, his skill in leading the people, one step at a time. If ever you are tempted to wonder about what I am doing in a crisis, you can guide yourself by the certainty that I am asking what Lincoln would have done. He saved the Union, he saved what he called 'government of the people, by the people, for the people'; and be sure he didn't do it solely for one people, but as an example to which all mankind would turn. Recall that to your mind when you are tempted to be lonely and discouraged, over there among the Nazi lions and the Fascist jackals."

XIII

So Lanny went out from the presence. Because he had a lesson to ponder, he did not go to his hotel at once, but took a long walk at random, lost in thought. When he came to, he observed in the distance a great marble structure which he knew to be the Lincoln Memorial; it stood, shining in a bright electric glow the whole night through. Lanny decided to begin his study of Abraham Lincoln without delay, and went to the building, entered, and stood looking at the nine-foot marble statue of the Great Emancipator sitting in the seat of judg-ment. At that late hour, there was no one in the building but the sentries, so his thoughts were undisturbed. He turned to the walls, where the Gettysburg Address is inscribed, and read the immortal closing words:

"It is rather for us here to be dedicated to the great task remaining before us; that from these honored dead we take increased devotion to that cause for which they gave the last full measure of devotion; that we here highly resolve that these dead shall not have died in vain; that this nation, under God, shall have a new birth of freedom, and that government of the people, by the people, for the people, shall not perish from the earth."

The son of Robbie Budd turned again to the great statue. There was exaltation in his heart; he was glad now that he was an American; he renewed his faith in democracy and resolved never again to waver. Once more his native land faced a crisis, and once more the people, with their deep understanding, had found a leader worthy of their trust.

Lanny's mind leaped back across the sea to that other man of great power whom he had come to know so well. Three times in the past year and a half he had traveled back and forth between Franklin Roosevelt and Adolf Hitler, and he knew that he had not made the last of these journeys. Suddenly the events of the time took shape in his imagination as a duel of wills between these two: one the champion of democracy, of government by popular consent, of the rights of the individual to think his own thoughts, to speak his own mind, to live his own life so long as he did not interfere with the equal rights of his fellows; the other the champion of those ancient dark forces of tyranny and oppression which had ruled the world before the concept of freedom had been born. It took no prophet to foresee that this struggle was not over; it was going on until it would involve the whole world and the whole future of mankind.

Roosevelt versus Hitler! These two had not created the forces, but led them and embodied them; they had made themselves, one the protagonist and the other the antagonist in a world drama, the like of which had never before been played in history. Lanny Budd resolved that as long as fate spared him he would play a part in that drama, the faithful friend and messenger of democracy's champion.

BOOKS BY UPTON SINCLAIR

Plays

Printed in the United States
117151LV00005B/159/A